LIFEBLOOD

by Gena Showalter

Recycling programs
for this product may
not exist in your area.

ISBN-13: 978-1-335-20835-4

Lifeblood

Copyright © 2017 by Gena Showalter

HARLEQUIN®TEEN
™ www.HarlequinTEEN.com

Printed in U.S.A.

To God, my rock, my fortress and my deliverer!

To Naomi at French 'N' Bookish—Thank you for all you do.
Your support and enthusiasm are absolutely priceless!

To Katy Evans and Sarah J. Maas—You guys are such a delight
and so freaking talented! I'm honored to know you.

To my earthly support team, Vicki Tolbert, Shonna Hurt,
Michelle Quine and Jill Monroe—You are divine blessings!

To Bryn Collier—You give good promo! Thank you, thank you
and a thousand times thank you!

To Siena Koncsol—You, brilliant lady, do so much behind the scenes
and I'm so very grateful!

To my editor, Natashya Wilson—The time and attention you give to me
and my work are so appreciated!

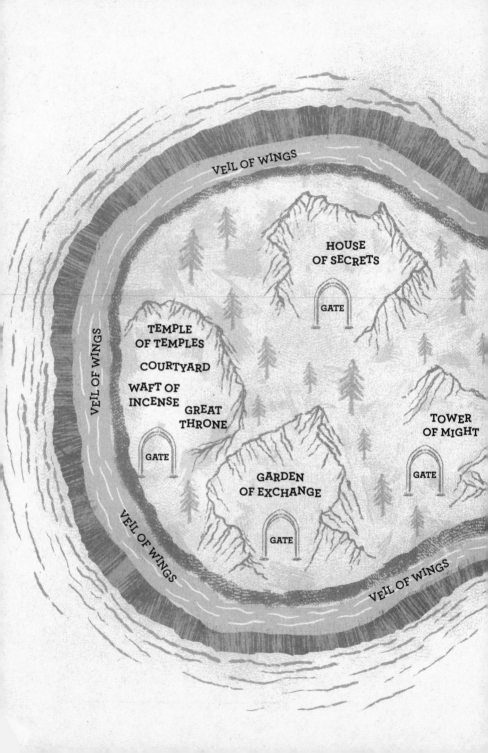

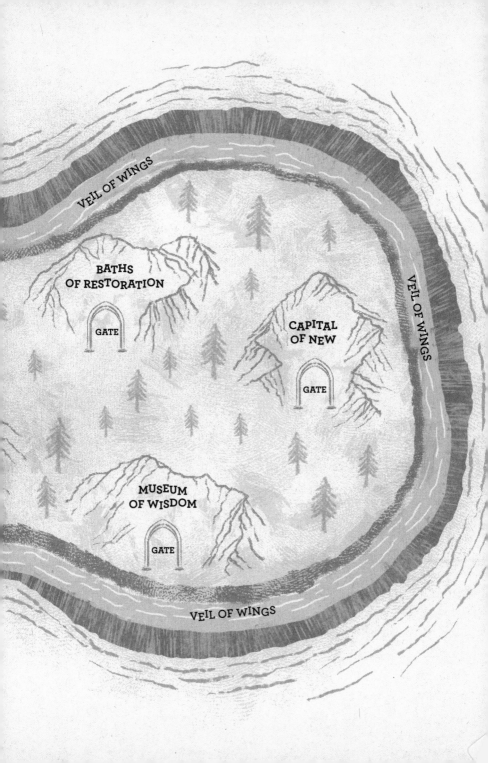

"*I see a beautiful city and a brilliant people rising from this abyss. I see the lives for which I lay down my life, peaceful, useful, prosperous and happy. I see that I hold a sanctuary in their hearts, and in the hearts of their descendants, generations hence. It is a far, far better thing that I do, than I have ever done; it is a far, far better rest that I go to than I have ever known.*"

— CHARLES DICKENS, *A TALE OF TWO CITIES*

The light Expands and the darkness Narrows

I've heard it said your entire life flashes before your eyes as you die. Those words comfort those who have loved and been loved but torment those who have failed and been failed.

I say, when you know where you're going to spend eternity, celebrate! Death has been defeated. Life forever reigns.

I am proof. My Firstlife is over, but my Everlife is now beginning.

My Light will shine...

The shadows will scatter...and every life will matter...

It's time to do what I was born to do. It's time to arise and shine.

Whatever I face—be it war, persecution, hunger, simple threats or my Second-death—I will not be deterred. Night will be replaced by day, and those who cry in the dark will rejoice in the morning.

The day is about to dawn. Time is short. Let the battle begin.

Glossary of Terms
excerpted from the *Book of the Law*

Abrogate—
Without hope, there is no Light.
* The highest rank of General in Myriad.
* Rare, none currently in existence.
* Those who extinguish the Light in others.

Conduit—
Day will forever chase away the night.
* The highest rank of General in Troika.
* Rare, only two currently in existence.
* Those who absorb the essence of sunlight from the Land of the Harvest and direct the beams to Troika.

Covenant—
So you shall say, and so it shall be.
* Any blood oath agreed upon between two separate parties (i.e. a human and an Everlife realm), legally voided only through court.
* If covenant terms are broken illegally, a human can be punished and put to death and a spirit can be enslaved.

Everlife—
Where there is no beginning and no end.
* The afterlife, where Troika and Myriad are in power and at war.
* Also known as the Unending.

Firstking—
He reigns with mercy and might evermore, evermore.
* Creator of Troika, Myriad, humans and their home, the Land of the Harvest.
* Father of the Secondkings: Eron the Prince of Doves, and Ambrosine the Prince of Ravens.

Firstlife—
What is isn't always what's supposed to be.
* A human life (i.e. a spirit encased inside a body).
* Dress rehearsal for the Everlife.

Firstdeath—
The end is merely the beginning.
* The demise of a human body.
* Occurs the moment a spirit cuts ties with its body.

Fused—
Believing a lie does not make it a truth.
* A Myriadian belief that a spirit is joined to another spirit (or even multiple spirits) after Second-death to be reborn in the Land of the Harvest.
* Disputed by Troikans.

General—
Learn the way, go the way, show the way.
* Next in command under the Secondking.
* Those who oversee specific teams of Leaders, Head-hunters, Laborers and Messengers within the realms.
* Responsible for planning battle strategies and leading armies into war.

Laborer—
Clear the way, make the paths straight.
* One of six main positions within the realms, directly under Leader.
* Responsible for returning to the Land of the Harvest to convince select humans to make covenant with their realm of choice.
* ML, the term for a Myriadian Laborer; TL, the term for a Troikan Laborer.

Land of the Harvest—
We shall sow, and we shall reap.
* Earth, home to humans.

Leader—
A helpmate is more valuable than diamonds.
* Assistants to the Generals.
* Responsible for delegating assignments to all other sub-positions within the realms.

Many Ends—
Ignore your future, pay the price.
* The realm where Unsigned are imprisoned after Firstdeath.
* Where happiness goes to die and nightmares come to terrible life.

Messenger—
Harken and deliver the good news.
* One of six main positions within the realms, directly under Laborer.
* Responsible for teaching humans about the realms, protecting others from the enemy and chronicling exploits within and without the realm.

Myriad—
Autonomy, bliss, indulgence.
★ The dark realm, ruled by the Prince of Ravens.
★ Magical forests whisper enchanted tales, and
secrets lurk in every corner...self-indulgence is
revered, and the party never stops...victors are
adored and failures are abhorred...emotion always
trumps logic.
★ Motto: Might Equals Right.

Penumbra—
In the dark, the blind lead the blind.
★ A disease born and spread in darkness,
capable of draining Troikans of Light.
★ Origin and cure unknown.

Realms—
Home is where the heart is nourished or starved.
★ Kingdoms in the Everlife: Troika, Myriad and Many Ends.

Second-death—
Another end, another new beginning.
★ When a spirit is drained of Lifeblood.
★ Myriad believes a spirit is Fused to another spirit(s)
in order to return to the Land of the Harvest; Troika
believes a spirit enters into the Rest forevermore.

Secondking—
The one you follow decides the roads you take.
★ One of two sons of the Firstking; Eron the Prince
of Doves, and Ambrosine the Prince of Ravens.
★ Ruler of a realm.

The Rest—
Peace beyond all understanding awaits.

* Troikans believe a spirit enters into this state of absolute tranquillity after Second-death, forever separated from the realms...with a few exceptions.

The Resurrection—
And so the dead shall rise again.

* Once every year, Troika holds a vote; one spirit within the Rest is brought back to spirit-life.
* The winner must exit the Rest even if he or she wishes to remain.

Troika—
Justice, equality, freedom of choice.

* The realm of Light, ruled by the Secondking Eron, the Prince of Doves.
* Untouched by gloom, where hard work isn't an expectation but a way of life, equality isn't an ideal but a standard and fear isn't a treasured friend but a hated foe...logic always trumps emotion...people are governed by a strict set of rules, and violators are punished.
* Motto: Light Brings Sight.

Unsigned—
Without hope, there can be no joy.

* A human who fails to make covenant with Troika or Myriad before Firstdeath.
* Damned to spend the Everlife inside Many Ends.

Veil—
All who enter are welcome.

* A doorway leading into and out of an Everlife realm.

TROIKA

From: L_N_3/19.1.1
To: M_C_4/2.17.12
Subject: Tenley Lockwood

You begged to take over Miss Lockwood's case, Madame Cordell, and vowed to always—always!—keep me updated on her progress. Since her Firstlife ended by poisoned spear, I have yet to receive a single report. Update me. Now!
  Light Brings Sight!
  General Levi Nanne

TROIKA

From: M_C_4/2.17.12
To: L_N_3/19.1.1
Subject: Your patience and trust humble me

My apologies for making you wait a whole 6.8 seconds for another report, sir. If you haven't noticed, my team is a little busy slaughtering Myriadian soldiers—and getting slaughtered in the process. By the way, Archer Prince has experienced Second-death. Not that you asked. I've lost track of Tenley and suspect Myriad is hiding her within their shadows. I'm doing my best to locate her, sir.

Light Brings Sight! ←maybe consider using yours?
Madame Meredith Cordell

TROIKA

From: L_N_3/19.1.1
To: M_C_4/2.17.12
Subject: Brrring! Brrring! This is your wake-up call

Find her!

And you had better not be crying for Archer. He lived a good life and died a warrior's death. His name has been added to the *Book of New Life*, and he's a candidate for the Resurrection. You just might see him again—and soon!

Light Brings Sight!

General Levi Nanne

TROIKA

From: M_C_4/2.17.12
To: L_N_3/19.1.1
Subject: Please leave a message at the beep

When has "might" ever been good enough?
   Light Brings Sight!
   Madame Meredith Cordell

MYRIAD

From: Z_C_4/23.43.2
To: R_O_3/2.17.12
Subject: The Conduit

It's certain. Miss Lockwood has made covenant with Troika. Foolish Madame Bennett! Her actions hurt us all. We appeared immoral and foul, so I can't blame Miss Lockwood for her choice. My question is: Does Killian Flynn protect Miss Lockwood for our benefit—or theirs?

How would you like me to proceed?

Might Equals Right!

Sir Zhi Chen

MYRIAD

From: R_O_3/2.17.12
To: Z_C_4/23.43.2
Subject: Instructions

You're right. Madame Pearl Bennett got us into this mess, but I'm happy to report Killian Flynn will get us out. I assure you, his every action is intentional and for our greater good. His mission is critical.

You will tell no one of his motivation. The fewer people who know, the less likely the information will spread, compromising everything he has done and has yet to do. Let today's battle play out without interference.

And fear not. All is not lost where Tenley Lockwood is concerned. Killian is working his magic to ensure she single-handedly wins the war—*for us*. Let him do what he needs to do. He knows what's at stake, and he won't let us down. He never has before.

Might Equals Right!
General Rosalind Oriana

chapter one

"Tribulation reveals your greatest strength...
or greatest weakness."
—Troika

Present day

Sand in the hourglass falls, one grain at a time...time...one
second bleeds into two...three... I try to piece together my
fragmented thoughts. A difficult task. My mind is hazy, my
thoughts blurred. Four...

A fact clicks into place. Numbers are my greatest obsession; they always tell a story, and they never lie.

Five...five...five. The numeral gets trapped in my head,
set on constant repeat. *Click.* Five minutes and fourteen seconds ago, I died.

Whoa. I'm dead?

I must be. My heart no longer beats, and my lungs are deflated. I can't breathe. I need to breathe. Sweat beads on my
nape and trickles down my spine, and yet my limbs remain
ice-cold.

Calm. Steady. Though my body is wrecked, my spirit lives
on. This is a new beginning. A new life.

Calm? Seriously? From now on, I'll have zero second chances. Zero do-overs. Everything I do will matter: every word I say, every action I take, every person I befriend and every enemy I slay will positively or negatively affect me. No ifs, ands or buts.

Welcome to the Everlife.

The words whisper on the wind, and a quiet ring erupts in my ears. In seconds, the volume cranks to high. I cringe. My bones vibrate, and a light tap registers against my ribs. *Tap, tap. Tap, tap. Bang, BANG!*

I gasp, taking my first breath, the real me awakening at last. My chest cools, and my lungs fill. I can breathe again. I'm dead, but still I live.

Arise! Arise and shine!

Another whisper drifts on the wind...or a voice is speaking inside my head.

I'm dead *and* crazy?

Inside, I wither and return to my default setting: counting. Six...seven...

Click. Seventeen! I'm seventeen years old. I was born on the tenth day of the tenth month at 10:10 a.m., and I died on the eleventh day of the eleventh month at 10:14 a.m.

$$1 + 1 + 1 + 1 + 1 + 0 + 1 + 4 = 10$$

The work of Fate, some would say. Wrong! Fate is a myth, an excuse, a way to cast blame. While we might have a divine purpose, not everything that happens is through divine intervention. Our actions change the course of our lives for good or for ill.

We are the final authority.

My present is the sum total of decisions made in my past— my own decisions, and even those made by the people around me. We are accountable...count...eight, nine... Ten!

Click, click. My name is Tenley Lockwood. "Ten" to my friends.

5 + 5 = 10. A representative of two equal parts.

The last piece of the puzzle snaps into place. Two realms in the Everlife—Troika and Myriad—are currently locked in a fierce, brutal battle.

Troika fought to save my Firstlife while Myriad strove to end it. Myriad proved successful. My body lies on a blood-drenched street in the heart of LA.

Congrats, Myriad. You won a battle. You won't win the war.

With my last breath, I pledged my allegiance to Troika, evermore, and I have no regrets. I value Firstlife. I like rules and enjoy structure. I understand every punishment is meant to teach rather than harm.

I'm a Troikan now, born anew in blood and violence. A soldier in a war as old as time. I've become enemies with people I've never met as well as people I know and love.

I've become enemies with Killian, a top Laborer in Myriad.

Killian! His name is a ragged cry from the depths of my soul. I'd say we dated, but *dated* is too mild a word. I craved him like a drug...and yet I still chose Troika over Myriad.

Home sweet home. Something I've never really had.

I'm supposed to hate him, but every fiber of my being flinches at the thought. I will never harm him. He means too much to me.

"Is she dead?" A harsh, unfamiliar voice claims my attention. "Did she make covenant with Troika?"

"Aye and aye." The husky Irish lilt I recognize, and relief is a cool cascade. Killian never left my side!

I want to see him so badly, I shake.

"Sucks to be you," Unfamiliar continues. In the distance, I hear the *clink-clank* of dueling swords. "Now that Madame

Bennett is dead, you fall under Zhi's command. When he learns you failed to recruit the Lockwood girl, he'll mount your head at the end of a pike."

Relief gives way to distress. Killian is in danger. Because of me. I need to help him, *have* to help him, but though I try to stand, I'm stuck, walled in. Useless!

What's the problem? My outer casing is dead, any ties to my spirit now broken. I should be able to ghost out, yes?

"Leave." Menace drips from Killian's command. "Protect our kinsmen from the Troikans."

"So you can kill Lockwood before her spirit escapes her body and collect the bounty on your own? No."

Bounty?

Buzzing noises erupt. Flames crackle. Smoke fills the air, sharp and pungent.

There's a pained gasp. A hard *thump.*

"Stay down," Killian spits.

He just attacked Unfamiliar?

Why would he harm his brother-by-realm to save an enemy? Why would he risk punishment?

The answer is simple: he wouldn't, except for me, only ever for me.

I vacillate between melting and rallying. *Get free, protect Killian.*

When he had the chance to seal the deal and convince me to make covenant with Myriad, he urged me to follow my heart instead. We'd both known I belonged in Troika. To him, my needs had been more important than his wants, a reward or a penalty.

He sacrificed his happiness for mine, but I failed to do the same for him. What kind of maybe, maybe not, girlfriend am I?

My final moments replay inside my head. Sloan Aubuchon,

once my enemy, then my friend, then my *bitter* enemy, nailed me with a poisoned spear.

I hate him more than I love you, she told me.

Him. Dr. Vans, the monster who oversaw every facet of our torture at Prynne Asylum, a "home" for wayward teens.

Myriad vowed to help Sloan punish Vans. *If* she made covenant with them and murdered me. She agreed to both.

Her treachery cuts as deeply as the spear. Granted, Vans did terrible things to her. Things no one should ever have to endure. But his behavior does not excuse hers. In her quest for vengeance, she became his mirror image, betraying my trust the way he betrayed hers.

Consequences were immediate. Killian yanked the spear out of me and, to protect me from further harm, impaled her.

Another reason he will be punished. I've *got* to help him.

I punch and kick, but even still, I make no progress.

"Where is she, Killian?" A new voice registers. This one is easy to recognize, too. "Where are you hiding her?"

Deacon, a TL. My friend. He's always reminded me of a die-hard warrior of old, his sense of honor as much a part of him as muscle and brawn.

If anyone can free me, it's Deacon.

"Over here," Killian croaks. "She's already...it's too late to save..."

Something hard and warm shackles my wrist. Suddenly I'm steady on my feet, and I can see!

I gasp, glimpsing the spirit world in operation around me for the first time. Dappled golden sunlight spills from a sky of sapphire silk. Fat clouds sprinkle the land below with a breathtaking rain of diamond dust.

Realization. They aren't just clouds, but an array of oddly

shaped buildings with armed soldiers marching along the parapets.

A floodgate opens in my mind, releasing a wave of information. *They are guard towers, from which humans can be watched and spiritual battles fought. They move between the realms and the Land of the Harvest, and ownership is ever-changing. Winner of every battle determines rights.*

I shake my head, my brow furrowed. I've never been taught about guard towers, and yet I now know all about them? I shouldn't—

I *have* been taught. Years ago. At the age of five, I attended a mandatory realm-history class. I had…had… Oh, wow, I'm being bathed by drugging warmth, my senses fogging with the most delectable scents: wildflowers, fruit trees and newly ripened berries. How am I supposed to concentrate? I inhale deeply, savoring.

"Don't let anyone near her until she's hooked," Killian says, jolting me.

Hooked?

"My men and I will keep the area clear as long as we can," Deacon says and rushes off.

My gaze finds Killian's, and my heart thuds. His eyes are gorgeous, soulful gold with flecks of electric blue. In one, there are five flecks. In the other, three. At our first meeting, I compared those flecks to an octave. The fifth and third notes create the basic foundation for all chords. Whenever he looks at me, my blood sings.

Today is not an exception.

A Myriadian soldier breaks through the protective ring created by Deacon and his men. Without disrupting our stare-down, Killian reaches out with a quick jab-jab, a dagger in hand. I gasp. He just killed one of his own. Savagely. Brutally.

Lifeblood coats the weapon, clear and glittering, a macabre but lovely sight. He closes in on me, menace in every step, but I remain rooted in place, unafraid. This boy will never harm me.

"Stop slaying your people on my behalf," I command.

"I'll protect you however I see fit, lass." He sheathes his dagger and cups my face, his palms calloused from years of combat.

Those calluses tickle my skin, creating friction—heat. Such delicious heat. Soon the battle is forgotten. I'm basically on fire for him, my blood steaming, tormenting me—thrilling me. All because of an innocent touch!

I've always reacted to this boy, but never this intensely. Maybe because we've never before experienced skin-to-skin contact, nothing between us. Not flesh, not a Shell. Not life-or-death stakes.

I lean into his grip like a kitten being petted for the first time.

Are the sensations this potent with all spirits?

I close my eyes and breathe him in. Peat smoke and heather. My favorites. My head fogs all over again, and I know he's intoxicating me without even trying.

"Look at me, lass."

I obey. He is studying me, as if he's memorizing my features. I study him right back, helpless to do otherwise. Shadows cling to him, but they fail to detract from his otherworldly beauty. Ebony silk hangs over a strong forehead and swoops to one side, creating a roguish frame for equally roguish features. His eyebrows are thick and black, his skin bronzed and poreless, as if his flesh has been painted on. His nose is blade-sharp and leads to a mouth so lush, it could be classified as feminine. His triangular jaw is dusted with sexy stubble.

"In the coming weeks," he says, agonized, "I need you to trust me, no matter what. Can you do that?"

Without hesitation, I reply, "Of course." I trace a fingertip over the seam of those lavish lips, acting without thought. He might be firm and muscled everywhere else, but he's soft as rose petals here, and I shiver.

His pupils dilate, a sign his awareness of me is deepening. "There's no *of course* about it. The situation will be bleak, but you must trust that I will always have your best interests at heart." His grip tightens. "Please."

I want to reassure him, and I totally mean to do so until a burst of wind blows a strand of hair in my eyes. I frown as I hold a lock up to the light. Cobalt blue? What the what? Before I died, my hair was black.

"I don't understand," I say.

"You should see the other changes." Killian's hand brushes mine as he sifts the strands between his fingers.

A sharp lance of pain sends me stumbling back, a cry parting my lips.

Was I just…stabbed?

"You're tense." Killian catches me, latching on to my wrists and holding me steady. "Relax." His *obey me or die* tone is usually reserved for everyone *but* me.

I bristle. "*You* relax! I—" Agony claws at my insides, and it's too much, far too much. "I don't know what's… I can't… I'm…" Dying for the second and final time? So soon?

"You're being hooked to your realm's Grid."

Grid? "I think something's wrong with the connection." I manage to push the words past the barbed lump growing in my throat.

"Nothing's wrong." He draws me against him, caresses the

ridges of my spine, offering comfort. "Everyone goes through this. Even Myriadians."

I rest my head on his shoulder, breathing in and out with purpose. Despite our efforts, I feel as if I'm trapped inside a never-ending pit, falling into one sword after another while taking an endless rain of bullets to the brain and torso.

Kill me! Let me die.

But…the pain is fading just as swiftly as it began.

Warmth envelops me, sinks into me and shines…shines so brightly that emotions I'd hidden in dark corners long ago are suddenly exposed. Those emotions scramble in every direction like tiny bugs. Hatred for my father. Rage for circumstances beyond my control. Sorrow over the loss of my mother and little brother.

Nothing can hide. I hiss and sob in unison. The sound a wounded animal must make.

"You're strong. You're brave," Killian tells me. "You've got this, lass."

As the warmth gathers in three distinct places—both hands and an arm—I squeeze him so tightly, I'm sure I bruise him. He never once complains. The warmth…it burns now. I think I'm being…marked?

In the center of each palm, a circle with three leaves appears. The Troikan symbol. They are pale at first but gradually darken. Along my right arm, three sets of numbers emerge.

"Spiritual brands," Killian says, passing his thumb over one of the symbols without actually touching me. "An outward sign of your inward loyalty."

Finally, blessedly, the remaining pain subsides, and I whimper with relief.

"A Key." Killian moves his attention—and his phantom-touch—to the numbers. "I'd heard rumors Troika forces their new recruits to work for their rewards, but no one has confirmed or denied."

"A Key?" When his thumb strokes my skin, I'm hit with a punch of cold. My jaw clenches, and my teeth chatter.

Fury contorts his features, startling me as much as the punch. He releases me and steps back, increasing the distance between us.

I'm not yet ready to part with him. Lifting my chin, I step toward him and flatten my hand over his precious heart. Another blast of cold hits, this one stronger, unbearable.

"Zero!" My favorite curse escapes, and I jump back. In a blink, the horrible cold vanishes.

"I tried to warn you," he grates.

As I gaze into his siren-eyes, the truth becomes clear. Physically, our bodies will forever reject each other. Darkness and Light cannot coexist. One will always chase the other away.

By siding with Troika, I doomed our relationship.

Tears well. "Killian," I say. He *did* try to warn me. I convinced myself we'd find a way to be together, not yet comprehending the obstacles we'd have to face.

"What's done is done." He gives an almost imperceptible shake of his head as he backs away from me. "If I fight for you, I help my realm lose the war. If I fight against you, I lose you. There's no middle ground. Not with us. Like you, I have to choose."

chapter two

Killian's words echo inside my mind. *If I fight for you, I help my realm lose the war. If I fight against you, I lose you.*

No middle ground.

Choose.

My tears—such silly, useless tears—spill over my cheeks, leaving hot, stinging tracks in their wake. I thought I was prepared to give up everything for my new home. I thought I could live with any consequences.

But the cost is already too high.

What am I supposed to do? Killian is more than the object of my fascination. He's my best friend. The only one I have left. Archer, a boy I loved like a brother, died trying to save my Firstlife. He died *today*. Worse, he died for nothing!

Grief rips through me. It grips me in a stranglehold and kicks me in the stomach. It whispers, *There's nothing you can do.*

Sorrow and helplessness join the pity party, and I despise both. These emotions are not innocent, but deadly. They devoured my past, eating at my happiness until nothing remained; I can't cede my present or my future, too.

I speak the promise burning a hole in my heart. "You matter to me, Killian. I'll fix this."

"Do I?" The rough disbelief in his tone guts me. "Will you?"

I've never ascribed to the notion that words are enough, and I've never trusted those who huff and puff, furious when someone dares to question another's claim of affection. I won't pretend otherwise just because a spotlight now shines on *me*.

My actions can make or break us.

"You do, and I will," I say, lifting my chin. "I'll prove it."

He gives a hard shake of his head. "Don't be putting yerself in danger on my behalf, lass. I'd rather you hate me and live than lo—like me and die. Deacon," he calls. "She's ready."

Deacon appears at my side. "Time to go." He takes my hand, and my spirit welcomes the connection, Light always a complement to Light. I warm rather than freeze—the way I should have done with Killian. The way I *used* to do with Killian.

What have I done?

Deacon appears to be my age, though he's infinitely older. He's black and beautiful, his dark hair shorn to his scalp, his green eyes pulsing with the very heartbeat of summer. His nose is a smidge too long and his mouth a smidge too thin, but neither matters. He looks like the bad boy he likes to accuse Killian of being: rough, tough and totally buff.

He's wearing a black leather vest with small silver blades pretending to be buttons. His matching leather pants have five zippers on each leg.

$5 + 5 = 10$

Wait. I saw him only minutes before I died, and he was

wearing a white robe with white trim. My brow furrows with confusion. Changing clothes during the heat of battle isn't impossible, but also isn't likely.

The answer rides a newly installed train track through my mind—the mysterious Grid, I suspect—and I rub my temples. His spirit was encased in a Shell that he has since shed.

"In case you haven't noticed," he says, "we're in the middle of a combat zone. You are weak, vulnerable. We need to get you to safety *now.*"

Leave? I shake my head. He wants to separate me from Killian.

Good idea. *Sworn enemy, remember?*

Once, these two boys worked together to save me from a madwoman, but Archer was the go-between. Deacon and Killian will never work together again, will they? They will never fully trust each other. One realm *can't* trust the other. Too many betrayals litter the past.

"No," I say, shaking my head. I won't abandon my friends when they need me most. I peer at Killian. "I'll stay. I'll help."

"Help?" He sneers at me. "Don't kid yerself, lass. Ye'll get hurt, and I'll be forced to watch. You are no longer mine to protect." His bitterness creates an invisible wall between us. He turns and slips inside his Shell. "Go! Before it's too late."

No longer mine…

The pain I felt before? Nothing compared to this. "I'm sorry." I did this. I broke us—broke him. The boy who risked his life to save mine.

Help him, help Troika. Two needs. One will always negate the other.

"An apology without a change in behavior is worthless." He doesn't glance in my direction. "Prove you mean yours and leave."

My determination to remain only strengthens. I will prove my affection for him by saving him from my realm.

I stand my ground and prepare to fight, scanning my surroundings. *Oh...zero.* I swallow hard.

Countless spirits and Shells who fought to either rescue or kill me are in pieces. Death should not be pretty, but the sight is as glorious as it is sickening. Lifeblood glitters in the sunlight, turning war into a twisted fairy tale.

During my Firstlife, I had trouble differentiating between humans and Shells. Now? I can tell with a single glance. Shells are dense with a plastic-like appearance I never before noticed. They are like life-size dolls. I can pick out the spirits and humans; spirits are luminescent and human flesh is dull. I can even tell who is Troikan and Myriadian. Troikans are the sunrise, a dawning illumination, while Myriadians are the sunset, a herald of darkness.

Light versus shadow. Bright versus gloom.

Those who haven't been chopped to bits are still locked in a gruesome battle. Grunts and groans blend with the pop of breaking bones and the gurgle of warriors choking on blood, creating a horrific sound track. My hand covers my mouth.

"You're not going to like this next part, lass." Killian grabs hold of a spear. The one Sloan used to kill me—the one still lodged in her lifeless chest.

He yanks. The weapon exits her body, taking pieces of rib with it. "After Firstdeath, most spirits remain trapped inside the body until freed by another spirit." He reaches into her torso, his fingers ghosting through her flesh. He yanks—

And there she is, the real Sloan. For a moment, rage overwhelms me. Behold, my betrayer! She looks the same, and yet completely different. The model-pretty blonde has morphed into an exquisite, incomparable beauty with hair as white as snow and lips as red as wine.

She killed an innocent human. She should be as haggard on the outside as she is on the inside.

My hands ball into fists. I can end her, the way she ended me. I can destroy her Everlife before it begins. Does she truly deserve a second chance?

Do you?

The question drifts through the train track in my mind, startling me.

Sloan gazes at the world around her with wide eyes the color of a morning sky. She's distracted and unaware of the danger. There's no better time to strike…

I'm going to do it, I decide. I don't care if I deserve a second chance or not. Don't care if my actions make me a hypocrite and contradict my beliefs.

What's wrong with me?

I don't care about that, either. I wrench free of Deacon and take a step toward her. Black shadows rise from the ground, covering her feet…her calves…her thighs. Pain twists her features.

"Help me." She reaches for me with a trembling hand.

I stop abruptly.

She reaches for Killian. He steps back, leaving her alone with her agony. Then she's gone, no hint of her anywhere.

"Where did she go?" I demand, only to fight a torrent of shame. Her absence is a gift, the temptation to harm her gone. I should let her go, not chase after her.

"Where else? Myriad." Deacon shackles my biceps in a firm grip and tugs me in the opposite direction. "*You* need to head to Troika. You're vulnerable here."

The war still rages, soldiers cutting each other down with

fiery swords, shooting each other with laser guns. Shells are disintegrating left and right, the sight *devastating*.

"I'm staying," I croak. Running away is cowardly. I am the cause of the battle. I will ensure it ends.

"What do you think you can do, Ten?" Deacon's grip tightens. "You're riding an emotional roller coaster right now."

"How do you—"

"I've been where you are. I know the Grid is exposing aspects of yourself you may not like. I also know you cannot help anyone but yourself right now. No speech, no matter how inspired, is going to penetrate the bloodlust currently plaguing these soldiers." He wrenches me to the side, startling and tripping me.

An arrow soars past me as I flail.

"See!" he shouts. "You're in danger."

"Go, Ten. Now!" Killian spins and swings the spear, stabbing a Troikan in the process of sneaking up behind him. "If you're killed, everything we've done to help you will be in vain."

I should be thrilled he's avoided injury, but his actions only feed the fury Sloan unearthed. I step toward him, intending to…what? I don't want to hurt him, but I can't allow him to kill another Troikan, either. These people…they're my brothers and sisters now.

Whoa. Such affinity for individuals I've never met?

Deacon tightens his hold. "I can't escort you to Troika without your permission. Say yes."

Free will matters, even in a war zone?

I struggle with duty and desire as more and more Troikans gather around Killian, attacking him en masse. He's strong and skilled, but is he skilled enough to survive this?

Fear for him—for everyone he's fighting—leaves me ice-cold.

A group of his comrades rush over to aid him, and I'm as relieved as I am ashamed. The group could harm my people.

More arrows zoom in my direction. Deacon uses a sword to deflect them, saving me from injury. Or worse.

Zero! If I throw myself into the fray, I can help Troika or I can help Killian, but not both.

No need to ponder. I have to help Killian. I recently lost my mom and brother. Earlier today I watched as my dad was gunned down. I lost Archer. I can't lose Killian, too.

Already lost him…

No. Absolutely not! And yet, hot tears blur my vision and streak down my cheeks. The Grid, whatever it is, has turned me into an emotional wreck.

Forget emotion. I need to act. Now or never.

Now! With a roar, I plow into the chaos. Grunts and groans. Limbs fly, some with purpose, a target in sight, others because they've been severed. The scent of blood saturates the air and zings with tension. Determined, I swipe up a sword.

The weapon is ten times heavier than I expected, and my arm shakes as I assume a battle stance.

"Stop," I shout. "Troikans love, forgive. Let's walk away and save lives. No one else has to die today."

I'm ignored. Deacon was right. A speech will never penetrate this blood-haze.

One of the Troikans notches an arrow and aims at Killian. I scream, diving at him, intending to shield him. As weak as I am, I fail to go the distance and hit the ground, useless. Killian doesn't need my help, anyway. Lightning fast, he uses the spear to block. The arrow pings, falls.

No time for relief. Other soldiers rush at him, trampling me in the process. Combat boots—

Miss me? Yes! I'm in spirit form while the soldiers are in Shells. We're intangible to each other.

Reeling, I climb to my feet. At warp speed, two other arrows hurl at Killian; he's fast enough to block both.

Behind him, a Troikan is coming in hot, a Stag aimed.

For a Shell, a Stag is the worst of the worst. A single dart traps a spirit inside its Shell, preventing any sort of mobility and rendering both defenseless.

I have no idea what a Stag will do to a spirit without a Shell, and I don't care. I put more pep in my step and jump. This go-round, my timing and efforts pay off. The dart flies through me and slows, giving Killian a chance to duck.

Agony sears me, and I scream. Seizing, I drop. Bolts of lightning set all of my organs ablaze.

The girl who pulled the trigger stares at me in horror. She just shot one of her own, and I just saved the enemy.

Her distraction puts her at a disadvantage, allowing a Myriadian to race in and swing a sword. Target: her head.

"Nooo!" Another Troikan shoves her out of the way. The sword slices through his shoulder, removing the arm of his Shell. Lifeblood spurts from the wound.

My horror mirrors the girl's. Shells and spirits are connected. Is the boy's spirit now missing an arm?

Above me, Killian whirls his spear, preventing several arrows from finding a new home in my chest. He kicks backward, nailing the Troikan sneaking up behind him.

"I told you to go, Ten."

I…can't. I can't leave him. Part of me fears I'll never see him again…and what you fear, you welcome into your life. I know it as surely as I know my name.

I try to stand, fail.

He ducks, avoiding the swing of a sword. Remaining low, he takes out his opponent at the ankles.

"If she's killed today," he says to Deacon, who is fending off a Myriadian soldier, "I'll blame you, aye. I'll retaliate by killing everyone you love." He is cold, merciless. And he's not done. He all but spits daggers at me after he clears the crowd around me and helps me stand. "Say yes to Deacon. From this moment on, every death I deliver is on your hands, not mine."

Contact is just as painful as before, but what's worse? My sense of disappointment. In his words. In my failure. In what this means for our future.

"Don't let me go." My knees are like jelly, yes, but I think the other part of me, the girl who hopes for the best, expects him to whisk me away. No more fighting, no need to choose between a home and a boy a second time.

I couldn't be more wrong. He holds me up with one arm and uses the other to quickly and brutally stop the next Troikan who challenges him.

My fault.

A contingent of MLs rushes over. Killian defends me from his own people, adding to his list of crimes.

My heart shrivels into a tiny ball of self-recrimination. By staying, I'm doing far more harm than good, aren't I?

"Yes," I shout at Deacon. "Yes, yes, yes."

The TL finishes off his newest attacker, closes the distance and drops his weapon to pull me from Killian's side and cradle me against his chest.

Killian holds on to my hand as long as possible. I cling to his.

Is this goodbye?

This can't be goodbye.

Deacon runs. He's injured, Lifeblood gushing from a wound in his shoulder and soaking his shirt. My shriveled heart aches. I'm not the one who wielded the sword, but I'm the one who placed him in its path.

Never slowing, he says something in a language I don't know but have heard him use with Archer. A special Troikan language the Myriadians can't understand.

My gaze locks on Killian. He pauses, the battle forgotten. He's so beautiful and strong, but he's haunted. A fallen angel with a thousand and one regrets.

He reaches for me. I extend my hand to him.

A beam of Light slams into me. I blink, and I'm standing atop the parapet of one of the guard towers with Deacon. TLs border us on every side, at the ready. Killian is gone. I swallow a whimper.

No future with Killian. No present with Archer.

"Stop thinking about everything you've lost," Deacon commands, "and start thinking about everything you've gained."

He's right. This isn't the time or place to break down. "Is that why you're so calm about Archer's death?"

"That, and I know there's a chance I'll see him again."

What? Surely I heard him incorrectly. Archer entered into the Rest. The end.

Questioning him isn't an option. Myriadians materialize, circling us, shadow-tipped arrows notched...and soon arching through the sky. Troikans use fiery swords to block, and the arrows burn to ash.

As the opposing forces leap together in a vicious tangle of limbs and weapons, Deacon drops me. I crash-land, still too weak to stand on my own. Scowling, he yanks a small vial hanging from his neck and throws it at me.

"Every drop," he insists.

I uncork the top, already knowing what swirls inside. Liquefied manna, everything a spirit needs to heal and thrive. The sweet scent teases me. I drain the contents.

Deacon stabs an ML, turns, and stabs another.

I begin to strengthen.

Two MLs rush at Deacon in unison. He throws himself at the taller one. I roll to my back and kick out my legs, knocking the shorter guy's ankles together. Deacon is there to finish him off before hefting me to my feet.

"Time to go."

No way! "I'm racer-ready. Let's stay and help."

"You're *that* eager to die again?"

Hey! "I've got skills." Both Killian and Archer worked with me before—

My shoulders hunch as a sense of dejection pierces me.

"You have *zero* skills," Deacon says, merciless. "Right now you're like an infant. All you can do is cry and crap your pants. So…" He turns, stabs an incoming ML. "If Her Majesty is ready to continue her travels…"

How can he stand to help me? Archer was his best friend, and I put him in the line of fire by requesting a Troikan army be sent to save Killian, who still defends Myriad despite being beaten by his bosses, and Sloan, who secretly had already made covenant with the enemy.

Archer wasn't just a Laborer, sent to the Land of the Harvest to protect his human charges. He wasn't just a negotiator of covenant terms or a guide for those who had signed with Troika. He was a man of great integrity, honor and kindness. A rarity. A hero in a time when villains are the norm.

Archer loved me when I was unlovable. Time and time again he could have disrespected me with a lie. It would have been easier for us both. Instead he told the truth, no matter how painful. He abandoned a centuries-old feud with his greatest enemy to help me. In the end, he died taking a blow meant for me.

The hunch in my shoulders deepens. "Yes," I say softly. "Let's go."

Deacon slings an arm around my waist. We dematerialize in a blaze of Light and reappear—

I inhale sharply. We're standing in the center of a crystal bridge. Before us is a crimson-colored waterfall framed by a wall of glistening ruby geodes. The layered sediment resembles feathers; those feathers stretch out on both sides, creating the illusion of wings. Framing those wings are stones of topaz, jasper and beryl.

The architecture is stunning, far too perfect to be man-made or even nature-made. Intelligent creation.

Firstking-made, then?

There are no Troikans or Myriadians here. No battles. Just me and Deacon and the cool kiss of mist on my cheeks. A scent sweeter than manna—sweeter even than Killian—permeates the air.

"Now that we're alone…" Deacon gets in my face, snapping, "Your first day in the Everlife, you aided Myriad. You protected the guy who was killing my soldiers. Soldiers who risked their lives to save you."

I look away from him, unable to meet his gaze. Shame is a deluge inside me, and my confidence crumbles like a condemned building. "Killian killed his own soldiers, too. He—"

"You're *still* protecting him!" Deacon bellows.

I bow my head. "I'm sorry."

"No, you're not. If you could go back, you'd do it all over again." His tone flattened, but even worse, his words were dead-on. "I told you there's a chance Archer will come back to us, and there is. A very small chance. Every year, the names of the people who die are placed in the *Book of New Life*. Troikan citizens vote for a slain spirit to exit the Rest. It's called the Resurrection. But we lost a Conduit this year, too. Conduits *always* win."

My hopes lift…and crash. "Maybe we can convince everyone to vote for Archer instead?" I love the big goof with all my heart. I want more seconds, days, weeks with him. I want years! Decades! "We can do anything if we—"

"Put our heads together? Work hard enough? Have faith?" He sneers at me. "Unsuccessful people work themselves into the grave every day. And have faith in what, Ten? Ourselves? Last time I checked, neither one of us had the ability to perform a miracle."

I wither, part of me wishing I could blame Fate for our predicament. If everything happened for a reason and our actions couldn't change what's coming, I wouldn't have to carry the blame. But every decision matters, leading down a specific road, and I know it.

"What do you want me to do?" I ask. "Tell me, and I'll do it."

"Don't bother." Still he shows me no mercy. "What you do tomorrow doesn't change what you did today."

Sorrow floods me, *drowns* me, and I wrap trembling arms around my middle.

At both the best and worst of times, my mind does one of two things: obsesses over numbers or drafts a poem.

Guess what I do now?

I am Ten, the completion of a cycle. Composed of two numbers. One and zero. One: solitary. Without companionship. Zero: neither a negative nor a positive, just a whole lot of nothing…like my status right now.

Ten out of ten people hate me right now.

Ten out of ten people will die during their lifetime.

The two most popular numbers in the world are three and seven. 3 + 7 = 10. Three is known as the trinity…or troika. Spirit, soul and body. Seven is often called the perfect number. Seven continents, seven layers of skin—three main layers, with four others in between—and seven colors in a rainbow. Seven notes of sound. Seven dimensions and directions—two opposite directions for each dimension, plus the center…the static…the one that never changes.

Everything has changed for me.

Deacon scrubs a hand down his face. "At least the battle in the Land of the Harvest ended the moment you cleared the guard tower."

"I'm glad." There would be no more deaths because of decisions I made. Not today, at least.

He stares at me for a long while. "Here's what is going to happen. I'm taking you into Troika, where your family and friends are waiting to greet you. You'll spend a week exploring the realm, getting to know the land and the people, and you'll attend a welcome party for those who recently experienced Firstdeath. Then you'll begin your training."

I'm to become a General. Actually a Conduit, the highest type of General. I'm supposed to save my realm from the horrors of Myriad's darkness.

There are six main positions in Troika—General, Leader, Headhunter, Laborer, Messenger and Healer—with hundreds of sub-positions under each.

Six positions, just as there are six fundamental virtues: love, wisdom, truth, goodness, mercy and justice.

"Through it all," he adds, "you'll stay away from me. I can't stand the sight of you."

Sandpaper rubs my throat raw. "Very well." I owe him. I'll respect his wishes—even if I'm currently losing respect for *him*. Troikans praise the merits of forgiveness and lament the hazards of retaliation. Two reasons I picked the realm. Two reasons I forsook Killian.

Am I a fool?

And did I really just think the word *Troikans* rather than *we*? I sigh. I'm part of the family, even if I feel alone.

Not that feelings are reliable. Feelings rarely provide a realistic picture, and often lead to destruction. I have to act on my heart-knowledge: what the heart understands, even if the mind—or logic—doesn't.

Hello, spiritual law. With Sloan, I acted on my feelings. What I dished, I'm now eating. Today's chef is Deacon.

Ann-nn-nd my shoulders roll in a little more. If left unchecked, my feelings can be a weapon more dangerous than a gun or a knife. They can send me sprinting down the wrong path and put me in the wrong place at the wrong time. They can hold me in darkness, blinding me to Light. They can make me soar one moment, and send me crashing the next. I must rise above. Must do what's right even when everything around me is wrong.

I won't forget again.

Deacon waves at the waterfall. "This is the Veil of Wings. The only way into Troika. Troikans can pass through without worry. If a Myriadian tries, he will burn to ash."

Tremors shake me. Message received. If I attempt to bring Killian inside, I'll kill him.

The weight of my decision to stand with one realm and rise against the other…to put everything I have, everything I am, into a single cause…to abandon the boy willing to kill for me, even willing to die for me…suddenly assails me. Panic crawls from the ashes of my despair, and slays my calm.

I try to distract myself with a poem.

Happiness is not obtainable
And I will never believe that
Love and Light will lead the way
Again and again, I've been shown that
Pain and darkness always win
It is a lie that
Happiness and joy are a choice
The truth is
There's no way out of the abyss.
I will never be convinced that
"Something better this way comes."
"You just have to fight the good fight."
Actually
I will say—
"Even worse is on the way."
Because there's no way that
We can escape the abyss.

So depressing! I flip the script and repeat the poem, starting at the bottom and working my way up. A new ray of hope dawns.

I cling to it. Right now, it's all I have.

"See the mist billowing from the waterfall?" Deacon asks. "It's part of the Veil and wraps around the entire realm. There's *nowhere* a Myriadian can safely enter." He marches across the bridge, never once glancing back to ensure I follow.

Resigned, I trail after him. Time to see my eternal home.

Time to meet the people I'll be sharing an Everlife with. My new family. The ones I'll be fighting to protect.

But a single question haunts me as I step underneath the spray of water.

I picked them…but what if they don't pick me?

MYRIAD

From: K_F_5/23.53.6
To: R_O_3/2.17.12
Subject: I'll go ahead and pat myself on the back

Consider Tenley Lockwood bagged and tagged. She trusts me implicitly, and she wants to be with me. Maybe she already regrets her covenant with Troika. The problem is, she's going to spend the next year holed up inside Troika, training. That is twelve months—or fifty-two weeks—before she's sent to the Land of the Harvest on assignment. Twelve months I won't get to see her or talk to her. Fifty-two weeks I won't get to "work my magic," as you like to say.

How am I supposed to convince her to spy for us? Unless... can you trick Troika into sending her on assignment sooner?

Never mind. My apologies for suggesting the impossible. I'll work my magic in a year, as promised.

Might Equals Right!

ML, Killian Flynn

MYRIAD

From: R_O_3/2.17.12
To: K_F_5/23.53.6
Subject: Never doubt me

I'm a General, Mr. Flynn. The best of the best. I can do anything. Mark my words: you will see Miss Lockwood sooner rather than later. I'll make sure of it.

In the meantime, you'll be training our newest recruit. Miss Aubuchon strikes me as resourceful young woman, willing to go the extra mile to get a job done.

Also, you've been assigned to a new Leader. Report your progress with Miss Aubuchon to Sir Zhi Chen. Report your progress with Miss Lockwood to us both.

Might Equals Right!
General Rosalind Oriana

MYRIAD

From: K_F_5/23.53.6
To: R_O_3/2.17.12
Subject: Is that a tear in my eye?

Thank you for gifting me with such an honor. I foresee *zero* problems training Sloan, the girl I just murdered. (Let me know if I need to explain sarcasm to you.) Elena and Charles are my Flankers/trainees. Adding a third is overkill, don't you think?

    Considering my recent successes, I have a favor to ask you. Before Madame Pearl Bennett died, she visited the Hall of Records to discover who is Fused with my mother, and where the girl is living in the Land of the Harvest. Will you look into Madame Bennett's notes? I'd be grateful.

    I'm sure I'll do a better job with Miss Lockwood if I'm focused on her, and only her.

    Might Equals Right!

    ML, Killian Flynn

MYRIAD

From: R_O_3/2.17.12
To: K_F_5/23.53.6
Subject: Aren't you adorable?

Next time you threaten me—however overtly—I'll have you returned to the Kennels.

Elena and Charles have been reassigned. As for your mother, I'll be happy to share her name with you…as soon as you do what you promised with Tenley Lockwood. That is our way. You help me, I help you.

Might Equals Right!

General Rosalind Oriana

chapter three

"Humility is your protection from self-deception.
Pride is your defeat."
—Troika

I'm bathed in liquid sunshine and bliss. The water doesn't soak
me or even dampen my clothing; it goes through me, somehow cleansing me from the inside out and, for one sublime
moment, washing away my problems. Peace settles over me.
There's no room for fear or melancholy.

I breathe in deeply…exhale slowly…and savor every second.

I'm certain Killian will overcome whatever obstacles are
thrown into his path. He's smart. Brilliant, actually. And I'm
ecstatic for Archer. He's entered into the Rest. Who *wouldn't*
enjoy a permanent vacation from war? I'm confident I'll overcome my own obstacles and quickly acclimate to my new circumstances…new structures, studies, traditions and people.

I'm not worried about my parents, who are Myriad loyalists, living in the other realm…hating me?

Maybe, maybe not. Before taking her final breath, my
mother reconciled with me. My father cursed me before his.
No matter. My peace endures. My worth isn't measured by his

feelings for me. I am who I am, and my worth is my worth. Life is that simple and that complicated.

I'm not even worried about the frigid cold I experience whenever Killian touches me. We've become two halves of a whole, and we'll find a way to be together.

A hard weight slams into me from behind and knocks me forward. I stumble, coming out the other side of the waterfall, my precious peace instantly replaced by worries and concerns, my warmth by cold and my hope by despair. Tremors ignite in my belly and quickly spread through the rest of me.

Deacon, despite his dislike of me, helps steady me as a guy who looks to be my age emerges from the Veil.

"Sorry, sorry," the guy says with a slight British accent. "Absolutely my fault, yeah. Wasn't watching where I was going."

He has dark blond hair and amber eyes—one of which is ringed with black. He's been in a fight. The battle we just left?

Guilt pricks at me.

There's something familiar about him, but I'm too jumbled by my wayward emotions to solve the puzzle. Despite the bruising, he's pretty enough to make a storybook princess weep with envy. At roughly five foot ten, he's not much taller than me. However, the breadth of his shoulders allows him to engulf me.

His gaze slides to Deacon, and I realize I've been staring at him in silence. "New recruit?" he asks, amused, and my cheeks heat.

"Yes," Deacon replies, his voice tight. He pats the guy on the shoulder and seems to fortify himself for an uncomfortable conversation. "There's something you need to know, Victor. Archer is…he's been…"

Victor holds up his hand and releases a heavy breath. "I've

been told, but I refuse to mourn. I'll be too busy fighting for his return."

Victor winks at me. "Welcome home, newbie. You're going to love it here. Come by my apartment later, and I'll personally make sure of it."

Deacon gives the guy's chest a light punch. "The sexual harassment seminar is going well, I see."

A grinning Victor salutes him before focusing on me. "I'm late for a debriefing or I'd stay and get to know you better. I know, I know. You're devastated. When you come by—you did agree to visit me, right?—I'll dry your tears." He rushes off.

"Is everyone I meet going to make me feel like I fell off the ugly tree and hit every branch?" I ask.

"Spirits are flawless. There isn't a can of dog food in the bunch."

Good to know. "So who was *that*?"

"Victor Prince. Archer's younger brother. They shared a special bond."

Archer's *brother*? Guilt *slashes* me, until I'm nothing but confetti.

Why didn't he curse at me? Or rail? Why didn't he demand I leave the realm forever? Something! Instead, he invited me over for, I'm guessing, a little light flirting.

Oh...zero. He must not know about my involvement in Archer's death.

I wish the ground would open up and swallow me.

"Behold." Deacon waves his arm to indicate the path Victor just took. "Troika."

My gaze follows the line of his finger, a drumroll going off in my head to herald the moment of truth. Is Troika as

lovely as Archer promised, or the scorched apocalyptic waste-
land Killian disdained?

I can't… I don't… I wasn't prepared for this. The beauty
before me is far lovelier than Archer described. Like nothing
I've ever seen. A gold brick wall frames an arched entrance
created from pearl; the exquisite design is broken only by the
Troikan symbol, which is carved into three separate locations.

Past the open archway is a thriving metropolis both fantas-
tic and futuristic, with buildings of every shape and design,
some made with a chrome-like substance, some with crystals. Interspersed throughout are castles and other buildings
straight from the pages of a storybook. Cinderella would *so*
approve; with the dewy foliage ascending many of the ram-
parts, Snow White wouldn't miss her woodland cottage and
the prince wouldn't need Rapunzel's hair to climb to the top.

I marvel as flowers bloom in a sky of clear, dappled water.
We're under an ocean? No. Realization: we're under the Veil
of Wings! Rose petals fall, twirling lazily through the air.

A ray of sunlight dances from a sun I cannot see. I reach
out…only to still. The Troikan symbol in the center of my
palm sparkles. Awed, I turn my arm. The numbers sparkle,
as well.

"So many changes," I mutter.

"You were living in an imperfect and tainted world," Deacon says. "Physical bodies reflect that. Spirits do not."

He ushers me past the pearl archway. A wall of mist parts
in the center, revealing seven smaller archways, each made
with a different precious gem and attached to a different—
massive—tube.

"These are Gates," he explains. "There are seven major cities within the realm, and every Gate leads to a different one.
You'll want to learn the transport system as soon as possible."

He takes my hand and leads me into a tube made of diamonds.

Those diamonds vanish in a blink, replaced by a searing display of fireworks. I'm cognizant of the fact that I'm still standing, still walking, and yet I feel as if I've been sucked into a vacuum. The array of lights blurs, whizzing past me, and a wave of dizziness causes me to sway.

With Deacon's help, I remain upright. The lights begin to fade, the diamond tube reappears. We step onto a gold brick street, surrounded by chrome-and-crystal buildings, no longer on the edge of the realm but in the middle of it. *Thousands* of people surround us. Male, female. Young, old. Well, not too old. No one tops thirty-five, I'd guess. There's a beautiful mix of colors and races, and yet they are one people. Different, but exactly the same: priceless.

Due to virtual reality tours I've taken through Myriad, I know their citizens wear clothing compatible with the era they lived in as a human. I've seen everything from Victorian ball gowns to loincloths. The same is not true for Troikans.

"Everyone is wearing a catsuit or robe," I say. "Why?"

"The robes are ceremonial. Needed for certain jobs," Deacon replies. "The suits are lightweight armor. The material protects us against certain weapons. We must always be ready for attack."

How…sad for us.

A clatter of voices hits my awareness, each light and cheerful. Smiles and laughter abound. No one seems to mind the threat Deacon described.

Envy cuts through me. Have I ever been so carefree?

First I was a girl sheltered by her parents, protected from any outside influence. Then I was a girl tortured at Prynne. Then I was a girl meant to save one realm and destroy the other. Always I was a means to an end. Until Killian and Archer transitioned from Laborers to friends.

Speaking past the lump in my throat, I ask, "How did we move from one location to another in mere seconds?"

"We're spirits, no longer bound by physical laws. The Gates allow us to travel at the speed of Light."

I struggle to process such an impossible revelation. The precise value of the speed of Light is 299,792,458 meters per second.

$2 + 9 + 9 + 7 + 9 + 2 + 4 + 5 + 8 = 55$

$5 + 5 = 10$

Stop counting! Deacon has moved on. I rush after him, trailing him through the crowd. Despite a seeming preoccupation with each other, the couples and families remain highly aware of those around them, and no one bumps into anyone else. Everyone is courteous, offering a genuine "Please" and "Thank you" whenever warranted.

Various perfumes scent the air, blending harmoniously with the fragrance of roses. Multicolored petals continue to rain from the sky.

Deacon enters a crystal building, whisking through a door of mist. The decor is breathtaking, the ceiling like a midnight sky filled with vibrant stars. The walls are aglow with hues plucked straight from a rainbow, and every piece of furniture—from dinner tables and chairs to sofas and coffee tables—extends from massive trees that have grown through the floor, as if carved from branches still attached to the trunks.

A woodland forest *inside* a building. This is where impossible meets miracle.

When the identity of the occupants registers, I come to an abrupt stop. People I knew and loved in Firstlife, and even family I never actually met.

There is my grandmother Meredith; since my parents disowned her before I was born, I've only ever seen her in pictures. She is so beautiful. Though she experienced Firstdeath in her forties, she now appears twenty-five, her skin unlined, her pale hair without a single strand of gray.

Mom once told me about the adventures she and her mother had. How they'd spent every weekend at homeless shelters to care for the less fortunate.

My palms sweat. Am I a disappointment to her?

Meredith is speaking with Clayton "Clay" Anders. Clay and I met and bonded at Prynne. During our escape, we trekked through ice-covered mountains and got caught in an avalanche.

I shudder. Clay and Sloan were swept to the edge of a cliff, terrified out of their minds, and I had to make a split second decision. Who to save first. At the time, Sloan was Unsigned, while Clay had a secure future with Troika.

I picked Sloan, pouring what little energy I'd had into pulling her to solid ground first. I hadn't wanted her sent to Many Ends, a realm of horrors and pain, to be tortured for eternity.

In the end, I hadn't had enough time to save Clay, too, and I regret—

No. Absolutely not. I don't regret. Yes, Sloan later betrayed me. Yes, Clay died too young. Considering the circumstances, I made the right call. I gave an Unsigned girl a chance Clay didn't need. *She* made the wrong choice afterward, and the fault is hers alone.

And look at Clay now. My hand flutters over my heart to contain a starburst of joy. He's thriving!

I spot General Levi Nanne, as handsome as ever in an immaculate pin-striped suit—no armor for him?—his dark hair brushed back from his chiseled features. He's holding Jeremy, my infant brother, and I squeal.

Jeremy is my little miracle. To protect the Everlife from overcrowding, the Land of the Harvest is strict about population control. Women are sterilized after giving birth to their first child. If someone heals and a second pregnancy occurs, the child is given to a childless family. If no family is found, the child is placed in an orphanage. If the orphanages are overcrowded, the child faces elimination.

My mother had Jeremy in secret. She died soon afterward, poisoned by Madame Pearl Bennett, and Jeremy died only minutes later; Mom had unwittingly shared the poison with him when she fed him.

Some of my happiness deflates.

Let go of the past, march into the future.

I don't recognize anyone else in the group, but I sense they are my blood relatives, ancestors who fought for me from behind the scenes during all the years of my Firstlife.

"Ten!" Clay catches sight of me and rushes over. I meet him halfway and throw my arms around him, clinging to him. With a laugh, he swings me around. "What did Zero say to Eight?"

At the asylum, he'd always greeted me with a number joke.

As I kiss his cheek, tears burn my eyes. My voice wobbles as I reply, "Hey! Nice belt."

He chuckles. "I'm never going to stump you, am I?"

"Not in *any* lifetime, my friend."

He tweaks my nose. The others join us, and I'm passed around like a hot potato.

By the time I make it back to Clay, his smile is gone. Sorrow peers at me. "You had so much more to do. You died too soon, Ten."

My chest constricts. "So did you, my friend. So did you." I lean my head on his shoulder. "Did Marlowe make it into Troika?" *Please, say yes. Please.*

Marlowe Dillinger is another of my Prynne friends. The sweetest, gentlest girl I've ever met. She ended up at the asylum because she stole money from her mother to—horror of horrors—pay for groceries.

She signed with Troika, hoping to escape the asylum. Her mom refused to spring her, and soon after, a guard sneaked into her cell to—

My mind shies away from the horrors she endured. The next morning, the girl with a heart of gold killed herself. Maybe she voided her contract, maybe she didn't. I'm unclear about the fine print.

Clay flinches. "I'm told suicides are decided on a case by case basis. Hers... She's in Many Ends."

Fresh tears well, but I blink them back. No more crying. Marlowe's Firstlife sucked, and guaranteed her Everlife is worse. It's not fair. But I will find a way to free her and all the others trapped inside Many Ends. I will! My determination will never wane.

"I know a little boy who is eager to say hello," Levi says, claiming my attention.

I give Clay another hug before stealing my little brother from the General. "Zero! He's changed."

Levi beams with pride, his love for the boy obvious. "He grows stronger every day."

Jeremy Eleven Lockwood. The last time we were together, he was missing patches of hair. His cheeks were sunken in, and his swollen lips had turned blue as he'd struggled to breathe. Now he has a headful of curls the same shade of cobalt as mine. His peaches-and-cream complexion speaks of health and vitality, and his eyes...they sparkle like precious gems, mesmerizing me. Like me, one of his eyes is blue and the other is green. Though he's only a few weeks old—spirits age just like humans, until reaching the Age of Perfection— both eyes regard me with intelligence and adoration.

A look I've received from only two other people: Killian and Archer.

Zero! I'm crying again, and I can't stop. Have I become the world's biggest sissy?

One of my tears splashes on Jeremy's cheek, and he giggles. He wraps his chubby little fingers around one of mine and brings it to his mouth for a toothless nibble.

"We're together forever now, baby bro." A vow from my innermost being.

—*Forever*—

"Ye—" I shake my head. A little boy's voice just whispered through my mind as surely as the wind had whispered earlier. Surely my brother didn't...surely he can't...

But maybe he can? New world, new rules. I don't yet know what's possible and what's not. There's no reason to stress over anything. One, I'll figure things out. Two, if I ask, I'll be given a cryptic answer that generates even more questions, guaranteed. That is Levi's MO. And three, I've got bigger problems than my brother maybe, maybe not, speaking to me telepathically.

Namely: How can I help free the people of Many Ends without Archer's and Killian's help?

Everything always comes back to my guys, doesn't it. And why not? Killian was my rock, the one who helped me stand when I wobbled. Archer was my guide. He showed me the way I should go every time I floundered.

Who else do I have? Clay is as new to this life as I am. I

have family I don't know, and I'm hated by the ones I do. I'm a soldier in a war I don't fully understand.

Oh, I know the story: the Firstking created Troika for his son Eron, the Prince of Doves, and Myriad for his son Ambrosine, the Prince of Ravens. Afterward, he created the Land of the Harvest and the humans who populated it—humans allowed to choose the realm where they would ultimately live.

One decision. An eternity of joy or regret.

But it wasn't long before Ambrosine plotted to destroy Eron, determined to rule both realms.

What I don't know is why the different citizens loathe each other. Or why, exactly, they decided to go to war. Were they simply following the orders of their kings?

Why can't we create friendships—relationships? If Troika and Myriad ever cease-fire, I can more easily save the people in Many Ends.

The portal to the realm of eternal horrors is hidden inside Myriad. But I can no longer enter Myriad...

I must find a way.

I could ask Killian to enter for me. And get him caught, punished or killed.

Not an option. If I can help Troika and Myriad reach a truce, I can enter Myriad again. Maybe. Possibly. I like my odds.

Levi pats my shoulder. "Guess what, lucky girl? I'm overseeing your training, and I'm giving you homework on your first day. Take a moment to boo and hiss if you'd like. No? Fine. Memorize the *Book of the Law*, write the words on your heart and see."

"Uh, care to finish your sentence? See *what*?" And how am I supposed to write words on my heart?

He winks at me, code for *figure it out for yourself, dummy.*

Fine. I arch a brow at him. "Please tell me the book is only a single page long, and part two of my assignment isn't literal."

Another wink.

Great!

"So sorry we're late," a familiar voice says. "Class ran over."

Excitement blooms as Kayla Brooks and Reed Haynesworth make their way through the throng. I met short, pale-haired Kayla and tall, dark-haired Reed in Many Ends. My first saves.

But not my last!

Like too many others, Kayla and Reed died too young. She's only eighteen, and he's a whopping nineteen.

Troika has been good to the pair. They glow.

In their Firstlife, they were Unsigned, refusing to choose a side and fight in a war they didn't understand. Instead, they joined HART. Humans Against Realm Turmoil.

They died when protestors bombed HART headquarters.

Had their deaths occurred before the age of sixteen, they could have entered either Troika or Myriad without problem. Anyone under sixteen—the Age of Accountability—has no ties to Many Ends, even if they are Unsigned.

Later, when the spirit-child reaches the AoA, he can choose to forsake whichever realm he's been living in and enter the other.

I'm not sure how much time Reed and Kayla spent in Many Ends before I showed up...once, twice, three times. Third time is the charm. We escaped together, forever changing the course of our Everlives; that's how I know the captives can be freed. There's a secret Gate or Veil or whatever inside Myriad—where we ended up.

"Hey, guys." I grin as I embrace them. "I'm so happy to see you."

"A word of warning, my friend." Reed gives me a pitying

look. "You've already made adversaries here. You're being blamed for the loss of several TLs."

My heart cracks down the center and leaks acid. "I made mistakes. I'll deal with the consequences."

"You're a new spirit in a new world," Levi says, and sighs. "None of us had a perfect start, and anyone who casts stones will have to deal with me."

The show of support both elates and depresses me. I don't want people to pretend to like me, fearing they'll get into trouble if they don't.

Jeremy waves his arms and kicks his legs in a bid for freedom. I've never been around babies, so I'm not sure what to do. My unease must show, because Levi gathers him close. In thanks, my brother upchucks all over his tie.

"Slob goblin." Levi laughs and gives Jeremy's butt a gentle tap. "That's what you are, isn't it, young man?"

Jeremy farts.

My grandmother moves to my side and nudges me with her shoulder. She's my mom's mom, strong but elegant, even regal, and up close she's more than beautiful. She's absolutely stunning. A gold catsuit makes her luminous from head to toe.

"I'm glad you finally saw the Light," she says.

Light Brings Sight is our realm's battle cry.

"Should I call you Granny?" I tease. "Or maybe Gran Gran?"

She snorts. "You refer to me by either name, and I'll put you over my knee to paddle the Light right out of you."

You can't take the old lady sass out of the young spirit, I see.

"Why don't you call me Meredith," she suggests, tugging on a lock of my blue hair.

"Sure. But I'm going to creep myself out every time I do it," I admit. "You aren't supposed to be so…"

"Hot?" She fluffs her glossy waves. "Just wait till you meet my mother—your *great*-grandmother—Hazel."

Curious, I scan the sea of faces. "Is she here?"

"No, she's out on an assignment. The job never sleeps."

To my knowledge, only two positions ever really leave the realm. "She's a Laborer, then? Or a Messenger?"

"Laborer. And a very good one."

So she works with human souls while I'll be working with Light. I'm supposed to absorb sunlight—which is more than just heat and illumination, I've been told—and direct the beams to Troika.

"And you are…what?" I ask.

"A Leader. I serve directly under Levi as one of his many assistants."

Meaning she's a step above a Laborer, and her official title is Madame. "Cool. But I kind of outrank you, right?" I say with a smile.

Another snort. "Honey, you outrank us all. Or rather, you will. You've got a lot to learn first. Here's proof." Moving too swiftly for me to track, she secures her leg behind my knee and gives me a push.

I topple to my butt, air leaving my lungs in a single heave. Before I can catch my breath, I'm lumbering to my feet. *Never stay down!*

Her eyes gleam with pride. She motions to my right arm with a tilt of her chin. "Have you decoded your Key yet?"

Only then do I realize I'm rubbing the numbers branded into my flesh. "Uh—no. I haven't. How am I supposed to decode my… Key? What Key?"

She ignores my questions. "You will. Until then, the Grid will provide an invisible link between you and every other

Troikan. We're all tied together, an army of millions with one true heart. Draw on our strength and peace."

I imagine the heart of Troika beating inside my chest, keeping me alive while my own weeps over losing Killian and Archer. "Why do I need to decode my Key?"

She shows me her right arm, where the words *Faith, Hope* and *Love* are etched. "When you do, you'll be able to open locked doors within the Grid."

Uh... "Why are the doors locked?"

"The information stored behind them is more than your puny brain can currently comprehend."

Puny brain? "How kind you are, Grandmother." I bat my lashes at her. "Your Key is three common words. Mine is a sequence of numbers with no rhyme or reason."

"Oh, there's a rhyme and reason all right. I had to do three things I'd never done before. Believe in myself, expect good things to happen to me and love the people around me, whether I felt like loving them or not. Easier said than done."

"I don't understand. You used to take my mother to homeless shelters."

"Appearances can be deceiving. I did what I did under duress. It was my husband, your grandfather, who so faithfully served others."

My grandfather Steven. A man I've never met. "Where is he?"

"Out on assignment with Hazel. He's eager to meet you." She blows me a kiss before strolling away.

A woman I've never met takes her place at my side, clutching my hands and gazing at me with pleading eyes. My heart knows something my mind doesn't: she's a blood relation from my father's side.

"My daughter," she says. The hem of her robe sways at her feet. "Please. You have to help her."

My stomach churns as if I've swallowed a mix of batteries and broken glass. "Help your daughter with what?"

"She is Unsigned. You will understand her better than most. You can convince her to choose Troika. She needs you—"

Deacon to the rescue! He wraps an arm around the woman's shoulders and whispers what I assume are words of comfort. She pales but nods, and he ushers her away. I watch them with wide eyes, wishing I knew more about this realm, my abilities, my responsibilities—or anything useful, really. Wishing I could help her, even though I can't seem to help myself.

I look to Levi and say, "How can I help her daughter choose Troika? I'm not a Laborer."

"You must crawl before you can walk."

Someone save me. "Thank you, Confucius." I really hate cryptic-speak.

"You'll be trained for *every* job here," he continues. "Through trials of your own, you'll better understand the people only you are to aid."

Great. Wonderful. But no pressure, right?

Levi waves Clay over. "Escort Ten to her new apartment. She's had a long day and could use a bit of rest."

My own apartment…an actual home. I've been without a home for over a year. The asylum was simply a building where I received a cot and three hots.

I say goodbye to the others, and Clay leads me outside. The crowd has thinned considerably. I'm so busy marveling at new sights, I have no idea how he gets me inside another tube.

The sides blaze and blur, and once again I experience the sensation of being sucked into a vacuum, only to step out a few seconds later into a maze of wildflowers. Fruit and nut trees are in full bloom, heavy with their bounty. Wisteria trees arch overhead, creating a ceiling of lavender petals.

"Where are we?" I ask.

"The Capital of New."

I nod, pretending I know what that means.

We clear the garden and come to a street peppered with homes from every era, from Egyptian pyramids to futuristic spaceships. When Clay stops in front of a Gothic cathedral, a chill sweeps over me.

Trepidation? Awe? I'm not sure!

"This," he says, "is where the most elite trainees live, no matter their field of study. You're on the top floor and, because you're so precious—" he snickers as he air-quotes the word "—you get me as a next-door neighbor. There are eight others on our floor. A mix of Messengers, Laborers and Healers."

I try to speak, I do, but all I manage are unintelligible sounds. The beauty *astounds* me. Up top are two towers with pointed pergolas, between them a crocket and a gable. A massive oval window consumes the center. Glistening in the sunlight are stained-glass windows interspersed with wrought iron twisted in the shape of a tree of life.

Clay presses two fingers under my jaw to help me close my mouth.

I noticed the brand on his wrist—three interlocking circles—and finally find my voice. "Have you decoded your Key?"

"Not yet," he grumbles.

I bump him with my shoulder. "Is it wrong how happy I am that we're in the same boat?"

"Yes! You should encourage me to kick your butt."

We share a laugh and enter the cathedral. The occupants

range in age, anywhere from sixteen to twenty. Some smile at me while others frown. A few scowl.

I distract myself, studying the magnificent architecture. Above every doorway are triptychs—paintings divided into three separate panels. Along every wall are marble columns, intricate mosaics—again in patterns of three—and murals. Above the farthest is a magnificent frieze ceiling with three tiers.

When we turn a corner, an elaborate staircase looms ahead. Both guys and girls race up and down. Again I receive a mixed bag of reactions.

I try to ignore the guy with the darkest glower. When I hear Killian's name whispered, I wonder if everyone's anger has more to do with my affiliation with a Myriadian than my actions on the battlefield.

"So coeds live here. Do we train here, too?" I ask.

"Nope. You're going crap yourself when you find out where we do train."

I snort. "Should I go ahead and order adult diapers?"

"The sooner the better."

I catch a glimpse of Victor, who is speaking with a pretty redhead. The two are wrapped up in each other and don't notice me. Then my gaze catches on a familiar face. The girl from today's battle. The dark-haired one who shot me with a dart when I dived in front of Killian.

She spots me, too, and stops in the middle of the staircase to glare at me.

I swallow a groan.

"That," Clay says, "is Miss Elizabeth Winchester. She's a bit of a wild card. Only speaks to a select group of people, but defends our weaker members with shocking ferocity."

"She's a trainee, right?" Meaning we're on equal footing? *Come on, throw me a bone.*

Nope, no bones today. A trainee wouldn't have gotten the green light to fight.

Clay confirms my suspicions, saying, "She's a new graduate. She'll be moving to a house soon. Until then, you might want to wear your armor. If looks could kill…"

I can't recover from a bad first impression. I can only work harder, do more and prove I'm better, wiser, stronger than I was before.

Am I better, wiser and stronger, though? I'm a girl with both feet in Troika and pieces of a broken heart in Myriad with Killian.

"Don't worry," Clay says. "One day, everyone will get behind you."

Yes. Let's just hope they aren't holding daggers in each hand.

Head high, I ascend the staircase.

When I reach Elizabeth, she grabs my arm and softly grates, "Watch out, Numbers. I owe you big-time, and I *always* pay my debts. Plus interest."

chapter four

"Pride will carry you when you're weak."
—Myriad

Clay shows me around my new apartment. He's beaming, excited to explain the ins and outs, and I try to concentrate on him, I really do, but...

Elizabeth's warning echoes inside my head. She called me Numbers. As if she knows me. Until today, we've never interacted. Someone who *does* know me must have told her about my obsession with numbers. Who? And what else was mentioned?

"Are any of my friends buddies with Elizabeth?" I ask, interrupting whatever tale Clay was spinning about a remote control.

He sighs and pats the top of my head. "As a suspected Conduit, you've been a topic of conversation among the masses for weeks. *A lot* of people know *a lot* about you. Messengers and Laborers—other than Archer—used to watch over you, protecting you, and when they returned to the realm, curious people asked questions."

My hands fist so tightly, my nails cut into my palm. Those Messengers and Laborers had been in spirit form. They had seen me, but I hadn't seen them. Now everyone I come across—strangers!—could know intimate details about my life. Embarrassing details.

Maybe I'll hole up here and never leave.

"If you'll show me the apartment again," I grate, "I'll pay attention this time."

He laughs. "I knew I'd lost you. All right. Thus begins the tour, take two."

He steers me to the front door and spreads his arms to indicate the small hallway leading to the living room. "This is your foyer."

I follow him through the rooms, attuned to his every word. What I learn: my new home is a diminutive but extravagant space, fully furnished with many of the creature comforts I was denied while locked in Prynne, and one bedroom. There's a cool hologram capable of following me anywhere, showcasing footage of newborns and new arrivals, promotional announcements, giveaways hosted by everyday average citizens, and Laborer interviews.

In those interviews, TLs talk about the humans they've most recently signed and any victories achieved in the Land of the Harvest. I wonder how many times I've been mentioned. A thought I do *not* allow myself to explore further. I'll rage.

The holograms are incredibility lifelike; the people appear to be inside my apartment.

Does Killian live like this?

"Take a seat on the couch," Clay says, his eyes twinkling.

Ooo-kay. As soon as I obey, a glowing book pops up in front of me, and I gasp.

"Go ahead." Clay does his best impression of an evil queen slash drug dealer and mimes what he wants me to do. "Touch it. You know you want to..."

I reach up. When my fingertip meets the illumination, the page flips. I huff and jerk back.

He laughs with delight. "Read."

I scan a page, and the numbers on my arm tingle. *Actions matter. Always. You are at the helm of your Everlife just as you were for your Firstlife. Take responsibility for your decisions. Be kind. You never know the details of another person's life. The pain they've suffered.*

"Wait! This is the *Book of the Law*, isn't it?" A manual about the Troikan way of life.

"Sure is."

Excited, I read on. *You are a treasure, a gift. There's no one like you. There are people in the world only you can help. Don't feel worthy? Just remember, no matter how far you've fallen, you can rise again. You can rise stronger. Your past weak link can be turned into tomorrow's strength.*

I'm trembling as I flip to the next page. *We have an enemy, and only one enemy. The Prince of the Ravens. Fight him, for he seeks your destruction. Never surrender. You—we—are the Light of the world.*

"All right, all right. That's enough for now." Clay helps me stand, and the book vanishes. "Your tour isn't over." But even as he speaks, he gives me a little push.

"Hey." I fall back onto the couch, the book reappearing.

Laughing, he helps me stand a second time, and the book vanishes. Well, okay then. There's an easy on-off switch.

"This," he says, holding up the fancy remote before passing it to me, "is your new favorite thing. It controls the holograms." *This* is made of metal and shaped in the Troikan symbol. The buttons are dispersed over the three outer leaves, while the center cutout allows a comfortable grip. "You can turn it on and off at will or watch a different hologram on every screen. You'll probably want to leave it running day and night. Levi told me you have a special link to Jeremy's nursery."

"What?" I thrust the remote back into his hands. "Show me."

With the press of a few buttons, the image on the nearest wall changes to reveal an empty room with a crib, rocking chair and a basket filled with toys.

"Dang, I'm good." Clay grins. "You should probably leave another screen on, as well. You don't want to miss the give-aways."

The giveaways. Need a brand-new hand-carved table? So-and-so just finished one, and he can't wait to gift it to you. Want a brand-new ceremonial robe sewed from authentic Victorian muslin? So-and-so just completed one, and she would love to gift it to you.

There has to be a catch, right? Or is this true kindness in action? Giving without expecting anything in return. The way Killian endangered his future to secure mine. The way Archer gave his life to save mine.

I rub my aching chest and say, "I don't need anything." Nothing materialistic, anyway.

As a distraction, I fiddle with the remote control and soon discover I can change the color of any wall or program an automatic change of sheets on the bed. Neat.

"You even have a treadmill." Clay motions to a portion of wall with strategically placed silver bulbs to fit my exact height and weight. Those bulbs rotate and vibrate every time I come near. "After you've run or walked at least five miles, the machine becomes a massager." He messes with the metal joints.

A small portion of the wall detaches from both the ceiling and floor, remaining hinged at the center while tilting to a steep incline. The rollers spin, creating the aforementioned treadmill. Up top are two handholds.

"Exercise is your friend," he states.

"If you said *extra fries*, you're right."

He snorts and drags me into the bedroom. The bed is small, a twin, but the mattress is as soft as clouds and cools or heats automatically, according to my body temperature. A door in back leads to a private bathroom. Inside is a sink, toilet and shower with settings to program a "gentle summer rain" or a "torrential downpour."

The bathroom opens to a closet already filled with clothes, everything from black leather catsuits to elaborate ceremonial robes, some white with green trim, some white with gold trim, some red with black trim, but all are in my size.

"These things...they're luxuries," I say. "Troikans are supposed to be dedicated taskmasters, all business and no pleasure. *Myriad* focuses on indulgence." Wait. Am I *complaining*? I suck.

He gives my head another pat. "Keeping the citizens comfortable is an important part of business. Happy people are productive people. And there's nothing wrong with pleasure." He leads me to the smallest room in the apartment. "All right. Last stop. The kitchen."

Seriously? "There's no stove or refrigerator."

"You'll never need to cook again. The only food your spirit craves is manna." He waves to a shelf where the manna is prepared in different ways: liquefied, cut into wafers, soft like ice cream, baked into little cakes. "We also have an abundance of honey, fruits and nuts to mix into your treat, better than anything you had as a human."

He opens a jar, dips a spoon inside and offers me the dripping treat. "This is manna with pecans and honey."

I accept, my eyes closing in rapture as the sweetness coats

my tongue. My Lifeblood fizzes with electricity. I could run ten races. No, twenty. A hundred! I could—

I yawn.

"Uh-oh. You're about to crash." He wraps an arm around my waist. "Your spirit isn't used to so much stimulation and demands a respite."

"No, I—" Fatigue pours through my veins, my limbs suddenly as heavy as boulders. Black dots wink through my vision, and my legs wobble.

"See!" He helps me to the bedroom and tucks me under the covers. "Sleep well, Number Girl."

I close my heavy eyelids, whispering, "One...two... threeee," and drift off...

I dream about my brands, only then realizing the numbers line up. One glows, then another and another. There's a clear sequence, I realize, and excitement sparks.

The number ten kicks off the first row, with seven numbers lined up after it, each bracketed by a period. Added up, those number equal 688. Eleven starts the second row, with seven numbers following it; when added, they equal 859. Twelve leads the final row, with seven numbers after it. When added, they equal 228.

And by adding the three totals, I get 1,775.

The year of the American Revolution. Any significance? I mean...am I supposed to start my own revolution? No, no. Why would I need to start one of those?

If my numbers are anything like Meredith's words, they represent three specific ideals.

The dream shifts, those ideals remaining at bay. Suddenly I'm standing on a mountaintop, the world at my feet, the wind dancing through my hair. I'm alone.

Above me, a squawk rings out.

My gaze jerks up, my insides twisting around pins and nee-dles. A flock of monstrous birds circles me. Spikes protrude from their beaks, and their wings look like a jumbled mess of razor blades, the rest of their bodies made from bone with-out muscle, flesh or feather. Metal claws glint in the sunlight.

Self-preservation screams, *Run!*

I take off in a mad sprint. I've encountered these birds be-fore, in Many Ends, when they attempted to eat me alive. How did they find me here? I need to hide. Where? My wild gaze darts through the forest stretched out below me. There's no place to hide, and I—

Crash into a wall of strength. Threat! I bow up, ready to fight for my life. I won't go down easily.

Fist balled, I throw a punch. The wall—is a boy, I realize. A boy my age. A boy I know. He catches my hand in his and chuckles.

"Killian!" I throw my arms around him, stealing a hug. My skin heats rather than chills, and currents of pleasure ripple through me. The scent of peat smoke and heather envelopes me. "Come on. We can't stay here. The birds. We have to—"

He presses a finger against my lips, quieting me. He smiles a devastating smile—a rare smile—his siren-song eyes glit-tering with undiluted joy. I go still. He's *never* looked at me like this, as if all his cares have been washed away. As if he is Light. My Light.

"Forget the birds," he says, his voice nothing but smoke and gravel. "Focus on me, lass."

Shivers course through me. Looking away from him is im-possible. He is my life raft. A promise of better.

Having died as an infant, he grew up in a Myriadian or-phanage. Adopted as a toddler, returned a few years later.

He's endured rejection after rejection, trial after trial, hardship after hardship. Now scars mar his soul.

How did I manage to sneak past his defenses?

He cups my nape to draw me closer and presses his forehead to mine. "I'm lost without ye, Ten."

"You'll never be lost." My fingers wrap around his wrists, my heart crying, *Never let go.* "I'll always find you."

Squawk, squawk.

Yelping, I look up, reminded of our audience. The birds are closer now, claws spread and ready to—

"Focus on me, lass." Killian kisses me, his mouth covering mine.

His taste tantalizes me, and I melt into him—

The dream shifts, Killian vanishing. A scream of frustration bubbles in my throat. *Noooo!* I want to be with Killian. I want to experience his kiss, enjoy his sweetness and bask in the beauty of his strength.

How do I return to him?

I spin, searching for a way out of this…orchard? Zero! I'm standing in the orchard I passed on the way to the cathedral. Something terrible has happened here. The leaves are withered, the fruit rotten, worms slithering from holes.

A crowd of people surrounds me, penning me in, everyone reaching for me, pulling at my clothing.

"Why didn't you help me?" someone cries.

"You could have saved me," another wails, "but you left me to my torment."

"You were supposed to sign my sister. You sent her to Myriad instead."

Bang, bang.

I jerk upright. I'm panting, damp with sweat despite the cooling wafts of air from my mattress. The overhead light kicks on automatically, illuminating an unfamiliar bedroom. My bedroom. My *new* bedroom. I'm trembling, my blood molten.

Those dreams…

They can mean only one of two things: something or nothing. How long was I out?

With a heavy exhalation, I fall onto my pillows. If I close my eyes, will I return to Killian? Will he kiss me? I hug the blanket to my chest.

Bang, bang.

Again I jerk upright. A picture of Meredith and Clay flashes over my bedroom wall; the two appear to be standing in the hallway outside the apartment. She's wearing an adorable pink catsuit with bows and ruffles, her golden hair fastened in a ponytail, and he's wearing solid black.

"I know you're in there," she calls.

Oh, yes. They are standing in my hallway.

I throw my legs over the side of the bed and make my way through the apartment. As I walk, bulbs flip on to guide my path.

With a yawn, I open the door. Meredith and Clay march inside.

She looks me up and down and *tsk-tsks*. "You've been here two days and you haven't changed out of your human clothes?"

What? "Two days? Does time pass more quickly here?"

"Time doesn't change until you enter the Rest." Clay nudges Meredith with his elbow. "Told you she'd still be sleeping."

"Well. You're up now, aren't you, my dear," she says. "And what perfect timing. I arranged for someone to cover my shift so I could show you around the realm."

"Wait. Back up. Time passes differently in the Rest?" I bounce on my heels. "Faster or slower?" In Archer's mind, how long has he been gone?

"One day is like a thousand years, and a thousand years is like a day."

Ugh. Her answers are as cryptic as Levi's.

"I'm more than happy to wait while you shower and change." Her nose wrinkles. "Please."

"Fine." Eager to see the rest of Troika, I brush my teeth and hurry through a shower.

"To save you the trouble of second-guessing yourself about what to wear, I placed an outfit on your bed," Meredith calls. "And a little manna."

When I emerge, I see a black catsuit, like Clay's. While living in Prynne, I only ever wore a pee-in-the-snow yellow jumpsuit, so this is a major improvement.

I eat the wafer of manna, delighted by the sweetness and accompanying jolt of energy, and don the skintight ensemble. Then I join my guests.

"Hot," Clay says with a thumbs-up.

"Meow." Meredith pretends to rake claws through the air.

My cheeks heat as they lead me out of the building. Along the way, every kid I pass glares at me. No more smiles or waves. I'm not gonna lie; it stings.

My companions fail to notice my subpar welcome, and I remain mute on the subject. I don't want the offenders in trouble, especially for anger they're entitled to feel. Besides, nothing Meredith or Clay says will change the minds of my haters.

But come on! I can't be the sole offender. Has no one else ever dated a Myriadian? What about spending time with family? A parent whose child signed with the other side? A husband and wife split by the war?

"In Troika," Meredith says, "there are seven major cities. The Garden of Exchange, the Baths of Restoration, the Temple of Temples, the Capital of New, where your apartment is based, the Museum of Wisdom, the House of Secrets and the Tower of Might."

We enter a tube—or Gate—and after traveling at the speed of Light, emerge in...

"The House of Secrets," she says with a proud grin.

We're standing on a teeming sidewalk. A *circular* sidewalk about the size of a football field. Along the outer edge stands one skyscraper after another. In the center, almost like an island, is a massive oval of glistening mist...or maybe melted glass? Surrounding the mist-glass is a jagged, unpolished frame made of diamonds; the upper and lower points extend outward, creating an eyelash effect.

I grew up with wealthy parents, but nothing they owned compares to this. Nothing found in the Land of the Harvest compares.

Among the masses, no one is wearing a catsuit. Everyone is draped in a plain white robe. My memory...or maybe the Grid...supplies the reason. This is a business district, and different-colored robes are reserved for different tasks and ceremonies.

Tension is tangible, hustle and bustle obviously mandatory. Both men and women rush in and out of different buildings, though only a handful approach the center island. No one is smiling or laughing. Only a rare few appear at ease, as if they know something the others do not.

"The Eye," Clay says, pointing to the mist-glass.

Meredith nods. "The Eye sees into the Land of the Harvest. Through it, Headhunters are able to monitor humans and compile dossiers for Leaders. Leaders then draft a recruitment game plan and figure out the best Laborer for every individual."

I'm torn between three emotions. Awe—knowledge is power, and these people wield theirs like a sword. A resurgence of anger. How many times was I spied on? And envy. Does the Eye peer into Myriad? The Rest? What about Many Ends? If I could catch a glimpse of Killian and Archer and study a future battleground...

My heart skips a beat. I'm a hypocrite. As bad as the people who spied on me. "Can the Eye—"

"No," she interrupts.

"You don't even know—"

"Don't I?" She arches a brow. "You aren't the first newbie I've shown around, and you all ask the same things."

Okay, yeah. She probably knows what I plan to ask. Disappointed, I change the subject. "I haven't seen any animals. Are pets allowed in the realm?" I've always wanted a dog or a cat, but my parents flat-out refused.

"Oh, baby, the animals!" Clay slings an arm around my shoulders. "There's a sanctuary in the Capital of New. Animals are allowed anywhere, anytime, but they usually prefer to stay in the sanctuary or visit the Sanatorium where Healers work. You're welcome to visit either place."

My brow furrows. "Why do animals prefer the sanctuary? Why don't they live with families?"

Meredith snorts. "Why don't you ask the animals? They'd *love* a chance to fill you in."

Is she implying the animals...talk? No, surely not. But... maybe? How cool would a talking dog or cat be?

I see you has manna, hooman. I has no manna. Give me your manna.

We stroll down the sidewalk and enter another Gate, this one posed between two buildings. I hardly notice a change in my surroundings before we exit. Or rather, try to exit. A mammoth crowd blocks our path.

"This," Meredith says, ramping up the volume in order to be heard over the crest of murmurs, "is the Temple of Temples, where the Secondking lives. There are three separate parts. The courtyard is located on the east side and opens to the Waft of Incense. The Waft of Incense—or WoI—leads to the Great Throne, where Eron presides."

"And when the Firstking visits Troika, he stays here," Clay adds, his tone wishful.

He wants to meet the Firstking, doesn't he?

I've seen both kings only once before, when Archer allowed me to view Troika through his eyes.

A twinge of grief causes me to hiss. "How often does the Firstking visit?"

"Once a month." Light flashes on the brands in the center of her palms. Frowning, she taps one, and a text message appears, hovering just over her hand. She sighs.

When she cants her head toward the Gate, I understand it's time to go. We enter, returning to the House of Secrets. Next stop—my apartment. The tour is over.

"Something wrong?" I ask her.

"Nope." She offers no more, and I decide not to press. I'm a newbie with, like, zero clearance.

However, I decide to ask questions about the realm while I have the chance. "Where does the Secondking's fiancée live?" I got a glimpse of Princess Mariée, and she is more exquisite than the realm itself, her hair as pale as a lily of the valley, her cheeks as pink as a rose, her eyes as blue as the clearest ocean. "How long have they been engaged? And why is she called princess when she's not yet married into the royal family? Are there other princesses here?"

Clay becomes waxen, disconcerting me.

Meredith wilts like a flower in summer heat. "Mariée is missing. I mean, we know she's here—and alive—because she's the other Conduit and her Light continues to shine through the Grid, but no one has seen or heard from her since your Firstdeath. Otherwise she would be overseeing your tour and training herself."

I rub the galloping pulse at the base of my neck. If she's out of commission, I'm needed now, not later.

But no pressure, right?

Am I wheezing? I think I'm wheezing.

"And no, there are no other princesses," my grandmother adds, probably to distract me from a possible panic attack. "The title denotes her engagement. After marriage, she'll become known as Secondqueen. Oh! They've been engaged for almost two thousand years."

I nearly choke on my tongue. "Um, that doesn't seem like an excessive wait time to you?" Like, put a ring on it already and lock that baby down.

"When you live forever, two thousand years is nothing. They say they'll seal the deal after we've won the war." A lock of my hair twirls in a sudden burst of wind, and she reaches out to shift the strands between her fingers. "What about you and your...boyfriend?"

"We are a classic example of *it's complicated*."

And yet, if he appeared in Troika right now, I'd pull him into a hidden corner and kiss the air from his lungs. I miss him as I'd miss a limb. He's one of my favorite things.

Two people rush past us, their conversation snagging my attention. I cling to the distraction with all my might. They are speaking... Russian, I'm pretty sure, reminding me of the special Troikan language. "Where can I go to learn Troikan?"

"Nowhere," Meredith says. "You'll learn it when you use your Key and not a second sooner."

Another light flashes on her brands. She checks the new message and stiffens. "Apparently I'm taking too long. We need to go." Steps quick, she ushers us to the first Gate we exited.

As soon as we reach the Capital of New, she kisses my cheek and says, "I'll pick you up tomorrow night at seven. I'm your date to the welcome party." She rushes off, disappearing inside another Gate.

"You ready to go home, Number Girl? No? Good, didn't think so. We're going to have some fun." Clay returns me to the woodland wonderland.

Reed and Kayla are seated at a table in back, looking at ease and without a care. The other tables are occupied by people I've never met...people who notice me and terminate their conversations. Silence descends.

I shift from one booted foot to the other. War is daunting, but this is worse.

Reed frowns. I gulp. Will he pretend not to know me?

"I should go," I whisper.

A second later, Reed waves us over.

In a show of solidarity, Clay takes my hand and leads me to our friends.

"—Archer," I hear someone say.

"I know. She's the reason he's dead," another replies.

The heat drains from my face.

My choice, my consequences.

Before my stay at Prynne, my parents decided everything for me. At Prynne, Dr. Vans did all the deciding. What I ate, what I wore, who I spoke with. When I finally claimed the reins of control, I crashed and burned. Archer paid the price.

He had a life here. A family. People who counted on him. Because of me, they lost him.

I want to shout, "We can bring him back in the Resurrection! Spread the word. Vote for Archer." But I don't know anything about the others in the running. Maybe these people hope to bring back a beloved family member.

"I should go," I repeat. I'm linked to these people through the Grid, so, I don't just feel the white-hot ping of their stares; I feel the sickening burn of their dislike.

How can I end the war between realms when I can't convince people predisposed to like me to actually like me?

Buck up. Find a way. The end result matters. Failure isn't an option. My mom lives in Myriad, along with family I never had the chance to meet. And then there's Killian, of course.

"We stay." Clay squeezes my hand. "What has six wheels and flies?"

I'm in no mood for a joke—so what better time to make one? "What else? A garbage truck."

He shakes a fist at the ceiling. "One day I'm going to stump her."

As we take our places at the table, Reed offers us a piece of manna from his plate. Clay accepts, but I shake my head. If I swallow a single bite, it will come right back up, guaranteed.

"So what is today's special?" Clay asks.

"Strawberry and honey," Kayla replies. "The best yet."

Okay. We're clearly in a manna restaurant. Curiosity gets the better of me. "Who farms the manna? And how, exactly, do we pay for it?"

"There's an agricultural section here in the Capital of New." Reed taps his palm, types into the Light glowing over his hand, and a map appears in the center of the table. He points to a long sweep of pastureland. "Agronomists, a subdivision of Laborer, plant and harvest the crops."

His ease with Troikan technology gives me hope. He hasn't been here long, but look at everything he's mastered.

"As for money," Kayla says, "trainees are given a weekly allowance for necessities."

Reed snorts. "An allowance you hoard, afraid the money will stop coming. When are you gonna realize this place isn't like the Land of the Harvest."

Kayla *hmphs* and flattens her hand on the side of the table. A Light flashes through her brand, and three beeps ring out. "There. I just paid for a fresh round of manna. You're welcome."

Sure enough, a waitress—another subdivision of Laborer—soon arrives with a smile and a plate of strawberry and honey manna.

"May you be ever enlightened," she says before moving off.

Kayla offers me a bite before polishing off two pieces. "If you'd arrived five minutes earlier, you could have met Victor Prince. He's—"

"Archer's brother. Yeah." I shift, uncomfortable again. "I met him when I first arrived."

"Oh." She traces a fingertip along the rim of her plate. "He's tutoring me. He—"

The restaurant is silent, her voice booming. Her cheeks darken. I glance to the entrance and do a double take. My stomach sinks.

Elizabeth is here, and there's a tall dark-haired guy at her side. She glares at me, and I lift my chin. If she wants to use me as a punching bag, fine. Go for it. Pain for pain. I'm willing, and I won't fight back. I deserve it. But I also won't be cowed.

Kayla trembles, as if she's the one on the receiving end of Elizabeth's vitriol. Confrontation of any kind is difficult for her. In Many Ends, she had recoiled from almost every fight.

"Either the Myriad supporter goes," Elizabeth announces, "or I go. Take your pick. But I suggest you choose wisely. One of us will help you. The other will stab you in the back."

Murmurs erupt. All eyes focus on me and narrow. Heat sears my cheeks, and I'm sure my color matches Kayla's. Lobster red.

"I choose you," Reed tells me. "I'll always choose you. You saved my life."

I'm overcome with gratitude. Problem is, I know Elizabeth will make life miserable for him. "No," I say. "Choose her." Nausea churns in my gut as I stand. "She's—"

"No way." Clay stands beside me, and Reed quickly follows suit. Kayla, too.

My sense of gratitude grows. "Sit down, you guys," I mutter, but they remain in place.

Killian would have laughed in Elizabeth's face, maybe flipped over a table after flipping her off and then he would have told *her* to go, because he would be staying.

Archer would have apologized with heartfelt regret and left without inciting an incident.

I miss my boys.

"I'll go. This time," I say with as much dignity as I can muster. "My actions led to Archer's death, and I take full responsibility. I accept punishment."

"Liar." Elizabeth hisses, "You expect forgiveness."

Her companion watches us with enigmatic eyes. I can't read his thoughts.

"One day, yes. I hope for forgiveness." *Can I ever forgive myself?* "Archer taught me the value Troika places on the act...and it is an act, a decision rather than a feeling." I hold up my hand and shout, "A round of second chances, everyone. On me."

Elizabeth glowers at me.

Having made my point, I stride past her. She balls her fists, clearly debating the merits of hitting me. In the end, she opts to stand down. Smart.

I don't start my fights, but I always finish them.

I make it out of the building without incident, my friends on my heels.

"I wish you'd stayed," I tell them.

"All for one, and one for all," Clay replies.

Kayla snorts. "So we're the Four Musketeers now?"

"Nah. I vote we call ourselves the Reed Raiders." Reed wiggles his brows.

"No way." Clay flexes his biceps. "We're the Clayminators."

"I'm on board for the Kayniacs," Kayla says.

"If we're called anything but a nerd herd, I'll be surprised," I say with a laugh. "Besides, when someone threatens us, we just have to say, *Do not make us count to Ten.* Bad guys will run away, crying for their mommies."

Chuckles abound.

My amusement doesn't last long, however. As we head to my apartment, I throw a furtive glance over my shoulder. Nothing and no one is there, but I feel as if my troubles are following me.

And why wouldn't they? They're chained to my ankles, bricks I've been dragging behind me for years.

chapter five

"There is power in consistency."
—Troika

At seven sharp the next evening, Meredith arrives at my doorstep. I've almost forgotten my encounter with Elizabeth.

Almost.

I spent the rest of the day holed up in my apartment, watching video feed of Jeremy and even Meredith, who visited him and Levi. Clay, Reed and Kayla spent an hour with me before they had to rush off to their classes. I'd asked questions about HART and their methods of operation, secretly brainstorming ways to stop the war with Myriad.

We gathered people from both realms and encouraged everyone to list their grievances so that changes could be made, preventing future clashes, Reed had said. *But the powers that be always stepped in and stopped the proceedings.*

He'd given me an idea, and I'd come up with steps one, two and three of what I'm sure will be a Ten-part plan.

Set a meeting with Elizabeth, allowing her to list her grievances with me. Win her over—and everyone else in the process. Convince Troikans that war with Myriad isn't in our best interest.

You know, *easy* stuff.

Maybe I'll host a Myriad Lovers Anonymous party.

T + M = TuisM

Tuism: the practice of putting the interests of another before one's own.

When the letters T and M are replaced by their numerical equivalents—20 and 13—they equal 33

Thirty-three is the atomic number of arsenic, a poison, but it is also the age often associated with the Age of Perfection.

Thirty-three is the numerical equivalent of AMEN: 1 + 13 + 5 + 14 = 33.

I'm going to need help with my Tuism. What if I can convince Killian to form an alliance with me? We could—

What? Convince others to join our cause? Prove Troikans and Myriadians can lo—like each other?

I tug at my collar. No need to throw words like *love* around, right? Killian would probably freak.

Zero! I need to contact him, but I have no way to do so.

Meredith clears her throat, and I realize I'm standing in the doorway, staring into the distance. My cheeks heat as I motion her inside. She sweeps past me, the scent of orchids fluttering in her wake.

She's wearing a formal white robe with black seams. The material conforms to her curves one moment but flows freely the next.

She holds up a bundle of metal links. "I brought you a dress."

That is supposed to be a dress? "You're kidding, right?"

"Usually, but never about fashion." She manhandles me, removing my catsuit and fitting me into the links. A wide smile blossoms. "You are ravishing."

"Thank you." I excuse myself and go into my bedroom, where I strap a kitchen knife to my thigh.

While I crave peace, I can't deny I have enemies. I have to be prepared for anything. A lesson I learned inside Prynne.

Curious about my "ravishing" appeal, I study my reflection. The top of the dress is made of small ovals, one laid over another to give the illusion of feathers. Those faux feathers form a deep V between my breasts before branching into multiple chains braided together and wrapped around my waist, the ends cascading to create an ankle-length skirt.

The entire ensemble should weigh a hundred pounds or more, but it's as light as a cotton T-shirt. Even more astounding, I have full range of motion.

I wish Killian were here. He would look me over slowly and say, "Nice dress. Now take it off." And I would laugh a throaty laugh to mask my shivers of need. I would ache to be in his arms.

I do ache.

Where is he at this precise moment? What's he doing? Who is he with?

I dreamed about him again last night, and I'm still raw. I felt the soft brush of his lips a split second before he vanished like morning mist.

I can't shake the feeling he needs me. That we need each other.

What if he's in some kind of trouble? What if he's trying to reach me, desperate for my help?

What if he's trapped in the Kennels?

I shudder. The Kennels are Myriad's number one choice for punishment. Cage is stacked upon cage, a different spirit locked inside each one. Men and women, boys and girls. Age doesn't matter. Everyone is degraded, cramped and starved.

I cover my eyes, as if I can somehow block the horrific image.

I *have* to find a way to contact Killian.

Head high, I rejoin Meredith. "Will everyone be dressed like this?" Good. I sounded normal, breezy.

In lieu of an answer, she says, "Oh, honey bunny. You have to dress for the job you want, not the job you have."

"Then I should wear a calculator." If I'd had a longer First-life, I'd planned to get an accounting degree.

"*Tsk-tsk.* Your nerd is showing."

"And your old lady is showing."

We share a smile, but I notice the merriment doesn't quite reach her eyes. Upon closer inspection, I notice the lines of tension bracketing her mouth.

Considering her reaction to yesterday's message, something bad has happened behind the scenes.

"Tell me what's wrong, Madame." I use my most authoritative tone. "That's an order from your exalted superior."

Her tension lessens, and she snorts. "You want to know? Fine. You're going to be briefed, anyway."

I am?

"Myriad has been guarding a girl they've already signed as if she's…well, as important as you. And she just might be. There are rumors she's infected with…" She shudders as she leans in to whisper a single word, "Penumbra."

I flip through mental files, find no reference. "What is—"

She slaps a hand over my mouth and shakes her head, her eyes wide as saucers.

All right, all right. I hold my hands up, all innocence. Top secret topic. Got it. "Why don't we call it the Bra?"

Her hand falls away, a half smile teasing one side of her mouth. "*The Bra* is a highly contagious disease we've only ever dealt with in rumor-form. There has never been a breakout. Half our population believes it's a scare tactic while the other half believes it's a time bomb waiting to blow. Humans are, supposedly, the only ones susceptible, but the infected can develop the abilities of an Abrogate."

Abrogate—the highest rank of General in Myriad. My counterpart. I draw Light—or rather, I will—and Abrogates drain it.

"Which camp are you?" I ask.

"Time bomb. The *Book of the Law* predicts the worlds as we know them will one day end. What better way than this? But that's another story for another time."

Maintaining a neutral expression requires a massive effort. The worlds are going to end? This is the first I've heard of any upcoming disasters!

What makes you think the changes will be disastrous?

The disembodied voice I heard the day I died, springing from the back of my mind. This is the Grid. My link to the heart of Troika. I'm certain now.

Deep breath in, out. "If the worlds as we know them change, they could change for the better." Like…peace could be achieved.

Her head cants to the side. "Very true. But because we've never dealt with this disease, we have no definite cure. However, we are certain Conduits are the key. If Pen—*the Bra* is total darkness, then the Light must chase it away."

Cold fingers of dread creep down my spine. With Princess Mariée MIA, Troikan powers that be will look to me for Penumbra containment, won't they? No wonder I'll be debriefed.

I'm supposed to save us. Me. All by my lonesome.

I'm not ready.

I'll never be ready. But I'm going to help, anyway.

"What causes a…*Bra* outbreak?" I ask. "Why can't other Troikans wield the necessary amount of Light?"

"Have you heard of Torchlight?" When I shake my head no, she adds, "For us, Light is power. Our version of electricity. If a human is hit with too much electricity, his body shuts down. Torchlight is the spiritual equivalent."

Stomach cramp. There's so much I don't know—so much I *need* to know if I'm going to survive. "This war," I say with a sigh. "The realms have been fighting for centuries. Do people even remember *why* they're fighting?"

"Of course. Right versus wrong. Values versus anarchy." She nudges my shoulder, saying, "Speaking of fights. I heard about your run-in with Elizabeth."

Recruit my grandmother to my peace plan—*strike one.* "She's angry with me. And I get it. I do. But I don't want to fight her. I don't want to fight anyone. Why can't we all just get along?"

"Easy. If we don't fight for what's right, we'll be overpowered by what's wrong."

Okay. *Strike two.*

She checks a wristwatch she isn't wearing and gives me a gentle shove toward the door. "Enough chatter. We should go."

"Fine," I grumble.

We exit my apartment. The hallway overflows with trainees just hanging out and talking. Most are wearing armor while a few are draped in robes. Everyone stops whatever they're doing to bow...to Meredith?

Ooo-kay. Here, we are all equals in terms of love and respect, but this is a show of respect for her position as Leader. The fact that I'm with her—or maybe the threats Levi voiced last night have spread like wildfire—earns me a handful of smiles and even more waves. No one glares at me. A few girls gaze at my dress with longing.

We take two Gates to the Temple of Temples. There's a crowd, but this one is much thinner, allowing me to note details previously missed. The courtyard teems with an abundance of roses in an array of colors. No petal is dry or withered, no leaf droops. The stems have no thorns.

The next chamber is the Waft of Incense, and I suddenly understand the reason for the name. A heavenly fragrance saturates the air. With every breath, I'm certain I'm inhaling pure life.

Fourteen men and women stand before the gold brick wall guarding the entrance. I scan each face, taking the measure of my peers, and scout out every possible exit.

Work now, relax later.

The fourteen represent a mix of nationalities and appear to be average Troikans, but they are the only ones wearing turquoise robes with short metal links sewn into the shoulders. Levi is among them.

Fourteen, a multiple of seven. A double portion. In numerology, it means deliverance from pain, problem and panic.

Long ago, when people married, they celebrated the wedding feast for fourteen days.

To the right of the fourteen, eight people form a line. Eight is the atomic number of oxygen. Meredith and I take a spot at the end, making us nine and ten. How appropriate.

"Spine straight, shoulders squared," she says as we make our way forward. "You're about to meet our mighty Generals."

Nervousness pricks at me. Will I be rejected or welcomed?

When we reach the front, Meredith takes care of introductions. Just when I think I'll never be able to remember their names, the Grid kicks in. Agape, Ying Wo, Tasanee, Bahari, Mykhail, John, Spike, Alejandro, Marcos, Jane, Chanel, Luciana, Shamus and of course, Levi. They hail from all over the globe, and they welcome me as they welcomed everyone, with genuine warmth and affection. I'm hugged, patted and teased about my obsession with numbers.

"You're going to do good things here," Alejandro tells me. I kinda sorta want to stare at him for the rest of eternity. He is beauty personified. Dark hair, dark eyes, dark skin. The poster boy for perfection.

"I hope so," I say. I really do.

I'm practically floating as Meredith escorts me into the courtyard, where she introduces me to the eight who stood in line with me. The other newbies.

Eight—looks like the symbol for infinity. A stop sign has eight sides. With me, we are nine. According to yoga, a human body has nine doors—two eyes, two ears, the mouth, two nostrils, and the openings for...um, waste removal and the one for procreation. A cat has nine lives. Happiness is found on cloud nine.

The newbies are Raanan—the guy who'd accompanied Elizabeth to the manna restaurant—Fatima, Winifred, Nico, Rebel, Hoshi, Sawyer and Clementine. They, too, come from all over the globe. Thankfully the Grid allows us to understand each other, no matter the language we speak.

At six—and a half, *foot stomp*—Fatima is the youngest, killed in a house fire. At seventy-three, Nico is the oldest. I feel like such a creep for thinking this but...he's hot.

To my delight, I'm not the only one with odd hair. Clementine has pink ringlets, Nico's mass of curls are fire-engine red and Hoshi's straight-as-a-pen locks are the color of plums, dark with purple undertones.

Everyone but Raanan offers an enthusiastic greeting; he remains mute, his expression contemplative. Despite him, I'm relieved by my easy camaraderie with the others, considering we are strangers. Strangers in a strange land flock together, I guess.

"By the way some of the others have been talking about you," Fatima says with an innocent grin, "I expected you to have horns, fangs and a forked tail."

"I know, right?" Rebel, who is fourteen, playfully elbows the little girl in the side. "I'm actually megadisappointed."

Raanan frowns as Hoshi and Clementine jump up and clap.

"He's here!" Clementine squeals. "Someone pinch me. No, don't! If this is a dream, I don't want to wake up."

"I've been praying for another glimpse of him," Hoshi admits.

I glance over my shoulder to discover...Victor Prince. He's involved in a deep conversation with a girl I've never met, and he hasn't yet noticed his admirers.

My good mood deflates like a balloon with a hole. Days have passed since Archer's death. My sweet, lovable Archer.

I haven't begun to heal.

I miss you every minute, every second
Are you near? Hope no longer beckons.
I want to sob, but here, now, I can only kneel.
Emptiness is the only thing I feel.
Tell me, please, how I'm supposed to go on.
For the rest of eternity, you, Little "Bow" Peep, are gone.

Has grief erased Victor's optimism? I've heard no more talk about the Resurrection. How can we convince others to vote for Archer? Do we even try?

Soft music drifts through the air. A live band plays amid the wealth of roses. Their instruments, like so many other things in Troika, are different than what I'm used to seeing, and the sounds...oh, wow, the sounds! The melody is haunt-ingly beautiful. My ears tingle. Tears well in my eyes.

"Have you ever heard anything so exquisite?" Winifred stares at the band with dreamy eyes.

"Excuse us, everyone. I'm going to steal Ten away." With an arm snaked around my waist, Meredith herds me toward the Great Throne room, even though the door is closed.

"Why—" I spot the Secondking to the right of the doors, speaking with a man and woman.

His violet robe is the most ornate I've ever seen, the seams bound together with gold thread, the hem glittering as if soaked in Lifeblood. He's tall, his face plain, but his eyes... they are bluer than a morning sky, brighter than a sapphire and lovelier than a blue jay.

The man and woman notice our approach and take a step back, clearing our path. My mouth dries, and my insides per-form a series of flip-flops. I'm about to meet Troika's king. In person.

Don't trip. Don't spit when you speak. Oh, zero, how's my breath?
Meredith bows, and I clumsily do the same.

He smiles at us, and I would swear the sun just rose over the entire realm. Plain? No, this man is the definition of beauti-ful. "I'm pleased you chose Troika, Tenley."

He knows my name! And though he spoke only six words, I jolt as if I just consumed an entire smorgasbord of manna. I'm electrified from the inside out. "Thank you..." Eron? Too casual. Great King? Perhaps too formal, considering our sur-roundings. Dang it, what's the proper way to address him? "Majesty."

He inclines his head. One point for Ten. I nailed it.

So...is now a good time to mention my thoughts on the war?

As if reading my mind, Meredith urges me away. As I huff

and puff with irritation, she says, "A party is *not* the time for politics." She stops in front of the pair who spoke to the Secondking before us.

"This," Meredith says, "is my mother. Your great-grandmother Hazel. She's a Laborer."

My eyes widen with surprise and pleasure. I should have guessed. Hazel is petite and blonde, just like Meredith, with a similar regal bearing. But…how is my dark-haired mother part of their familial line?

Hazel *tsks* at her daughter. "What have I told you about playing Barbie with the new recruits?" Her voice reminds me of a lullaby: soft, sweet and calming.

Meredith snorts. "You said to wait for you so you could play, too."

Hazel nods and looks me over, a smile twitching at the corners of her mouth. "I hope you don't expect me to call you Ten. I refuse to refer to my great-granddaughter as a number. I'll call you Blue."

She refuses to call me a number, even though it's my name, but she's fine with a color? I take a page from Clay's book and pat the top of her head. Only family can get away with such illogical logic.

"I'm good with Blue. How about I call you Meemaw?"

"Yes!" She fist-pumps the sky. "Meemaw it is."

"And this," Meredith says with a laugh, "is Steven, your grandfather. He's a Laborer, though a different subset. He harvests manna."

Steven smiles and shakes my hand. He's on the tall side with clear Native American roots. "So wonderful to meet you, Tenley."

"Call me Ten. Or Blue," I add with a wink. I wonder if he and my grandmother are still married.

What the heck. I go ahead and ask.

"During a human marriage, two bodies are bound together, not two spirits." She pats Steven on the shoulder. "Upon Firstdeath, the bond is voided. But no worries. We're best friends now."

With her gaze on something—or someone—behind us, Hazel frowns. "What is *she* doing here?" Annoyance drips from her tone. "Only friends and family of the newbies received invitations."

Foreboding rushes through me, a river without a dam. I turn...and spot Elizabeth. Great!

She whispers something to the freckled redhead at her side, and the two glare at me before making their way to Nico, Raanan and Sawyer, who have congregated in a corner.

"She's distantly related to Raanan." Meredith wags a finger in her mother's face, and I begin to understand why she's a Leader. "And we're happy she's here, aren't we? We hope she has fun. Right? Right! Because we love our fellow Troikans, no matter what."

Well. Raanan's silent treatment now makes sense.

"Right," Hazel grumbles. "Happy. Fun. Love."

I catch sight of Clay, Reed and Kayla as they enter the courtyard, and a spark of happiness ignites. "Over here!"

They spot me and rush over. Before I dole out hugs, they notice Meredith and bow their heads in greeting. Hazel and Steven receive handshakes.

Clay wiggles his brows at me. "Hey, baby. You must be the square root of negative one, because you can't possibly be real."

I bark out a laugh.

Meredith rolls her eyes. "Your pickup lines need serious work, Clayton."

"So you keep telling me." His smiles widens as he focuses on her. "But that wasn't a pickup line. This is. On a scale of one to ten, you're a nine...and I'm the one you need."

She throws back her head and laughs with delight.

Whoa. Full stop. Did eighteen-year-old Clay just try to pick up my *grandmother*? Gross! Killian, at least, is nineteen and only a year and a half older than me.

Killian...

Forget contacting him. I want to see him, breathe him in. I want to touch, hug and kiss him. I want his skin pressed against mine, without a flicker of pain. And the desires do not spring from my crush on him. Not entirely. I think... I think the Grid is trying to tell me I'm not supposed to be here without him.

Impossible. Right? The Troikan Grid would never welcome a Myriadian.

Still my heart cries, *Killian*.

There are seven letters in his name. The numerical equivalent is $11 + 9 + 12 + 12 + 9 + 1 + 14 = 68$

68 is a code meaning "put it back," while 86 is a code meaning "remove it."

Kayla waves a hand in front of my face and says, "If your plan is to discourage Elizabeth from seeking revenge by making yourself look miserable, mission accomplished."

"I miss Killian," I confess softly. She's never met him, and I'm glad. Before me, he slept with his assignments. His method of choice. The quickest and easiest way to convince a girl to make covenant with Myriad, desperate to stay with him.

What can I say? The boy gives good romance.

At first, I feared I was just another number to him (har har). Just another conquest to be won. But he willingly entered the Kennels for me in order to buy me more time, so I could make a decision about my future in peace. He disobeyed his Leader's orders to hurt me, protecting me instead. Finally, he urged me to make covenant with Troika, despite the war.

How can I ever doubt his affections for me?

"You won't be allowed to leave the realm for a year," Kayla tells me. "You have to complete your training first."

I open my mouth to respond, but the girl who arrived with Elizabeth approaches our circle—sans Elizabeth—and zeros in on Clay.

If she thinks to strike at me by hurting my friend…

He's a good guy with a good heart, and I will play Ten Ways To Die if her intentions are anything but honorable.

After a few minutes of back and forth teasing, the two wander off. I'm tempted to follow, but Clay looks so happy. I let him go without comment, and the conversation behind me snags my attention.

"—so excited to make my first kill." I recognize Clementine's voice.

"I know!" Hoshi replies. "Those Myriadians are going *dooown*."

They talk about ending a life as if it's easy, as if there are no consequences. I know better. I've killed before. A guard at the asylum sneaked into my cell, expecting a *good time*. I choked him with his own belt. Another guard beat inmates for attempting to escape. I stabbed him in the gut.

Both were acts of self-defense, and yet I haven't been able to wash the dark stains from my soul.

Soon I'll be expected to slaughter entire armies.

Sweat beads over my nape, even as my insides chill.

Victor moves to my side, handsome in a white robe with black embroidery. He shakes hands with everyone in our group. Kayla brightens when he kisses her knuckles.

He winks at me. "You want to dance, New Girl?"

Overjoyed by his ease with me, I nod. Only as he draws me away do I notice no one else is dancing. "Wait," I begin.

"Nope. No take-backs." He swings me around and tugs me against him, catching me and laughing. "This is happening."

He looks so much like his brother I can't help but soften against him.

"How do you like Troika so far?" he asks.

I scan the sea of faces for Elizabeth, but she's nowhere to be found. Kayla is frowning at me. When she notices my gaze, she spins away.

Odd. "The land or the people?" I ask Victor.

"I'll take that to mean you love the land but want to throat-punch some of the people." He flattens a hand on my shoulder and the other at my lower back, careful not to delve anywhere he shouldn't. "Here's what you don't know. One of the soldiers Killian killed—Elizabeth was dating him."

Oh…zero. My shoulders roll in. "How do I earn her forgiveness?"

"If forgiveness has to be earned, it isn't forgiveness."

A high-pitched scream assaults my ears, and panic sweeps through the crowd.

"Help," a girl shouts. Young Fatima? "Help them! Please!"

Another newbie rushes past me, a look of terror on her face.

"It's all right." A guy chases after her. "It's not what it seems."

I wrench from Victor's arms and dart in the opposite direction, closing in on the still-screaming Fatima. She's on the floor, curled into a ball, staring ahead as if she's just come face-to-face with her worst fear. Multiple people attempt to comfort her.

"What—" I spot the reason for her upset and cry out.

Killian. Killian is here. He's chained to a column, his feet engulfed in flames, his features contorted in agony. He screams. Clay is chained to the column next to him, his feet also engulfed by flames. He jerks at his bonds to no avail.

As I sprint over, three facts occur to me. 1) Not a single General, Leader or Laborer is concerned for the boys. 2) The flames emit zero heat. 3) The air is fresh, no hint of burning leather or flesh.

However, there's no time to ponder the reasons. No time to waste with a debate about whom to save first. Clay is Troikan. Any soldier here will happily rush to his aid. No one but me will free Killian.

I unsheathe the knife discreetly hidden under my skirt and slide the rest of the way across the marble pathway to stop behind Killian. I reach for the lock on his chains and—

Go still. My hand ghosted through him.

Confused, I pat at him. He is 100 percent intangible to me.

I don't understand. I lean over and reach for Clay. My hand ghosts through him, too.

A hologram, I realize. Only a hologram.

Relief blends with a potent mix of anger and dread. Who would create such a sickening scenario? And why?

No need to ponder the answers for long. A smug Elizabeth stands nearby. Her friend is with her—and so is the real Clay. Hurt shimmers in his eyes. Even though he wasn't in any kind of danger, he knows what I know: once again, I opted to save someone else first.

"I told you," Elizabeth announces. "We aren't safe with our new Conduit around. She will *always* choose a Myriadian over a Troikan."

MYRIAD

From: Z_C_4/23.43.2
To: K_F_5/23.53.6
Subject: An introduction, a request and a question

Our first assignment together! I hope you're as excited as I am, Mr. Flynn. I've heard good things about you, and I'm looking forward to seeing you in action. I know it will take time for you to fully trust me, and I understand. I'm currently an unknown to you.

Going forward, there are two things you should know about me: I love my realm, and I will cross any line to protect those placed in my care. I encourage you to reach our goal—freedom for all—any way you see fit. I will never oppress you with ridiculous rules; I ask only that you show me the respect my position is due and keep me informed.

Now, about our assignment. I hope you comprehend victory isn't our only end goal. We are fighting for our very way of life. The right to feel our emotions rather than ignore them. The right to play after a hard day of work and enjoy the time we've been given. The right to shuck conformity, to no longer be mindless drones but individuals with singular needs and wants.

We must prove to Miss Tenley Lockwood just how much better Myriad is for her. For everyone!

I'd love to hear your plans to accomplish this, and I'd appreciate confirmation that your seeming affection for Miss Lockwood is exaggerated for the sake of the mission. What you tell me, I'll believe. I'll trust you until you give me reason to doubt you, and you'll trust me. I believe in give-and-take.

Oh! One final note. I received an incident report early this morning. Apparently you tossed Sloan Aubuchon across the training room. Was such violence against your charge necessary?

Might Equals Right!

Sir Zhi Chen

MYRIAD

From: K_F_5/23.53.6
To: Z_C_4/23.43.2
Subject: A statement, a truth and a pat on the back

Rest assured, I understand the importance of my mission. If Troika loses Miss Lockwood, they will fall and Myriad will rise.

If you've read my file, you know I've lied, cheated and seduced for our realm. I'm good at it. Very good. But I will always be honest with you.

Question: Do you truly believe my affection for a Troikan could be genuine? Rest assured I'm more determined than ever, and I'll do whatever I must to reach my goal.

As for Sloan Aubuchon, I didn't toss her across the training room once—I tossed her across the training room *three times*. She will never again attack an instructor from behind, no matter how much she hates him. You're welcome, Myriad.

Might Equals Right!
ML, Killian Flynn

MYRIAD

From: Z_C_4/23.43.2
To: K_F_5/23.53.6
Subject: I'm impressed

We could all take a lesson from you, Mr. Flynn. You live with passion and fight for what you want. The true Myriadian way. Carry on!

You'll be pleased to know our efforts to draw Miss Lockwood out of Troika are progressing nicely. I predict you'll see her in a matter of days.

Might Equals Right!

Sir Zhi Chen

chapter six

"Change is the bedrock of success."
—Myriad

I spend the next day at home, trying to forget yesterday's walk of shame. After Elizabeth's announcement, I left the party and, after taking a few wrong Gates, managed to find my way back to the cathedral. No one came after me.

Last night my dreams turned into nightmares. Killian never appeared on the mountaintop, and the birds attacked me en masse. Within minutes, they tore me to shreds and feasted on my organs. Organs that quickly regenerated, ready to be eaten again. The pain... I still feel a twinge in my side.

After I managed to fight my way free, I dragged my broken, bloody body into the cornfield, the throng of people absent. I was alone. No one had needed or wanted my help, and I'd fallen to my knees, sobbing.

I'm considering forgoing sleep for the rest of my Everlife.

Today, no visitors come knocking on my door, and I'm glad. So far, all I've done is anger and upset the people I'm supposed to protect. I haven't done anything right.

I'm Ten, the rarity. Ten, the necessary ingredient for victory. Ten, the special one. But...what if Levi and Archer and everyone else got it wrong? What if I'm *not* special? What if I'm the necessary ingredient for failure?

Dejected, I plop onto the couch. The *Book of the Law* appears, glowing just in front of me, all, *ta-da, here I am, the answer to your problems.* As if.

I'm not in the mood to read, but I decide to do it, anyway. Knowledge is power. Maybe I'll do a better job here.

If you forget all else, remember this: love is always the answer. Love your realm. Love your people. Love yourself. This is right. This is good. Only when you choose love are you living in Light.

My number brands throb as I turn to the next page. Someone needs to remind the rest of the realm about choosing love!

Other people are not the source of your problem. Your own thoughts are your—

I flip the page.

Let this word take root inside the rich soil of your heart so that, when a storm comes—and it will—you have something firmly planted to hold on to.

Enough! This isn't helping.

Frustrated, I press a series of buttons on the miracle remote and the book vanishes. Another series of buttons and a detailed map of Troika materializes on the ceiling.

I discovered the map last night and memorized the locations of the Gates. Besides the seven main Gates leading to different cities within the realm, there are multiple smaller Gates—Stairwells—for travel within each specific city. Every city is hundreds of thousands of square miles.

I decided to spend quality time with a favorite pastime: counting. On the map, only sixty-six trees are marked—thirty-nine on one side and twenty-seven on the other. Why?

Sixty-six is the atomic number of dysprosium, a lanthanide.

A lanthanide is any series of fifteen metallic elements, often collectively known as the rare earth elements.

Fifteen is a triangular number: 1+2+3+4+5=15

Thirty-nine is the atomic number of yttrium. Equal to three trimesters, the length of a human pregnancy.

Twenty-seven, the atomic number of cobalt. The number of bones in the human hand. The number of "cubies" in a Rubik's cube.

Boom!

My front door bursts open, wood splinters flying. Three masked assailants march inside my apartment, and I jackknife into a sitting position, my mind and heart racing.

Fight-or-flight?

The intruders can't be Myriadians; Myriadians can't pass through the Veil of Wings.

Is the trio planning to throw me out of the realm?

Fight!

As the intruders approach, I kick the vase perched on the coffee table. It nails Middle Man in the face. He's tall and muscled and the porcelain explodes into fragments; he grunts, stumbling backward.

I roll to the floor, flowing under the table, and jump to my feet on the other side. Leftie—who was diving for me—smacks into the couch and plops onto the table.

I rush into the kitchen, but Rightie catches me before I can grab a knife, wrapping strong arms around my waist and holding me prisoner. No matter how hard I struggle, I'm unable to break free.

No. No! The other two grab my ankles to help cart me out of the apartment. I buck and flail and shout for help. This is no time for pride. Whatever they have planned for me, I won't make it easy.

Apartments doors open. Three trainees peek out to see what's going on. The only male pales and retreats. One of the girls—Winifred—steps into the hall.

Leftie shoots her with a Dazer, and she freezes. Jerk! I know the spirit stun gun causes no pain or lasting harm, but he's left a young girl vulnerable.

And why the heck wasn't the Dazer used on me?

Maybe I'm going to be tortured before I'm thrown out?

Fear claws at me, but still I fight. The last girl in the hall—Elizabeth, who needs to move her butt out of the trainees' section—watches my abduction with an air of amused satisfaction. The fear morphs into fury.

"Have fun, Numbers," she calls. "I know I am."

There's no sign of Clay, my next-door neighbor. It's early. He's here, and he has ears; no way he's missed the commotion. Has he washed his hands of me?

I deserve this.

Go ahead, guys. Take me away.

I'm carried into the elevator. Soft music drifts from overhead speakers.

I should have nutted up and gone to see Clay last night. Instead I took the coward's way out and avoided him. I should have apologized on my knees. He's my best friend. I should have explained the reason for my choice.

He should have…given me the benefit of the doubt?

Is it wrong of me to think so? Maybe. The problem is, someone else's response—supposed or otherwise—should never dictate my actions. Isn't that what I claim to believe?

Dang it! I'm going to escape, and I'm going to tell him how much he means to me.

The elevator dings, and the doors slide open. As I'm hauled

into the lobby, I spring into action, bucking and kicking with every ounce of my strength.

"Can you just be still for a second?" a familiar voice grumbles.

Hold up. Clay?

"I think you broke my ribs." Definitely Clay.

I waffle between relief and confusion. Clay would never hurt me, even while supremely disappointed in me. This must be some sort of...test?

"You aren't supposed to speak," another guy snaps.

Deacon? He's successfully avoided me since the day of my arrival and now he's part of this...whatever *this* is?

"Sorry, man," Clay mutters.

We make it outside. Light spills over me, greeting me as if we're old friends, warming me from the inside out.

As we continue on, I bring the map of Troika to the forefront of my mind to track our progress. A Stairwell is used to take us deeper into the Capital of New, where the higher-ups must live. Mansions, mansions, everywhere. We enter a Gate and exit in the Museum of Wisdom. This is my first time here, and I'm... Wow. An Egyptian pyramid, a Russian palace, a Romanian fortress. A tepee.

The absolute majesty of every edifice dumbfounds me.

We travel through another Stairwell, then another Gate, and finally end up in the Tower of Might, a city given its name because of the numerous skyscrapers with...loading docks rather than balconies? Flying cars come and go. I shake my head, awed.

I'm carted to one of many coliseum-type arenas surrounding the skyscrapers and dropped on a sandy ground. I jump up, ignoring the black spots flashing in my eyes and the empty state of my lungs. The masked men remain in place as Levi, Meredith, Kayla and Reed join us; the entire group forms a circle around me.

Tremors shoot through me, but I raise my chin. *Want a piece? Come and get it.*

"Gentlemen," Levi says with a nod.

The "gentlemen" in question remove their masks, revealing Deacon, Clay and Victor.

There are seven people in total.

Seven days in a week. A heptagon. Lucky number seven.

I scowl at Levi, the General who obviously issued the order to abscond with me. "There are better ways to invite me to… whatever this is."

"Yes, but there was no better way to show you just how weak you are."

"Well, consider me shown." I spread my arms wide, all, *Bring it.* "Anyone else want a go at me?"

"Oh, don't worry. Everyone will get a go at you." He crosses his arms. "Please tell me you spent the morning using your Key, unlocking doors in the Grid."

"I'd tell you, but I'd be lying."

He frowns at me. "You should spend less time pitying yourself and more time on what matters. We need you, and people in the Land of the Harvest need us. See how that works?"

So irritating, but so right.

He walks around me, drawing a circle in the sand. "A gift given can do nothing unless it's received."

My hands ball into fists. "If you're hoping to confuse me, A-plus. You nailed it."

He smiles at me, but there's no amusement in the deed. "You have to forgive yourself for Archer's death. Otherwise you'll be in breach of contract. Did you know that? Hold a grudge, earn a punishment. Even when the grudge is self-directed."

I bristle, retorting, "Has anyone informed Elizabeth of this?"

"How about you focus on you, eh?" He winks at me. "Since you're new, I'll throw you a bone and explain a few things. Elizabeth has entered a grace period. A time *without* punishment to reflect and forgive. While you might curse *her* grace period, I have a feeling you'll rejoice when you are shown the same mercy."

Ugh! He's more irritating by the second. "What constitutes a punishment here?" I know about the Exchange, when we see our crime through the eyes of our victim. But there must be others.

"Loss of home or job. Solitary confinement. Yes, we have a prison here, and resentment is a serious crime. Antipathy of any kind casts a shadow over the Grid and affects us all."

Well. Time to do my part to keep the Grid bright and shiny, then. I face Clay. "I'm sorry. I knew someone else would rush to your rescue but feared no one else would—"

He holds up a hand to stop me. "*I'm* sorry. Meredith explained the situation to me. I should have trusted you."

Meredith knows me and sees the best in me. The realization *is* bright and shiny.

My gaze finds hers. *Thank you*, I mouth.

She blows me a kiss.

"You are a Conduit," Levi says, taking the reins of control.

"Am I?" I ask softly. "I've shown no signs of extraordinary power."

"A few setbacks, and you doubt my word and your own abilities. Perhaps you *are* ordinary."

I scowl at him. "A *few* setbacks?"

"Anyone can start a marathon. Only the strongest will finish it, even after they fall."

Ann-nn-nnd he's right again. Zero! "Please stop doing your impersonation of a motivational poster."

"Very well. We'll get down to business." He wipes an invisible piece of lint from his shoulder. "Normally we wouldn't send a trainee into the field, but a unique case has come to our attention, and you, Tenley Lockwood, are the only one who can do the job."

"Also, we would *never* send a Conduit into the field when our only other Conduit is MIA," Meredith adds, her voice now brittle with tension.

Trepidation flash-freezes my Lifeblood. I can guess where this is headed. The girl Meredith mentioned before the welcome party. The one infected with Penumbra.

"The princess isn't missing," Levi informs us. "The Secondking spoke with his Generals this morning. Myriad has placed a large bounty on the princess's head. Unwilling to risk one of our own people turning against her for personal gain, the Secondking has hidden her, as we suspected."

I'm disgusted by Myriad's daring, but relieved the princess is safe.

Levi pins me in place with a hard stare. "As for the case. The worst has happened. A day so many feared. Myriad has successfully infected a human with a disease known as Penumbra."

Knew it!

Gasps of horror rise from the others.

"It's real?" Reed asks.

"This isn't a drill?" Kayla seems to crumble into herself and shrink.

Levi nods and continues. "This information goes no further

than our circle. Understand?" After everyone verbally agrees, he adds, "You're the only one who can stop an outbreak, Miss Lockwood, which means I have to give you a crash course in the field of...everything. We'll also work on your quirks and help you grow through every problem you encounter."

Grow through, he said. Not just *go through*. I like it. "But I'm just a girl. One girl, newly dead. How can I—"

"All you lack is the proper motivation." A shrewd gleam enters his eyes. "Perhaps this will help. Killian Flynn has been placed in charge of the infected girl's care."

I jump as if I've been hit by a freak bolt of lightning. Catching my breath is suddenly impossible. My blood heats. I'll get to see Killian, speak with him...fight with him?

Wah, wah, wah. Way to ruin a mood. We'll be on opposite sides of the war, with far different goals.

"Why would you pair me against him?" I ask.

Expression grave, Levi says, "The importance of this mission...the consequences if you fail... I will do *anything* to ensure you do *everything* you can to save us. If you can convince Mr. Flynn to help us, even better."

My stomach twists. *But no pressure, right?*

"Train me," I tell him. "I'll do whatever I can to help."

A glint of approval. "Meet your teammates. The ones you'll be working with directly. Everyone has a different specialty, and I believe you'll complement each other well, despite the lack of experience. Like Archer, Victor spent time with Killian before he defected. And considering Killian helped you rescue Kayla and Reed from Many Ends, they're the least likely to attack him and the most likely to aid you. Clay and Meredith love you and will guard you with their lives."

No one will be giving up their life for me ever again!

"Why don't you go ahead and say *goodbye* to your teammates, too. Killian will murder us all—with your help, I'm sure." Elizabeth enters the coliseum and approaches the circle. "Whether you're witting or unwitting."

I glare at Levi. "What's she doing here?"

"Hey! Numbers!" she snaps. "You don't talk to a General that way. Even children know—"

He glares, and she goes quiet. "Elizabeth is a member of your team, Miss Lockwood. Grace period or not, antipathy, rancor and malice always come with a price." He doesn't raise his voice, but his irritation is clear. "The two of you will learn to work together, to trust each other, or you'll fail your charges when you're in the field."

I toss my hands up. "So why even risk it?"

"If you can't overlook your emotions with each other, how will you overlook your emotions when something else goes wrong? And something *will* go wrong. We risk you by *not* teaching you to transcend what you feel."

"I will *never* trust you," Elizabeth spits at me. "I'd rather spend eternity in Myriad's Kennels than work with—"

"Enough, Miss Winchester," Levi snaps. "You've already been warned. As a graduate, you are an example to trainees. Be a good one."

In a surprising display of respect, she lowers her head.

I'm in no position to gloat over her chastisement. I'm already struggling with the reality of what I'm supposed to do, what I *need* to do. Now I have to deal with Elizabeth, too? Wonderful.

The past can't be changed, and her opinion does not—will not—define my reality. A judgment rendered is an affirmation of the judger's character, not mine. But I need this girl to work with me, not against me.

"I can't defend Killian's past," I tell her. "He did what he did, just as you and I have done what we've done. You've asked for second, third and fourth chances, I'm sure. Shouldn't he receive the same? Shouldn't I?"

She glowers at me, and mutters, "Go count yourself."

Um. I'm...not sure what to say to that.

"All right. Let's get started." Levi taps the top of his hand, and a blue glow appears. He types into the glow, and a few seconds later, a Shell materializes beside me. A Shell created to resemble me. "Everywhere you go, veteran Laborers will be securing the perimeter. You will never be without an armed guard. They'll be able to track you through the Shell."

I barely hear him. I'm too busy marveling at the Shell itself. She—it—has straight black hair and no brands, the only real differences between us. The eye sockets are empty and clear, but that will change the moment my spirit is inside. Humans and spirits alike will see my real eyes.

The eyes are the windows to the soul, after all.

The Shell even has— Hey! "Was the pimple really necessary?" I demand.

"The key to blending in," Levi replies, "is actually blending in."

"Wow. Such wisdom." Humans won't know I'm a Shell unless and until I'm physically touched; Shells produce no body heat.

Not that the truth will register even with contact. Until I got to know Killian and Archer, I'd had no idea I was interacting with Shells, and blamed their cold flesh on a glandular problem.

Oh, the power of rationalization.

"Archer's Shell was perfect," I grumble. "Meaning, without flaw, in case you need the definition."

Levi arches a brow. "Pimples are not flaws, they are pim-

ples. People come in all types, shapes and sizes. Are you for-
getting the time Archer used Bow?"

Bow, a rotund female Shell and my first introduction to
a boy who would change the course of my Everlife. "No."
I'm still grumbling. "I'll never forget Bow." I took showers
in front of her/him.

To Archer's credit, he always used the time to marvel over
his own breasts.

"Archer knew how to blend in without trying to blend
in." He claps his hands. "Now. Every Shell comes with three
cases for weapons. One each for swords, daggers and guns.
They are called Whells—Weapon Hull with Enhanced Link
and Load—and if you acquire a different type of weapon,
you'll need to have a custom Whell made. Whells are useless
until you anchor inside the Shell. In conclusion, if you want
to fight with a sword, your Shell needs to be clutching the
Whell meant for swords. Understand?"

I nod, even as my head spins. "What about swords of fire?"
Like I saw the day I died.

"Pyres do not require a Whell. When you decode your
Key, you'll be able to create a Pyre of your own. An outward
manifestation of your Light. Until then... We're moving on."

"Wait! Myriadians produce Pyres, too, but they have no
Light."

"A cheap perversion, I assure you. Their swords are called
Glaciers and they smoke because they are made of something
akin to frozen carbon dioxide. *Now*. A spirit cannot interact
with humans without a Shell," he says, "which means lesson
number one is vital. Staying inside the Shell."

Sounds simple enough.

He motions to my Shell. "Go ahead. Give it a shot."

Confident I've got this, I walk into mine, as if I'm walking into an elevator—and I'm immediately ejected, propelled by a great force. Frowning, I try again, walking into it and—

I'm ejected.

My audience experiences different reactions.

Deacon remains stoic.

Clay grins. "Had the same problem myself."

Meredith and Victor cheer me on. "You can do it!"

Kayla and Reed regard me worriedly.

"Give up, Numbers," Elizabeth calls. "You're going to fail, and we all know it."

Levi doesn't correct her. "Don't ask yourself how you anchor," he tells me. "Ask yourself why you haven't *already* anchored."

Is he freaking kidding me? "Just so you know, my class evaluation will read, *totally sucked.*"

Others snort, but he rolls his eyes. "What is explained is often forgotten. What is experienced is remembered forever."

Fine. Why *haven't* I anchored?

To anchor. A verb. To secure, fasten, attach or affix. So… I haven't secured, fastened, attached or affixed my spirit to the inside of the Shell because…I haven't *tried* to secure, fasten, attach or affix my spirit to the inside of the Shell?

I square my shoulders and lift my chin.

"There she is," Levi says with a smile. "The warrior I know and sometimes like."

My fingers curl, preparing to dig in as I walk forward. My third attempt. The third time is the charm. My determination acts like glue, a suction developing between the animate and the inanimate. A suction that doesn't last more than a few seconds; I'm ejected, but I don't care. I did it once. I can do it again.

Levi's grin widens. "Next time you're in, slap the top of

your hand. A one-handed keyboard will appear. My address is preprogrammed into your database. Send me a message."

Shall I pull a rabbit out of my butt while I'm at it? "What do you want the message to say?"

"Anything you'd like. This is your one and only chance to tell me off without repercussions for disrespecting your superior."

I bat my lashes at him and for the first time since my death, I'm without even the minutest hint of despondency. "Is that because I'll be *your* superior one day soon?" He's a General, yes, but a Conduit outranks him. A fact I think I'm going to enjoy. A lot.

He looks up at the exquisite heavens, a sky of dappled water that surrounds the entire realm. "Take me into the Rest! Please!"

"She's definitely Archer's recruit, isn't she?" Meredith asks with a chuckle.

The pang of grief returns to my chest.

"Miss Lockwood," Levi says and pushes out a heavy breath. "A single thought can lead to absolute destruction or ultimate victory. Close your eyes and imagine staying inside the Shell. If you can see it, you can do it. So repeat after me. See it, do it. See it, do it."

"See it, do it. See it, do it." To humor him, I picture my spirit remaining inside the Shell...to my surprise and delight, a bolt of power hits me. A tide of determination and excitement buoys me. I *can* do this! I can stay inside the Shell.

I step into my Shell...and this time, I stay put.

TROIKA

From: T_L_2/23.43.2
To: L_N_3/19.1.1
Subject: rwat trey

Soed
A
S
S
Seow gpc/ehceo fo e y echd iiiii
EOC.SOECC EPOS.Sdl clwo dowleo wos w w ro.s
kr.

TROIKA

From: L_N_3/19.1.1
To: T_L_2/23.43.2
Subject: Your message skills—or lack thereof

Wow, Miss Lockwood. You really know how to insult a man. Too bad I haven't learned to read complete gibberish. But keep practicing. You (obviously) can't get any worse.

Light Brings Sight!

General Levi Nanne

PS: I usually end my transmissions with *Light Brings Sight!* For you, I'm ending with: *Bend or Break!*

TROIKA

From: T_L_2/23.43.2
To: L_N_3/19.1.1
Subject: Tesy Tesr Test

Yo cab shove yor light ip tour add.
    But srrioualy. hiw ia yhis??//?
    General-in-training,
    Twn Lockqood

TROIKA

From: L_N_3/19.1.1
To: T_L_2/23.43.2
Subject: Yawn!

I guess you're ready to admit Killian isn't the right partner for your Everlife. Obviously you don't want to see him again. And perhaps that's for the best. At this rate, the reunion will happen when you're both in your six thousands. A diaper is never a good look.
  Light Brings Sight!
  General Levi Nanne

MYRIAD

From: K_F_5/23.53.6
To: T_L_2/23.43.2
Subject: Tenley Lockwood

This is a test. Try to ace it.
  ML, KF

MYRIAD

From: K_F_5/23.53.6
To: T_L_2/23.43.2
Subject: Some days I think I hate you

1. But only because I miss you more with every breath I take.
2. Never forget your messages are monitored. Do not reply to this.
3. You're probably wondering how I contacted you. Archer gave me a Troikan comm before he died. And don't worry. His rep won't suffer. The action was approved by his superiors to help us help you.
4. I'm awesome. You like numbers, you get numbers.
5. I know you had trouble with your dad, but I also know you're the forgiving type. Something I'm grateful for only when it applies to me. But. You'll be happy to know he's being treated with nothing but respect. On the flip side, your mother requested a court date, hoping to defect to Troika, and she's currently in hiding. I have friends seeing

to her protection every second of every day. No harm will come to her, you have my word. You will, of course, owe me big-time, and I will, of course, expect payment. I'm sweet like that.

6. You said you'd always trust me. Never forget.
7. Guess who gets to mentor Sloan? I'll give you a hint. He dreams about you every night.
8. You are the best friend I've ever had. I miss looking at you, talking to you, laughing with you. If I could sneak into your room and watch you sleep, I would. Screw the creep factor.
9. The next time we're together, we will fight. There's no way to avoid it. Be ready.
10. 143

ML, KF

TROIKA

From: T_L_2/23.43.2
To: K_F_5/23.53.6
Subject: o miss you top

1) Thank you gor caring dor my mother.
2) I am heafed to land of Harvess—I will see you therr and thank you properly.
3) What does 143 mean/

If it's your way of telling ne we're over, sorry boyo, but it's not going tp work out for you.

Conduit-in-training,
Ten Lockwood

TROIKA

_____

From: Mailer-Erratum
To: T_L_2/23.43.2 K_F_5/23.53.6
Subject: THIS MESSAGE HAS BEEN DEEMED UNDELIVERABLE

A report of this exchange has been sent to your superior, General Levi Nanne.

chapter seven

"What you seek, you will find. Good or bad."
—Troika

For over a week, I practice with my Shell, a plethora of Whells/weapons and my teammates at all hours of the day and night, driven by unwavering determination. Several Generals stop by periodically to watch my progress, or lack thereof. Alejandro, who I'd swear was an Italian model in his Firstlife. Luciana, who is short, curvy and covered in adorable freckles. Shamus, who is the epitome of a Scottish warrior. And Ying Wo, who is as graceful as a sunbeam.

Each of the Generals oversees a different part of Troikan security and well-being. Everything from war planning to communications to the well-being of our citizens. They are the leading experts in their fields.

But no pressure for me to perform without error, right?

Every day Levi says, "Take my hands. Send a stream of Light to me through the Grid." Every day I fail, and frustration is riding me hard.

In what little spare time I have, I read the *Book of the Law*. If there's power in knowledge and strength in consistency, I'm going to be the strongest, most powerful girl ever to live!

Confession: half the time I don't understand what I'm reading.

Page one states: *The law does not define your life. The condition of our heart does that. You can only walk in the Light you know. Never violate your Light.*

So the laws aren't as important as our intentions...or the laws are just as important as our intentions, but if we mean well, we'll be forgiven for our mistakes? And how do you violate Light? Doing the wrong thing when you know what the right thing is? Or simply doing the wrong thing?

Either way, my brands throb as I read, so I figure some part of me gets the gist. Kind of like when I eat manna. I don't know what vitamins and minerals I'm putting into my spirit, but my cells absorb the nutrients all the same.

Every part of me understands the importance of forgiveness. My bitterness is poison—but only to me.

I force myself to let go of my anger with Elizabeth. When the feeling resurfaces, and it does, I focus on her good qualities. Her loyalty and passion. She hasn't returned the favor; she's holding on to her anger like it's a new boyfriend, putting me down at every opportunity.

She'll say, "If you're our savior, I weep for the fate of our realm." Or, "I wonder if the Firstking looks at you and regrets the creation of all humans." Oh, and I loved this one, "I bet your name stands for all the ways you make those around you miserable. Numbers one through ten, existing."

Thankfully, the rest of the realm has pardoned me. I'm greeted with smiles.

I wonder what everyone would think if they knew I'd received a message from Killian. I wonder what they'd think if they witnessed my reaction to the message.

Every time I think about it, I laugh, spread my arms and

twirl. The untouchable, indomitable Killian Flynn might maybe possibly be in love with me!

In the middle of my apartment, I do my thing. Laugh. Spread arms. Twirl. I have come to believe 143 is the numerical equivalent of *I love you*. 1—a one-letter word. 4—a four-letter word. 3—a three-letter word.

Until I received Killian's note, I constantly shied away from the word *love*. But why? My aversion seems so silly now. I mean, what's so frightening about four little letters? *L-O-V-E*.

Love gives. Love protects. Love lifts up and never tears down. Love empowers.

I think I might 143 Killian right back. My heart softens at the mere mention of his name. He is strong, smart and witty. He is courageous. He is learning how to be kind. When he looks at me, I don't see the pain of the past, but the brightness of the future.

I will tear the world apart to be with him.

But how can we be together?

We will have to brave the hostility of two worlds. I'll have to be stronger physically and mentally. A soldier capable of defending those under my protection and ignoring insults.

Yesterday Elizabeth said, "What if you're wrong about your Myriadian boy toy, huh? What if, when you compete with him, he uses your feelings for him against you? Who am I kidding? He will."

She hopes to ignite doubt. I have to be careful. Doubt is an insidious creature. It can creep in, set up a tent and ruin *everything*.

Killian has more than proved his loyalty to me. He deserves my trust. He's hiding my mother, even guarding her so that she can defect.

One day, she might walk the streets of Troika at my side, her hand in mine. Because of Killian's efforts and love.

Maybe he'll go a step further and work with me to end the war. Together, we can do anything! After all, not every Myriadian is a representative of darkness, and not every Troikan is a representative of Light. There are good and bad people in both realms.

The brands in my hands vibrate, and I jolt, preparing to— oh. Right. My internal clock. Ever since I learned to move in and out of a Shell, I've been able to produce a glowing keyboard above the center of my wrist. I can type whether I'm in or out of a Shell. I've learned to set an alarm.

Time to head to the Tower of Might for my next training session with Levi.

I stuff the arsenal I've collected into a backpack and blow my brother's hologram a kiss. He's reclined in a beautiful walnut crib. Four posts stretch toward the ceiling, each carved to resemble a tree trunk with curving branches up top. He kicks his legs as he giggles at me.

A feed of me plays on *his* walls, and he likes to watch me. I'm a source of entertainment.

My heart swells with love for him, strengthening my determination to end the war between realms. One day, he'll be old enough to join the army. If peace reigns, he'll never have to fight. He can enjoy the fruits of my labors.

"I'll come see you when my session ends," I tell him.

He farts.

Meredith visited with him a little while ago. Now his nanny sits in a rocking chair beside the crib, reading a passage from the *Book of the Law*. Nose wrinkling, she waves a hand in front of her face. "That was more than gas, wasn't it, my lovely," she says and stands. She's a beautiful girl, with red hair and a wealth of freckles. "I bet you filled your little diaper with toxic waste."

Ann-nn-nnd that's my cue to go. "Bye, guys," I say.

"Bye, Ten," she replies. I like her. She's been nice to me from the start. "Have an enlightened practice."

"I will, thank you." I'm smiling as I exit my apartment…the cathedral. Light spills from the exquisite watery sky, stroking and warming me. My insides hum with energy.

I might not be ready for my first mission, but I'm eager to help the girl infected with Penumbra. While rotting inside Prynne Asylum, I often fantasized about someone swooping in to save me. Then came Archer and Killian.

A familiar pang of guilt—*I miss you so much, Archer.* A electrifying thrill of anticipation—*I crave you like air, Killian.*

Levi hasn't mentioned my email exchange with "the Myriadian," and I haven't brought it up. If I'm going to be penalized for consorting with the enemy, I'd rather wait until after my first assignment…because I have every intention of consorting again.

I take my usual route through two different Stairwells and three Gates. The first Stairwell leads me to the manna fields. I count one hundred thirty-seven people hard at work this bright and sunny morning.

My name—well my preferred name, Ten Lockwood— equals one hundred thirty-seven when the letters are changed to their numerical counterpart.

$$20 + 5 + 14 + 12 + 15 + 3 + 11 + 23 + 15 + 15 + 4 = 137$$

I pluck a purple petal from a nearby branch and nibble as I walk to the first Gate. The breakfast of champions who are on the go. I receive nods, waves and smiles.

I spot redhead Nico, adorable Rebel and the charming Clementine. The boys give me a thumbs-up.

"How's training going?" Clementine asks.

"Slowly," I reply. "How's it going for you guys?"

"I'm rocking it." Nico flexes his biceps. "Unfortunately, I can't say the same for these two clowns."

Snickering, Rebel punches him in the shoulder. "You're only good with a musket, old man."

Clementine crosses fisted hands over her heart. "We're going to be Laborers under General Chanel's command. She's the best!"

"Unless we're late," Nico adds.

She looks at the comm on her wrist. "Oh, crap! Gotta run."

"Have an enlightened day," I call as we hurry our separate ways.

The next Gate takes me to the House of Secrets. In my black catsuit, I stand out. Everyone else is wearing a white robe. Some robes have gold thread, some have red, blue or green. The Grid supplies the reason: the threads denote different sub-positions. Gold—those who are in charge. Red—assistants. Blue—assistants to the assistants. Green—trainees.

Hoshi, Sawyer and Winifred are here, their heads bent over a table of books. Oh, look. Fatima is here, too. She's in the middle, almost too short to distinguish. The little girl has begun training already?

I take another Stairwell to a different section of the city, and the brands in my palms vibrate. Great! I have five minutes to make it to the Tower of Might.

I pick up the pace. My brands continue to glow as if...are they absorbing Light?

As a Conduit, I have the ability to absorb sunlight and turn it into Light, then project it to others. Or I *should* have the ability. The rays energize me before fizzling. The very reason I can't send any Light to Levi when our hands are joined.

Frustration and disappointment plague me. But come on, what did I expect? I haven't deciphered my Key, haven't unlocked the secret doors inside the Grid. Whatever that freaking means! I'm still at a complete loss, and no one knows how to help me. My code isn't like theirs, and theirs isn't like mine.

I reach the third Gate...exit and—

Bang!

I careen to the side and land on my hands and knees. Sharp pain explodes through my head, dizziness following. I come close to blacking out. Lifeblood leaks into my eyes, hazing my vision. A high-pitched ring assaults my ears, but even still I think I hear gleeful laughter from two different sources. A boy and a girl.

A whistle of air catches my attention. Incoming! I roll to my back, kicking up to knock— A board slams into my calf, another burst of pain exploding inside me. The board sticks to me, spiked tips sinking past flesh to bite into muscle.

I gag as I pull out the board, but I don't hesitate to swing at anyone or thing in my vicinity.

Thunk!

There's a grunt. Shuffling footsteps. Who'd I hit? I stand on shaky legs in time to watch three retreating figures; my mind is desperate to reject the idea I've been attacked. But I was. Three against one. The shock nearly sends me to my knees.

Troikans physically attacked a fellow citizen.

The knowledge leaves a dark, sticky film over my skin. A shadow?

A strong arm enfolds me, but I wrench backward, severing contact. Friend or foe?

"Hey, hey. Are you all right?"

I know the voice, at least. Victor. "I'm fine. I'll be fine." Will I, though? Whether in body or spirit, people are people;

where there is free will, there is potential for ultimate good or ultimate evil. I could be attacked at any moment.

"Tell me what happened," he demands.

I relate the story as best I can.

He gives me a gentle push toward the Gate. "Let's get you to a Healer. You'll be patched up heart, mind and body."

Most of—cough *all* cough—my training sessions have ended with me bruised and bloody, but I ate manna and boom, my spirit patched up all on its own. I had no reason to visit a Healer. Now I consider Victor's words. *Patched up heart, mind and body.* I guess Healers do more than deal with physical injuries.

"No." Teeth chattering, I sidestep him. What if I'm deemed unfit to train? What if I'm ordered to take time off? "I'll be all right. I'm due to practice with Levi. And so are you." We're *overdue* now.

"When you visit a Healer, a report is filed and an investigation launched. The Grid can be used to find out everyone in the vicinity of your attack. Your assailants will be caught and disciplined. Probably with an Exchange."

The Exchange is the best way to teach us the importance of doing unto others as we want them to do unto us.

"If those kinds of details can be unearthed, who would ever dare break the rules?" I ask.

"Well...some people know how to hide their location from the Grid," he admits. "But it's always best to check."

No doubt my attackers hid their location. "Did you see what happened?" I drop the board and rub my temple, hoping to ease the pain and pressure.

A heavy pause before he sighs. "When I came through the Gate, you were standing alone with a spiked log in hand."

"So that would be a no." I wipe my eyes to clear my vision. Victor is in front of me, his hair a mess, his amber gaze glittering with concern. "I still don't want to visit a Healer."

He bends to pick up the log. "This is a pretty abysmal start to your Everlife, yeah?"

"I'm sure there have been worse."

"None that I've seen."

Great. Wonderful. I lumber toward the coliseum, and he stays by my side. "Why would someone do this?"

"Before your arrival, we lost a Conduit," he says. "Ever since, our Light has been dimmed."

"Exactly! Why would anyone risk killing me? I'm needed!" Whether I'm liked or not.

"Darkness makes people...cranky. Besides, I'm not sure your Second-death was the endgame today. I'm guessing your attackers simply took satisfaction in your pain."

One of my number brands tingles, the same way it tingles when I read from the *Book of the Law*, and I frown. I look left then right, up then down, but notice nothing amiss.

One possible explanation...his words caused the reaction? But is he right or he is wrong?

The tingle becomes an ache, but I'm in no shape to puzzle out the reason. "Forget about me. Let's talk about you. I've been training with you, but I have no idea what your position is."

"I'm a Messenger." He practically pounds his chest like a gorilla. "One of the best. I whisper words of encouragement to Troikan loyalists, inspire Unsigned humans to speak with TLs and report any findings to Laborers."

Archer was the best at his job, too. "I know why your brother defected to Troika. Why did you?"

He tenses before he admits, "I wanted more time with him."

Oh…ouch. A barbed lump grows in my throat. "Because of me, he's gone."

"Every day I'm more convinced he can win the Resurrection, despite the fact a Conduit is in the running. The way everyone reacted to your involvement in his demise…he was more loved than I realized."

His words both tear me down and lift me up.

To me, the Resurrection proves Myriad is wrong and souls of the dead never Fuse with human souls in order to return to the Land of the Harvest. To someone like, say, Killian, it might prove only Myriadians experience Fusion.

A lie. Only a lie. One of so many.

Killian, like everyone else in Myriad, believes my spirit is Fused with one of their great Generals. He also believes his mother's spirit is Fused with a human, that she's a new person, alive and well.

Will he see this situation as I do, or as I suspect? The answer is so important. After all, our beliefs direct our steps, leading us along certain paths.

Lies are shackles. Truth is freedom.

Lies will keep us apart. Truth can bring us together.

"Can any spirit win, or only the ones who died this year?" I ask. "And when does the Resurrection take place?

"Only the spirits who died this year. And in less than a month."

What? Hardly any time to enact a plan of action. "Why do it? I mean, don't get me wrong. I'm overjoyed it happens. I just don't understand the reason."

"You just named the reason. Our joy."

I chew on my bottom lip. "I'd like to speak with those who have been resurrected in the past."

He sighs. "I figured you'd be asking for an introduction

and already made inquiries. Don't take this the wrong way, okay, but those I've spoken to so far refuse to meet with you. Free will, you know."

There's a *right* way to take that? Talk about kicking a girl while she's down. "How many still live?"

"Not as many as you'd think. Once they experience the Rest, they are ready to go back. They aren't exactly motivated to stick around."

Great! My odds of success are dwindling fast. "What happens when the resurrected die again?"

"They reenter the Rest, and they are excluded from the next vote."

We pass through the arched doorway leading to the coliseum, where Levi and the others are waiting.

"I still can't believe I'm working with a General," Victor says quietly. "While I trained with Messengers, I worked with a Leader. And really, you should be trained by the princess, and what an honor that would be, but—don't tell anyone I said this—Levi is better. He's stronger, smarter and in charge of our first line of defense. The fact that you're working with him...that you'll one day outrank him... I'm in awe."

There's no time to respond. Not that I know what to say. I didn't have a clue we'd been so highly honored.

Clay and Meredith notice my poor condition and rush over to worry and demand answers. Elizabeth doesn't reveal a hint of emotion, and I wonder...is she the owner of the board? Did she perform the hit-and-run?

"Back in line," Levi calls.

With a wince and muttered apology, my friends return to their positions.

He turns his scowl to me. "You're late." When he sees the Lifeblood soaking my top, he barks, "What happened?"

I watch Elizabeth as I say, "I was attacked."

Her expression never wavers. If she's the culprit, she expresses zero guilt or glee.

Levi taps his palm, his keyboard glowing. "Why haven't you had any manna? Why haven't I received a medical report?"

"I don't have any manna on hand, and I didn't visit a Healer." I change the subject before he can insist I take time out to visit one. I'll never risk being benched. "So where are Reed and Kayla?" My wingmen.

"Elsewhere," he says, and offers nothing more. "Why didn't you visit a Healer?" He removes a necklace from his neck and tosses it my way. "They're here to help you."

"I'm fine." I catch the chain and find a vial of manna dangling from the end. "I'll *be* fine."

"Whoever did this… I will find out, and I will ensure justice is done." The fierceness of his tone… I shudder, kind of feeling sorry for the culprit now. "In the meantime, drink the manna, get the vial refilled after practice, and wear the necklace without fail in case something like this ever happens again."

I drain the contents and hang the now-empty vial from my neck. My wounds…fail to heal. Disappointment knocks at my door.

Before Levi notices and decides to go ahead and send me to the Healer, I say, "Where's Deacon?"

"Out on assignment." Levi's gaze slides over me, his frown deepening. As if he sees something I don't. "Have you decoded your Key?"

Ugh! He has a one-track mind. "You know the answer. Why do you continue to ask?"

Alejandro walks up behind him and pats him on the shoulder, but smiles at me. "He continues to ask so your determination to succeed will grow—or at least your determination to shout *yes* in his face so he'll finally stop asking."

The two Generals shake hands and share a look of concern. For me?

"Time to build your stamina," Levi tells me. "Run around the columns until you collapse."

I *hate* building my stamina, but today I do it without complaint. I gotta get stronger. Gotta get tougher. I run and run, pushing myself to my limits.

All the while Levi and Alejandro chat, and neither seems happy about what they are discussing. I wonder…has the Penumbra situation gotten worse?

When I trip over my own foot, I force my attention to remain on the track. I run like the wind. A sickly, dying wind. To my consternation, my wounds continue leaking Lifeblood.

Just like bodies, spirits sweat with exertion, and all too soon I'm drenched. My limbs burn and tremble, exhaustion settling in, but something amazing happens, too. The sticky film I noticed earlier finally fades. I don't have the strength to hold on to my resentment about the attack—and that's exactly what had adhered to me. Resentment. Levi must have seen it.

My wounds heal at last, every hint of pain fading.

Lesson learned. Resentment blocks the effects of manna. Emotions matter.

I run another lap…and another. I'm certain I'm about to fall over when Meredith appears on the sidelines to cheer me on. Victor joins her, the two giving me a mental and physical boost. I make it another three laps. Clay throws water on my face, cooling me down, and I make it another two.

Elizabeth stands in the distance, watching with thinly

veiled dislike until Levi commands the entire group to follow me. Alejandro has left him in a bad mood.

With my teammates around me, I run another lap...four... six...

A thousand times, I want to give up, but there's no way I'll be the first to go down. A good soldier endures hardship, and that's that. I will endure.

"All right," Levi finally calls. "Enough."

Still I run another lap. When I go for a second, my body screams, "That's it, no more." I collapse. Grass and dirt fill my mouth, but I'm too busy wheezing to care.

Levi marches over extends his arms. "Take my hands. Send a stream of Light into me."

Though I'm *soaked* in sweat, I sit up and link my fingers through his. I close my eyes to better concentrate on the vivid rays and swirling warmth in my heart and mind. The home of the Grid.

I reach out with every intention of latching on to...nothing. I latch on to nothing, the Light dancing just out of my reach.

Levi releases me, and I open my eyes. I expect to see disappointment, but he smiles encouragingly and gives me a freaking noogie.

"You've proved you can persevere when you're injured and tired. You've proved you can let go of upset feelings to do what needs doing. I'm pleased, Miss Lockwood."

I struggle to tamp down the urge to preen and quip, "Try to contain your excitement on my behalf. Too many compliments will go to my head."

One corner of his mouth curves up. "Tomorrow morning, you and your teammates will visit the infected human. You will observe her, nothing more. Unless she threatens human life, you will not speak to her or interact with her in any way. Not yet. Understand?"

Finally! Progress! I mask my eagerness and give him a jaunty salute. "Sir, yes, sir."

"Head to the Hall of Records in the Museum of Wisdom. Study our files on Dior Nichols."

Whoa. Slam the breaks. "Did you say *Dior Nichols*?"

"Yes. She is the one infected with Penumbra."

I reel, a girl stuck on a spinning carnival ride. Dior is the twenty-year-old med student Archer tried to win for Troika. He fell in love with her in the process and would have succeeded if Killian hadn't stolen her away, convincing her to make covenant with Myriad and tricking her into agreeing to the worst terms of all time.

The *old* Killian, I mean.

"If you've never dealt with Penumbra," I say, "how can you be sure she's infected?"

"I personally entered the Land of the Harvest to observe Miss Nichols. I saw the darkness writhing underneath her skin, watched that darkness attempt to jump on one of her friends. I have no doubts we're dealing with Penumbra."

Dior Nichols, patient zero. This can't be a coincidence.

Archer didn't just love her; he adored her, and he despised Killian for ruining her future.

Killian hadn't used his usual method—straight-up seduction—so I'm not sure how he won her over. I only know he's expressed massive guilt.

According to Dior's contract, she cannot help Troikan loyalists without earning a punishment. However, hospital policy states she can't turn anyone away due to their realm affiliation. A terrible catch-22.

Twenty-two, the atomic number of titanium, which is

harder than any rock. The number of players permitted on the field in American football. The number of letters in the Hebrew alphabet.

"Do I have time to take a shower?" I ask Levi.

He looks me over and winkles his nose. "No, but you're going to make time."

Funny. I head to the locker room only to pause to look at him over my shoulder. "Do you ever wish the war would end?"

"Yes. Of course," he replies without hesitation. "But the day we stop fighting is the day we're conquered."

Didn't Meredith say the same? "What if Myriad wants to stop fighting, too?"

"The citizens might crave peace, but their king will never allow it. He won't stop until he's dead—or every Troikan is."

chapter eight

"When you cease seeking, you will find."
—Myriad

After a quick scrubbing, I emerge from the stall to find Meredith standing guard at the door. She hands me a white robe with white trim, a combination I haven't seen before, and exchanges the empty vial on my necklace for a full one.

"Thank you," I say.

She nods, her expression grave. "During Elizabeth's Firstlife, she lost her family at a young age and ended up bouncing from foster home to foster home. She wasn't always treated well. In her last home, it was so bad she ran away and ended up in all kinds of trouble. Archer was her TL, and he changed her life. When she came here a little over a year ago, she fell hard for a boy named Claus. She felt for him what you feel for Killian. The day you died, Killian killed Claus."

I want to cover my ears and shake my head, no, no, no. I'd known Killian had ended her boyfriend's life. I hadn't known the rest. I hadn't known about the horrors of her Firstlife.

My grandmother is forcing me to see Elizabeth as a person rather than a villain. A person with hopes, dreams and hurts, just like me.

I want to snarl at her and tell her it will never work. I've been ridiculed, insulted and beaten by a heartless bitch.

I want to hug Elizabeth close and comfort her while she cries.

"Go on," Meredith says in an act of compassion. "You have a job to do."

I force Elizabeth to the back of my mind. I'll figure out my feelings later. I kiss Meredith's cheek. "I love you," I say and haul butt to the Hall of Records.

I remain on alert for any sort of attack. Catch me by surprise once, shame on me. Catch me by surprise twice, experience my wrath.

When I reach my destination, I take a moment to appreciate the massive Victorian Gothic. Tall and sprawling, it is enclosed by a black brick-and-granite wall. A multitude of people rush in and out.

In total, there are ten stained-glass windows. The three biggest depict (1) the Firstking, (2) the Secondking and (3) Princess Mariée with doves rising over her shoulders, their lovely white wings extended. The other seven windows line up in a single row, divided only by larger windows with clear glass.

Between the Firstking and the Secondking are panels showing the Land of the Harvest, the sun and a tree in full bloom. Between the Prince of Doves and Princess Mariée are panels depicting the four seasons inside a single circle. A bird flies above it while a fish swims below it. The next panels feature a spirit on the upper half and a human on the lower half, the two reaching for each other. Finally, there's a window without an image, a simple pane of a glass with different shades of blue.

Before me, an iron balustrade offers seven different openings that lead to a grand staircase in the center of the building. On each side is a picturesque bridge that climbs to the second floor, where seven columns create different archways. Between each arch is a roundel featuring a bronzed dove in various positions. On the ground, eating. On a bench. On a tree. In flight. Soaring through the clouds, soaring above the clouds and, finally, surrounded by a beam of amber Light.

So much symbolism here. Too much to decipher all at once.

I scale the steps, finding three granite panels between the columns attached to the wall, revealing carved friezes portraying fierce battle scenes. There are four pediment niches where flowers overflow, and between two are Reed and Kayla, who are holding stacks of books and vibrating with excitement.

"This way." Kayla turns on a sandaled foot, the hem of her robe swaying with the movement. The material is light green with dark green trim, and labels her a Leader-in-training.

Reed trails her, and I trail Reed. He's wearing a white robe with a green trim, signifying his status as a Laborer-in-training.

The deeper we go, the more awed I am, the inside of the Hall even more elaborate than the outside, with domed ceilings and life-size sculptures of Generals who have led our armies into battle throughout the centuries. There are multiple chandeliers, but they aren't connected to the ceiling. The glowing teardrops are suspended in the air, dancing together to create different shapes and patterns.

I'm mesmerized and trip over my own feet—twice.

"Good going, *graceful*," a male quips.

I turn, meeting Raanan's hard gaze. He's at a table, surrounded by books—and he just spoke to me, I realize. This is the first time I've ever heard his voice.

"I'm hot, I know," he mutters. "No need to stare. Later, your fantasies will remind you of what I look like."

I prefer him silent. And seriously, is he hitting on me—or himself? "What are you doing here?"

"Studying for a test. I assume you're doing the same." His wry tone suggests I'm an idiot. Or at least borderline.

"You assume wrong. I'm studying for a *mission*." Ooo-kay. *My* tone suggests I'm smug and prideful, two things a Troikan is not supposed to be. I end the conversation before I can throw witchy into the mix, giving him my back as I face my friends.

Kayla and Reed have settled at the glass table next to Raanan's—great!—and they are arranging their books in rows of three. When they finish, sections of the glass depress, hiding the books beneath the surface while magnifying the pages over the surface.

"Amazing." My voice echoes, and I cover my mouth with my fingers. "Sorry."

"If you think that's cool, just wait." The strange thing is, *her* voice doesn't echo. To the table, she says, "Show me the text I've highlighted about Tenley Lockwood." She grins at me. "Everyone always wants to know what can be learned about them, but more than that, there is no better way to prove the information you read about others is correct."

My cheeks flush as text appears on the glass. "Anyone can read about my life history? My mistakes?"

Someone shushes me.

Grin widening, Kayla takes my hand, places my palm on the table and, after a few seconds of confusion as a neon colors flash over my skin, she releases me.

"There. You're now connected," she says.

Connected?

"After you've dealt with your bad decisions and embarrassing moments," she says, "they're redacted."

"Dealt with?" I parrot. This time, my voice doesn't carry. I don't understand, but I can deal with only one mystery at a time.

"You know...worked through, forgiven yourself and others, apologized, that kind of thing. Whatever you haven't dealt with, well, you still don't have to worry. Only Generals can access the bulk of that information."

My heart pounds as I read the mostly-redacted file, *Tenley Lockwood—thick black line—during her escape from Prynne Asylum. After—thick black line—with Archer Prince. Thick black line—with ML Killian Flynn. Thick black line—Prynne Asylum closed down.*

The asylum closed down?

Well. Something becomes clear: no one ever gets away with a crime, and no secret will ever remain a secret. Whether in Firstlife or the Everlife, there will be a punishment or a reward.

"Per Levi's request, I've already searched for your attacker," Kayla says. "So far, the incident hasn't appeared in anyone's file."

"Okay, I've seen enough. Dismiss my file."

She types into an invisible keyboard, and says, "Please show every sentence I've highlighted about Dior Nichols and reveal the accompanying photos."

The text is replaced, and photographs of Dior Nichols in different stages of her life appear.

Dior Magnolia Nichols visited with TL Elizabeth Winchester on November 1 seeking a way to break covenant with Myriad. We are proceeding accordingly.

Court. Of course! The one and only way to null and void an Everlife covenant.

Myriad must have learned about her possible defection and found a way to infect her with Penumbra.

"What happens if Dior defects, but I fail to cleanse her of—you know?" I ask, back inside the pressure cooker, the setting jacked to high.

"You won't fail," Reed says, but there's a catch in his voice.

"Help me understand. Why make covenant with Dior now?" I croak. "Why not wait until she's been cleansed?" I know Penumbra is said to only affect humans, but what will happen to our Grid if she dies? Can't be good for us.

"We do not cherry-pick our humans." Kayla wags a finger in my face. "We offer sanctuary to one and *all*. Always. We are equals, one life just as important as any other, and circumstances do not dictate our behavior."

A philosophy I believe with all my heart. And yet... "By accepting Dior, I suspect we'll be endangering millions of other lives. Troikan lives."

"We'll be endangering millions of other lives if we reject her." Reed pinches the bridge of his nose. "If there's a reason to reject one, then there will be a reason to reject others. When we place restrictions on our aspirants, we break the laws we were built upon. We become Myriad."

Kayla twines her fingers with mine and presses our joined hands against her raging heartbeat. Desperation radiates from her. "You must cleanse her of Pen—darkness. You *must*. That is the solution to every problem."

The pressure cooker just might blow.

I release her and massage the back of my neck. "Is there anything here that will help me decode my Key?"

"Are you kidding? I haven't unlocked mine." She holds up her arm, revealing three symbols descending from elbow to wrist. A raindrop, a winding line and a flame.

Reed holds out his arm, rolls up his sleeve, and shows me three animals branded into his flesh: a lion, a lamb and a fish.

"I'm still locked as well, but I've done some digging. Our Keys are some type of cipher."

He's…right. Excitement sparks. I can't believe I overlooked the key to our Key. Hope unfurls, and it's kindling for the excitement. Somewhere in Troika there's a note…maybe a letter to trainees, or a specific book…even a speech that's been given. Something! Those words will correspond with my numbers and their symbols and unlock the Grid.

My number brands throb, and I know beyond a doubt I'm on the right track.

"Where is Dior now?" I ask.

"Elizabeth convinced her to go into hiding," Reed says.

If this isn't proof Troika values free will, nothing is. Lives are at stake, and yet we allowed Dior to make her own decision.

He points to a line of text that's been redacted. "We won't know where she is, exactly, until Elizabeth meets with Madame Meredith tomorrow morning. That's when the rest of us will be sent to her."

I fought some of my roughest battles outside a Troikan safe house. Looking back, I'm glad they happened. They tested my limits, pushed me to change and to grow. To toughen up.

"How am I supposed to fight the big P?" I ask.

"According to Levi, we're to observe only." Kayla nudges me. "Remember?"

Right. When we observe, we learn. And I desperately need to learn.

"Dior has had a terrible couple of years." Kayla's chin trembles. "We need to help her. If we don't, who will?"

Zero! She's right. If any of my friends were in her position, I would move heaven and earth to help. How can I do less for Dior? Besides, I promised Archer I would do everything I could to ease her burden.

So that's what I'll do.

"I will find a way to help her," I say. "Is there anything else I need to know before I take off?"

"Yes." Warm breath strokes my nape. "You can take the rest of the information with you."

I whip around to glare at Raanan, who is now standing behind me. "Personal boundaries are invisible but real. Please use yours."

Amusement sparkles in his eyes. He holds up his hands, all innocence, his robe falling to his elbows to reveal *his* Key, three different types of swords. I'm not sure if he's trying to torment me or make peace.

"He's right." Reed takes my hand and presses my palm to the edge of the table, where my Troikan brand meets a brand that's been etched into the glass. "Here are a few little tidbits. You can study them tonight."

Just as quickly as the pages appeared on the table surface, the information they contain uploads into my data pad. Or maybe directly into my mind. Dizziness overwhelms me. Too much, too much. Too fast!

A few little tidbits? my brain cells shout.

"Isn't osmosis fun?" Kayla says with a laugh.

"No!" I grate.

"Give it moment," Reed replies.

Raanan adds, "Everything will settle into place in three… two…one."

Thank the Firstking, the dizziness fades. I draw in a deep breath, slowly release it, and comprehend the information overload is in the process of nestling, settling to the back of my mind to await my study.

"Okay, I think I'm a fan of osmosis." I rub my temples in an effort to ward off a weird tingling sensation. "Thanks for—"

Raanan walks away without another word. What an odd duck. When he decides to stop being standoffish, he goes all the way. I'm still not sure what to make of him.

"Hey, do you want to come over later to go through the information with me?" I ask. "You can bring manna since I'm almost out..." *Hint, hint.*

"Oh, I wish," Kayla says, "but I made plans." She opens her mouth to say more, thinks better of it and snaps her jaw closed.

Interesting.

"Got other plans myself," Reed says with a shrug.

Very interesting. Would their plans happen to be together... a secret romance brewing, perhaps?

"No problem. I hope you have fun." I hug one, then the other. "I'll see you guys later." I'll go home, flip through my new mental files and work on decoding my Key so that I can better help Dior.

As I make my way out of the Hall, again remaining on alert, an azure glow springs from my palm.

Curious, I tap the brand. A message from Victor appears. How about we get together and come up with a campaign to ensure Archer wins the Resurrection?

My heartbeat speeds up. Yes! I need Archer. He will help me decode my Key. He will help me save Dior—and in the process, save Troika.

I send a response, one-handed typing still harder than I ever could have imagined. My place? And brung manna.

His response appears a few seconds later. Your typing still sucks, I see. (Thankfully I can read Ten.) I'm on my way.

He beats me there, a bag of manna wafers in hand.

Victor, I soon learn, is far different than his older brother.

Archer gave new meaning to the phrase "in your face," while Victor is all about subtlety and even misdirection.

"After our session with Levi, I asked around," he says. "Everyone wants the Conduit to return. I failed to make them understand we don't need the Conduit. We have you, and Archer is clearly the optimum choice."

"What makes you think so?" The question awakens a tide of guilt inside me. Shouldn't I agree flat-out? Why do I need proof my friend is the optimum choice?

He rolls his eyes. "One day, you're going to have serious power in this realm. You need to be surrounded by people you can trust."

And I can't trust the Conduit?

"We have to let people know why Archer is the better choice without actually saying so," Victor continues. "The moment we start *claiming* he's the best, people will stop listening. Arguing never changes anyone's mind."

We sprawl on my living room floor and dig in to the manna. When every crumb is gone, I lean against the couch. Victor lies back on the rug and throws a small ball into the air. Catch and release. Catch and release. I think the simple rhythm helps him to focus.

I wonder what the other newbies are doing tonight, if they've made new friends. If they have a new purpose.

"What do you suggest?" I finally ask, picking up our conversation as if it hasn't lagged. "I've never tried to reach people without stating my desire up front."

"First, we figure out who's currently the most influential person in the realm, and we target him. Or her. One person can lead thousands. Second, we're going to have to leverage Dior. She's sick with the Troikan version of the boogeyman, and while another Conduit could help combat that sickness,

Dior has to *agree* to be cleansed. Will she? Since she loved Archer, he might be the only one capable of convincing her to say yes."

"I...don't know how I feel about that." Am I being ultra-sensitive, or is this something the old Killian would have suggested? 1) We would be playing on everyone's fears. Fear is the enemy at your back with a knife at your throat.

2) The Resurrection takes place in less than a month. What if we can convince Dior to be cleansed—neutralizing Penumbra—much sooner? If that happens, Archer won't be needed. Not the way Victor suggests, anyway.

His plan strikes me as underhanded. But this is Archer's brother I'm dealing with; he grew up in Myriad, a child of the Secondking—he's a literal prince. He learned his MO from the same people who taught Killian.

A glow springs from his brands. He checks the message and groans. "I've got to go." He sits up and wiggles his brows at me. "I've got a hot date."

Frustration takes a big bite out of my calm. Archer's fate hangs in the balance, and we have yet to develop a workable idea to save him. I can't do this alone, and Victor is bailing on me?

"You're going on a date, and yet you groaned, as if in pain," I say.

He gently bounces the ball off my nose. "Because you girls are a lot of work."

I twist my fists under my eyes, mimicking tears. "Poor baby. So who's the girl?"

"None of your business, Miss Lockwood."

"So you're protecting her identity. The relationship must be serious, then." The *Book of the Law* says it's best to date a person selected for us by the Grid. 1) It's supposed to keep the peace between, well, everyone. No more fighting over a mate, or thinking you belong with someone who would be better off with someone else. 2) It's supposed to keep our focus where it belongs. On the war. And 3) it's supposed to prevent messy breakups.

Is Victor's date not Grid-approved? Because of free will, we can date whomever we want. Grid-approved or not. Either way, he has nothing to hide.

I wonder if my recurring dream about Killian is the Grid's version of permission.

Wishful thinking? I mean, why choose Killian, a Myriadian? Why not select a Troikan for me?

"Just...think about what I said, okay?" He stands. "Help me with this, and I'll help you with something you really, really want...finding a way to stop the war."

I purse my lips. "How do you know I want to stop the war?"

"Doesn't everyone?" He hikes his shoulders. "Face it. You're not exactly subtle."

He takes off before I can lob a million questions at him. How would he help me? Why hasn't he helped me already? Can he list at least three ways I've been less than subtle? Gotta work on my game.

I remain in the living room, playing catch with his ball. There's really no need to think about his offer, I decide. I'm not going to help him with his plan. I'm not going to feed other people's fears. Archer would *rage* if I did. There has to be another way to win everyone over.

As for stopping the war...my chat with Victor *has* helped me in that regard. I've been thinking on too large a scale. Because he's right about one thing. Want to reach a thousand people? Start with one. That one will help you reach others. Those others will reach others, and so on and so forth.

A whisper can become a roar.

Excitement sparks, hotter than before. *One by one.*

My first—Dior.

I can help her. I must. The fate of Troika depends on it.

I head to the Veil of Wings, my spirit tucked securely inside my Shell, Whells strapped all over me. Just in case. My hold is secure. I'm not going to be kicked out by anyone or anything; in fact, I'll die before I let go. I stayed up all night, practicing with my Shell and reviewing information about Dior, as if I was cramming for a test.

Before being taken to the safe house, Dior Nichols lived in Oklahoma City, Oklahoma. She was a resident at Baptist Hospital, assigned to triage in the ER. On her days off, she played with her dog, Gingerbread, and volunteered at a Myriadian homeless shelter.

She has a kind heart, almost too good to be true, but her life is far from perfect. Every time she's helped a Troikan loyalist, Myriad has taken away something precious to her—a right she gave them when she made covenant.

The once-happy girl is now miserable. Court is her only chance.

She's considered killing herself, a notion that cuts deep into my compassion. I want to shake her and say, "Never give up! If you're breathing, there's hope!" The only reason Dior hasn't ended her life is a clause in her contract. Fine print states she'll have to spend one hundred years locked inside the Kennels if ever she commits suicide.

One hundred years trapped in a tiny cage.

Did she not read her contract before signing? Or did she just not care at the time?

I know how Killian won her over, at least. He approached her when she was at her most vulnerable, after her father, her only guardian, had broken his spine in a car accident. After multiple surgeries, his health had declined and death seemed imminent.

Archer told her: *Trust us to make it right.*

And she had. For a little while. But the situation had grown worse instead of better. At least in Dior's eyes. As a human, she hadn't seen the things happening in the spirit realm. The small fixes for big changes being set into motion.

Killian told her: *No more waiting. Your father will walk out of the hospital, and he'll go home today. Just sign here.*

Patience is a virtue for a reason.

*Im*patient, she'd done it, and her father *had* walked out of the hospital, as promised. Only, he'd collapsed right outside the doors, his heart bursting from strain. He'd died right there on the dirty concrete.

He'd gone home, again as promised, but he'd gone home to Myriad, his realm of choice. Another reason she'd agreed to their terms. She'd wanted to spend her Everlife with her beloved father.

What Killian did to her...it was ugly. So very ugly. To hurt Archer, he distorted the truth in the worst possible way. A despicable act from a despicable boy who'd laughed in Archer's face immediately after Dior made covenant—laughed at the heartache he'd caused.

I know deep in my heart he isn't that boy anymore, but I'm still sickened by his actions—which makes me angry with myself. Who am I to judge anyone for anything? I've made mistakes. Many, many mistakes. I've hurt people, unintentionally and intentionally. I've *killed* people. I've ruined lives and broken up families.

I never want people to judge me for the person I used to be, so I shouldn't judge Killian for the person *he* used to be.

Troikan rule one: *love everyone, even yourself.*

Troikan rule two: *forgive everyone, even yourself.*

I get it now. Though there are many other laws, number one is the be all and end all. The *reason* for the other rules. Number two helps us do the first.

I'm not dealing with Past Killian anymore. I'm dealing with Present Killian. He's searching for Dior right now, and he won't stop until he finds her. It's his job. Chances are, we're going to fight. And fight hard, just as he warned.

No matter what, I will do what needs doing. I'll do what's right, and I won't quit.

Victor, Clay and Elizabeth beat me to the Veil of Wings. Elizabeth won't meet my gaze. Meredith's description of her life rings in my head, and I begin to melt.

I destroyed her in the worst possible way.

Everyone is in a brand-new Shell, dressed in a plain T-shirts and a pair of jeans. The Shells look as if they were made with wax, making it obvious they are, in fact, Shells. But then, we aren't supposed to blend in with humans today. We are supposed to stand out.

I stop beside Clay, who clasps my hand and squeezes.

"How does this work?" he asks. This is his first mission, too.

"Madame Meredith has a lock on our Shells," Victor says. "As soon as we step through the Veil, she'll send us on a beam of Light to a specific location in the Land of the Harvest. Clay and I will stand guard outside the safe house, along with a hundred or so Laborers we probably won't be able to see. They're already in place, and Reed is among them."

"You, Numbers." Elizabeth snaps her fingers without glancing my way. "You will observe Dior inside the safe house. The goal is to learn the feel of your Shell in the Land of the Harvest and communicate with your teammates without alerting humans you're doing so." Finally her gaze meets mine. Her eyelids narrow to tiny slits, her lashes nearly fusing together. "Remain calm at all times. Fear draws Myriadians like flies."

This girl is hurting. She's lost everything. She needs compassion rather than censure. I nod. "I'll do my best."

"No. You'll do, plain and simple. And," she continues, "before you start thinking you'll scare Dior to draw out Killian, expecting him to *help* you with your job—"

"I would never," I interject, bristling.

"Don't," she finishes. "The last time he helped you, he still had a chance to win your soul. He doesn't anymore. Which means he's going to betray you faster than you can say, *Please, Killian, no.*"

"You don't know him," I say softly. I'll probably have to repeat the words to everyone in Troika at some point or another.

"Oh, but I do. I've seen how he works firsthand. He's seduced a lot of girls. What makes you think you're special to him?"

"What makes you think I'm not?"

Her nostrils flare as she huffs and puffs. "I've gone against him. I've watched my friends die at his hand. I watched Claus die." Her rage is replaced by grief. "Killian uses, lies and tricks. The only thing you're going to get from him... is heartache."

MYRIAD

From: Z_C_4/23.43.2
To: K_F_5/23.53.6
Subject: The fruit of our efforts!

My spy inside Troika informs me Tenley Lockwood will be in the Land of the Harvest today. She'll be visiting a human you signed. Miss Dior Nichols. The two will be inside a Troikan safe house. The coordinates are attached.

I'm excited about your next move. Is there anything I can do to help you, Mr. Flynn?

Might Equals Right!

Sir Zhi Chen

MYRIAD

From: K_F_5/23.53.6
To: Z_C_4/23.43.2
Subject: I've got this

I know exactly what to do to win over Miss Lockwood.

But there is something you can do to help me. Miss Lockwood might seem as tough as nails, but she's actually a bleeding heart. After she meets with Miss Nichols, she'll be desperate to ease the girl's pain and suffering. She'll want Gingerbread returned—not just a little slice but the full loaf. If you'll release the dog, I can show my "affection" by offering the little mutt as a gift. I can use this to my advantage.

Might Equals Right!

ML, Killian Flynn

MYRIAD

From: Z_C_4/23.43.2
To: K_F_5/23.53.6
Subject: Good thinking!

I will ensure Gingerbread is released into your care.

Also, as you know, our precious General Oriana died three days ago in an ambush. Before her death, she mentioned your desire to know the name of the human Fused with your mother and her promise to blaze through red tape *after* we've won Miss Lockwood's loyalty. (Shhh, just between us, I'm doing my own digging on your behalf.)

Oh! I'd like Miss Aubuchon to accompany you on today's mission. I suspect Miss Lockwood has yet to embrace the Troikan concept of forgiveness. Why should she? Miss Aubuchon killed her. If you can, subtly encourage Miss Lockwood to seek revenge. Help her discover the satisfaction of getting even.

Might Equals Right!
Sir Zhi Chen

chapter nine

―――――――

"Without love, action is meaningless."
—Troika

The word *heartache* loops through my mind, and I shake my head to dislodge it. Everyone has a story, and I will be the author of mine. Every day begins with a blank page. Today, I will fill my page with hope and hustle. One hundred percent, nothing held back.

In fact, I'll begin my new story right now.

The girl who is special to Killian Flynn is going to save the day. She steps through the Veil of Wings.

I trek under the spray of crimson water, the droplets raining over me. Peace and Light encompass me. I breathe in... out... I'm still moving forward, knowing the others are behind me, and then—

I fall.

There's no time to scream or flail. One moment I'm whooshing across an expanse of blazing stars, pulled by a force I can't control, the next I'm standing in front of a quaint little farmhouse in Texas with a wraparound porch, shuttered windows and a tin roof.

My heart pounds as if I've run a race. I did it. I returned to the Land of the Harvest.

A thousand details flood my awareness at once, big and small. In the corner, a basket of strawberries rests at the feet of an ancient rocker. A wealth of pecan trees casts clusters of shade. I can see the individual pieces of bark on the trunks, every grain on the rocker, and the threads used to weave the basket. I can hear the creaking of the rocker as gusts of wind blow, the chirp of grasshoppers and locusts, the scamper of feet as squirrels run for cover.

Encasing the entire farmhouse and surrounding forest is a dome of jellyair—a faint blue Light that sparkles with diamond dust, just like our sky, keeping Myriadians out. Myriadians can't even *see* what's behind the Light, and if they try to walk through it, they will burn to ash.

My vision blurs, sand blowing into my eyes. I blink rapidly to clear the Shell's lenses.

The wind brushes against me, and the sensation is…odd, as if it hits a wall, and I feel only the vibration of impact. Also, I have no perception of hot or cold. I remain the perfect temperature, outside factors inconsequential.

Birds chirp, but unlike the other noises—nope, the other noises, too—the sound is muted, giving me the impression I'm hearing an audio recording on low.

I sniff…and smell nothing. Are earthly fragrances somehow filtered out through the Shell?

Clay grins from ear to ear as he takes a post on the left side of the porch. Victor moves to the far right.

Elizabeth marches to the door. —*Try not to mess this up.*—

Her voice drifts from the Grid, filling my mind. I've learned not to react when Troikans speak to me without moving their mouths. —*I never try. I do.*—

—*Funny.*— She opens the door. Hinges squeak.

I enter behind her. Inside, there's a couch, two recliners, an ottoman and a coffee table. Everything is utilitarian.

Elizabeth crosses her arms and watches a human pace.

The human. Dior Nichols in the flesh. The woman who won Archer's heart. The beauty used as rope in the tug-of-war between Archer and Killian.

From her file, I know her mother is black, her father white. Dark hair frames a baby-doll face, with a small nose and adorable, Cupid's bow lips. Humans might come with flaws, but she's pretty close to perfect. Her skin is a few shades lighter than her hair, and her eyes are a few shades lighter than her skin, almost gold.

But Levi is right. I can see the disease. Shadows slither across her cheeks, down her neck. They are thin, almost like veins…only filled with what looks to be toxic sludge. I don't think she's aware of them; otherwise she would be screaming or maybe even setting herself on fire.

How did she become infected?

"Who's the girl?" she asks Elizabeth.

"I'm—" I begin.

"She's no one," Elizabeth interjects, flicking a narrowed glance my way. "She's here to observe."

Oops. Gonna zip my lips now.

Dior continues to pace, unaware a Messenger keeps pace beside her. A boy I've never met. Through Levi, I know he's one of the best, hand-chosen by the Generals.

He's in spirit form, and he whispers to Dior, "Firstlife is an opportunity. The past is the past. You have a bright future. Do not fear. Fight for what you want."

Having trained with Victor and Clay, I know Dior doesn't

hear the words but somehow internalizes them, as if she's just had an idea. She chooses whether to follow it or discard it.

I'm tempted to introduce myself to *him*, but I don't want to interrupt him. Or freak out Dior. She has no idea he's here.

"Why are *you* here?" Dior demands. "Has the court date been set?"

"No. I'm sorry." Elizabeth looks genuinely remorseful.

Dior stops to glare at her. "Why? What's the holdup? I don't want to spend the Unending in Myriad."

The Unending. Another term for the Everlife, used by humans more than spirits.

"I told you Myriad would contest the trial, and I was right. They have. Meanwhile, we need to prepare you for the hardships to come."

Elizabeth's gaze zings to mine. —*Too many fail. The process is difficult, with both realms examining and cross-examining the defector. All the while scenes from the human's life play over a screen for everyone in court to see. If she's not ready, she'll crumble and we'll suffer a loss.*—

The loss of Dior?

A bitter laugh escapes the human. "Thanks to Killian Flynn, I've endured hardships for the past two years. He's a monster, and I'm ready."

Oh, no she didn't! "*You* are responsible for the pain you suffer. Your decision, your consequences."

Elizabeth sucks in a sharp breath. The Messenger I still haven't met finally looks in my direction, his eyes wide.

Dior balls her fist and steps toward me.

One of my number brands throbs. A warning to stay quiet? Too late. "Don't," I say. "I don't want to hurt you, but I will if I must. When it comes to fight-or-flight, I fight. Every time. Continue down this path, and it won't end well for you."

Levi told me I must temper my strength with humans. I'm stronger than they can ever hope to be.

To be honest, I'm not as strong as I could be. I've got to push myself harder. My one-on-one with the spiked board proves I have to be ready for anything, anytime. And considering my aspirations for peace, I have to be prepared for pushback.

Elizabeth jumps between us, her gaze remaining on me. "Threatening a human won't end well for *you*, Ten."

Zero! She's right. I'm allowing my emotions to steer me. It's time for head-smarts to take the wheel. Proceeding with caution, I say, "Troikans are love. The true Lights of the world. Myriad embraces hate. Do you want to be Troikan, as you claim, or remain Myriadian? You can't be both."

Dior closes her eyes and drags in a deep breath. If the actions are supposed to calm her, they fail. Her eyelids pop open, and she glares at me. "You're *already* Troikan, an advocate against judging others, and yet here you stand, judging me."

I should fade into the background. I'm not observing, I'm participating. But what the heck? I've already violated orders. "I've stated facts, nothing more, nothing less."

"You're as cold as Killian. I would never—"

"Tsk, tsk," I interject. I am *not* cold, and neither is Killian. "Those three words—*I would never*—are an attempt to disguise judgment as opinion."

"Enough, Ten." Elizabeth wraps an arm around Dior's shoulders to draw her away while whispering words of comfort.

Dang her! Is the TL brave or foolish? —*What if Dior inadvertently drains your Light?*— I throw the words at her through the Grid.

She doesn't miss a step. —*Dior hasn't exhibited any signs of becoming an Abrogate. Until she does, she can't hurt me. I'm going to treat her as I would treat anyone else.*—

I almost say, *So you're going to smack her with a spiked board?* I remain quiet instead.

"Oh, my gosh. I'm sorry." Dior wrenches from Elizabeth's hold. "I forgot. I'm so sorry."

"No reason to be sorry. I give you permission," Elizabeth says, her voice gentle. Once again she wraps an arm around the girl's shoulders, and this time Dior allows it without protest.

Long ago, the realms instituted a law stating humans are never to touch Shells. This saves the shelled spirits who are working in recruitment centers, the House of Troikan Representatives and other places throughout the world to do their jobs without interference, and allows more natural-looking Shells to blend in, hiding in plain sight.

There are only two caveats to the rule. 1) When the human doesn't know the other person is a Shell, and 2) when the human does know and has permission from the Shell.

I stalk to the far window and gaze out, removing myself from temptation. But I'm not alone for long. Dior joins me.

I tense, expecting some kind of attack. She simply says, "I'm sorry. You did nothing wrong, and yet I took my frustrations out on you."

Oh…zero. Levi would tell me the first to apologize is the strongest. Dior is human, but despite my earlier boasts she's stronger than me in the way that matters most.

What remains of my anger instantly deflates. "I'm sorry, too. Archer loved you. He wanted me to make your life better, not worse."

A warm ray of Light shines through the glass, coils around my brands and…strokes me?

I wonder if the beams are the Troikan counterpart to Penumbra. Or perhaps the rays are normal, and *I'm* the one who's changed.

"Archer." Tears fill her golden eyes, and her chin quakes. "Elizabeth told me he died in battle."

My heart squeezes in my chest. "Yes."

"I loved him so much." The tears streak down her cheeks. "I've tried to move on. Since I signed with Myriad, I mean. I've dated. I even have a boyfriend. But…"

"I know. It's hard to get over Archer."

Her head cants to the side. "You loved him, too." A statement, not a question.

"Very much. He was like an annoying older brother."

She laughs softly. Then her tears flow faster, harder.

The Grid buzzes inside my head, pricking like bee stings. *Remember the year you spent as an Unsigned, torn between Troika and Myriad, unsure what was best for you? Every time someone pushed you one way, you pushed back and ended up further away from a conclusion. Be the Laborer you needed someone else to be.*

The suggestion grounds me. Deep breath in…out… "Before he died, Archer forgave Killian for what he did to you. They worked together to recruit me to Troika."

Her eyes widen. "He worked with Killian? Seriously?"

I nod. "You define Killian by the worst of his actions. Actions that are part of his past. Mistakes he made and now regrets. By the end, Archer defined him by his current actions, which proved how much he'd changed. He's different, Dior. He feels remorse for what he did to you. He even searched your contract for a way to free you from your punishments."

"But he couldn't find one." She slumps a little. "He wrote the contract, and he's very good with fine print." She presses her palm against her neck. "Despite the contract, I decided to continue on with the life I'd planned. I accepted a residency and dedicated myself to saving others. Which I can do. But only if my patients are Myriadian. And I know, I know. I'm told I shouldn't have any problem turning Troikans away. They'll only hurt my realm later, right? But people I like and admire are Troikan. If they scream in agony and I turn away, I'm a monster."

"I'm sorry." I am. Her struggle is agonizing.

"My contract states I'll be a Laborer in the Unending, not a Healer. I've only ever wanted to be a Healer." She shudders, and finally, she breaks down, her knees crumbling. She lands on the floor with a hard thud, sobbing into her hands.

I'm angry on her behalf. Her choices led her down a terrible road filled with bumps and potholes. She's bruised and broken, clinging to the only life raft she's been thrown. A court date.

Compassion overtakes me. This girl doesn't know me, but I know her. I can help her. I know I can!

I crouch beside her and comb my fingers through her hair. She hisses and scrambles away from me. *I* hiss, sharp pain exploding at the ends of my fingertips, shooting through the rest of me.

"What was *that*?" she demands.

I rub my arms, feeling as if lightning is now striking on the underside of my Shell. "I don't—" But I do. I do know, and I look to Elizabeth, my jaw clenched.

Penumbra.

How am I supposed to cleanse her?

I cast my voice to Elizabeth. —*Is that a sign she's becoming an Abrogate?*—

—*No. I'm guessing that is Penumbra's defense against a Conduit. That is why you weren't supposed to touch her.*—

Right. Rules are rules for reasons. Whether I know the

reasons or not. "I'm sorry, Dior. I'll be more careful in the future." I stand. "And I *will* help you, even if I have to work myself to the bone." I will act like the woman Archer expected me to be.

"Ten," Elizabeth snaps, reminding me I've overstepped my bounds yet again.

I don't care. This girl needs me. And I get it now. I understand why Troika will go to so much trouble to save a single soul. Everyone is precious. Everyone is someone's child or loved one. Everyone has potential.

"When is the last time you spoke with someone from Myriad?" I ask.

Dior calms enough to say, "Three days ago."

I run my bottom lip between my teeth. "Killian?"

"No. Rosalind Oriana and Zhi Chen."

Instant relief; Killian wasn't involved. "Did they say or do anything unusual?"

"Like what?" She wipes away her tears.

"You tell me."

Now she frowns. "They came to my house and chatted about nothing for what seemed an eternity. Then they left."

I consider the timing and ask, "Why did you contact Troika afterward?"

She bristles, as if I've insulted her. If I did insult her, it was unintentional. I only want answers.

"Is this necessary?" Elizabeth demands.

"Yes," I reply without looking away from Dior.

"I'd had enough," she says. "I'd reached the boiling point. I remembered Archer told me to contact Elizabeth if ever I needed anything, so I called her."

But how did Rosalind and Zhi—assuming they did it—

infect her? "Who else have you spoken with? Any strangers? Did you notice any odd behavior from your patients?"

"No. I haven't been to the hospital in a week. The only other person I've spoken to is my boyfriend, Javier Diez."

"Is he Myriadian?"

"He's Unsigned. Why?"

I look to Elizabeth. —*Does she know she's sick?*—

—*No. And we're not to tell her.*—

Because she would freak out? Who wouldn't? "Where's Gingerbread?" Dior could use a special friend right now.

Dior starts sobbing all over again.

Zero! What'd I do wrong this time?

"The dog was taken by her ML." Steam practically curls from Elizabeth's nostrils. Either I've pushed her too far or— "By Killian, in case you require clarification."

That.

I flinch. "How long does it take to set a court date?" We've got to get Dior out from under Myriad's control. Once she's made covenant with Troika, we can safeguard her until she's been cleansed, ensuring she doesn't enter the Everlife with Penumbra, potentially harming the Grid.

"Could take months, depending on how hard Myriad continues to fight us," Elizabeth replies.

"Well. You take care of that, and I'll take care of the dog. And you," I say to Dior, remembering tidbits I read about her. "You've been dealt a raw deal, there's no question about that, but self-pity isn't your friend. See past it and fight for what you want, like Elizabeth said."

She peers at me through eyelashes beaded with her tears, her face red and blotchy. "You can find Ginger? Really?"

Elizabeth stomps over and gets in my face. —*This is a watch and observe assignment for you, not a command and do whatever the hell you want.—*

I respond. —*You are free to make your own choices, just as I'm free to make mine.—*

Stiff as a board—har har—she types a message into her keyboard. Probably contacting Meredith. Maybe even Levi. No...chain of command is important in Troika. She's *definitely* contacting Meredith.

Any second now, I should receive a message telling me to stand down. Well, I won't. I absolutely will not! There's hope in Dior's eyes for the first time since we arrived. It's fragile, and it needs tending. Doing anything but what I promised will destroy her, and she might not be able to weld the pieces back together.

My palm glows, and Elizabeth smirks at me.

Meredith has sent me a text. I brace myself to read it...and a fiery lance of shock nearly splits me in two.

Proceed.

Whooo hoooo! Thank you, Granny.

Elizabeth growls as she reads a message of her own, one telling her I can do what I want. "This is why family shouldn't work together," she grumbles.

Suck it. "A good plan is a good plan."

The front door swings open, and a determined Victor enters the farmhouse. "Killian and an ML-in-training found us. They're just outside our security wall."

Everything inside me goes haywire. My heartbeat slips out of rhythm. My blood heats, melting my spirit inside my Shell. Different parts of me tremble...all the places Killian has touched... I ache in the most delicious way.

Finally! He is nearby. The boy who 143s me is within reach.

I smooth my hair, my clothing. How do I look? How will he react when he sees me?

Dior pales. Her eyes chill to frostbite-cold.

"How did he get past our guard?" Elizabeth demands. "How did he find us?"

Dior's fear, maybe? But I doubt she's in the mood to hear my opinion.

"I don't know," Victor replies.

"Let's go." She grabs hold of Dior's arm and pulls her to her feet. "I'm taking you to a new safe house."

"Stop and think this through." Victor crosses his arms. "You take Dior away, and the Myriadians will leave. She stays, and we can send Ten out to talk with Killian. For her, he might let good intel slip. Like how he managed to track us. You still want to know, right?"

Elizabeth throws a death-glare at me. "Apparently we're doing things her way today. If Numbers wants to risk Dior's safety in order to talk with the guy who will destroy us, she can."

He high-fives me. "Way to go, Ten. You're in training, but you're being trusted to lead. What an honor!"

Stomach cramp. What if this is a test, and I'm failing?

"If you go out there," Elizabeth tells me, her tone grave, "you will endanger us."

Dior steps forward, her hands balled into fists. "My fate hangs in the balance. *I* should be the one to decide."

Uh, no. That would be a huge mistake. She doesn't see the whole picture.

Do I? Not even close. Am I allowing my desire to see Killian to direct my actions?

I zip my lips. *Testing, one, two, three.*

I nod at Dior. She's right. Her future, her decision.

At first, she says nothing else, and I shift from one booted foot to the other. If she says no…

"You can go out there." She expels a deep breath. "You do what you promised me. You bring back Gingerbread, alive and well."

My knees nearly buckle with relief. "I will."

"You heard her." A victorious Victor hikes his thumb at the door. "Go out there and get answers, Ten."

I rush forward, stopping abruptly when Elizabeth grabs my arm. Eyes now resolved, she says, "You're about to learn the harsh reality of the war between realms, and the betrayal you will *always* face at the hands of our enemy. Not because you're facing Killian, but because you're facing a Myriadian. Good luck."

chapter ten

"Action without love is still action."
—Myriad

I rush out of the farmhouse, certain of only one thing. I don't believe in luck.

When something good happens, someone has been working behind the scenes to see it through. Luck will not dictate Killian's treatment of me. His character will.

On the porch, I look past the Buckler—aka jellyair—and search for Killian.

Clay races to my side. "I know what you're planning, and I'm asking—no, I'm *begging* you to stay within our Buckler. I've been in Troika longer than you. I've heard rumors about Killian—"

"I know what you've heard. He's mad and bad to the bone. He wins whatever the cost." *Until me.* "He's changed."

"No. I mean, yes. I've heard those rumors, too. But there are others. New ones." His tone drips with trepidation. "Worse ones."

Searching… "I don't care about gossip. Rumors are a disease, usually started by people with an ax to grind, and they mutate as they spread."

"You're right. And that's the reason I never said anything until now. But this... I think Killian's life hinges on his ability to neutralize you."

"No." I give a vehement shake of my head. Killian would have told me when he messaged me. "How could anyone in Troika know what a Myriadian has or has not been ordered to do?"

"I'm not sure. I just know I overheard Levi and Meredith talking."

Shock kicks me back a step. If Levi and Meredith truly believed Killian intends to "neutralize" me, they wouldn't have used him as an incentive for me to work harder, to learn faster.

Searching... "You must have misunderstood."

The next time we're together, we will fight. There's no way to avoid it. Be ready.

My chest hollows out, but again, I shake my head. He would never hurt me. "I'm going to talk with him."

"Then I'm coming with you."

"No. You're in danger, I'm not." Still searching... Dang it, where is he? "Stay here, and stay safe."

There! A tall, dark blur through the jellyair. I race off the porch and through the trees, closing in on the shield... almost there.

The ground quakes, as if a giant fist just smacked into the planet. I trip and land on my knees. My gaze lifts to the sky. The dome is gone, and a guard tower hovers above the farmhouse.

Like clouds, towers are mobile, steered wherever the action is.

Along the parapet, TLs and MLs are locked in a fierce battle—for rights to Dior? Fiery swords swing, appearing like bursts of lightning.

Such violence. When will it end? How many lives will be lost today?

Within seconds, the Buckler reappears, the battle nothing but a blob on the horizon.

I stand and kick into motion, finally exiting the dome. Surrounded by trees, I'm sheltered from the battle by a canopy of leaves.

Adrenaline surges as I search nearby thickets. Where is Killian? Was he attacked by patrolling TLs? Hurt? For that matter, where are the TLs? Now in the guard tower?

I spin, calling, "Killian!"

In the distance, leaves rattle. I palm the dagger sheathed in the side of my boot. Branches part...and Killian emerges, the rest of the world forgotten. His dark hair is messy, his shirt and battle leathers ripped in several places. He holds a sword in a tight grip.

There's a rope tied around his waist, the end stretched behind him like a tail. Whatever he's dragging is hidden behind the line of trees.

Our gazes meet, and we both go still. His savage intensity threatens to unravel my calm. His blue-gold eyes sing to me...always they sing, and the anguished melody haunts me.

"Ten." The huskiness of his Irish lilt turns my name into a thousand other words. The one I cling to—*Love*.

I can't catch my breath, and I'm not sure I want to. Every inhalation marks the passage of time. A second closer to our parting. I want to stay here forever.

"Killian." His name is a soft invocation. He's here, and he's in front of me. A literal dream come true. I wish I could scent his peat smoke and heather, my two favorite scents in the world.

I wish I could touch him.

I remember the bone-deep cold a single graze of skin-to-skin contact causes, but I can't bring myself to care. I know the agony of being without him, and I would endure *anything* to hold him in my arms again.

I sheathe my dagger and step forward.

"What are you doing? Arm up not down." Expression hardening, he lifts his chin, squares his shoulders and straightens his spine. He angles the sword, pointing the tip in my direction. "I told you what would happen the next time we were together."

I've seen him do this with others, and I know he's preparing himself for battle. For the horrors to come.

Unease pricks the back of my neck. Elizabeth's warning… Clay's warning… Am I a fool to ignore them?

Stop! Why am I entertaining doubt? When it came time to pick a realm, doubt kept me imprisoned with indecision. I have to trust my instincts.

Right now my instincts are screaming: *remember the dream.* The birds attacked me only when my attention veered away from Killian.

What if the birds represent misgivings and other people's expectations?

"I'm not going to fight you," I tell him.

"Your new family hasn't convinced you to hate me, then?" His voice is devoid of emotion. "They must not have shared the worst of my sins with you."

Does he fear my disdain? "You're a horrible person, blah, blah, blah. I've heard it all. Can we move on to the happy to see you portion of our reunion?"

A flash of hope—of Light?—before he scowls. "Still your stubborn self, I see. Your instructors must mourn the day they met you."

Does he? "You can't stay here. TLs are stationed around the perimeter, commanded to kill Myriadians on sight."

Now there's a flash of surprise. "I've done a sweep. We're clear—for now." His gaze roves over me...and heats. "How are you, lass?"

I shiver and lick my lips. "I'm curious. What does 143 mean?"

A smile flashes, gone within a single heartbeat. "What do you think it means?"

"I...love you," I say and shift from one foot to the other.

"Do you, then?" He sheathes his sword at last, a gleam of wickedness in his siren-song eyes. "I had no idea. Thank you."

"Killian." I anchor my fists on my hips. "Do you love me or not?"

He extends his arm and holds his wrist under a ray of golden sunlight. I notice his slight tremor and melt. I— His Shell has been tattooed. The numbers 143,10 stare at me, and I gasp.

I love you, Ten.

My hand flutters to my heart.

Killian closes the distance and frames my face with his big hands. I expect pain, but there's none. I expect a chill, but the temperature of my Shell never changes.

A Troikan and Myriadian Shell can touch without complications?

He presses his forehead to mine and breathes me in. "I love you so much I hurt."

My pulse points hammer. Suspecting his feelings isn't the same as *knowing* his feelings, and I... I'm... I throw my arms around him, embracing him the way I've longed to do since we parted. I hold him tight, so tight I would bruise him without the insulation of the Shell.

He runs his fingers through my hair. "I've missed you. I've thought about you every day, dreamed about you every night. I've had to play my bosses to keep myself out of trouble and assigned to your case."

"I'm still a case?"

"You're a Conduit, lass. You'll always be a case." He rubs his cheek against mine. "I'm supposed to romance you and convince you to betray your realm."

Elizabeth would insist he's playing me *now*, only telling me what I want to hear while explaining any actions he takes against me. Clay would insist he hadn't misunderstood Levi and Meredith.

My trust never wavers. "How can I help you stay out of trouble with your bosses without harming Troika or a human?"

He straightens, as if he's been jerked by an invisible chain. His beautiful eyes fill with amazement as they search my face. "Convince your Generals to deny Dior's request for a day in court."

Wait, wait, wait. "How will that keep you safe? How doesn't that harm Troika? Or Dior! If she's with you through duress, she's not really with you."

"Forget trying to keep me safe. Myriad is using Dior against you."

"How?"

"I don't know."

You're about to learn the harsh reality of the war between realms, and the betrayal you will always face at the hands of our enemy.

What possible motive could Killian have for—

Um, hello! That's easy. He's already given me the answer—to stop Dior from going to court.

I grind my teeth. Enough! Instinct over circumstance. Heart over logic.

"I believe you," I tell him. People can call me foolish and judge my decisions all they want. They will be looking at the situation through the dusty lens of the past. I see who this boy has become. "But I can't abandon Dior. You haven't seen her sobbing on the floor. If you're worried about Penumbra—"

"Yes. No. I don't know," he repeats. He gives a single shake of his head. "Penumbra is above my pay grade. A well-kept secret among our Generals. The fewer people who know the ins and outs, the less Troika can discover."

"So you don't know how Dior was infected?"

"All I know is that General Rosalind Oriana left Myriad to meet with Dior and never returned. Word is Rosalind was ambushed by TLs when she stopped in a guard tower on her way home. And she's not the only General we've lost this week. This morning, General Abdul Ibqal visited Javier Diez—Dior's boyfriend—and like Rosalind, he died during an ambush on the way home."

I arch a brow. "You sound skeptical."

"I am. If Troika were responsible, they would have taken credit. Maybe gloated. So far, they've been silent, as if they have no idea what happened."

There's another option, I suppose; Myriad could have taken out their own Generals.

Impossible. They wouldn't...would they?

"Dior is desperate to escape her contract, Killian. I can't turn my back on her just because we don't know what's going on behind the scenes. If I can help her get to court, I will. I must." I have to act while I have the opportunity.

His sigh is heavy. "I knew you'd say that." His hands travel the ridges of my spine and stop just above my bottom, leaving me tingling with anticipation. The perfect torment. "Be careful who you trust. There's a spy among you. That's how we found your location."

A spy? "Who in their right mind would agree to live in Troika while remaining loyal to Myriad?"

"Someone who *isn't* in their right mind."

Right. "But how would we not know? I mean, we're all hooked to…" I go quiet as tendrils of dread coil around me. We *aren't* all hooked to the Grid, are we? Some Troikans… like my attackers…can unhook to hide their location. "I'll be careful," I croak.

He reaches up to trace his knuckles along my jaw, and I wish, I wish so hard, I could feel him skin-to-skin rather than Shell-to-Shell. His touch is like the wind. I know it's happening, but I only experience a vibration…like the ghost of a memory. But it's enough. Today, it's enough.

"I should go," he says, but remains in place.

Every cell in my body screams *No! Stay!* But I reply with a soft, "I know." I flatten my palm on his chest and imagine I feel the echo of his heartbeat through his Shell.

He utters a bitter laugh. "I'm not ready to leave you. I'll never be ready."

A familiar pang cuts through me. "We'll see each other again, right?"

His eyes heat like a thousand suns. "With us, there will *always* be a next time."

Shivers consume me. His words…they are beauty incarnate, poetry and passion. They are hope.

Before Killian, I wasn't a romantic girl. I existed with no real purpose, anger directing my actions. He's changed me for the better.

The rope attached to his waist jiggles. Scowling, he grabs

hold of the center and tugs…and I discover Sloan Aubuchon hog-tied at the end.

I grab my dagger, a curse brewing in the back of my throat.

"Behold," Killian says. "My new partner."

His…partner? I swallow bile, suddenly sickened in body and soul. My boyfriend and my killer are teammates. He's teaching her how to fight, the way he once taught me. Worse, he's teaching her how to defend herself *from me*.

Decisions…consequences. What did I expect when I picked Troika over Killian? Smooth sailing? No storms along the way?

She frees her ankles and hands and, with a moan of relief, rips the blindfold from her eyes and the plugs from her ears. Spotting me, she palms a dagger and leaps to her feet. Her narrowed gaze zooms from me to Killian and back again. She's pale and panting. Dirt streaks her from top to bottom.

I know it's wrong of me, but I like seeing her in this condition.

"If you harm Ten," Killian says, the menace in his tone almost frightening, "I will hurt you in ways you cannot fathom."

Even now, he defends me. My hurt begins to fade.

A thousand different emotions flicker over her features; shame, remorse and guilt are the front-runners. Finally she returns the blade to its holder. "I'm not going to… I know you won't believe me but…"

"Sir Zhi Chen, our Leader, extends his blessing. He'd like you to punish Sloan for her crimes against you." Killian's hands fall away from me. "Proceed any way you see fit."

I mourn the loss of his touch.

Sloan's jaw drops. "Wh-what?"

I'm tempted to accept, I admit it. But if I hurt her, I'll be *worse* than she was—than she is. She lashed out at me, yes, but she never wanted to harm me. I *yearn* to harm her.

Desire will not prevail over duty. I, too, sheathe my weapon.

Her sky blue gaze widens and she points an accusing finger at Killian. "He's using you. Trying to win your affections so you'll betray your realm."

Killian doesn't lash out at her but cants his head to the side and studies her more intently, as if he can't quite understand what just happened.

"Why are you telling me this?" I ask her. She has no idea he already admitted Myriad has a hidden agenda. Then I shake my head. "You know what? Never mind. I don't trust *you*, so your answer is moot." I placed my faith in her once, and paid the ultimate price. This could be another set up. Pretend to help me now, destroy me later.

Tearing up, she rubs at the center of her chest. "I'm sorry I hurt you. I loved you. I still love you, despite everything."

"But you hated Dr. Vans more. I *know.* I received your message loud and clear. And you're not sorry. Not really. Words without actions mean nothing. You wouldn't change the outcome, even if you could."

She trembles and wraps her arms around her middle. A position of defeat. What doesn't she do? Refute my claim.

"Tell me. Did Myriad live up to their end of your unholy bargain?" I ask. "Did they deliver Dr. Vans?"

"Yes," she whispers. "He lives in a cage in my apartment."

He'd been Unsigned. He should have gone to Many Ends. More proof Myriad has access into the third realm.

"Where is your satisfaction?" I demand. "Where is your happiness?"

Sniffle, sniffle. "I don't know. I've hurt him, again and

again, the way he hurt us, but I can't...nothing I do fixes *this*." She thumps a fist above her heart.

If she's faking her turmoil, she's the best actress in the Everlife. Her shame and guilt are almost tangible.

My anger begins to deflate. In that moment, I understand her distress, and part of me pities her.

There was a time I hated my parents more than I loved myself. They locked me in Prynne. They paid to have me tortured. Later, my dad paid to have me killed, thinking he could use Jeremy as a contractual substitute.

Hate never kept me warm at night. Never held me when I cried. Never patched me up when I was injured.

Like bitterness, hate is poison. It hurt me, not the ones I despised. Worse, hating my parents had made me exactly like them. I was doing to them what they'd done to me. Had I continued down that road, I would have had to deal with guilt and remorse the rest of my life.

I much prefer love.

Still. I don't feel like letting go of my resentment; I do it, anyway, imagining it floating away like a balloon. "I hope you find peace," I say, and I mean those words from the bottom of my heart.

My number brands tingle and throb, the sensations too strong to ignore. I know I've done the right thing, and the Grid is pleased.

Sloan blinks with confusion, fat tears raining down her cheeks. Is it possible my compassion is doing what my anger never could and...changing her?

"I don't trust you," I tell her gently. "But I want peace between our realms." One by one... "Let it start here, with us. I'll stay out of your way, and you'll stay out of mine." I offer her my hand, intending to shake. "Deal?"

Killian steps between us. "You're right, Ten." He takes my hand and kisses my knuckles, making me shiver all over again. "You can't trust her."

What is he—

Comprehension dawns. *Now* he's playing a part.

"Can I trust *you*?" I say to him for Sloan's benefit. "You'll need to prove your good intentions and return Gingerbread to Dior."

The corners of his mouth quirk up. He reaches out to pinch a strand of my hair, the darkness perfectly contrasting with the flawless bronzed beauty of his Shell. "I knew you'd demand the dog's return, which is why I've already made arrangements."

Sweet Killian. I barely contain the urge to throw myself back in his arms.

Stiffening, Sloan swivels around to inspect the line of trees. "I think someone's coming." She closes her eyes, her expression taut as she concentrates. "Six MLs. I sense they're angry and heavily armed."

She's *that* connected to Myriad's version of the Grid? Zero! She's a step ahead of me.

Killian curses and unsheathes a gun—a gun he aims at me.

I frown, certain I'm misreading the situation. "Hey. What are you—"

"You can't stay here. I'm sorry, lass, but this might sting a bit." He squeezes the trigger, nailing me between the eyes.

chapter eleven

"Mercy and correction forever walk hand in hand."
—Troika

Zero!

He did it. He actually did it. Killian Flynn shot me.

Yes, you can shoot a Shell in a specific spot, destroying the outer casing while ejecting the spirit, unharmed. The spirit returns home in a split second. There are also ways to destroy the Shell while injuring the spirit, as well as ways to trap a spirit inside a Shell, causing the spirit to hemorrhage to death.

Killian went with option A.

My Shell explodes, every nerve in my body hit with a sudden blast of heat. For a moment, I'm in limbo, Shell-less but trapped in a vacuum of air I can't escape.

My mind whirls. In the past, Killian did everything in his power to protect me, and that kind of vigilance can give a girl certain expectations. Like, *he wants to kiss me* and not *he wants to blow me to smithereens.*

I know, I know. By shooting me, he prevented a battle between me and the MLs headed our way. He protected the image he's worked so hard to cultivate: a dedicated Myriadian willing to turn on me whenever necessary.

I can't throw a hissy fit over this, can I? On the flip side, I might have to award him a gold star of excellence.

The vacuum tightens until I feel as if I'm being expelled from a birth canal, sliding into the welcome arms of…the Veil of Wings.

I rush through the crimson water and, to my absolute delight, the fires cool and every lingering ache leaves me. I intend to find Meredith or Levi. Someone to send me back.

I *have* to go back. Not for Killian, not this time, but for Dior. I promised to deliver Gingerbread, and I will.

I come out the other side and discover Kayla waiting for me, a Shell standing beside her. A new Shell for me, with new Whells attached. This one is a replica of the first, with only one major difference. There are *two* zits on her chin.

Hilarious, Levi. Simply hilarious.

"How did Meredith know I'd need a new one?" I step inside the Shell and anchor.

"She didn't. She suspected. As soon as she gave you permission to lead the mission. Oh!" Kayla says. "I'm supposed to tell you Gingerbread is tied to the pecan tree near the spot where you met with Killian and Sloan. The dog was hidden by a Myriad shield, but that shield has since been removed."

He did it. He really did it. Warm honey spills over my heart. "How do you—never mind. I can guess. The Eye."

I kiss her cheek and rush through the Veil—

I end up where I started: in front of the farmhouse door. Clay, Victor and Elizabeth pace the porch, arguing about me while typing into their keyboards.

Elizabeth spots me first and scowls. "I told you. *I told you* he'd choose his realm over you. You are now what his breed of slimeball likes to call *nothing special.*"

Her venom misses its target—my heart—and doesn't even

rouse my anger. I know she's wrong. Besides, we're teammates, she and I, and we've got to find a way to get along…which means someone has to make the first move.

Together we'll stand or one by one we'll fall.

The ground quakes with greater force, and dust plumes the air. Obviously the battle still rages in the sky, the damage spilling into the Land of the Harvest.

Clay pulls me close for a hug. "Thank the Firstking you're all right."

"Yeah, well, my job isn't over. Kayla told me Gingerbread is just beyond the wall." Is Killian still there? Is Sloan? Looking between Clay and Victor I say, "Back me up?" Just in case the MLs haven't moved on.

"Of course." Victor nods.

"*Now* you want my help?" Clay quips.

"Yes, please, and thank you."

We stalk down the yard, side by side, each of us clasping a weapon. I scan the area beyond the Buckler for any indication that Killian and Sloan have lagged behind, but I find none. Good. That's good. If they threatened or hurt my friends…

If my friends threatened or hurt them…

Remain calm. Deep breath in…out…

When we reach the edge of the perimeter, Victor holds out his arms to block me. "You're in charge, Ten, and you can go first, if that's what you want, but I don't like the thought of a Conduit in danger. Let me check things out per protocol? Just in case?"

"No. I would much rather place myself—"

"Thanks for understanding." He pats my shoulder and rushes through the Buckler, gun aimed and at the ready.

Well. Irritation flares, but I tamp it down. Is this how I come across to Elizabeth? Pushy and relentless?

Sow and reap.

I have to start working *with* my team rather than bulldozing over everyone. They have more experience, collectively and individually. I can take a backseat...upon occasion.

Victor peeks through the glittery wall and smiles. "All clear."

I remain on alert as I move forward, Clay at my side. Out of habit, I conduct a search of my own. No twigs snap to signal a coming approach. Up ahead, a jiggling rope is tied to the base of a tree.

"Over here," I say, already running.

"Could be a trap," Victor says. "Slow down."

Clay almost passes me. Almost. Just before we reach our destination, a gorgeous white-and-ginger pit bull chases a butterfly around the trunk.

She spots us and wiggles her butt. There are no marks on her fur to suggest she's suffered any kind of abuse, and she has meat on her bones. She's been fed and cared for.

So happy I could burst—mission complete!—I crouch to scratch behind the ears. "Hey, pretty girl."

I laugh as she licks my face. No wonder Dior missed her. This animal offers unconditional love. No judgment or snide remarks. No stinging rejections.

There's a note attached to her collar, addressed to *10*. Curious, a little suspicious, I unfold it.

You wanted the dog, you got the dog. You're welcome. Now you owe me two favors, and I WILL collect. Yours, K

I snort.

"What's it say?" Clay asks.

There's a spy among you.

Killian's warning sounds an alarm in the back of my head.

I trust Clay. Victor, too, for that matter. He is Archer's brother, for goodness sake. But I'm not going to gamble with Killian's life.

I stuff the note in my mouth, chew and swallow before anyone can snatch it. Shells are able to eat to better blend in with humans, but the food—or note, whatever—goes into a tube we have to empty later.

Clay regards me with a blend of annoyance and exasperation before cutting the dog's leash from the tree. Victor eyes me quizzically.

I'm stuck on Clay's reaction, though. Why annoyance?

Because he plans to report to Myriad?

I swallow a groan. Rampant paranoia would be a beautiful way for me to ruin my relationship with my team. What if *that's* how I'm supposed to help Myriad?

Ugh. Now I suspect Killian?

No! My decision has been made. Instincts matter. I'm not changing my mind.

We walk Gingerbread to the farmhouse, each of us lost in thought. The moment we're inside, the pittie scents Dior and whimpers.

At the kitchen table, Dior jumps to her feet. With a bark of delight, Gingerbread bounds over.

"Gingy bear!" Dior drops to her knees and opens her arms. She chants, "Thank you. Thank you so much" as she sobs into the dog's fur.

The sight is balm to the scars on my soul. *This* is why I'm here. This is why I picked Troika. To help people. To make their lives better.

"Next up, your court date," I say, blocking Killian's other warning from my head. "How do we bypass the obstacles Myriad created and set a date?"

"There are twelve judges, and each presides over a specific territory in the Land of the Harvest," Victor says. "In two weeks, we'll present the facts to Dior's judge, and he'll decide if the case can go to trial."

Time is measured in units of twelve—twelve hours equals half a day. Humans have twelve pairs of cranial nerves. There are twelve months in a year.

"Are the judges Troikan or Myriadian?" In other words, is there bias?

"They are neither. Like humans, spirits and realms, they were created by the Firstking for a specific purpose."

Oookay. "If they aren't human or spirit, what are they? What do they do when they aren't being judgy?"

Stymied, he looks to Elizabeth. "How do we explain? They're a mix of both human and spirit, I guess. And no one knows what they do after court. We only ever interact with them during a case."

"Also, I believe I mentioned the injunctions Myriad has filed against us," Elizabeth says. "We have to deal with those as soon as a Barrister is found."

There's so much I don't know. So much I need to learn. "Barrister?"

Clay motions to Dior, who is now watching us avidly, her eyes filled with concern. "That's a conversation for another day."

Right.

The house shakes. Furniture scoots across the floor and knickknacks clink together.

Will the battle never end? "I'm ready to move Dior and Gingerbread to another safe house."

"You?" Elizabeth scowls at me.

"Yes, me. I know where I want to take her." To a secret place. To borrow Killian's words: the fewer people who know, the better.

I send Meredith a message, asking if my chosen location is sound. Her response is instantaneous.

Yes. I've had it cleaned.

I ask her to hide the coordinates from everyone else, even those tracking me through the Eye.

Done.

Love her! "Clay will come with me as my personal Messenger," I tell the group. I trust him more than I trust the others.

"Levi isn't going to like this," Elizabeth mutters.

"Ten….buddy. Pal," Clay says. "Are you sure this is wise? We're both so green."

"Why don't I act as your Messenger," Victor says.

"No. I'm sorry. Not this time." Instinct demands I take Clay.

I don't wait for another chorus but move to Dior's side. She hasn't stopped hugging her dog. A treasured friend, given new life.

I smile at her. "The change of scenery might be jarring."

She wipes away the happy tears and stands, Gingerbread dancing at her feet. "I'll adjust."

Elizabeth comes up behind me. "Let's hope you arrive in one piece. Ten," she says, patting my shoulders, "has never traveled at the speed of Light with a human in tow."

Dang her! Free will matters, even in times of danger. She's hoping Dior will protest and force me to abandon my plan. "Like it's hard," I snap.

Chalk white, Dior says, "You loved Archer, and he loved

you. What you tell me to do, I'll do. If you think this is best, I'll do it. If you think you can do this, I'll believe you."

Her confidence empowers me. "I'm not even the one who will be doing the work. Someone in Troika will. All I have to do? Hold your hand. So easy even *Elizabeth* can do it." Zing!

Elizabeth flips me off.

"Such a fine representative of your realm," I tell her, earning another scowl.

I offer my hand to Dior, remember our reaction to the Penumbra, and drop my arm to my side. "Does anyone have a glove?"

Of course, the answer is no. I stride into the kitchen and select a pink oven mitt. Good enough. Before I put it on, I send another message to Meredith, asking her to send us to my location of choice in sixty seconds. She agrees.

One. I take Clay's hand, counting the seconds in my head. *Ten...*

I offer Dior the hand with the oven mitt. *Fifteen...* "Don't let go of me, okay? Also, maintain a tight hold on Gingerbread's leash." *Twenty...*

"The leash is enough?" Straight white teeth worry on her bottom lip. "Are you sure?" *Thirty...*

"I'm positive." *Right? Right!* "Anything connected to you in any way goes with us." *Forty...*

"Where are we going?" Clay asks, only to press his mouth shut. "Never mind. I'll know soon enough."

Fifty... "Ready?" I ask Dior.

A tremor rocks her, but she nods.

Sixty!

Meredith can't track Dior, specifically; she can only base her measurements on the girl's proximity to me and Clay, and she nails it. In unison, a beam of Light hits the three of us and the dog, surrounding us with a Buckler to stabilize Dior's fragile human body while sucking us up and carrying us away.

Dior screams and tries to wrench from my hold.

She's in pain? How? We're not touching.

The oven mitt allows a slippery grip, and I almost panic. If we're separated, she'll be flung from the jellyair, and she'll die. I yank Clay against me and spin toward her, using him as a shield between us.

"Grab her," I shout.

He obeys, and we land in the Urals…in Prynne Asylum. Together. Success!

Dior collapses, and Gingerbread licks her face, offering comfort. She whimpers, Penumbra writhing under her skin. I suck in a breath. Penumbra. Of course! It reacted to the Light used to transport us.

The same Light inside of me.

"I'm so sorry." I wonder if manna will help her or make her worse. After the way she reacted to me? Probably worse. "Penum—you had a bad reaction to the Light." If we have to move her again, we'll knock her out first.

"Are you all right?" Clay pats her back.

"I'm fine," she rasps. "I'll be fine. The pain is fading."

He straightens and looks around. "You've got to be kidding me, Ten."

"No one will ever believe we'd come back here." Too many people avoid their fears. I face them. Only by looking fear in the eye do we see it for what it really is: a coward afraid of *us*. When we fight back, fear flees.

"What is this place? It's creepy." Dior eases up. "And freezing."

The fortress once used to torture kids into doing whatever their guardians desired is now a skeleton of its former self. The walls are cracked, the floors bloodstained.

"It'll warm up once we get you settled in the staff's quarters, where you'll have all the comforts of home. As for what it is…it's a nut house. Or a whack shack, according to Killian. Happiness once came here to die."

She shudders and leans into Gingerbread, seeking more comfort and warmth. "Did you live here?"

"Clay and I both did for well over a year."

"Is this where you died, then?" she asks softly.

"Close," Clay says, but he doesn't sound upset. "I escaped and fell off a cliff a few miles away."

He's clearly satisfied with his new life, and with his words, a weight lifts from my shoulders. The burden I'd carried for choosing to save Sloan first.

"I died in LA," I tell her, and leave it at that. No reason to outline all the gory details.

"So…what happened here?" Dior asks, her features pinched. "Exactly."

"Torture, and a lot of it," Clay says. "Whips. Chains. There's even a rack."

"That's it. Get me out of here!" she demands.

"We are horrible salesmen," I mumble to Clay. To Dior, I say, "Don't worry. You're going to make this place a sanctuary, where victory begins. Besides, the asylum's reputation gives you an extra layer of protection. No one will visit the place."

"True." She breathes a weary sigh. "All right. I'll stay."

"Excellent." I should probably feel something as I look around. There are the tables where I ate slop. The halls where I was stripped and whipped and dragged, leered at by guards.

There, Archer chatted me up about Troika. There, Killian winked at me.

Those boys…they were the catalyst I desperately needed, helping me transition from victim to victor.

Dior stands on unsteady legs, and we make our way to the

staff quarters. Thanks to Meredith, there are no dead, rotting bodies along the way.

As predicted, the staff quarters contain everything Dior will need. Plush couches and chairs, different-sized beds, holoscreen TVs still in working order, since they use batteries made by the realms, and cabinets stocked with food. There's a bathroom with a door—a luxury the inmates were never provided.

Gingerbread inspects every inch.

"I'll visit as often as I can," I promise. "Clay will stay here. He'll contact me if anyone approaches, and of course, you can tell him to summon me if you need me. Oh! And whatever you do, fight your fear. Apparently fear draws Myriadians like flies."

"I can't help how I feel," she says, clearly offended by my instructions.

"Actually, you can. You can help what you think about. Focus on the positive rather than the negative. Remember you aren't alone. You've got all of Troika on your side."

"All right." She flattens a hand over her heart. "Thank you."

"My pleasure."

A pretty smile blooms. "I know only eleven percent of people win their court case, but I do feel better about my chances now that you're here."

I turn away before she can see the color drain from my cheeks. So much trust...so much pressure!

How many times have I cracked under pressure in the past? Too many!

Buck up! I'm stronger every day. I won't crack this time. Not again. Never again.

—*We don't know a lot about Penumbra.*— I send my voice to Clay through the Grid. —*Keep your hands to yourself at all times, just in case. And watch her closely. Report anything unusual. Absolutely anything!*—

—Will do.—

She comes up behind me, and though I stiffen, I don't pro-test. I don't like having people at my back. Abhor it, in fact. Too many have struck at me while my head was turned.

"Elizabeth's team tried to get Gingerbread back from Killian for over a week. You did it in fifteen minutes. If he aided you—and I suspect that he did—he's setting you up or he cares for you."

143,10. "He cares for me," I say with certainty.

"I hope you're right. I hope he's changed. If so, I won't pro-test if he works my case with you. But if you're wrong, and he's doing this to make you *think* he's changed, make you think he's willing to help you, well… I'm sorry. You deserve better."

My mind whirrs with questions and yes, even secret fears as Clay and I set up the perimeter. An easy task, considering we simply place a disk in each corner of the room, press a button and, *boom!* A Buckler forms.

As for my fears…before Killian, another ML pretended to be a guard at Prynne, simply to play me. He made me think he loved me, that everything he did was meant to help me.

I fell for his act. And why not? He comforted me when I was beaten, ensured I was given food when I was supposed to be starved, and pretended to aid my escape. Actions meant to prove his feelings for me…to prove I was his soul mate and belonged in Myriad with him.

Dr. Vans killed him before we cleared the building. Or so I thought. It was just another set up. James was a Shell, and his spirit returned to Myriad.

For the first time, I'd seriously considered making covenant with Myriad. I'd wanted to be with him. What a mistake that would have been. I'd been one of thousands to him.

What number am I to Killian?

TROIKA

From: T_L_2/23.43.2
To: L_N_3/19.1.1
Subject: Rant alert

I've decided to trust you with my life, Levi Nanne, because I've trusted you with something far more precious to me and you've exceeded my expectations. (My brother's life, in case you're wondering.)

There's a spy among us. Don't ask me who it is; I don't know. (Possible spoiler alert: it's not me.)

What I do know? Everything I learn about everything opens a Pandora's box of questions, and everything I thought I knew I know I never really knew. Now I'm a walking question mark and I do not like it, so you need to help me.

Light Brings Sight!

Conduit-in-training,

Tenley Lockwood

PS: thanks for letting me take the lead with Dior
PPS: Did you notice the complete lack of typos????
PPPS: I am *so* rocking thes

TROIKA

From: T_L_2/23.43.2
To: L_N_3/19.1.1
Subject: Argh!

I meant this.
  I am rocking *this*.
  This, this, this

TROIKA

From: L_N_3/19.1.1
To: T_L_2/23.43.2
Subject: Good thing I speak Teen Girl.

You can think or know something in your mind but until you know it deep in your heart, you don't really know anything. Also, making a decision based on fear is the fastest way to arrive at the wrong place at the wrong time. Where there's peace, there's your answer.

I know there's a spy among us, but I appreciate the heads-up. (And I never thought it was you.)

I can predict what your next message will say. *How did you know about the spy, oh, magnificent General?* Let me save us both a little time. The answer is: I'm very good at my job.

General Levi Nanne

Light Brings Sight!

PS: I'm half impressed with your cojones and half disappointed. We'll discuss my reasons at your debriefing.

PPS: before you freak out, debriefings are standard operating procedure...and yours is scheduled to take place five minutes before now. Hustle!

chapter twelve

"Mercy forever walks hand in hand with your doom."
—Myriad

Five minutes *before* now? A fancy way of saying I'm late. Great!

I return to Troika, my heart pounding. There's no one waiting for me on the other side of the Veil, but I receive a message from Kayla with directions to the Tribunal, located inside
the Temple of Temples. I do as Levi commanded and hustle
my bustle, even though I would prefer to avoid any kind of
debriefing.

I've never attended one, but I can guess how this one will
go down. I'll explain what I did and why I did it, and Levi
will tell me what I did wrong...which will be...oh, absolutely everything.

I rush through Gates and Stairwells, my mind whirling.
Levi knows about the spy. That's good. It's a burden I don't
have to carry alone. I just have to keep my head on a swivel,
note anything out of the ordinary—not that I know what's
ordinary in Troika—and sleep with one eye open.

I smack into Raanan, Nico and Hoshi. The trio catches
me, though it's Raanan who prevents me from falling. His
eyes glint with amusement.

"Cool your jets, little girl," Nico says with a laugh. "We're about to—"

"Sorry, no time to talk. But thank you." I keep going, staggered by the difference our training has made in our attitudes.

The trio exuded relaxation; they were probably out having fun between classes. I'm constantly on the go, constantly working to save Troika and stop a war. I both envy and pity them. Action today prevents regret tomorrow.

I throw a glance over my shoulder. Nico and Hoshi have moved on, but Raanan is exactly where I left him, his gaze glued to me. Intense, curious. I wonder... Is *he* envious of *me*?

By the time I reach my destination, I'm sweating buckets. The Tribunal is a chrome-and-glass building with, I'm guessing, ten bazillion stories. At the reception desk, I'm told a courier will take my Shell to my apartment, and I'm given a visitor pass. The debriefing is taking place in room 1010.

The number gives me pause. Double tens.

If ten means *complete*, does 1010 mean *doubly complete*? If complete means *one door has closed*, does doubly complete mean *a new door will open*?

Is this a coincidence?

Trick question. I don't believe in coincidences.

There are Laborers in the lobby and elevators, though no one speaks or looks anywhere but at the floor. Got it. This is a somber, nerve-racking affair.

Ding.

The doors open on my floor, and I step into a spacious room where Levi, Kayla, Reed, Elizabeth and Victor are lined up in front of seven desks. They are wearing white robes while I'm in my catsuit armor.

Double zero! Someone should have sent me a dress-code memo.

Behind each desk is a fellow Troikan. People I've never met.

I take my place at the end of the line, and search for clues about the men and women—and boys and girls—before me. Only the desks hint at individual personalities. One looks like the wing of a plane. Another is made entirely of hand-carved wooden roses while another looks like a simple stack of logs. The youngest boy, who can be no more than ten, has a desk shaped like a car and the youngest girl, who can be no more than eight, has a desk shaped like a glass slipper. The final two are absolute opposites of each other. One offers clean lines and sharp edges while the other is a mash-up of different metals that have been bowed.

"Children?" I whisper to Levi.

"Haven't you heard?" he whispers back. "Lo, that we all had the innocence of a child."

Innocence—great. But I'm supposed to tell these kids everything I did and why I did it, and they're going to understand?

He bumps my shoulder with his own. "One day, after your training has been concluded, you'll be summoned once a year for a week behind a desk, overseeing debriefings like this."

Kind of like jury duty for spirits. Which means these people might not want to be here. How wonderful for us.

He says no more, and silence thickens the air, soon cracking my calm veneer. I release a shaky laugh and whisper, "This is right on par with whipping hour at Prynne."

The oldest juror regards me with keen displeasure. He is black, with swirling tattoos along his temples and jawline. "Being kept waiting is never fun, is it?" He bangs a gavel. "We shall begin."

I sputter for a response. "I got here as soon as I could. I only found out about the meeting a few minutes ago."

"Had you observed Dior Nichols as ordered, you would have been on time," he states.

"I had permission to—"

"Only after you had disobeyed."

Levi gives me a gentle push forward. "We'll each have a turn at the wheel, but you, the self-proclaimed Leader, get to go first."

"Are you kidding?" I squeak. "You had better be kidding."

"If I give you the key to a car, Miss Lockwood, and you crash it, which of us is at fault?"

Zero! This is going to be a trial by fire, isn't it?

A tall man I failed to notice when I entered steps from the corner to take my hand. My trembling embarrasses me, but I don't pull away. He leads me directly in front of the desks, where an elaborately carved podium rises from the floor. My mouth dries. He helps me step up before returning to his post in the corner.

"Watch," someone says.

Jellyair spills down each wall, and video feed of what transpired during the mission plays across them, everything on fast-forward. Funny thing. My mind processes the images and sounds at warp speed, courtesy of the Grid. What should have taken hours takes only a few minutes.

By the end, my critics—and that's what these people are, if their scowls are any indication—know every word that was spoken and every action that was made, with the exception of Dior's trip to Prynne and every mention of Penumbra.

Why were those deleted? And who did the deleting? Meredith, who'd witnessed the events? Or someone higher up on the food chain? Levi? Or maybe even the Secondking?

One of the main reasons I selected Troika as my Everlife home was the promise of justice for all. Here, there are no favorites. Everyone lives by the same set of rules, faces the same consequences and truth always prevails. I take comfort in that.

When the jellyair evaporates, every gaze glues to me. The urge to fidget is strong, but I press my weight into my heels, remaining still.

"Do you consider the mission a success, Miss Lockwood?" The voice comes from the left.

Well. We're going to start with a bang. My opinion versus their perception. No prob. I can roll. "Yes, I do. Dior Nichols is safe, and she has reclaimed ownership of her beloved dog."

"But you yourself once said a victory achieved by the wrong means is not a victory at all," another male pipes up.

I did say that, yes. To Killian. In private. As a human.

My mind spins and rattles. "I…" Have no idea how to respond to an admission of such rampant voyeurism. *Hope you got a good view of my ass* seems inappropriate.

"Today your Shell was destroyed by a known Troikan enemy. Is Killian Flynn a boy you trust without exception?" This voice comes from the right, courtesy of a gorgeous Asian man with hair dyed green. "Oh, and in case you haven't been told, if you lie during these proceedings, you will be stripped of your duties indefinitely."

Harsh, but understandable. A lie—big or small, well-intentioned or not—is the ultimate sign of disrespect. If I cannot be trusted, I'm a liability rather than an asset. "When dealing with people who are inherently flawed by nature, nothing is without exception." I do not mention Killian's intention to save me from harm. He has to maintain his pro-Myriad, anti-Ten facade. "But I think you question my feelings for him more than anything. You want to know if I love him. The answer is yes. I do."

Gasps sound behind me, but I hold my head high. I won't be shamed.

"Troikans are supposed to love others," I say and blink. I didn't tell Killian I love him, did I?

I was so overwhelmed by his declaration, I lost sight of my own. But I do. I love him. He owns my heart. There's no need to ponder or weigh the pros and cons. *143, 11.9.12.12.9.1.14.*

Does he know I return his feelings?

Every fiber of my being demands I hunt him down, but I plant my feet into the floor. First things first.

"He has harmed and killed many Troikans," one of the jurors says. "People *we* loved."

"He's never killed in cold blood." Not to my knowledge. "Like everyone here, he strikes in the midst of battle. And haven't we all made mistakes? Aren't we all grateful for the second...fifth...tenth chances we've been given?"

"My mother used to say the same." The youngest girl speaks Spanish, yet I understand every word, despite never having learned the language. She smiles at me—she has the most adorable crooked tooth—before wiggling her brows. "Plus, Killian Flynn is cuuute."

I suppress a smile of my own. "Yes, he is."

Going from dreamy to stern in a blink, she wags a finger at me. "A pretty face shouldn't affect us. A pretty face can often hide a monster. Beauty fades. Character lasts forever."

"Killian isn't a monster." *He isn't!*

I wrap my fingers around the edge of the podium and squeeze, the color quickly leeching from my knuckles. "We cannot say love is the answer to every problem and not love *everyone*. Including Myriadians. We must see past the realm to the innocent men, women and children who populate it.

We are supposed to help others. Shouldn't we help even those who have hated us?"

More gasps erupt behind me, but I'm past the point of caring.

"Perhaps you're right, Miss Lockwood. But how can you know for sure? You are overconfident without actual experience, and you refuse to listen to those who do have experience." The oldest woman folds her arms over her desktop. With her dark hair, eyes and skin, she could pass for Cleopatra. "You were told to watch and observe, and yet you dived headfirst into action right from the start. You need seasoning."

"I had permission," I say, and one of my number brands throbs. I think... I think it's telling me to stand down.

"You had permission after you'd broken your commander's order. Now I must wonder. How quickly will you break rank during your next assignment?"

"Why don't we wait until I actually break rank before casting blame," I say with a little bite. "Also, I think we can all agree today's mission had a happy ending."

The oldest male leans forward, his pierced brows winging into his hairline. "Yes. Today's happy ending could be tomorrow's tearjerker. You look at the here and now while we look ahead to the endgame."

"Maybe our endgame needs to change," I reply.

He ignores me, saying, "Have we reached a verdict?"

"We have," the others call in unison.

"Tenley Lockwood." The intensity of Oldest's gaze pierces me. "You will not be benched. However. During your next mission, you will not issue a single order. You will do as your commander tells you without complaint."

My spine fuses with a bar of steel, my brands throbbing harder, faster. "What if I disagree with my commander?"

"A baby must crawl before she can walk. A subpar Conduit will never defeat Myriad."

Throb. I grind my teeth. "You're asking me to surrender my free will." Something I will never do. I fought too hard for the right to choose.

"No, Miss Lockwood. We're asking you to willingly submit your will to another's. There is a difference. We're giving you the opportunity to plant seeds, to be a good helper so that one day you will have good help. Sow and harvest, the foundation of our realm. Enjoy a bountiful return, or lament a rotten one. There are no other options."

Throb, throb. "No way, no how. I won't obey an order I disagree with."

His stare remains unwavering. "What makes you think you know what's best? You, who have many questions but few answers. What makes you think you can lead your teammates when you cannot even lead yourself? Here's the truth, unvarnished. If you cannot accept discipline, you cannot grow."

Does everything he says have to be treated like a precious pearl of wisdom?

THROB! "You're right. I don't have all the answers, and I'll never know what would have happened to Dior if I'd remained in the background as ordered. So. I'll submit myself to whatever punishment you deem fit. But let the others go. I'm responsible for any wrongs committed."

"Agreed." He bangs a gavel. "So you have said, so it shall be done."

The man in the corner returns to take my hand. He ushers me to the end of the line. My knees tremble, but I lock them in place.

Levi is escorted to the podium...where he is praised for using every circumstance as a teaching moment.

Elizabeth goes next. I'm shocked when she *doesn't* say anything negative about me.

After they are questioned, Victor, Reed and Kayla are thanked for their service. Meredith is last, and she's warned about the perils of favoritism.

As soon as she rejoins the line, we're dismissed. Levi leads us out of the room…the building. Outside, warm sunlight strokes me, soothing my razed nerves.

Elizabeth mutters a hasty goodbye to everyone but me and hurries off. Doesn't want me to ask why she supported me in front of witnesses?

Reed has a class and heads in the other direction.

Meredith gives me a hug. "I'm proud of you. I wish I could stay and celebrate your first mission, but I need to watch over Clay and Dior." Off she goes. A workaholic's job is never done.

That woman…oh, that woman! I love her more every day.

Victor and Kayla hang back.

"I received permission to take you on a tour of Archer's place," Victor tells me. "Want to go?"

The griminess left over from the debriefing sloughs off me. "Yes!" A thousand times yes. I'll get to see where Archer lived, walk among his things and breathe in his beloved scent. "But why did you have to receive permission?"

"Until the Resurrection, the homes of the dead are preserved."

Kayla stiffens, saying, "I thought we—" Whatever she sees in Victor's expression quiets her. "I've, uh, got to go. Things to do," she says with false brightness. She scurries off before I can question her about her odd behavior.

"A word first, Miss Lockwood." Levi draws me aside, and I expect a reprimand for my behavior. Instead, he peers down at me with pride. "You held your own today. Good job."

"I...thank you?"

He nudges me with his elbow. "If only you did so well with your Key, eh?"

I bristle. "Hey! I'm close. Well, closer." I hold up my right arm to trace a fingertip over each numerical sequence. "They are cyphers. I just have to find out *what* they decode. Any hints?"

"Yes."

I wait for him to say more. He doesn't. "And?" I prompt.

"And what? You've been given plenty of hints. Just...look to your heart. The answer is there."

My lashes fuse as I glare at him. "Gee. Thanks."

"We need our Conduit," he says, "and until you've unlocked access to the entire Grid, you're just another soldier."

"There's nothing wrong with being a soldier," I sputter.

"Very true—when you're meant to be a soldier. A hand can never be a foot and a foot can never be an ear. You are a Conduit. A born leader. You are meant to start a wildfire with a single spark."

My head falls back, and I stare up at the beautiful, bright sky. "Another teaching moment? Seriously? More cryptic words of wisdom that *do not help*? Why can't I have a normal teacher who assigns me a ten-page essay about all the ways I can improve my sucky attitude?"

"Excellent idea." He tweaks my nose. "Have the essay on my desk by eight tomorrow morning."

I cross my arms. "Why didn't you tell me what would happen when I touched Dior?"

"Because you weren't supposed to touch Dior."

A simple answer, and yet sharp enough to pop the air in my balloon of confidence. I should have obeyed. I should have trusted.

"Now," he says. "If you're wondering why I haven't mentioned your messages with Killian…"

Zero! I barely swallow a moan. "Do we have to do this here?"

"Shhh. Levi's in the middle of a teaching moment."

I give him a brutal side-eye, and he laughs.

"If anyone can convince him to defect, it's you," he says, shocking me. "Archer tried, wanted it to happen so badly. But more than that, you would no longer be in danger of consorting with the enemy. And miracle of miracles, I think you're making real progress with Killian. Keep up the good work."

What? I'm flummoxed by this. His mind-set is a complete 180. Unless, of course, Levi is the one working with Myriad, and he secretly wants—

Nope. Not going there! Not traveling the paranoia path.

"Now, my final thought for the day," Levi says. "Your aunt Lina lives in the Land of the Harvest, and she's incapable of taking care of herself. When she helped you evade Myriad, she violated the terms of her contract. Myriad has the right to punish her, and word is they've chosen to end her Firstlife."

"No!" They'll try to use her Everlife against me. "They can't just—how can they—no one should—"

"She visited the Troikan HQ in LA and asked for sanctuary. Your covenant with us allows us to protect any extended family members, even Myriadians, so we were able to hide her in one of our institutions. But it's a temporary measure. Unless and until she agrees to go to court, our umbrella of protection is limited. Do yourself a favor and go see her. Convince her to agree. The institution is surrounded by TLs, so you'll be safe."

Aunt Lina. My dad's twin sister. Loony Lina. Every member of our family thought she was crazy. Including me! Until recently, I'd had no idea she wasn't insane—she saw into the future.

"She tried to kill me," I remind him. Scratch that. She *did* kill me. At the time, I was Unsigned, and I wound up in Many Ends.

Okay, okay. In her defense, she first ensured I had the resources I needed to rescue Kayla and Reed, and she even made arrangements for Archer to find and revive me.

Do I want one of my killers in Troika *forever*?

"Also," I add, "Archer told me the newly dead aren't supposed to visit their relatives in the Land of the Living. It creates too many problems."

"In Lina's fragile mind, you've been dead all your life. No rules will be broken." He uses his knuckles to gently tap my chin. "Go see her. If you don't, you'll regret it for all of eternity."

"Is that an order, sir?" My next mission, perhaps? The one during which I'm supposed to obey my superior without question?

"A suggestion."

"Then I need time to consider your suggestion. Are we done here?"

He sighs. "For now."

I return to Victor, who links our arms and draws me away.

"What was *that* about?" he asks.

"Levi told me—"

Be careful who you trust.

For the time being, Levi is my go-to guy, and I'm not going to invite anyone else into my inner circle. Better keep the information about Lina close to my heart.

"Just another teaching moment," I finally say. It's the truth without revealing any of the damning details. "A single spark can start a conflagration, or something like that."

Victor snorts. "Good to know I'm not the only one who finds the constant lessons tedious."

I don't find them tedious, exactly, but I do find them uncomfortable. They, in themselves, are Light. The very spark Levi mentioned. They chase away shadows of confusion, revealing weaknesses I need to conquer.

Just once I'd like to find out about a hidden strength, though.

"Are debriefings always so brutal?" I ask.

He snickers as he pats the top of my head. "That wasn't brutal, honey. That was the equivalent of Sunday brunch with your girlfriends."

I knock his arm away, which turns his snicker into a chuckle. "Remind me never to accept an invitation to Sunday brunch with you."

In the Capital of New, I spot Raanan, Nico and Hoshi again as we pass my apartment building. This time, Rebel, Clementine, Sawyer and Winifred are with them. A reunion? Only the too-young Fatima is missing.

I experience a twinge of longing. How fun it would be to blow off my duties and join them.

Killian wouldn't think twice about attending a party.

Enjoy the moment, he'd say.

But I'm not sure I know how to relax. I'd probably ruin everyone's good time.

I force myself to continue on and enter a Stairwell with Victor. We end up on the ritzier side of the city, where mansions regally line the streets, each boasting a different design. My favorites are the medieval fortress, the Disneyland castle and the Southern antebellum.

Victor stops in front of the antebellum, where a cobblestone walkway is canopied by a huge violet wisteria tree and leads to double doors with stained-glass centers. On either side is a winding staircase that climbs to the second-floor balcony, where a glistening wrought-iron bow and arrow hangs.

A bow and arrow. How appropriate.

"What's going to happen to this masterpiece if Archer doesn't win the Resurrection?" I ask.

"It will be bulldozed, a new home built for a new graduate." He lightly taps my shoulder. "But we're going to make sure he wins, aren't we?"

"If he doesn't, it won't be because I didn't give the vote my all." I just haven't found the right way to go about it.

We enter the abode, and all I can do is gape. A wide entrance hall spills into a formal parlor, which leads to a polished library, an opulent dining room, and a cheery sitting room.

"Archer lived *here*? *My* Archer?"

"He earned the right." Victor sounds proud. "Because we have free will, the work we do carries great significance. We choose, and so we are rewarded for our successes."

I wander about, enamored by the antique furnishings, and snared by the portraits on the wall. There's one of Victor... a handful of people I've never met... Levi... Deacon... Killian—

Killian?

My heart stutters against my ribs. Oh, yes. Killian's beautiful face peers at me with a mixture of sadness and hope.

This is how Archer saw him. As someone worth saving. And—no way! Beside Killian's portrait is one of me. On the canvas, I am sunlight and fire. I burn with the kind of passion I'm not sure I've ever felt.

"Who painted these?" I ask, somehow able to speak past my awe.

"Archer. He worked while others slept."

What? He never told me he had such amazing talent.

"I knew who you were the day I ran into you," Victor admits with a sheepish grin. "He talked about you all the time. The girl who would change the worlds. He is the reason I volunteered to be on your team."

A lump grows in my throat. *The girl who would change the worlds.*

Not one, maybe not two. Possibly three. Pressure…

I wonder if Archer is disappointed in me right now.

"Tell me your story," I say in an effort to distract myself from the haunting thought. "How did you die?"

"In the womb. I never had a Firstlife, only an Everlife."

He goes silent. I wave my hand in a command for more information.

"My mother met Ambrosine, the Prince of Ravens, at a party he attended in the Land of the Harvest. She fell in love with him, and they…*dated* isn't the right word. They spent time together. He bought her a house and, for a time, visited her regularly. She survived a car crash, I didn't. Her family in Myriad raised me, and Ambrosine ensured we had the best of everything."

"You were loved?"

"Very much so."

I can't help but juxtapose his life of privilege to Killian's life of poverty and rejection.

Killian spent most of his early years in the Center of Learning, an orphanage. He was unwanted, possibly abused. I'm not clear on the details, and I haven't pushed him for more. He'll share when he's ready.

A prince adored by his people, Archer often visited the orphanage to play with the children, and he'd eventually befriended Killian. A friendship that raised Killian's social standing. Soon after, Killian was adopted by Pearl Bennett, a Leader who'd acted as my original ML; she'd wanted Killian to be a companion to her daughter.

A short time later, Pearl's daughter died, and she decided the orphan boy was a nuisance.

She returned him, as if he were an ill-fitting shirt.

Killian experienced another deep-rooted sense of betrayal when Archer, his best friend, reached the Age of Accountability and defected to Troika. Archer Prince had everything he'd ever wanted—a father who doted on him, money, prestige— and yet he eschewed it all, leaving Myriad and Killian behind.

Killian had raged, unable to forgive him.

Everyone has scars. "How well do you know Killian?"

"I knew of him, but I never spent time with him. Archer and I had different mothers, and we weren't raised together."

I'm confused. "If you weren't raised with Archer, why did you follow him to Troika?"

"Before I reached the Age of Accountability, I'd finished my training to become a Messenger. Every time I was sent to the Land of the Harvest, Archer found me and told me of the happiness he enjoyed in the Light."

A small smile blooms. Archer had talk—talk—talked about happiness with me, too.

I enter a second sitting room, where multiple weapons are on display. A long, golden staff practically *begs* for my attention.

"May I?" I motion to the staff.

Victor is watching me with a curious expression. "Out of all the guns, daggers, chains and swords, *that's* the weapon you pick? Did you not see the wristband over there? It controls the four elements in the Land of the Harvest."

"Neat." I make grabby hands at the staff. "Gimme."

He barks out a laugh. "Fine. Go for it."

I tremble as I lift the staff, certain I'm holding something precious. I wrap my fingers around two distinct indentations—perfectly spaced handholds—and lift. It's solid, heavy, and all too soon my biceps protest.

Upon closer inspection, I find a crack in the center of the staff, too precise to be an accident. With a frown, I tug the two sides in opposite directions. The crack widens, revealing two separate swords made of...opaque glass? Precious gemstones?

The dark sheen glistens with different colors, but inside one, there are three Troikan symbols and inside the other, there are seven.

$3 + 7 = 10$

"It's yours," Victor says. "Levi told me to tell you to pick a weapon, any weapon. Archer had planned to give you one as a welcome home gift."

Tears well in my eyes. Uh, oh. Here come the waterworks. "Really?"

He nods. "Really."

I don't know why or when accepting gifts of great monetary value became taboo among humans, but there's no way I'm rejecting this one. I say, "Thank you." I will cherish this gift, and I will learn to use it. I will make Archer proud. When he returns—and he will, I'll accept nothing less—I'll show him how good I've become by knocking him on his butt...in the grass...because I'm a mean little lass...who's taking her opponent to class...because she's all about sass.

One of the tears escapes, gliding down my cheek.

A high-pitched alarm suddenly screeches to life inside my head. I nearly jump out of my skin. I do drop the staff in order to clutch my ears, my heart hammering. "Something's wrong."

Victor pales. "The alarm. Do you hear the message coming through the Grid? TLs and MLs are engaged in combat in the Land of the Harvest. We're losing, and more soldiers are needed. Location...near the home of Javier Diez." He pauses to rub his temple. "Only our group is to know Javier has been infected with Penumbra, like Dior, and there's a chance he's already spread it to someone else."

No, no, no. After all our precautions...

This is bad. This is very, very bad.

"We don't have a moment to waste." Victor heads for the door. "Let's go!"

chapter thirteen

"Fate says: when a door closes, you're not meant to go in.
We say: kick down the door."
—Troika

Messengers and Laborers sprint down the streets, Victor and I among them, and every single one of us is barreling toward the nearest Gate. Shells and spirits alike are armed for battle. I even spot two Generals. Tall, thin Jane and the dark, bald Spike. Those in noncombative positions—Headhunters and Healers—watch us with trepidation.

Fueled by adrenaline, I clutch my new staff to my chest. When one of the ends accidentally knocks someone to the ground, I yank the sides apart, content to have a sword in each hand.

Levi is posted at the Veil of Wings, shouting words of encouragement as TLs and TMs race through.

Without a pause in his step, Victor vanishes through the waterfall. I'm right on his heels, determined to do my part and—

A hand shackles my wrist, wrenching me to the side, out of the way, before I can follow.

Levi is ashen. "Only you and the princess are equipped

to deal with this threat, but we can't risk both our Conduits at the same time. We also can't allow the darkness to spread to any other humans. Even though you're not ready for this fight, we need you down there. But I'm not going to force you. The choice is yours."

"This is my next mission," I say. "My will is yours."

"And I'm commanding you to choose."

Sometimes war is the only path to peace.

The words play on a loop in the back of my mind. War is never a good thing, but as history has proved, it can be a necessary thing. When one group tries to harm another, it is inevitable, and the only way to prevent something worse from happening.

War is never pretty. It is bloody and brutal and violent. People die. *Innocents* die. We, the soldiers—we must do what we think is right.

"I'll fight." I can't allow darkness to snuff out Light. I *won't*.

"Thank you," Levi croaks. "Once you're down there, we won't be able to whisk you in and out at will." The urgency in his tone leaves a cold film over my skin. "The earthquakes you feel? They happen when one of the realms engages a Buckler. You also feel a quake when the other realm *disables* a Buckler. You can tell them apart with a glance. Myriad's Bucklers are shadowed, ours glow. But you won't need to guess which is which today. Only Myriad will be using a Buckler. They'll enclose our soldiers in an effort to pick them off. If you see one, do *not* attempt to leave the Land of the Harvest. Stay where you are until it falls. Understand?"

I'm struggling to breathe, but I nod. "I still don't know how to cleanse—you know." Penumbra. "When I touched Dior, I hurt her. I hurt *myself*."

He scrubs a hand down his face. "Don't worry about cleansing anyone today. We simply want the infected out of Myriad's control. Plus, we think your presence alone will prevent the spread of the disease. That's why we want you near Mr. Diez until we're able to transport him to an unpopulated area."

I square my shoulders. To save Troika, I'll do whatever proves necessary. "I'll do it. I'll get to him, and I won't leave his side."

"Good. Anytime you're injured, take a drink of your manna." He checks the vial around my neck to ensure it's been filled. "Go. Go!" He waves me off. "The Buckler is down, and your location is set. Mr. Diez is on the move, so we can only transport you within a one-mile radius of him. But our Laborers know you're on the way. They'll protect and guide you."

Heart hammering, I slip back into the crowd and race through the Veil of Wings…

Whoosh…a blur of stars…a tide of dizziness…impact.

The landing jars my knees, but I don't pause. I take stock. Night has fallen, and yet it's far from dark. TLs are perched on guard towers, shining halogen lights in every direction. Light that isn't exactly the Light we need, if that makes sense. MLs are there, too, doing everything in their power to destroy the halogens.

So. Many. Spirits. They are in the towers, on top of nearby buildings and on the ground. Swords of fire—*Pyres*—swing this way, that way, every way. Glaciers, too.

We're in Seattle, in the middle of a busy street. Shells are in the process of ushering humans away from the battle zone. Not that the humans see the spirits around them.

We are nothing but wind and mist.

I search for Javier, his picture hanging in the back of my mind. Troikans glow while Myriadians wear small, dark clouds like cloaks. I see fellow citizens I've never met... Myriadians... I see my great-grandmother Hazel... And oh, wow. General Jane is a killing machine. She swings a pair of short swords, moving through the crowd as if she's floating on water. Around her, Myriadians fall, dropping like dominoes set in imperfect rows. Her strength and speed are incredible.

General Spike drops to his knees and slides across the ground, cutting through Myriadian ranks with ease. Before he stops, he swings a Pyre, and the fiery tip slices through the underside of a Myriadian's chin—the ML who just decapitated a TL.

A Glacier—incoming! With a yelp, I duck and roll. The smoking ice misses me by an inch. Reed rushes to my side and blocks the next strike, saving me from injury. Or worse.

"Thank you." As I stand, another Myriadian appears out of nowhere and strikes.

Contact! Acid licks my neck. My flesh sizzles and bubbles like cheese on a pizza. I scream in agony but remain on my feet.

Reed kills my attacker, but can't help me with my wound. The next threat has arrived, and the two engage.

Despite my pain, I step into the fray, thrusting and parrying the way I've been taught, maintaining a wide circle of personal space—until a dead body trips me, and I fall.

Three Troikans rush to the rescue, Hazel among them.

She shoves me into a wall. Impact knocks my brain into my skull. Stars overtake my vision, but they can't obscure the fact that she saved me from another Glacier, taking the wound herself. Her comrades fend off two burly males while I pour manna down her throat.

"No, no." She tries to turn her head away. Lifeblood leaks from the corners of her mouth. "You need—"

"You need it more. You're going to be all right," I tell her. It's a command.

Several other Troikans spot us and rush over. Hazel is escorted away. Home, I hope. The other TLs surround me. One of them jabs a needle in my neck, jolting me—energizing me.

"A concentrated dose of manna," she explains.

She removes a thick leather belt from her waist and secures it to mine. Multiple daggers and guns are sheathed in the pockets. Whoa! She disarmed herself to arm me? No way. I try to return the belt, but she's already moved on, fighting an ML.

The rest of my protectors plow through the masses, steering me toward Javier. But one by one, they are taken out, and my guilt proves sharper than any sword. I'm the reason they're targeted.

When I'm on my own, a young ML launches an attack against me. I maneuver him into a wall and point a sword at his throat.

"I don't want to hurt you," I tell him, and despite the burst of energy provided by the manna, I'm panting. "Let's—"

"Shut up and die!" He kicks me, knocking my ankles together.

I stumble but remain upright and block his sword with my own.

Where are the Generals?

With a growl, the ML goes for my throat. The instinct to survive is ingrained, and the need to protect my people and the humans around us surges through my veins. I dodge his blow and lunge, extending my arms and ramming both of my swords into his torso. The tips stick out the other side of him.

He grunts with pain, his pupils flaring with surprise.

We never expect to reach the end, do we?

Questions bombard me. Is he leaving a family behind? Will children be without their father? Brothers and sisters without their best friend? A mother without her son?

Stop! Move on. Reach Javier.

I yank, but one of my blades remains trapped in his bone; the handle begins to vibrate. Or *he* is vibrating? The color drains from his skin, leaving him chalk white...no, no, his skin is darkening. He's now gray. Stone gray...stone that cracks, crumbles, and explodes. Ash rains.

I gape, confused and revolted.

To the left, a blaze of Light appears, nearly blinding me. In the center, Meredith appears, a Pyre in hand.

She slays the Myriadian in front of her—the one who'd been sneaking up on me. "The human is this way." Her gaze slides past my shoulder and widens. "Look out!"

I dive. Too late. From behind, a Glacier nicks my thigh. My skin splits and Lifeblood hemorrhages. Instant pain and weakness. Bile rises up, but I swallow it back.

Meredith closes in. My attacker has two metal swords; he uses one to take another stab at me and the other to slash at my grandmother. *No! Not her!* We both manage to block.

She kicks and nails him between the legs. In this, spirits react as humans. He howls as he hunches over.

With a single swing, she removes his head. It's a bloody, violent death, but I have no more regret to give. I want my grandmother safe.

When Meredith releases the Pyre, it vanishes. She helps me to wobbly legs, then palms two axes. Together, we surge onward. She hacks at three...four...six MLs who make a play for me, effectively dividing their attention.

This woman...she is a true warrior. A magnificent sight to behold. Every spin, slash and kick is almost too swift to track.

"Be ready," she shouts over the craze. Then she pushes an ML at me.

Knowing what she wants, I mimic her earlier move and ram my knee into the guy's midsection; as he hunches over desperate for breath, I swing one of my swords. His head detaches, and his body crumbles, Lifeblood glittering, spurting and pooling.

Meredith shoves someone else my way, but familiar blond hair and blue eyes bring me to a halt.

Sloan?

She's sallow and trembling, unprepared for the horrors of war.

Is anyone ever prepared?

Lifeblood streaks her face and chest and soaks her hands. Her mouth is hanging open at an odd angle, her jaw broken. Mewling sounds escape her.

Strike! What if she turns around and kills other Troikans?

Still I hesitate. There's good in her. I know it. I can't punish her for it.

"I'm sorry," she slurs and backs away from me. "I'm so, so sorry."

I plant my feet, refusing to give chase.

Meredith shoves another ML in my direction. He bows his back to avoid my kick, and my leg flies through the air. My momentum spins me. Laughing, he lifts a sword. His mistake. Instead of attempting to slow my momentum, I go with it, continuing to whirl. My swords slice through his middle, one after the other before he can deliver a single strike.

Entrails spill onto the ground. I gag, not because the sight disgusts me. It doesn't. His organs are hauntingly beautiful, glittering like jewels. The fact that I *like* the look of them— that is the problem.

A whoosh of wind, then a loud *boom*! The ground shakes, a Buckler engaged.

I trip over my victim, and I'm too weak to catch myself. Zero! I'm still hemorrhaging. At this rate, I'll soon experience a total collapse.

Determination took me further than skill, but I've reached my limit. I don't have the strength to stand.

"They're closing in on us!" Meredith shouts.

Her warning comes too late. We're *already* enclosed. MLs form a wide circle around us, caging us in. Behind them, TLs struggle to reach us.

A shot rings out—

"Nooo!" Meredith jumps in front of me, meaning to block the bullet with the swing of her sword, but in her panic her aim is off and the bullet cuts through her chest. She cries out, her body jerking as it falls.

The moment she hits, three daggers sink into her stomach.

No. No! I scream with an agony of the heart rather than the body. *Leave her alone! Please!*

Rage driving me, I swing my swords at the offenders. While the tips miss the MLs by a hairsbreadth, it doesn't matter. A shower of Light—flaming metal shards?—flies from the ends of my weapons and slashes every offender across the throat.

As they gasp for breath they can't catch, I position myself over Meredith's body to act as her shield. I will protect my grandmother with my life.

An arrow flies at me, and I stop it with my swords. Another arrow follows, then another. Too many, too fast. A sharp pain suddenly explodes between my shoulder blades, and I cry out. I've been hit!

Agony swims in my veins, and black dots wink through my eyes.

I ignore the terrible sensations and keep swinging my weapons. Once again, blazing shards fly from the tips. The surrounding MLs expect the deluge this time and duck. Zero!

A dagger is hurled at me. Despite my pain, I manage to block, and the blade pings to my feet. From the corner of my eye, I detect a blur of red. I pivot, but I'm not swift enough—an arrow lodges in my shoulder.

The new flood of pain is quickly overshadowed by a surge of acid. Poison? I hiss as spiderwebs of black weave through my mind.

The world shakes, and I sway. My ankles buckle, the tendons suddenly detaching, and I scream as I fall. I can't breathe. Can't see. The pain...it's too great, and it's only getting worse. The swords tumble from my grip.

I try to yank out the arrows, but I don't have the strength. Lifeblood gushes from me. Frigid cold envelops me.

With a whimper, my grandmother turns her head. Judging by the pinch of her lips, the action is torture. Our gazes meet, my mismatched eyes suddenly linked to the beautiful amber windows to her soul, a soul now filled with regret and sorrow. White-hot tears catch on my lashes, and her image blurs.

This can't be the end of her—of us. Someone will swoop in. Someone will come to our rescue. Or we'll be beamed back to Troika, out of danger before a deathblow can be delivered.

Yes. —*Beam us up!*— I scream at anyone who might be able to hear me. —*Please!*—

Meredith mouths a single word. *Live.* Then she closes her eyes. Muted Light begins to glow from her ears...nose... mouth...the tips of her fingers...her pores...so much Light, only growing brighter and brighter. Confusion grips me. What's happening? What's she doing?

MLs scramble backward. Then...

Her body—utterly—explodes.

MLs wail and topple as Light and Lifeblood splash over them. Light and Lifeblood rain over me, too, but they are warm and welcoming.

I have the strength to remove the arrows and dagger. My wounds begin to cauterize, and the cold leaves me.

She did this…she did this to heal me…she did this to save me.

She died.

No, no, no. She isn't gone. She isn't entering into the Rest. Not Meredith. My wonderful, amazing Meredith.

I need her. I need her now. *I need her always!*

She was kind to me when others were not. She loved me when others could not. But she is…she's gone, isn't she? She's joined Archer in the Rest, because I failed to stop the war. Because I failed to protect her. Because I failed her—period.

TLs encircle me, shielding me from further attack. I hate that they are endangered. I don't deserve their help.

"Get her up," a voice yells from a distance. General Spike, I think.

"You can't stay down, Ten." Reed's voice, closer than the General's but still far away. "Hurry!"

He's right. I can't stay down. I have to do what Meredith came here to help me do. I have to get to Javier. Then I'll mourn. Then I'll cry… I'll cry and never stop.

I'm trembling as I sit up. My shield of TLs has already thinned; only three are still standing…and Reed is the next to fall. I suck in a breath as an ML pins him to the ground, smiles and readies a blade.

No!

With a roar, I swipe up my swords and swing. He blocks, but he isn't prepared for my second swing. The blade cuts through his shoulder, and he howls. Reed works his legs up and kicks the ML in the chest. He flies backward, and I follow, menace in every step, both of my ankles healed and steady. The moment he hits the ground, I'm there to meet him.

I remove his head without a moment of hesitation.

"Thank you." Reed and the other two TLs bound off to meet a new group of MLs headed my way.

The trio is quickly trampled, the soldiers surging past them. If I'm going to die, I'm going to take as many MLs as I can with me. Bring it!

Something cold and hard suddenly presses against my back. I stiffen, preparing to turn and strike. I catch the scent of peat smoke and heather and my heart leaps. *Killian*. Killian is here.

To help…or to hurt?

No time! As another ML closes in from the front, I detect the cock of a gun behind me.

Grinding my teeth, I fake left, swing with my right, spin— block—and swing with my left. Like his comrade, the big brute avoids the first but not the second. The blade slices through his middle. He falls, revealing another ML.

Killian shoots the new one between the eyes.

He keeps shooting. In quick succession, eight Myriadians join the others on the ground.

Killian is helping me, at the same time ensuring there are no witnesses to his deeds.

The earth shakes, the Buckler vanishing. Injured TLs begin to vanish, as well.

Killian leads me into an alley hidden between two towering buildings. TLs are driving MLs farther down the road, away from me.

At the moment, I'm safe. But I'm too keyed up to sheathe my swords.

Killian doesn't seem to mind their presence. He presses his forehead against mine and whispers, "Remember your trust in me."

"I remember." I long to sink into his arms, to cling to him and forget the horrors of the day. Forget the loss I've suffered, and the broken heart dying inside my chest.

"Good." He straightens and glares at me, as inflexible as steel. Fury radiates from him. "Your realm should have known better than to send you. It's what Myriad wanted. It's why they had an army watching Javier."

I blink at him. "I don't—"

But he's not done. "If I save ye again, lass, my boss is going to know I'm not working to win ye to the Myriadian cause but simply protecting ye." His accent thickens with every word. "I'll be punished in the worst possible way. Do ye ken? Do ye even care? Do ye want me harmed?"

He *knows* I don't want him harmed. To suggest otherwise can only be an attempt to manipulate me. But why would he—

Remember your trust in me...

Frowning, I stare up at him. I think I understand. He's playing his part...which must mean we're being watched.

"I care about you. I love you," I tell him, my voice soft. Whoever lurks nearby won't be able to doubt my claims. The truth saturates my voice. "I love you with every fiber of my being."

Killian inhales sharply, his nostrils flaring. His hands settle on my waist, his grip strong enough to hold me up if I fall.

"Ten." My name is a benediction on his lips.

"I don't want you in danger, Killian. Not now, not ever." More truth. But I have a part to play, too. One meant to keep this boy out of harm's way. "Just...don't help me again, okay?"

He searches my gaze, and whatever he sees seems to undo him. Again he presses his forehead to mine, our exhalations mingling. "I'm sorry about your friend."

A crack in my chest. "My grandmother," I croak.

He brushes the tip of his nose against mine. "I'm sorry, lass."

"Ten!" Victor comes barreling around the corner. He spots Killian and lifts a Stag. He takes aim, demanding, "Where's Javier? Where did your people move him?"

I sheathe my swords at last and spread my arms, covering as much of Killian as I can. "Don't shoot," I command. "Please." I'm speaking to both of them. I can't tell Victor what Killian has done, so, I'm sure this comes across as a major betrayal to Troika. Again. But I won't back down and allow Killian to be hurt.

Victor's gaze darts between us; he's clearly unsure about his next move.

"Javier's gone?" All this pain and death for nothing! "Do you know where he is?" I ask Killian.

"No, but I'll do what I can to find out."

Maybe Meredith could use the Eye to search—

No. No, she can't. My chin trembles.

"What about the person he infected?" I ask.

The space between Killian's eyes crinkles. "To my knowledge, only Javier and Dior are infected. If you heard otherwise, I'm thinking you heard a lie."

Something in our favor. There are two infected people rather than three. "Let's go home, Victor. Please." I don't want to leave Killian, I need him, but I have no other choice. I'll see him again. I have to see him again. I'm breaking down from the inside out, and I don't know if I'll be able to put myself back together. But he can. He's done it before. "We have to go while the Buckler is down. We need to regroup."

Killian backs away from me. Every cell in my body screams in protest. *Chase him!* I don't. The separation allows Victor to approach him unimpeded.

Victor's finger twitches on the trigger, spurring me into action.

I jerk up my knee, nailing his wrist, using one hand to push his arm to the side and the other to take possession of the weapon. He has no defense against me. He's a Messenger, not a Laborer, and fighting isn't his specialty.

"No more killing," I tell him.

He glares at me. "You want to go home, we'll go home." He punches a code into his data pad and takes my hand.

"Ten," Killian calls.

Too late. I'm caught up in a beam of Light.

MYRIAD

From: Z_C_4/23.43.2
To: K_F_5/23.53.6
Subject: Excellent job!

Your skill continues to amaze me, Mr. Flynn. One small quibble. You were supposed to pretend to kill our soldiers in order to "save" Miss Lockwood's life, thereby placing her in your debt. You actually killed them. Why?

Whatever the reason, I can't bring myself to punish you. Miss Lockwood seems willing to do anything to keep you safe.

Do you think she's ready to take the next step and betray her realm for your sake?

Might Equals Right!

Sir Zhi Chen

MYRIAD

From: K_F_5/23.53.6
To: Z_C_4/23.43.2
Subject: No!

I need more time.

As for your men—oops. My bad. No, you know what? It's *their* bad. They held me back at knifepoint and REPEATEDLY INJURED TENLEY LOCKWOOD. She was not supposed to be injured in ANY way. They could have killed her. If they had, you would have lost your ace. Is that what you want?

Might Equals Right!

ML, Killian Flynn

MYRIAD

From: Z_C_4/23.43.2
To: K_F_5/23.53.6
Subject: Focus on the details that matter

None of the injuries Miss Lockwood sustained were life-threatening. How do I know? She survived. But without some type of injury, she could have saved herself. You wouldn't have been needed.

I'm beginning to wonder if your feelings for Miss Lockwood are genuine, after all. I'm also beginning to wonder why you've been disconnecting from the Grid so often, preventing me from reviewing your daily activities. I've given you great leeway and let you do your thing. Now we do things my way. Explain yourself.

Might Equals Right!
Sir Zhi Chen

MYRIAD

From: K_F_5/23.53.6
To: Z_C_4/23.43.2
Subject: Was the risk truly worth it?

ANY injury has the potential to be life-threatening. What if Miss Lockwood had been unable to obtain manna and hemorrhaged to death?

What happened to your plan to trust me?

Let me be clear about this, in case any other opportunities to harm her arise. Hurt her, and I hurt you. News flash: you *cannot* defeat Troika without her. Myriad has tried for centuries. If she dies, the entire realm will be forced to pay a high price. Myriad will lose the war. Citizens will lose their realm, homes and families. And why will this happen? Because of *your* orders.

You once told me you love your realm. Do you really want to be the one who destroys it?

As for my disconnection from the Grid. The reason should

answer both of your concerns. If you haven't noticed, Miss Aubuchon's feed has been going dark at the exact same time. What can you deduce from that?

Might Equals Right!

ML, Killian Flynn

MYRIAD

From: Z_C_4/23.43.2
To: K_F_5/23.53.6
Subject: You're right

I shouldn't have doubted your motives. Your passion is clear. For Myriad and for Miss Aubuchon. I support your romantic relationship. There's no need to go dark again.

I apologize for my actions. In my zeal to reach our goal, I placed our realm in danger. I won't do so again, you have my word.

However, what's done is done. This is the perfect opportunity to reap the fruits provided by our labors. Whether you feel ready to take the next step or not. Because, if Miss Lockwood doesn't begin to aid our cause, she will only continue to hurt it, and we will be forced to consider elimination.

Might Equals Right!
Sir Zhi Chen

chapter fourteen

"Trust in Fate. If one door closes, simply wait.
Another will open."
—Myriad

As I exit the Veil of Wings, the sense of calm and rightness I usually experience gives way to grief. Without Killian's arms around me, holding the world at bay, I begin to spiral.

"I'm sorry," I say as Victor releases me. "I didn't mean—"

"No need to apologize. I understand. You love him. You wanted to protect him."

Does he understand? His voice is unruffled, but a muscle is jumping under his eye.

I hand him the gun I stole from him. "Meredith is dead. I lost her." The words are glass shards in my throat. I didn't just lose her—I lost my way.

"I know. Troika lost a great Leader today."

I don't care about her station or her title. To me, she wasn't a Leader. She was an amazing grandmother.

"You'll see her again, Ten." Victor pats my shoulder. "You know you will. It's only a matter of time."

He doesn't mention the Resurrection, and I don't have to wonder why. He still wants Archer to win.

Do I?

"She saved me. I'd rather she lived, and I died." I wrap my arms around my middle. The hated position of defeat.

"She knew, and she felt the same about you."

Love is the single most essential part of our lives, a need we all share, and yet it's always been invisible to the naked eye. Until today. Today I saw love in its purest form.

Meredith loved me enough to die for me.

A sob climbs up my throat, a poem drifting through my mind.

I can't say goodbye. This isn't goodbye.
You're gone, but you're still here.
You're still here with me, deep in my heart.
I'll hold you close. I won't let you go.
When I train, you'll be with me.
When I shine, it's your Light others will see.
When I hurt, your memory will be my comfort.
We'll be together. You and me. Forever.
But not today. Today you're gone.
No matter where I look, you're not here.
When I cry, you're not here to hold me.
When I sob, you're not here to comfort me.
When I quiet, you're not here.
Why aren't you here?
Today I'm alone.

Usually my poems have a double meaning. A negative and positive side. I can think of nothing positive about this situation. Hot tears flow down my cheeks.

"Meredith is in a better place. And so are you," Victor says. "Everyone in Troika will trust you now. Your wants—and the Laborers you desire to have on your team—will matter."

I frown at him. "What are you talking about?"

He grins. Grins! "You'll be able to sway the Resurrection."

I don't care! "I still don't understand," I say, managing to temper my voice.

"I saw the Myriad soldiers you slayed. You should be proud. You should be celebrating."

My hands ball into fists. His words are a slap in the face. Killian is the one who killed the soldiers, but I can't praise him without exposing his secret, and *that* I will not do.

I want to scream. I want to scream until my voice is gone. I'm supposed to save us all, but I couldn't even save my grandmother. I couldn't save *one person*. A person I loved. A special woman with a special purpose of her own.

Everything starts and ends with one. If I'm Troika's last hope, we're all doomed.

I can't deal with this. It's too much.

"I'm going home," I croak.

"You can't. We have to visit the Sanatorium. The Troikan version of a hospital. After every battle, we're required to see a Healer."

I have zero desire to undergo a physical checkup, but I don't argue. I don't have the energy.

Thankfully, as Victor herds me to the nearest Gate, a sheen of ice numbs me. The only way I can get through this.

The Grid attempts to warm me, gently prompting me to feel and heal, but I don't want to be warmed. I don't want to feel or heal.

Victor is silent as we exit the Gate in the Capital of New. Other soldiers stride ahead of us and behind us, and everyone is headed in the same direction.

In every section of the realm, the people who stayed behind line the streets, cheering us for our efforts.

Fatima rushes from the crowd to throw her arms around me. My cold threatens to crack.

"I'm so glad you're alive," she says, her dark eyes filled with relief.

I wish I could say the same.

She rushes off, then, to rejoin her group.

The Sanatorium is housed in a building similar to the cathedral, with a plethora of stained-glass windows, a pergola covered in clinging ivy and a rose garden leading to the entrance.

Dogs and cats play chase along the cobblestone paths, pausing to offer licks and purrs—and conversation—to anyone willing to stop.

It's true, then. The animals talk. I'm amazed, fascinated and curious, but I don't deserve their brand of comfort and sidestep the creatures in my path.

As soon as we enter the cathedral, two Healers step forward, as if they've been waiting for us. We're led down a hallway. Victor is escorted into a room on the left and I'm escorted into a room on the right.

The word *room* is somewhat inaccurate, however. *Closet* works better. There's enough space for a gurney and a medical cart with wheels, nothing more.

Despite the diminutive size, the area is designed to inspire relaxation; a waterfall cascades down the center of each wall, splashing into bowls of amethyst geodes.

My Healer removes the belt around my waist and in a gentle voice says, "Lie down, please."

Fine. Whatever. Let's get this over with. I peer up at the ceiling mural. Doves in flight.

She checks my vitals and injects me with liquid manna. She

asks me questions—*how do you feel, what happened, what do you need?* I remain silent. Answers will only invite more questions.

She refills the vial around my neck. When she lifts a rag to clean Meredith's Lifeblood from my skin, I latch on to her wrist, stopping her. She flinches.

"Sorry," I say and release her.

"I only wish to cleanse you," she says in her gentle, soothing voice.

"No." The Lifeblood is all I have left of my grandmother. I'm going to wear it with pride.

The look she gives me is filled with tenderness. "Visit the Baths of Restoration, then. The water will buoy you, spirit, soul and body."

I have no desire to be buoyed. "Are we done?"

She sighs. "Yes."

I thank her, stand and walk out. I don't wait for Victor; I go home.

By the time I'm locked inside my apartment, the ice is threatening to crack for good. I want to cry. Oh, I want so badly to cry, but tears are a luxury I shouldn't be allowed to experience.

The sunlight streaming in through the window calls to me. I need it like air, but I avoid every golden, glorious beam. Another luxury I shouldn't be allowed. I flop onto my couch.

When the *Book of the Law* appears, I stab at it with my fingers until it fades. I hate this. Right now I think I hate myself, too. If I'd taken Levi's out and refused the mission, Meredith would still be alive.

A hard knock sounds at my front door.

"Go away," I call.

Someone picks the lock, or maybe uses a key. Hinges squeak as the door opens.

Levi leans against the frame, his arms crossed. "We have Mr. Diez. Two of our Laborers followed the group hiding the human. They called for backup, and a new team of Laborers swept in to squire Mr. Diez away. He's staying in one of our safe houses, away from other humans."

So I wasn't needed, after all. *Meredith* wasn't needed.

My nails bite into my thighs. "Thanks for the info." I motion to the hall; a not-too-subtle hint I'd like to be alone.

"I'm not done," he says, unaffected by my rudeness. "We suspect we were given Mr. Diez's location in the first place, and told another human had been infected, in order to lure you out of Troika. I apologize for asking you to fight."

My throat tightens, air wheezing in and out. He has no reason to apologize. My decision, my consequences.

"The situation has been explained to Miss Nichols," he continues. "She's upset, could use a friend."

Silent, I turn away from him. Dior has Clay. I'll only make things worse for her.

He sighs. "Tomorrow, your training starts again. You will not hide here. You will practice with me until you've decoded your Key and have full use of your Light."

"What if I can't?" I rub the number brands on my arm.

He strides over, crouches in front of me and gives my chin a gentle tap. "You can. You will."

Will I? Another crack in the ice. No, no, no. My eyes burn. I press my lips together to contain a whimper.

He places a ring in my palm. A very unusual ring. "She wanted you to have this. A six-shot pinfire cylinder that can be fired straight from your hand. Notice the notch on one side."

I tremble as I slip the ring on my index finger and hug it close to my chest.

"Her grandfather gifted her with the ring before his Second-death, along with a message. *So often we are given the tools to fight against evil but fail to use them. Use this.*" Levi pats my shoulder. "Joy is strength, Miss Lockwood, and you need to find yours."

My eyes burn *hotter*. "How? Meredith died today."

"Yes, and you are parted. For now. But true joy isn't a state of mind or even a feeling. It's a weapon you wield. It stands up to fear and says *No. You won't come near me.* It butts heads with defeat and says *I can do anything, despite the odds.* You have it inside you, desperate for release, but you must choose to see your situation through its eyes. You must be diligent and watch over your land. Pull the weeds—grief and sorrow—when they try to grow."

I scrub a hand down my face. "Why did you send Meredith to battle? You had to know she would—"

"We didn't. We told her to stay in Troika. She disobeyed."

The news shrivels my insides. I'm looking for someone to blame, aren't I? But our present will always be the sum total of decisions made in our past.

"I think it's time we ask ourselves the hard question, Levi. What if I'm not a Conduit? What if I'm a time bomb waiting to blow? Just…" I motion to the door a second time, my arm shaking. "Go. Please."

"I'm leaving." He straightens and holds out his hand. "But you're coming with me. You're going to experience an Exchange."

Of course I am. "I'm being punished."

"The Exchange isn't always about punishment, Miss Lockwood. See the battle through Meredith's eyes, begin to heal."

I lick my lips as dread bubbles up inside me. I've witnessed someone else's Exchange, and the experience scarred me.

"Come," he says, waving his fingers.

I know I have the right to refuse him. Free will. But I place my hand in his. This is something I deserve. A non-punishment punishment.

He tugs me to my feet and ushers me into the hallway, where Kayla is waiting, a blue robe draped over her arm. She's fighting tears as she fits the material over my shoulders, and she won't meet my gaze.

She blames me. She must.

Neither of us speaks. There's a ball of sorrow stuck in my throat.

She doesn't follow us from the cathedral.

After taking two Gates, we end up in the Temple of Temples. For the first time, the entire section of the city is emptied out.

"Why aren't we in the Garden of Exchange?" I ask softly.

"This Exchange is a gift. We go to the giver."

In the back of the Waft of Incense, doors open. Tremors sweep through me as we enter the Great Throne room. The air is sweetly scented air, almost intoxicating.

Two creatures fly overhead, drawing us deeper inside. Both have a single head with a different face on every side. A man, a lion, a ram and an eagle. Both have two sets of wings. One set arches over a pair of wide shoulders while the other set covers the groin area. One wears gold armor, the other silver.

My gaze returns to their wings. At first glance the feathers look like a peacock's, but the ends...a human eye tips every single one. I gasp. Those eyes watch me.

The creatures dance around seven towering lamp stands, and I know without asking the stands represent different cities in the realm. Two glow brighter than others, and the reason

hits me with the force of a jackhammer. Seven cities, seven Conduits needed.

The princess and I are working overtime, being drained faster than we should, two women doing the job of seven.

A puzzle to work out another day.

Marble steps lead to two alabaster columns. Between the columns are thrones. A rainbow arcs behind both, and crimson-colored water flows from the feet of the smaller one, down the stairs and through the center of the entire room. Just like the Veil of Wings.

A man dressed in dented armor sits in the smaller throne. Light shines from him, the most glorious Light. I know I've met the Secondking, Eron, Prince of Doves and firstborn of the Firstking, but this feels like the first time. I'm still in awe of him.

His beautiful eyes peer at me with sympathy I don't deserve. The ice melts. Tears finally pour down my cheeks, leaving stinging tracks in their wake.

As long as he's been alive, as many people as he's lost, he probably understands grief better than anyone.

He is the essence of Troika itself; in one glance, there is no doubt he is everything the realm represents. Love. Forgiveness. Strength. Equality. And that armor…he is also a warrior, something I hadn't known. He fights alongside his people. He fights *for* his people.

He stands with fluid grace and descends the steps. At the bottom, he stops to stretch his arms toward me.

Do I curtsy?

"Your Majesty," I say, and suddenly I don't have to wonder what to do. Through the Grid, my heart knows what my mind doesn't. I go to him and kneel, my arms crossed over

my chest. Next I raise and uncross my arms, offering him my hands in a show of fealty.

A sign I was once bound by darkness, but now, because of Light, I'm free.

He clasps my hands and in an instant, a blink, a breath, a second, the Lifeblood coating me rises from my skin, the glittering particles hovering in the air around me.

Those particles float away as the Secondking gently pulls me to my feet, and my heart shudders. "You are brave, Ten. You are mighty. A Conduit with unmatched determination."

The tears flow faster as I shake my head. "No. I'm stubborn and foolish. A maker of incomparable mistakes."

He frowns at me. "If that is what you believe, that is what you will be."

I say nothing more. I can't. There's another ball of sorrow in my throat.

"Do you see?" he asks, his grip on me tightening. *"Do you see?"*

See...as Levi once told me to do? To meditate on the outcome I want rather than the outcome I fear? My chin trembles as I shake my head. "Not yet."

"See."

I bow my head, my eyes closing, and suddenly I'm no longer Ten; I'm Meredith. I see the world through her eyes. I feel her emotions and hear her thoughts.

I'm standing at the Eye, watching my worst fear come to life. Ten is in trouble, MLs killing anyone who gets close to her.

If she's hurt, or worse...

No! When she finally taps into the power that is locked inside her, she will send legions of enemy soldiers fleeing in terror. Troika needs her. *I* need her.

Months ago, when Ten lived at the asylum, her mother sent me a message. *Take care of my girl.*

Truth is, I vowed to take care of her long before that day. I've watched over Ten since her birth, have *loved* her since her birth. Every time danger dared approach her, I petitioned my General, seeking aid for her. Aid that was always granted. Not that she ever knew it.

Can I really hold my position now, as ordered, when she needs me most?

"Kayla," I shout. "Take my place."

She pales. "I... I can't. I'm not ready."

When Kayla first arrived in Troika, she was assigned to the Laborers. I took notice of her because of her connection to Ten, but it didn't take me long to see the Leader caged inside her, waiting to be freed.

"You are. You're stronger than you realize. And your comm will keep a log of Laborers who enter the fray. When one is weakened, let others know backup is required. If your messages fail to go through, it's because a Myriadian Buckler is in place. Continue to resend. At some point, the Buckler will fall." I run, as fast as my feet will carry me, a Pyre in hand, a manifestation of my Light.

I reach the Veil of Wings and—

Land in the center of the action. I scan the sea of faces, searching...searching...there!

Ten has killed an ML, and it's clear she's wallowing in guilt.

I quickly dispatch an ML of my own. I've got to help my granddaughter reach Javier; once she's touched him, the way she touched Dior, he'll be unable to infect anyone else, at least for a while, his Penumbra too busy repairing the damage Ten caused. Then my girl can go home. We can figure out our next move without an army breathing down our necks.

"The boy is this way." A shadow moves behind her, a soldier gunning for her. "Look out!"

She doesn't hesitate. She dives out of the way—

But the tip of a Glacier grazes her, cold and sharp enough
to slice through her armor and into her leg. I wince as glittering Lifeblood gushes from her.

My sympathy quickly morphs into rage. Hurt my grandbaby? Die badly.

The soldier makes another play for her. Thank the Firstking
she's strong enough to block. I'm there a second later, blocking a blow cast *my* way. But splitting his focus costs him, as I
knew it would. Instincts well-honed, I kick him—and then
I remove his head.

I release the Pyre and help her stand. I want so badly to
tell her it's never a crime to protect yourself from evil, but
conversation will only distract us. With my axes in hand, I
lead her through the masses standing between us and the infected human.

Years of training allow me to focus, to kill without hesitation, and continue on. With only weeks of training, Ten is
well able to keep up with me. Soon she's able to free herself
from a defensive position and go on the offensive.

No wonder she's going to lead us to victory!

Deciding we'll get further if we work in tandem, I push
an ML in her direction, getting him out of my way so I can
take down the next one.

Ten for the win! She does what's necessary to remove his
head.

The next soldier she…allows to walk away?

Only takes a moment for comprehension to dawn. I recognize the ML. A girl named Sloan. Having watched over

Ten throughout her life, I know this is the one who betrayed her after escaping the asylum.

Her heart is so soft. We should…nurture that?

I push another ML at her instead. Survive now. Nurture later. She's ready, but she's weakening, her motions slowing.

I finish off the two MLs in front of me and take a post at her side. More and more soldiers are converging on us. No matter how many we slay, their numbers only multiply.

"They're closing in on us!" I shout. But I'm wrong. We're *already* enclosed.

Fellow Troikans will have to perform a miracle to reach us—but even still, they won't succeed in time. The circle is simply too thick, every ML peering at us with murderous glee.

Unacceptable! I will *not* fail my precious granddaughter.

When I notice a soldier aiming a gun at Ten, a scream leaves me unbidden, and I jump in front of her.

Boom!

A bullet cuts through my chest. I crash-land, and I'm quickly hit with three daggers. Agonizing pain rips through me, a wrecking ball to my calm. I'm utterly consumed, barely able to breathe. My veins fill with poison. A special concoction Myriadians use to dull Light.

Ten shouts in denial, leaping in front of me in an effort to protect me.

No, sweet girl. No. I open my mouth to voice my protest, to tell her to run…to run and never look back, but only a whimper escapes me.

To my horror, an arrow embeds in her shoulder. Even still, my brave girl continues to fight.

The boy behind her goes low, severing her Achilles tendons without her seeing. With a grunt, she falls. She loses her grip on her swords.

Shadows...shadows all around her, cast by the swarm of MLs.

As a Troikan—as a Conduit—she needs Light if she's going to survive this. I have to give her Light...where is Light... there's no Light here...

I gasp as the answer strikes me. There *is* Light...it's just trapped inside me.

I can give it to her—through Torchlight. In doing so, I'll die, and there will be nothing left of me to save. But that's okay. I've lived a good life. Now she can live hers.

My body jolts once, twice, a third time, and the poison surges through my veins with renewed strength. I'm running out of time...*she's* running out of time...

Soon I won't have any Light to give.

Resolved, I turn my head. My gaze connects with hers. Her eyes—those lovely mismatched eyes—are filled with pain, guilt and remorse. I want to tell her goodbye. This is it. The end. I want to tell her this isn't her fault. My decision, my consequences. I've heard her say those words. She'll understand. I want to tell her I'm sorry. I'm sorry I won't get to spend more time with her. I'm sorry I couldn't get her out of this mess. I'm sorry I'm going to miss the amazing life she's going to lead. I'm sorry I won't be there to see the boy she marries, the family she raises. I'm sorry...

But the only word that leaves me is, "Live."

Live well, my Ten. Live well.

I close my eyes and send my conscious mind along the Grid, gathering every ray of Light I've stored and hidden in case of an emergency. I draw the Light up, up until every ray bumps against the undersurface of my skin. Warmth bathes me. Such beautiful warmth.

More Light. Too hot now. I'm burning up.

Still more. The rays...there are too many, and they're too

strong. I'm not a Conduit, and my body isn't equipped to handle such a massive upwelling. Any second now, I'm going to—

I gasp.

I'm Ten once again, the Exchange over, and I'm crying. I'm crying so hard my nose is running, my chest heaving. I choke on a sob.

The Secondking's grip keeps me upright. He squeezes my hands. "She loved you, and my hope is that you will heed her desire to live well, Ten. Live well."

chapter fifteen

"You can't fight fire with fire. You must fight fire with water."
—Troika

The next morning, a memorial service is held in Meredith's honor. The courtyard of the Temple of Temples fills with people. I'd rather mourn alone, but Levi tells me attendance is part of my training, so I go. At my side, Hazel squeezes my hand and sobs. Steven reaches up to wipe away the tear tracks on his cheek.

Behind me, Kayla snot-cries.

"This is my fault," she says between sniffles.

She blames herself, not me? What a pair we make.

Grief is a fire in my chest, burning and agonizing me. Sorrow is a bitter pill lodged in the back of my throat. My already broken heart is torn in two once again, one half in the Rest with Meredith. But I have my memories of her I will forever cherish. She loved me all the days of my life. She fought for me, and believed in me.

For her, I will live. I will live well.

I put my emotions on lockdown and stand back, watching the congregation. Surprisingly the other newbies are here. Raanan, Fatima, Winifred, Nico, Hoshi, Rebel, Sawyer and

Clementine. If they'd spent any time with Meredith, I wasn't aware of it.

Or maybe they're here to support me? They take turns hugging me. Raanan even says, "I'm sorry for your loss."

I'm touched, I really am, and it threatens to raze my defenses, but I somehow find the strength to remain stoic. I won't break down. Not here, not now.

Meredith touched so many lives, but most of the crowd laughs as funny stories are shared about her.

Death ends a life, but it doesn't end a love.

Mightier than a sword
Eager to bless those around her
Radiant, a Light for the world
Eternally loving and loved
Devoted to the end, she
Illuminated my life
Thankful, humble, true
Hopeful till the end...

After the service, after my training session, I spend a few hours in the Museum of Wisdom, searching for information about cyphers: secret or disguised ways of writing; codes. To put a message into secret writing; to encode. I look up each specific number branded in my arm...to no avail.

Clay keeps me updated on Dior. She's doing well. And so is he. I expected tears when he learned about Meredith's death, but he remained unaffected. "I'll see her again," he told me. "This isn't goodbye."

As the days pass, strangers in the street stop me to ask me who I want to win the Resurrection. Every time I answer with an uninspiring, "I don't know." I can't think about me, me, me anymore; I have to think about my realm. What's best for the people who so loved my grandmother?

When another battle breaks out in the Land of the Harvest—again over Dior's boyfriend—I'm told to stay behind. I obey.

We experience a crushing defeat, more of our brave soldiers killed and Javier taken away from us.

Elizabeth returns from the battle injured.

Victor doesn't return at all.

We search among the dead but find no trace of him. Leaders and Headhunters use the Eye to search for a signal from his comm, but again, there's no trace of him. Has he been forcibly unhooked from the Grid? Where is he? Is he okay?

I hate that I can't do more for him. For anyone!

"I don't understand how he can just disappear," Kayla says, her worry feeding my own.

I try to remain positive. "We'll find him." We must. He's a valued member of our team.

"How?" she demands.

"I don't know, but we won't stop until we succeed." I've also studied how to unhook from the Grid and/or vanish from the Eye. There are only three known ways. 1) Shove a hot poker through the comm. Without manna, it won't heal. While it's damaged, you're off the Grid. 2) Surround yourself with a Buckler. Apparently there are degrees of thickness, and some stop all forms of communication and tracking. 3) Go to court and defect to Myriad.

My guess? Victor is a prisoner of war, and his comm has been purposely damaged. He's probably being starved and tortured for information.

This newest defeat… I *burn* with helplessness.

Lockdown.

My dreams remain the same. I'm saved from a horde of

skeleton birds when I concentrate on Killian, and a mass of people surround me, begging for help. Last night I began to recognize their faces. All the Troikans who have died in battle. Archer. Meredith. So many others. They are joined by all the Troikans who *could* die in battle if I remain static.

Frustrated, I head to the coliseum for my next training session. Levi is preoccupied and commands me to run—and run and run—as if I'm part of a marathon. By the third hour, I'm pretty sure he's forgotten I'm nearby. I'm drenched in sweat, every muscle in my body burning and trembling. But I don't stop. I push myself until I collapse right there in the sand.

Finally he closes the distance. He stands at my side, my swords clutched in his hands.

I look away from them. "You broke into my apartment, I see." I'd hidden the weapons under my coffee table, not wanting to be reminded of the deeds I'd committed with them.

"Yes. You're welcome."

"What are they, exactly? They turned a spirit into stone and sprayed flaming metal into crowds of people."

"No, they sprayed pure light, not metal. The swords are known as the Blessing and Cursing. One offers a second chance. The other offers instant judgment. Both offer protection to the one who wields them."

Um… "How do you tell which is which? How does a *weapon* offer a second chance or judgment? Are they sentient? For that matter, how did Archer acquire them?"

"The Secondking gifted the swords to Archer for successfully completing a mission. They aren't sentient but an extension of you. Everything you need to know about the Blessing and Cursing can be found on the Grid, in a special room only their owner can unlock. Even without decoding her Key."

Really?

"Go ahead. Give it a try."

I do. I close my eyes and concentrate on the Grid, just as Meredith did when she searched for all the places she'd hidden her Light.

My chin trembles.

Lockdown!

A glowing crimson river flows in the back of my mind, reminding me of the waterfall in front of the Veil of Wings... and the water flowing from the second throne. That water rushes toward me, rising up, up, and finally sweeping me away.

I'm carried to a door and placed on my feet as the water drains. The door glows, beckoning me closer. Excitement sparks as I twist the knob...in an instant, a stream of data floods my mind. A vast sea. I cringe. Too much! But suddenly I understand why I have to work to decode my Key. I have to be ready for what I learn.

I concentrate on the barest facts.

The Blessing offers a do-over. A second chance, wiping away one set of deeds to make way for a new choice.

The Cursing causes the condition of the heart to manifest in the body. If a heart is as hard as stone—figuratively speaking— the body turns to stone. If a heart is an inferno of hate, the body burns to ash.

"All right. You've been buried inside your head for over an hour," Levi says, pulling me from my thoughts. "Time to practice with the swords."

Over an hour? He's got to be kidding.

He wasn't kidding. My knees are the consistency of pudding as I rise.

He hands me the swords and shows me how to twirl my wrists. At first, I drop the weapons more than I twirl them, but I continue until I can smoothly swing the two in opposite directions.

"Good," he says. "You also need to learn how to connect the pair. A staff doesn't get trapped in bone, and it has a much longer range. You can take out more people at once."

Right. I slide the swords together, and the center locks. As I twirl the staff—far more clumsily—the outer casing grows hot...almost too hot. Definitely too hot. Literal flames crackle at the ends. My eyes widen. Despite the heat, my hands remain uninjured...until I shift my thumb out of the handhold. One of the flames licks over my skin, blistering me.

Hissing, I drop the staff. The flames vanish.

Levi grins. "I've got to get me one of those."

I snatch up the weapon, surprised to find the metal is already cool. "Mine." My sore muscles protest the action, but not by word or deed do I reveal my pain. The moment I do, I suspect Levi will call a halt to the session.

Teach me more! Teach me everything!

He snickers at me. "What of generosity, Miss Lockwood?"

"I'll think about saving your life with my weapon. Can't get more generous than that."

As he chuckles, a shadow falls over us. I spin and spot—

Deacon. A *smiling* Deacon.

Have I entered Bizzaro world? Last time we were together, he gave me the stinky boot.

"I hear you killed an entire contingent of Myriad soldiers," he says to me. "Good job."

I bite my tongue until I taste the sweetness of my Lifeblood. *Cannot talk about Killian. Cannot admit the truth.* I change the subject. "Where have you been?"

His smile slips. "I was part of a select group guarding Javier. During the last battle, I had a chance to escort him to a new safe house, but he refused. At that point, I could do nothing to help him without violating his free will."

"How is he?" Levi asks.

"The disease is stronger in him than in Dior. He rages out, and nothing calms him."

For once, I lament free will. If a human doesn't want us near, we cannot go near. The only exceptions? When a family or friend inside the realm asks on behalf of the human. Like Meredith so often did for me.

Lockdown!

Even with a family member's interference, there are codes of conduct all TLs must respect.

"I received word before you arrived at the coliseum," Levi says. "One of the reasons we lost the battle is Javier himself. Our soldiers were weakened in his presence. We believe he's begun the transition. He will become an Abrogate."

A sound I don't recognize slips from my lips. If Javier becomes an Abrogate... "Could he be cleansed and become a Conduit for Troika?"

"It's...possible."

A chance is better than nothing.

Javier could be the one, then. He could save Troika and win the war. Because Javier Diez is—

In my mind, the Grid translates the word *Diez*. In Spanish, *diez* means ten.

He is Javier Ten.

The knowledge comes with a strange mix of dismay and hope. And pressure. A whole lot of pressure. If he signs with Myriad, he'll become a General. Before the deaths of Rosalind and Abdul, he would have been the tenth. The complete set.

Myriadians have always favored the numbers one and zero.

They have ten cities within their realm. Ten festivals of cele-bration. Ten points on their brand.

The day of my birth, nine of their Generals were killed. Their Leaders believe the spirits of those Generals immedi-ately Fused with humans. Beginning with me.

With the loss of Rosalind and Abdul, Myriad desperately needs two new Generals. Javier is a nice start. Do they be-lieve Javier is the one they've been searching for, instead of me? After all, ten is ten, and there are always different ways to say the same thing:

$2 \times 5 = 10$

1.2.3.4.5.6.7.8.9.10

Greater than 9 but less than 11.

★ ★ ★ ★ ★ ★ ★ ★ ★ ★

X

$11-1 = 10$

A dime.

A decade.

Decem.

Dix.

An insidious monster with fangs and claws prowls through me—his name is Envy. I actually envy Javier. He might be the one my realms need. Him, not me.

I've bewailed my status for weeks and now, when it might be taken from me, I want it back? Wow. I suck.

"I wonder if our s—" Remembering our audience, I press my lips together.

"It's okay. Deacon knows there's a spy in our midst," Levi says, understanding the direction my mind had traveled. "We've checked out everyone who knew where we were keeping Javier, but have come up with no concrete evidence any information was leaked. But all that means is he or she is very, very good at hiding his or her activities."

"Maybe Myriad is fighting so hard to keep Dior on their side because she influences Javier." Once Levi told me I wasn't seeing the full picture. He was right. But my eyes are beginning to open.

"They aren't fighting to keep her anymore," Deacon says. "This morning they voided their petition to stop her trial. A court date has been set for two weeks from today."

Unease prickles at the back of my neck, but I say, "That's wonderful." She'll be pleased. And I did promise to help her. But I can't help remembering Killian's warning...

Deacon rubs the back of his neck as if he feels the same sense of unease. "I don't think she's ready."

"Why? I still don't understand the in and outs of court," I admit.

He looks to Levi.

Levi thinks for a moment, sighs. "It'll be better if you show her. Do you have time?"

"I'll make time. But first things first. We're stopping by your apartment, Ten." Deacon wrinkles his nose. "You have to shower and change into a ceremonial robe."

"No problem. And no need to go home. I can use the locker room—"

"Robes aren't stored there."

Right. Meredith would have fetched one while I showered and waited for me to finish. She would have offered me pearls of wisdom and—

Lock. Down. Now.

"All right. Let's go." Using Stairwells and Gates, we travel thousands of miles in seconds, stopping at Deacon's house—

mansion—to acquire a robe for him, then at an outdoor market to buy manna since both our cupboards are bare.

I hurry through a shower. Deacon eats half the food and takes a power nap on my couch.

Clean and dry, I weapon-up, strapping blades to my waist, thighs and ankles. I slide Meredith's ring on my finger—*lockdown*—and pull a white robe over my head. The material is feather-soft. As I anchor my hair in a knot on the crown of my head, I head to the living room.

"Let's go," I say, and stuff my mouth full of manna. Energy zings me.

Deacon looks me over and shakes his head. "No weapons." He pushes a few keys on his keyboard. In a flash of Light, his Shell appears. "You'll need yours."

I reluctantly remove Meredith's ring and all the daggers and step inside my Shell, which is flush against the massage wall. We make our way to the Veil of Wings. People smile and wave at us. A few try to stop and chat with me, but Deacon sends them off as kindly as possible.

Everyone thinks I'm a hero, despite Meredith's death. They think I've finally proved myself loyal to the realm. I want to lift my head to the sky and scream, *It wasn't me. I did nothing right and everything wrong. I'm a failure.*

"You're tense," Deacon says with a frown. "Why?"

I ignore his question and ask, "Where are we going?" I won't lie to him, not even a small, innocent lie. Actually, there are no small, innocent lies. Saving his feelings today will only hurt him in the future.

I know this firsthand. My parents lied to me often. So did the people in charge at Prynne. Madame Bennett. Even friends, and once, Killian. Trust is precious. Once lost, it's difficult to rebuild.

But I won't tell Deacon about Killian, either.

"We're headed to the Courthouse. It's neutral territory, overseen by the Firstking. We do not break the Firstking's rules. Ever. Ignorance is not an excuse."

"Enlighten me, then."

"No weapons of any kind inside the building. No fighting anywhere, either verbally or physically. He is the judge supreme. When one of his delegates rules on a case, it is final. There are no appeals. Both Troikans and Myriadians attend the sessions, so be prepared for killing glares. We attend in Shells for the benefit of humans—they're usually the ones on trial."

Usually...

I think of my mother, desperate to switch sides to spend time with her infant son. I think of Killian...who might not be as happy in Myriad as he used to be?

If he would go to trial... I close my eyes, imagining the joy of having him nearby, of touching him and being touched by him, of working cases with him rather than against him, and I smile. I don't want to be parted from him. I want him out of danger, mine to protect. I want...him. I just want him.

Live well. When you step toward a dream, you step away from a regret. *I'm coming for you, Killian.*

"This way." Quickly and efficiently—like the boy himself—Deacon leads me to the outside edge of the realm.

We step through what looks to be a dense fog, and end up directly in front of the Veil of Wings.

Another step, and we're whisked to the border of a guard tower, where sunlight shines on one side and shadows cloak the other. Stone steps lead to the tallest skyscraper I've ever seen.

As we make our way up, Troikans nod at us. As predicted,

Myriadians glare at us. Just past the towering double-door entrance, a guard pats me down. I'm unarmed and expect to be sent on my way, but he tugs the band from my hair.

I frown at him. "Seriously?"

"Choking hazard." He shrugs and throws the band at an oval mirror hanging on a wall. Only, the band ghosts through the glass, because it isn't glass; it's a Buckler hiding a...trash can?

Gimme!

Deacon and I move forward. The lobby is devoid of color or decoration. In fact, there isn't a single piece of furniture, just more stairs and what must be a thousand doorways. Our footsteps echo as we make our way up...up... The staircase moves with us, twisting and turning around corners. On every floor, we pass through a veil of jellyair, and I suspect we are traveling through a maze as well as a building.

Finally Deacon stops and taps a screen with a flashing digital number. 1001.

In *The Book of One Thousand and One Nights*, the heroine tells her husband the king a new story every night for one thousand and one nights to pique his curiosity and stave off her execution.

Stomach cramp.

"Game face on," Deacon mutters.

We quietly tiptoe past the doors and—

I don't know what I expected, but this isn't it. It looks like a courtroom found in the Land of the Harvest. There's a viewing section with benches. A waist-high wall with a swinging gate in the center divides the front section from the back. Beyond it is a desk for Troikan representatives and a desk for Myriadian representatives.

The judge's desk consumes the back wall, with a court reporter on one side and a witness seat on the other. There is a second seat beside the witness. The only noticeable difference? The floor is concrete, with several drains.

I go cold. The "punishment" rooms at Prynne had drains.

The judge isn't the Firstking. I've seen our creator only once, when Archer allowed me to glimpse Troika through his eyes, but he left a strong impression. He's tall and strong, but Light, such intense Light, radiates from his eyes, even his pores, making it impossible to distinguish his individual features. He carries a rainbow on his back as if it's a weapon, an actual bow. Power radiates from him, and as I'd gazed upon him, my blood fizzed; my skin felt as if lightning zipped over the surface.

This man is...odd. Half human and half spirit, as Victor and Elizabeth explained. He looks like he's made of wind and flesh. A ghost, but dappled, like water is raining over him.

—*Here.*— Deacon's voice whispers over the Grid. He waves to an open section on the bench, and we ease into place.

—*So, what's going on?*— I ask, thankful no one else can hear me.

—*In the witness seat is the human on trial. She's the only human in the room. Her TB is the one seated beside her.*—

The human. A thirtysomething female currently sobbing into her hands.

Deacon continues. —*The ML, who works within the temporary sub-position of Barrister, is the one slapping the metal wand at the hologram playing beside the human.*—

The judge gives us a fierce side-eye, as if he knows we're having a conversation inside our minds. Then, focusing on the TB, he says, "You are certain you're willing to do this?"

After a slight hesitation, the TB nods and says, "Yes, sir."

"Very well. You may proceed."

—*Do what?*— I ask Deacon.

—*Every court case must be paid in blood. Since both realms agree the human isn't to be harmed, the Barrister on the losing side pays the price.*—

—*But why is blood demanded, of all things?*— I struggle to understand.

—*One way or another, a contract is paid in full, even when it's voided. Blood contains cells, nourishment for tissues, oxygen, antibodies for disease, hormones and other substances that help maintain health. Blood is the life of all flesh, and there is nothing more precious or priceless. Only blood can bind this woman to her contract—or set her free from it.*—

Oh…zero. I get it. One way or another, someone is going to die today.

The hologram changes to reveal…a section of her life? Maybe her past? In it, a younger version of her looks over her shoulder before taking money from a grease-stained purse.

"Are you watching?" the MB demands of the TB. "Her mother worked hard for her cash. Cash she needed to pay for medicine. She had cancer. She existed rather than lived and her pain pills were her only source of relief. This girl, the one you hope to add to your flock of sheeple, stole her dying mother's money—to get high."

—*Um, why does Myriad want to keep her?*— The question springs from me, not out of a place of judgment but out of a need to understand the proceedings. —*Why does Troika want her? Why are we willing to risk one of our citizens for her?*—

—*Love is never about a person's actions. Love is about the person. This girl is loved. She has family in both Myriad and Troika. Family who will do anything to keep her or win her. More than that, the crimes mentioned…they are things that have eaten at her for years. Today, she's not the girl she was yesterday. We know it.*

*Myriad knows it, too. They mention these things only as a means
of winning the case.—*

The scene changes. The human is speaking with another
girl. "Tammy is such a slut. I don't know why we're friends
with her. Payton snapped his fingers, and she came running."
Snicker, snicker.

Another scene change. The human is in bed, snuggled
against a boy's side. She calls him Payton. The boy she ridiculed Tammy for sleeping with.

"You consider yourself a horrible person, don't you?" the
MB asks at her, and she only cries harder. "You steal. You lie.
You degrade your supposed friends. Worse, you're a hypocrite.
You cut others down for things you yourself have done. Shall
I go on? Does Troika need to know more about your despi-
cable character before you call a halt to these proceedings?"

I shift in my seat, uncomfortable. My gaze locks on the
Troikan Barrister, who remains silent in the witness seat.

—*Why isn't the Troikan objecting?—* My tone is fierce. *I'm*
struggling not to object.

—*He's only allowed to answer questions about his intent. The
human must answer all others.—*

—*But why?—*

Before Deacon can reply, the MB says to the TB, "You
can't want this piece of garbage in your realm. Tell me you're
not that foolish."

"I want this beautiful life in my realm, yes." The Troikan
Barrister's voice is firm, assured.

"Beautiful," the MB sneers. "Did you fail to watch the
feed?"

—*Even if we win, the human must meet the requirements of our
contract. She must forgive herself and even the people who hurt her
today. If she can't do so, we fought for nothing.—* Sadness tinged

with dread adds a heavy weight to Deacon's words. They hang in my mind like a noose.

"And you." The MB sneers at the human. He's treating her like she's scum on the bottom of his shoe. "Do you wish to be ransomed from Myriad and given into the hands of Troikans? Those who have been your enemy for so long? Do you truly believe you can forgive yourself for the pain and anguish you caused their people? Do you think *they* will forgive you?"

She trembles. The MB is attempting to strip her of her humanity, to reduce her to raw nerves and the very anguish she's been accused of causing others. I grip the edge of my seat.

"What if Troikans expect perfection from you?" the MB continues. "With their countless rules and regulations, how can they not? Can you be perfect?"

She licks her lips, shakes her head. "No one can." A whisper. He's getting to her.

"That's right. No one can. If you return with us, we will accept you for who and what you are, no matter what you've done. You must simply admit you made a mistake asking for a court date and denounce Troika."

"Tell him you have no crimes," Deacon whispers, as caught up in the drama as I am. "Tell him you are free from your past. Tell him you are ready to start over."

I tremble as if I'm the one on trial. —*Surely our Barrister prepped her for this?*—

—*He did. But knowing what's coming isn't the same as experiencing it.*—

The noose tightens.

Radiating sorrow and regret, tears running down her cheeks and snot pouring from her nose, the human chokes out, "I've done despicable things. Unforgivable things."

The TB sheds a tear of his own.

"I'm sorry," she whispers. "I made a mistake. I can't risk the hatred of your people. I choose to remain with Myriad."

Cheers erupt from one side, groans from the other.

"So you have said." The judge bangs, bangs the gavel. "So it shall be."

A wiry blanket of disappointment wraps around me.

"This." Deacon's hands curl around his knees, his knuckles turning white. "This is how eighty-nine percent of cases end up."

And this is what Dior will face. Dior, who harbors resentment against Myriad. Who hates herself for the things she's done and the people she's allowed to suffer.

We have to prepare her. We have to prepare her *hard*, until the only sentence she's willing to speak is "I choose Troika."

Determined, burning with urgency, I jump to my feet.

—*Come on. We've got work to do, a case to win and a girl to save.*—

—*Not yet.*— Deacon clasps my wrist and draws me back to the bench. —*The proceeding isn't yet over.*—

—*But the judge banged the gavel.*— And I know what's coming next, what Deacon warned me about. I don't want to watch. —*Let's go. Please.*—

—*The Barrister had the strength to risk his life. We must have the strength to witness his death.*—

My chest tightens as the MB smirks at the TB, who is standing, moving around the dais. He stops in front of the MB, his hands clenched at his sides. My throat threatens to close.

Pity darkens the TB's eyes. Pity, and a determination that is far more powerful than mine.

What I don't see? Regret.

Tremors rock me as the judge unscrews the top from the

gavel, revealing a blade hidden underneath. A blade he hands to the MB.

"Weapons aren't allowed," I call, willing to risk punishment to stop this. My words go unheeded.

Deacon reaches over to squeeze my knee. "His name is Tom. He has a wife he adores. He works in the orphanage in his free time, teaching children how to play baseball. He is kind."

I want to scream at Deacon to shut up. I don't need to know. I don't *want* to know. I want to leave. But the TB—his name is Tom, kind Tom with a wife—doesn't deserve my cowardice.

Then…oh, then…

With a single motion, the MB slashes the TB's throat. I cry out, the reason for the drain suddenly, vividly clear.

Tom presses his hands against his wound. Lifeblood spills between his fingers and from his mouth. Though pain fills his eyes, the pity and determination never falter.

The human hunches over and vomits. Tom topples, lands with a heavy thump. He shakes…shakes, fighting death… and finally stills.

"The price is paid," Deacon rasps. "Even though it was paid in vain."

MYRIAD

From: K_F_5/23.53.6
To: S_A_5/46.15.33
Subject: Let's get together

Come to my place. There are things I'd like to do in the dark...
  Might Equals Right!
  ML, Killian Flynn

MYRIAD

From: S_A_5/46.15.33
To: K_F_5/23.53.6
Subject: On my way

Hopefully you're better with your hands this time.
   Might Equals Right!
   ML-in-training,
   Sloan Aubuchon

MYRIAD

From: K_F_5/23.53.6
To: Z_C_4/23.43.2
Subject: Things are gonna get freaky

So I'm going to disconnect and take a little time out with
Sloan. I know, I know. You'd rather we remained connected.
Thing is, I'm giving you a heads-up, not asking for permis-
sion. We'd rather have privacy. And yeah, I know everyone
claims intimate moments aren't recorded, but we'd rather
not take any chances. I'm irresistible enough as it is.
   Might Equals Right!
   ML, Killian Flynn

MYRIAD

From: Z_C_4/23.43.2
To: K_F_5/23.53.6
Subject: Very well

I'll give you and Miss Aubuchon the rest of the weekend off, no questions asked. Be together, be pampered. Drink, be merry, relax and enjoy life. First, I have a new mission for you. Miss Lockwood is in a vulnerable state. You will remind her of the comfort she can find in your arms. Details attached.

   Might Equals Right!
   Sir Zhi Chen

chapter sixteen

"Let the fire burn. You will rise from the ashes,
and you will be stronger."
—Myriad

How am I supposed to prepare Dior for what's to come? *I'm not prepared.*

Who's to be her Troikan Barrister? Who will risk his—or her—life for a human who might cave under pressure? No one has volunteered yet.

Archer would step up to the plate in a heartbeat, but he's not here. Who does that leave? Me? The only things I know about court proceedings, I witnessed today. Would I be a help or hindrance?

Is Dior strong enough to persist as an audience views the worst deeds she's ever committed? Is she ready for her deepest secrets to be revealed?

Molten fire burns the center of my chest, and yet ice crystallizes in my veins. Is she ready to live a nightmare? Is she willing to forgive herself and start fresh? Or does the past hold her too tightly, determined to tug her back into the darkness?

No, scratch that. Does *she* hold *the past* too tightly?

The wise will rise, and the fools will duel.

There isn't an easy way to prep her. There's only a hard way. But even that might not work!

I'm too dazed to protest as Deacon steers me out of the courtroom. A Myriadian walks past us and snickers.

My hands ball, but remain at my sides. *Fools will duel.*

Insight from the Grid. And true! Breaking one of the First-king's rules will do me no good.

We say goodbye to the guard tower and step into the Gate. When we exit, Levi is blocking the Veil of Wings, his expression stern.

"We received intel," he says in lieu of a greeting. "Javier Diez has an appointment with Mr. Flynn in roughly one hour. We'd like you to meet with him, Miss Lockwood."

Killian. My heart flutters. See him? Yes. Please. Deal with Javier Diez? No way.

"I'm not ready." Inadequacy delivers a one-two punch to my throat. What if I screw everything up? Alienate him? Get him killed? "I'd rather search for Victor." I haven't done nearly enough for my friend.

"Search and rescue isn't your job, Miss Lockwood." Levi pins me with a hard stare. A look he's got nailed. "Your job is whatever I assign you. Remember that."

I disappointed him. Zero! "What if this is another trap?"

"It's not." He pivots on his heel and strides under the water.

I follow him, entering Troika, and breathe deeply of the sweetened air, better able to center my thoughts…to focus on who and what I am. The brave and mighty Ten Lockwood. The Secondking said so. Twice!

The only way to fail is to quit. I can help Javier and Dior. I can and I must.

"How do you know?" I insist.

"You're just going to have to trust me."

"All right. I'll go," I say. "But what about Javier's free will? He refused our aid."

"His three-greats grandfather petitioned for a second chance."

I spot Reed and Kayla standing under a tree. He's holding a bundle of clothes, and she's clutching three Whells and two weapons. Wait. Those are *my* weapons. My staff and my ring.

"Why?" I ask.

"We stopped by your apartment, picked up a few things." Kayla shoves the weapons at Deacon and tugs at my robe. In unison, the boys turn, presenting me with their backs while also providing a shield from any nearby observers. "Hope you don't mind."

"Hey!" I exclaim as the robe hits the floor. "The wardrobe change can wait."

"Would it have killed you to wear matching underwear?" she mutters, taking the bundle of clothes from Reed.

"Maybe. If I ever did laundry and the machine fell on top of me," I retort.

Smiling, she helps me dress in one of my black catsuits. One of the scantier catsuits. I knock her hands out of the way to finish the chore myself, and as I work, she brushes and twines my hair into… I don't even know what kind of style.

Kayla straps a double-sided pouch to my back, and stores two Whells. Then she breaks the staff in two and hands me the pieces. "You're up, Reed."

"Here." He turns and slips a small round Whell on the Shell's finger and Meredith's ring on mine. "Just don't go getting any ideas," he mutters.

"Dream on, buddy. Or don't. Yeah, probably don't dream about me. I'd have to smack you."

I slide the swords into the Whells.

Gena Showalter

Kayla slaps her hands together in a job well done gesture. "You're ready."

"So, what do you want me to do with Javier?" I ask Levi.

"Succeed," he commands. "Help him. Show him Troikan love. Prove our realm is home." He taps his palm, types in the glowing keyboard. "You've been practicing hard, and your stamina is almost mediocre. You can do this."

"Wow. I sound ah-maz-ing," I quip, my tone as dry as the desert. "Practically indestructible."

"Stay in the Light and allow the Grid to guide you."

Right.

"You're probably curious about the reason Mr. Diez is meeting with Mr. Flynn," Levi says, his eyes gleaming. "Mr. Flynn is now Mr. Diez's ML. That means you will be competing with your old flame for Mr. Diez's Everlife."

My nerve endings buzz with a potent mix of anxiety and excitement. "Way to bury the lead, sir."

Kayla takes me by the shoulders and peers deep into my eyes. "Ask Killian about Victor. Please. He'll tell you whatever you want to know. He's putty in your hands. Just...bring Victor home, okay?"

I'd argue the word *putty*. And such vehemence is rare for her. Does she *like* like Victor? I thought she had a thing with Reed.

"I'll ask," I promise, wondering if Killian will be punished for answering. Before anyone can request any more favors that could prove detrimental to the boy I love, I return to our original subject. "Let's go to the Hall of Records so I can research Javier." I'm going to do this the right way.

Levi nods, and Kayla links her arm with mine.

We reach our destination. General Agape is waiting for us

at a table in back. In the human realm, she might be classified as plain, but all I see is beautiful dark eyes filled with strength.

She stands and motions us over. I'm not as at ease with her as I am with Levi and in deference to her station, I bow my head.

"I've spoken with General Nanne about the situation. I've ensured you have a table and all necessary resources." She is regal in a metal dress, her innate strength on display. "I command the majority of spies who act as humans in the Land of the Living. I've personally compiled all the information we have on Javier Diez."

"Thank you, General," I say.

Kayla peers at her, slack-jawed and silent.

General Agape gives us a curt nod and strides off.

When Kayla recovers, she loads me with all the info the General provided. The highlights? Javier is twenty years old, and we share a birthday. October 10 at 10:10.

What are the odds?

Well, that's actually very easy to answer. The odds are 100 percent, since it actually happened.

I've been told my spirit glowed with incomparable Light the moment of my birth. I wonder if his spirit glowed, too.

Multiple Myriadian Generals died the day Javier was born. Multiple Myriadian Generals died the day I was born, too.

I wonder, again, if Javier is *the one*. The tipping factor in the war.

How many times have I postulated Troika made a huge mistake by selecting me? Now there might be proof to back up my claim.

Zero! I'm wheezing.

What the heck is wrong with me? I should be glad about this. The pressure to win—to save—will be his. *If* he chooses Troika. Will he? He remains Unsigned.

His mother is Myriadian, but his Troikan father raised him after the divorce; surely the father has more influence over him.

Over the years, Javier grew into a hard-core guy's guy, sleeping around, drinking as if alcohol poisoning was a myth to be challenged and making money by stealing cars.

Well. Now I understand why my pals dressed me up like a good time girl. I'm supposed to be some kind of eye candy for the dangerous man-child.

I'm both offended and flattered. And okay, okay. I'm grateful. I need every edge I can get.

I'm going against Killian. He's better with females, sure. There's no one better at seducing the opposite sex to his side. But he's also the kind of guy Javier appreciates most; a hard-core guy's guy, rough and tough, mad and bad to the bone.

In the end, there will be a winner and a loser. We both hate to lose.

If I'm victorious, will he be sent to the Kennels?

If *he's* victorious, will I resent him?

I shudder, wondering if this time—with us—love will be enough to keep us together. Lives hang in the balance.

"All right." Enough wallowing about what could or might be. Fear will never be my friend. "I've got about forty minutes to spare before crashing Javier's meeting with Killian. I'd like to visit Dior and Clay. Help me?"

And afterward… I'd like to visit with Aunt Lina.

I mean, I'm heading into dangerous territory. What if I'm killed? If I don't see Lina today, I might not get another chance. More than that, I'm trusting Levi in every other area of my life. Why not this? If he thinks I can make a difference in Lina's Everlife, I'll set aside my grievances and speak with her.

"Of course." Kayla squeezes my hand. "May your visit and your mission be enlightened."

As I race to the Veil of Wings, Kayla heads to the Eye, where she'll be watching my progress, warning me of incoming attacks and doing her best to anticipate my needs. A job Meredith should be doing.

The thought jolts me, and I lose my footing. This will be my first mission without my grandmother.

I wince as a hot poker of grief stabs into my chest.

Lockdown!

I message Levi, telling him my plan to spend half my time with Dior and the other half with my aunt. He grants his permission, even arranging for an escort to meet me at the Veil.

Sure enough, Deacon is there. Like me, he's still in a Shell.

"Today I'm your Flanker," he says.

A Flanker is sub-position of Laborer, meaning to guard and chronicle my exploits.

"Thank you." He once flanked Archer, and he is the best of the best. "Feel free to ignore the troubadour aspects of your job."

He snorts. "Already planned on it."

"All right. First on the menu," I say. "A visit with Dior and Clay."

We pass through the portal—

Whoosh. We're falling. A blaze of Lights erupts...then a solid foundation settles at our feet. The Lights fade. I experience a brief moment of dizziness before I steady.

I look around. The staff quarters at Prynne are homier than ever, with blankets and pillows, games, toys for Gingerbread and even a string of twinkling Christmas bulbs hanging from the ceiling.

We're months away from the holiday, but pretty is pretty.

Clay and Dior sit at a small round table, playing cards and laughing. She's lost a little weight, her cheeks now slightly hollowed. Her skin is dry and flaking, and there are bruises under her eyes. Her dark hair is limp and lifeless.

An alarm goes off in my head, and I know beyond any doubt. If left unchecked, Penumbra will *destroy* her.

Gingerbread, who is resting at her momma's feet, notices us and barks. Clay jumps up, and Dior stiffens.

"Ten." Clay relaxes.

"Good to see you again," Dior says.

Deacon tells her about her upcoming court date, and she smiles with genuine relief. Meanwhile, dread blows through me, a cold, damaging wind.

I stuff my hands in my pockets and jut my hip, forcing my body to say, *I'm not worried about a thing, nope, not me.*

—*How has she been?*— I cast my voice through the Grid.

Clay's grim gaze meets mine. —*She tosses and turns all night. If she does manage to fall asleep, she has nightmares.*—

—*She hasn't drained your Light?*— If I placed him in a hazardous situation...

—*Not even a little.*—

Thank the Firstking! "You'll be pleased to know I'll be speaking with Javier in roughly forty minutes," I say to Dior. "We'd like to offer him a covenant with Troika."

She places a hand over her heart, and the action reminds me of a baby bird too weak to take flight. "Thank you. I know he can be difficult sometimes, but he can also be sweet and kind, and he's *always* protective." She nibbles on her bottom lip. "He's been offered a covenant with Troika before but declined to accept. He believes equality is overrated. It has nothing to do with race," she rushes to add. "He despises laziness. His father was a drunk and relied on Javier and his stepmom to pay the bills. Javier says he can never support a realm that rewards the lazy and hardworking alike."

"We accept the lazy into our realm, yes, but the lazy are not rewarded." Deacon's tone is stiff.

"Something his TL has explained to him on several occasions," she says with a sigh.

"Why hasn't he signed with Myriad, then?" At the very least, I'd think he'd want to be with his girlfriend.

"They promote indulgence and, according to Javier, that's just another form of laziness."

Um, stealing cars from hardworking citizens to make easy money is another form of laziness, but I keep that little nugget to myself.

I make my way to the table and ease into the chair across from her. Up close, I can see the darkened veins branching out just under the surface of her skin; they are thicker, longer and *active*, like rushing rivers.

"How are you feeling?" I ask.

Her gaze looks anywhere but my direction. "Tired, weak. A little achy."

I lick my lips. "Things might get worse before they get better, but if you'll refuse to give up, they *will* get better." One day I'll be able to cleanse her.

She white-knuckles the edge of the table. "Clay told me about Penumbra. How did Myriad infect me?"

My gaze darts to Clay.

"Levi wanted her to know," he says with a shrug.

Information I should have received before my arrival. "We don't know," I tell Dior. A General visited her, then died in a supposed ambush. Dior became infected. Later a General visited Javier, then died in a supposed ambush. Javier became infected. Coincidence? No and no. But what is the actual connection?

Deacon's comm glows. He checks the message and regards me with expectation. "I'm taking you to your aunt? The one who tried to kill you?"

So soon? "She didn't try." I look to Dior, who is crying into her hands. I reach over to pat her on the back but stop myself just before contact.

Frustration takes a big bite out of my calm.

"I'll be back," I tell her. "We'll get through this together."

Deacon types into his comm, takes my hand and pulls me to my feet. Within seconds, we're transported to the corner of a small room. To the right, there's a comfortable-looking bed and a toilet with a privacy screen. To the left, there's a panel of what I assume is two-way glass. A human with dark, graying hair paces from one side to the other.

"I'll let you know when your time is up." Deacon exits the room, the door closing behind him.

Lina doesn't react to our presence. She continues to pace, the hem of her paper-thin hospital gown ripped and dragging across the floor.

"I cheered. I cheered," she chants. "Then I cried."

This is Loony Lina.

I don't know why I'm surprised by the compassion wrapping me in a warm embrace. I'm Troikan. Sympathy is hardwired into my DNA.

This woman killed me, yes, but long before the madness drove her to strike, we shared a wealth of love and laughter. When my father refused to spend time with me, she played games with me. When my mother was too busy painting to listen to my childish babble, Lina sang songs to me. To the best of her ability, she warned me about the dangers I would face in the future.

Ten tears fall, and I call. Nine hundred trees, but only one is for me. Eight times eight times eight they fly, whatever you do, don't stay dry. Seven ladies dancing, ignore their sweet romancing. Six seconds to hide, up, up, and you'll survive. Five times four times three, and that is where he'll be. Two I'll save, I'll be brave, brave, brave. The one I adore, I'll come back for.

The silly song was a road map to salvation. It saved me. Saved Kayla and Reed, too, every line an instruction we'd desperately needed to navigate Many Ends and escape Myriad.

And…I haven't completed the instructions, I realize. A tremor nearly rocks me off my feet. I left Killian behind, locked in the Kennels. He's free now, but he might not be free later. I haven't gone back for him.

One day I'll go back for him!

The knowledge stirs something deep inside me. Hope, maybe. Or excitement. I will make it back inside Myriad, maybe even Many Ends, and I will leave with Killian at my side. Perhaps Marlowe, too.

A wide smile blooms. *This.* This has to be one of the reasons Levi asked me to seek out Lina. To be reminded of a future I've been promised. A goal I've had since before my Firstdeath.

Lina stops, her head snapping in my direction, her milky eyes locking on me. "I was ready. I was ready to die. Why didn't you let me die?"

"Lina," I say, and my chin quavers. She almost always speaks as if events have already happened, even when they haven't. "I want you to live, and live well. And when you die, I want you to live with me in Troika. Would you like that?"

Silence.

I reach out to clasp her hand, but she rears back, as if she knows I'm a Shell. "It's okay. You can touch me. I give you permission."

I step closer, giving her time to get used to me but keeping my hands at my sides. Her eyes clear of milk, revealing blue irises that pierce as sharply as daggers.

"One fox in the henhouse," she says. "In two days he'll try to eat his mouse."

Another rhyme. Another set of instructions? My jaw aches as I bite down to avoid asking questions. Through experience I know her answers will only confuse me more. "Lina, let me help you the way you helped me. Let me ensure your future is a good one."

"I stayed."

Okay. We're back to speaking in past tense. "You stayed... here?"

"No, no. I was home. Home!"

Panic radiates from her, and I hold my hands palms out in a sign of surrender. Frightening her wasn't my intention. "All right," I say. "You stayed home."

She backs farther away from me. "One fox in the henhouse. In two days, he'll try to eat his mouse. Three, yes, three warnings will come. By four five six, you'll be glum. Look, look, look, for the seven. Eight, nine, Ten is in heaven."

It *is* another set of instructions, and my mind whirls. Who is the fox? And who is the mouse?

Why will I be glum? What does she mean by *heaven*?

"Sleep now," she says, sitting...then lying down. I want to stroke her forehead, the way she used to do for me, but I don't want to upset her.

"Lina," I say, my heart constricting as if someone has reached inside my chest and squeezed the organ in their hands. "I want you to know I forgive you." One of my number tattoos tingles and glows. At the same time, a weight lifts from my shoulders, a weight I hadn't even known I'd been carrying. "I forgive you for everything."

She yawns. "The Key...in your heart all along."

I jolt. "The Key? It's in my heart?" A second row of numbers tingles and glows.

"Written in blood." Another yawn. She closes her eyes, her features softening, the strain fading. "Sleep now."

I flatten a hand over my heart. For all intents and purposes, this woman is supposed to be my enemy. But she's not. She'll never be. I will love her always.

How have other families hated each other over the centuries? How have husbands and wives warred each other? How have mothers turned their backs on their children?

I don't want to hurt Lina. I want to saturate her in Light.

Is her fragile mind capable of withstanding court? What if she buckles under pressure?

A soft knock sounds at the door. A courtesy knock, only. Deacon doesn't wait for my response but strides into the room.

"It's time for us to go."

I push my grief and confusion to the back of my mind, along with the new riddle. *Lockdown!*

I know I need to deal with everything. I can't continue to suppress my feelings. The lockbox is so full the hinges are threatening to bust.

Later. I'll deal later.

Today, I have a mission to complete, and it deserves my all.

"I'll be back," I tell my aunt and move to Deacon's side. In a matter of minutes, I'll meet Javier Diez...and spar with Killian.

Ready or not, here I come.

chapter seventeen

"You cannot accept what's right if you're happy
doing what's wrong."
—Troika

Deacon transports us to...a gym? Oookay. The location is a bit underwhelming considering I expected Killian and Javier to be inside a strip club. But no prob. I can roll.

There's a boxing ring in the center, where six scantily clad women are hanging over the ropes, watching two muscular guys attempt to punch each other into pulp and powder.

Someone save me! One of those guys is Killian.

He's inside a Shell, tall, cut and without flaws. His dark hair is slicked back, his beautiful body glistening with sweat.

Shells can be programmed to sweat as well as shiver; they can also be programmed *not* to sweat and shiver.

I'm glad Killian flipped the On switch.

Am I drooling? I think I'm drooling.

He's teaching Javier how to box his way—no rules, no honor, anything for victory. Both boys are shirtless, wearing only boxing gloves and shorts. Both are brawny and defined with sinew—though Killian is far more ripped—and covered in tattoos.

The 143,10 tattoo causes the most feminine parts of me to flutter and heat.

To be fair, I'm fascinated by *every* image etched into Killian's skin. Underneath the array of lines, stars and severed heads, I sometimes think I spot a map. What I can't figure out—is it a map of Myriad? Or somewhere in the Land of the Harvest? He's never said.

Concentrate now, ogle later.

Right.

—*Javier looks to be in much better condition today.*— Deacon's voice comes from the Grid, claiming my attention. —*In fact, he almost appears...healthy.*—

We're standing in a shadowed corner, unnoticed by the occupants. Cheers ring out, and Deacon sighs.

—*He's going to be a pain to deal with. Put on your big girl panties, Ten.*—

Before we arrived, Deacon had told me, "We'll appear inside a building. There will be MLs inside and outside. As soon as we're noticed, I'll put up a Buckler, but for the love of life, try not to get us noticed."

"Why hasn't *Myriad* erected a Buckler around the building?" I'd asked.

"It would give away their location. TLs would see it."

"Wait. We put a Buckler around Dior's safe house. How did we not give away her location?"

"You didn't see behind the scenes. We erected other Bucklers all over the world at the exact same time. It's a complicated strategy and not one we execute often. There are other ways to mask one, but let's move on to what matters right now. If you can, lure Javier away and tell him whatever you plan to tell him. If Killian spots you, he'll try to stop you. So will the other MLs. I'll take out as many as I can. Just remember, as soon as our Buckler goes up, an army of MLs will be dispatched to disable our shield and pin us in."

Deep breath in...out. —*Big girl panties...on.*— They better be. I've got one shot at this. Only one.

Bile agitates my stomach. I think I could wash a load of laundry in there. Well, ruin a load of laundry at least. I'm about to sneak past Killian Flynn or challenge him. And I'm about to do it simply for a chance to speak with Javier.

As a girlfriend, I currently suck eggs.

Can't make any progress standing here. On your mark, get set, go!

Adrenaline surges through me as I move toward the boxing ring, weaving around treadmills, elliptical machines, weight benches and recumbent bikes. There are no other MLs present—not that I can see, anyway—and only three other humans are working out.

What's my first move? *Think, think.*

"Hands up," Killian tells Javier. The closer I get, the more I feel as if I've been snared by an unbreakable gravitational pull. "Aye. Like that."

I love when his Irish accent comes out to play.

For a moment, I imagine the war is over, and we're openly dating. I see myself pressed against him, his warm breath fanning my skin as his husky voice whispers my name. A promise. A passion. Goose bumps spread over my spirit but thankfully not my Shell.

Stop mooning!

I'm not. Really. See it, do it. Right?

I pause, my mind whirling. The second I'm standing behind the ropes, Killian will notice me. How will he react? Will he shout for reinforcements?

No. Not his style.

Javier will notice me, too. He might or might not know

I'm a Shell. *He* might call for reinforcements. The Buckler will go up and the countdown clock will start. Ticktock, ticktock. As soon as the MLs disable the Buckler, Deacon and I will have to leave or risk being overrun.

Think, think. What's the best way to proceed? To intrigue the human *and* protect Killian?

"This is merely the beginning of what Myriad has to offer," Killian says now. "Strength like you've never known. The ability to defeat anyone who challenges you—even those who don't. And as you can probably tell, win any woman you want."

Well. The sales pitch has officially begun.

"I can win any woman I want *now*," Javier replies, throwing another punch.

He is very handsome, despite the Penumbra writhing under the surface of his skin. A guy's good looks would never be enough to help a girl get over Archer, but I guess this particular guy gave good distraction.

The girls stationed around the ring giggle and wave at him. They blow kisses to Killian.

Mine! Eyes off!

Well, well. Who knew Tenley Lockwood would mutate into the Hulk when jealous?

To his credit, Killian appears unaffected and unimpressed.

"Riches and fame," Killian continues. "Whatever you desire, we will procure for you."

What of love, compassion and peace? The kind of bone-deep peace I feel every time I pass through the Veil of Wings is worth anything. Everything. And it's a peace Killian has never known.

What I wouldn't give to share it with him.

First things first. Win Javier, protect my man. In the back of my mind, an idea springs to life. At first, I dismiss it. Too crazy! But also kind of…cool? Could it work?

I guess we'll find out.

Determined, I hide behind one of the four corners of the boxing ring and step out of my Shell. As stealthily as possible, I climb up to the ropes. I hold my breath.

If anyone walks around the corner, they'll see my Shell, and my efforts will be moot.

Chewing on my bottom lip, I step *into* one of the spectators—a pretty blonde—to use her as a shield. I don't treat her as a Shell and attempt to anchor because I don't want to control her movements.

Anchoring to a human is called Possession, and it's against Troikan law.

I can almost feel Levi's uncertainty pulse along the Grid. He is at the Eye with Kayla, the two watching my process in real time. My protectors.

Killian stiffens. He sniffs the air as his gaze roves over the entire room. Does he sense me? Is he *that* aware of me?

I melt a little.

Javier uses Killian's distraction to his advantage and punches. Target: Killian's jaw. My guy stumbles back.

When he steadies, he pops the bones of his Shell into place. "Good job."

"Again." Javier hops from one foot to the other, his eyes wild, glittering.

"You're too amped. We're taking a break." He unwinds the tape from his gloves, his gaze rescanning the room…those blue-gold eyes slide over the blonde only to zoom back and narrow.

Does he see me peeking out underneath her skin? I gulp.

I think the blonde frowns at him—or smiles, I can't tell which. He blinks, as if confused.

No, he doesn't see me…exactly. Good. That's good.

Javier removes his gloves. "I said *again*." He punches Killian bare-knuckled.

Killian bounces on the ropes. I swallow a snarl of rage and a grunt of concern.

Calm, steady. He's in a Shell. He's fine.

With a scowl, Killian jumps up. "The first, I let you have. This one? Not so much." He slams a bare fist into Javier's smiling face. The human whips to the side, blood leaking from the corner of his mouth.

Javier wipes the drops away before laughing. "More."

Killian gives him more, punch, punch, punching—every strike focused and contained, delivered for maximum impact—until the human is sprawled across the mat, unable to stand but still smiling.

"*Now* it's break time," Javier says between panting breaths, crimson smeared over his teeth.

I grimace. Penumbra hasn't had such a sinister effect on Dior and I wonder if personality dictates severity.

The building shakes, and I stiffen. Either a battle has kicked off outside, or someone just erected a Buckler.

A second later, four MLs rush into the room—two in Shells, two in spirit—each holding a weapon. Got my answer. A Buckler was erected, and it's Troikan. I feel a sweet pulse of Light.

Deacon sprints from the shadows and rams into the Shells. The trio slams to the floor, the MLs absorbing the brunt of impact.

My blonde squeals and dives through the ropes to join the

boys, abandoning me. Killian spots me, his narrowed gaze drilling holes in me.

"Go to the locker room," he commands Javier. "Do not talk to anyone but me. Do not leave with anyone but me."

The younger male clearly isn't used to taking orders and remains prone; he's panting but smiling again.

Gaze never leaving me, Killian throws a hard punch. Javier's entire body jolts as he's rendered unconscious.

The blonde alternates between patting his face and peering up at Killian with a combination of awe and fear.

I race toward the MLs who are in spirit form and lift my arm, aiming Meredith's ring.

Boom, boom!

The bigger male falls. Without missing a beat, the other guy tosses a dagger at me. I dodge, wishing I had time to aim—too late, we collide, hurtling halfway across the room. I use his neck as an anchor and swing myself around him.

Upon impact, he's dazed. Easy to pin. With my knees in his shoulders, I jab the ring into his throat and fire.

Guilt. Sorrow. I experience both as Lifeblood pours from his motionless body.

I know he's past the point of hearing me, but I say, "It didn't have to be this way."

He's dead and gone, and he won't Fuse with a newborn human; he won't enter into the Rest, which is open only to Troikans. That leaves...

Many Ends?

Surely I haven't sent this man...and all the others I've killed in battle...to Many Ends. Surely *Killian* won't one day find himself in the nightmarish realm.

I suck air between my clenched teeth, struggling to maintain my composure. Killian...trapped in Many Ends...

My blood curdles.

From the corner of my eye, I notice a Myriadian exiting his Shell as he approaches me.

Dang it! I've got to keep my head in the game!

As I jump up, he swings a Glacier. I bow back, narrowly avoiding injury, and reach for *my* swords. Straightening, I extend my arms, my body forming a T. He punches me in the stomach, as I expected, and I hunch over, wheezing for breath, at the same time drawing my wrists together to create a pair of makeshift scissors.

Off with his head.

My signature move is swift, painless and permanent.

"I don't want to hurt anyone else, but I will if I must." I spin as I speak, addressing the entire room.

I'm ignored. Six other MLs are here, and one of them is Sloan, the traitor; they're working together to take out Deacon. He's doing his best to neutralize the eager beavers *without* hurting Sloan, a girl he once crushed on.

Humans scurry for cover, chaos quickly reigning. Killian remains in front of Javier, acting as his guard.

"Look out," Killian shouts at me.

I pivot as two Shell-less MLs race toward me. I'm ready, but Deacon sheds his Shell and blazes over, knocking the two to the ground. His previous opponents charge his now defenseless Shell, not yet realizing he's left it—except for Sloan. She whips out two .44s, one for each hand, and nails her own teammates in the back of the head.

Deacon and I jolt with shock.

"You got this?" I ask Deacon.

"Without a doubt."

I rush to my Shell, sheathe the Blessing and Cursing—I won't risk cursing Killian—and slip inside the casing. After swiping up two new swords, I climb into the ring. Time is running out.

Killian looks me over and arches a dark brow. "You planning on stabbing me, lass?"

"With Cupid's arrow maybe, but nothing else."

His features soften. As he circles me, his gaze lingers on my cleavage. His hands curl into fists—to stop himself from reaching out to touch me? His pupils dilate. "Did you come here to seduce me, then?"

Does he realize he's rubbing his 143,10 tattoo?

Beyond the ring, grunts and groans sound as Deacon and Sloan take out the remaining MLs.

"Why are you doing this?" the TL says between ragged breaths.

"Just shut up and kill the witnesses," she snaps.

I move with Killian, wishing he would close the distance and yank me into his arms. "When I decide to seduce you, Killian Flynn, you won't have to ask. Actually, you won't even have enough breath to ask."

"Well, then." His eyes glitter with wicked intent. "I look forward to your attempt."

"You mean my success."

"Finished," Sloan calls. She yanks a sword out of the last ML standing…well, falling, and stalks to a desk in back. She checks the security system. "The humans made it outside to safety."

Humans can pass through Bucklers, no problem.

And sure enough, the rest of the MLs have been finished off. Sixteen in total. I expected more.

In a blink, Killian's entire countenance darkens. He goes from pleasure to business, every mask gone. No longer a charmer, he's a boy who's devastated beyond repair.

"Let's talk frankly, Ten. With your Buckler over the gym, my comm is disabled, and my boss can't listen in."

"What about Sloan? She—"

"Is on our side."

I shake my head in an effort to dismiss my confusion. "Please don't tell me you trust my murderer." I know she aided me today. I know I let her live during our previous battle. But we're discussing matters of the heart right now.

"Why not? She's there for me when you aren't," he snarls.

Every ounce of heat drains from me, leaving me rigid with cold. "Are you...are you two..."

"And now you insult me!" He spits the words at me. "I would *never* betray you. And she won't, either. She could have turned on me a thousand times, but she's helped me in order to help you. Lets our boss believe we're screwing so we can disable our comms and sneak around the realm, counteracting every plan Myriad has for you."

Too much. Too much information to process while I combat far too many conflicting emotions. Betrayed but beloved. In peril but protected. Out of control but steady.

"You're here for Javier," he adds, "but I'm not going to let you have him. He's too dangerous to you."

No way I'll let him play that particular card. "While you're sneaking around, actively putting *your* life in danger, I'm supposed to ignore my job to *avoid* danger? Do you have any idea how devastated I'd be if something were to happen to you?"

He disregards my questions, rasping, "Javier doesn't want to speak with a Troikan. You need to go, and you need to trust me as you promised."

I admit it. This card is harder to discount. "I'm staying here. I'm speaking with him."

A flash of fury in eyes still capable of making my blood

sing. "How do you think Troika found us, Ten? Because we're bad at hiding? I assure you we're not. Or because someone informed your realm?"

"The latter, but—"

"I'm supposed to put up a fight before I let you have him."

"Why? Why would Myriad willingly give him up?"

"I don't know the plan. I only know you risk your life every time you're around him."

"Or you want to keep him, so you're tricking me into leaving," I snap, and Killian scowls at me. "Javier has a blood relation who asked us to speak with him, so I'm going to speak with him."

"The relative isn't the final authority," he snaps back.

I breathe in...out...calming. This is Killian I'm talking to. My love. He's not lying to me. He believes what he says.

"You're right," I tell him. "The relative doesn't get to pick for Javier. So Javier can tell me to go—*if* that's what he wants. He can even tell me to stay away forever. But he *will* hear me out first. I'm certain he'll want an update on Dior."

"He's slept with two different girls in two consecutive days." His tone is dry. "I think it's safe to say Javier is over Dior."

I purse my lips. How easily Killian speaks of a relationship's death.

Forget Javier. For the moment, anyway. I made a promise to Kayla. "Do you know where Victor Prince is being kept?"

Killian smiles a cold smile. "Yes...because I abducted him."

What? "Is he alive?" My grip tightens on the swords.

"Yes." A single nod of his head. "For now."

There aren't many reasons Killian would have kept a Troikan Messenger alive. In fact, there's only one. His weakness—for me. "You think you're helping me." What I don't understand is how Victor's imprisonment helps me. "I'd rather you stay safe and Victor goes home."

Now he gives a clipped headshake. "You don't get a say in this."

I try a different route. "His friends miss him. *I* miss him."

Mistake! He tenses. "You gonna stop loving me if I keep him?"

"No," I say, but he's far from pacified.

A muscle jumps beneath his eye. "Maybe there's something about him I don't like. Something I've *never* liked, even when he lived in Myriad."

"Maybe he doesn't like the fact that Victor can touch you and he can't," Sloan calls.

"Shut up, inferior," he grates.

"Killian—" I begin.

"No." Rage vibrates from him. "We're on opposite sides of a war, lass. A choice *you* made. Do you expect me to lay down my weapons and accept defeat?"

"No, I—"

"Good. Because I haven't. I won't. I'm too busy fighting for ye." His accent thickens. "Everything I've done, I've done to give ye a better *eternity*, not just a better present. I'm protecting ye the only way I can. And I'm doing it without lying. Do know how difficult that is? But I do it because I know ye despise liars. Because I want to be a man worthy of ye, even if I can't have ye."

"I'm nothing special. I'm not yet worthy of *you*. But I'm here. I'm yours."

Abject longing stares at me through those blue-gold eyes… until his expression hardens. "I'm not going to get out of this alive, lass, and I know it."

"You're not going to die." Panic grabs me by the neck and squeezes. "Do you understand?"

He offers me a small, sad smile. "I'm living on borrowed time. When this is over, my crimes will be exposed and punishment will come. I'll be kept alive only as an insurance policy against you, my life used to control yours—to stop you from leading your armies into battle."

"I don't have armies!"

He plows on. "Do you really think I'll let that happen? No, lass. No. I'd rather die than hurt you, and I will. I'll make sure I go out in a blaze of glory." He laughs now, but the sound lacks any hint of amusement. "What I did to Dior is being done to me, only a hundredfold worse. Your realm says we reap what we sow. Karma. Justice has come for her due, wouldn't you say?"

"Killian." I take a step toward him.

He jumps back, avoiding contact. "I have always believed what's meant to be will be, and everything will work out the way it's supposed to work out. This," he says, spreading his arms, "is my fate."

"No." I stomp my foot. "Everything works out when we fight for what's right. Choice matters. You say you don't want to lay down your weapons and accept defeat, but that's what you're doing. What you're choosing to do. You have options. You can defect to Troika."

"Impossible. Your realm would *never* accept me."

"Maybe not at first. But fight *with* them instead of against them, and they'll grow to love you."

"To fight with them, I'd have to go to court. Who would be my Barrister, lass?" Another bitter laugh. "You?"

"Yes!" I shout. "Yes! It would be my honor and privilege. I love you."

"No. I would never allow you to—"

The entire building shakes, the foundation rattling at our feet. Dust plumes the air as I stagger backward, actually falling out of my Shell. Killian races over, abandoning his Shell to catch me before I hit the ground. The shaking continues, and we both fall. I release the swords and cling to him.

He twists in midair, absorbing the impact. "Sorry, I'm sorry," he mutters when he catches his breath, and I'm not sure why he's apologizing.

"No, I'm sorry." The Buckler has been disabled, and it's time for us to part. I'm not ready. I'm not even close to ready. I don't want to leave him like this. And zero! I haven't spoken to Javier. I can't leave without completing my mission.

Killian must not want to part with me, either. He rolls me over, pinning me in place. Where we touch, I grow chilled. He hisses, and I know he's being burned. Even still, awareness sizzles inside me. He's so beautiful. I ghost my fingers over his cheekbone. I love the line of his jaw, adore the sweep of his brows, marvel at the long length of his lashes, and take comfort in the stubborn jut of his chin.

"Everything I do, I do for ye," he repeats, his accent back. It returns every time his emotions overtake him. "I would do anything—except put ye in danger."

My chest aches. My brands tingle. Every step toward a dream is a step away from a regret. "Do you want out of Myriad?" Let me rephrase. "Do you want to join me in Troika?"

"Ye would be—"

"Don't think about consequences, only desire. Do you want to join me?"

Those blue-gold eyes lower and snag on my lips. He says one word, only one, but it seals his fate. "Yes."

I want to shout with joy. One word, but I'm forever changed.

"But," he says, and I shake my head.

"No buts." I press my lips into his, despite the pain. The kiss, like the one in my dreams, is over far too quickly. "If I must, I'll force your hand. And you should want me to do so, eh? After all, as long as you're in Myriad, my life is in danger."

His eyes narrow to tiny slits. "Are ye manipulating me, lass?"

"I did learn from the master."

The tender moment ends with a bang, the front door swinging open, countless MLs rushing inside. They aren't alone. Countless TLs rush in behind them.

The two armies clash together. Grunts, groans and clangs sound. Spears and arrows fly.

Killian and I roll apart, and he moves to block me from my Shell.

"Get out of here," he commands.

I end up next to the unconscious Javier...and an idea strikes. "You're right. It's time for me to go. Just know that everything *I* do, I do for you."

As I talk, I type into my data pad, sending Kayla an urgent message. Help! Can you transport my Shell next to me? Also, I need a location switch with a human in tow. Like, now!

Javier is infected with Penumbra, yes, and the Light will hurt him, but he's sleeping so—fingers crossed—he'll never know.

My Shell appears at my side in a blaze of Light. Kayla did it! With a quick spin, I slip inside and anchor. Then I reach out, clasping Javier's hand.

"Ten!" Killian shouts, realizing what I'm planning. "Don't! They'll never let ye—"

His voice cuts off as a blaze of Light slams into me. The gym disappears, and a new location takes shape around me.

MYRIAD

From: Z_C_4/23.43.2
To: K_F_5/23.53.6
Subject: You have some explaining to do

Reports have come in, and my soldiers tell me you tried to stop Miss Lockwood from taking Mr. Diez from the gym. Why is that, Mr. Flynn? For our plan to work, the two need to be together.

Might Equals Right!
Sir Zhi Chen

MYRIAD

From: K_F_5/23.53.6
To: Z_C_4/23.43.2
Subject: I'm really tired of having to explain myself

Dude. Chill. Miss Lockwood is a smart girl. She suspects we're planning to use the infected humans against her. What's wrong with making it look like I objected?
    Anyway.
    I know you told me to take the weekend off and enjoy a little sexy time with Sloan. For a job well done today I'd rather be rewarded with another assignment. What would you like me to do?
    Might Equals Right!
    ML, Killian Flynn

MYRIAD

From: Z_C_4/23.43.2
To: K_F_5/23.53.6
Subject: I still have doubts

There's a girl in Paris. A distant relative of Miss Lockwood. She's Unsigned. You want to prove your loyalty beyond any doubt? Sign her.

Afterward, return to Myriad so we can chat about your abduction of Victor Prince.

Might Equals Right!

Sir Zhi Chen

TROIKA

From: T_L_2/23.43.2
To: L_N_3/19.1.1
Subject: I have Javier Diez

What am I supposed to do with him?
   Light Brings Sight!
   Conduit-in-training,
   Ten Lockwood
   PS: Peace by Piece ←Possible new motto for our realm?????

TROIKA

From: L_N_3/19.1.1
To: T_L_2/23.43.2
Subject: What do you think?

Talk some sense into him.

Light Brings Sight! ←Let's stick with the old one. It actually works.

General Levi Nanne

chapter eighteen

"Sometimes good people have to do bad things."
—Myriad

Kayla, for whatever reason, decides to send me to a ratty motel room. I grimace as I look around. The ceiling is spotted with mold, the carpet is stained with...something I don't want to contemplate and the furniture is top-of-the-line Goodwill.

A snoring Javier appears on the floor at my feet.

As I wait for him to wake, I send a message to Kayla: Couldn't we have sprung for a 3-star place?

I'm pretty sure there are STDs on every bangable surface of the room. Not that I'll complain...much. My Shell can be bleached. Or burned. Yeah. Burning is probably the way to go. I just hope the next one is pimple free.

My comm glows, and I read her reply: You asked for a location switch ASAP. I gave you ASAP, the closest public housing owned by a Troikan. It shouldn't be in need of repairs. According to our records, we paid to have the entire place refurbished. BTW Levi has TLs and TMs posted around the building.

The owner must have used the money for other purposes. I wonder how that will be dealt with.

Not important right now. Maybe Javier will wake in a

good mood if he's on the bed instead of the floor? Since my Shell is stronger than a human body, I have no trouble lifting him onto one of the twin beds. By the time I straighten, however, I'm trembling.

Weakened by Penumbra?

I back away from him. At the window, I stand between the curtains, letting golden rays of sunlight strengthen me.

Five minutes stretches into ten. I perch at the end of the vacant bed. Amid the silence, Lina's newest song plays through my mind. *One fox in the henhouse. In two days, he'll try to eat his mouse. Three, yes, three warnings will come. By four five six, you'll be glum. Look, look, look, for the seven. Eight, nine, Ten is in heaven...*

Could *Javier* be the fox? He's the closest thing to an Abrogate, after all.

What warnings will sound, and why will I be glum? What is *the seven*?

My brain must be fried, because I'm stumped.

Finally Javier arches his back, stretching his arms over his head. My heart pounds a wild beat as he blinks open his eyes.

When he sees me, he jolts upright and frowns. "Who are you?" His gaze darts through the room. "Where are we?"

Let the games begin.

"I'm Ten, your Troikan Laborer. As to our location... I suspect we're in a human petri dish."

He rubs the palms of his hands into his eyes. "I told the last guy I want nothing to do with your realm."

"And I forgive you," I say, batting my lashes at him. "I'm sure you didn't mean it. Otherwise you would have already signed with Myriad."

"Wrong. I like to keep my options open."

"So I hear."

He eases onto the pillows and pats the spot next to him.

"You want to stay and talk about where I'll live in the Unending, you'll have to get naked."

Do women actually find him charming?

I'm not shy—how could I be? During my year in Prynne, cameras watched me every second of every day, even while I showered. Guards, who were allowed to view the feed, often propositioned me.

"No thanks. I'm dating Killian. You remember him, right? The guy who popped you in the face."

"So what?" Another pat. "You and I can still be...friendly."

Irritation flares. "*You* are dating Dior Nichols."

At last he backs down. "Is she here?"

"Nope. Sorry. But she's safe."

He throws his legs over the edge of the bed and sits up. He's shirtless, his knuckles cracked and scabbed. "Take me to her. I want to see her."

A buzz in the Grid gives me pause. "Not yet," I say. I'm supposed to keep the couple apart?

He glares at me, probably trying to decide how to proceed. The black veins under his skin are thicker than Dior's, and even spill into his eyes. "How did I get here?"

"I carried you." The truth without revealing more than he needs to know.

He looks me over and barks out a laugh. "Yeah. Right."

I'm tempted to give him a demonstration. *Possible Abrogate, remember?* "Look. Dior is in trouble. And so are you."

In an instant, he sobers. "Is that a threat?" His voice lashes like a whip.

He doesn't give me a chance to respond but launches a surprise attack, lunging at me, pushing me to my back and pinning me to the mattress. I'm not afraid, but I won't be manhandled, either. I work my legs between us and shove with enough force to send him flying onto the other bed.

I hop to my feet, my knees close to buckling. Zero! Weakened again. I study him and realize he's trembling, too. He's not immune to my Light.

We face off. His gaze spits fire at me.

"If you've harmed a single hair on Dior's head—"

Oh, now he cares about having a girlfriend? "I would never harm her." But, uh, considering I've done so—twice—I rush to add, "Not purposely."

He pops his jaw. "I've been told your realm is encouraging her go to court. If that's true, you're not saving her, you're endangering her. According to my ML, most people lose."

Well played, Killian. Well played. He erected roadblocks just in case I got my hands on Javier.

He's not done. "Dior's Firstlife *and* Everlife will be worse when she loses."

When, he said. Not if. "Great risk, great reward. She's sick, and so are you. You've both been infected with Penumbra, a disease—"

He shakes his head. "No."

"Yes."

"No. I'm healthy."

"You might feel that way now, but—"

"I'm healthy," he insists. "So is she."

And the award for most stubborn guy in the Land of the Harvest goes to…

Is this how I came across to Archer? How I come across to Killian and Levi? Yeah, probably. So frustrating! It's a miracle I haven't been stabbed.

Okay. I can handle this one of two ways. The hard way,

trying to reason with him, or the harder way, touching him and proving he's filled with darkness.

What the heck? I'll take my own advice. *Great risk, great reward.*

I close in on him. He stiffens, as if he expects me to throw a punch. Not giving myself time to change my mind—and gearing for a kick of pain—I reach out and flatten my hand on his check. Skin-to-skin contact.

Boom!

A violent current of air throws me across the room. I slam into a wall, cracking the plaster before sliding onto the floor. Something pops in my ears. A high-pitched ring fills my head. I blink, trying to clear the sudden haze from my eyes, but the world remains black-and-white, as if I've lost all sense of color, and Javier—

He's on the other side of the room, slumped over. Crimson leaks from his eyes, nose and ears.

What have I done?

Warm liquid trickles from the corners of my mouth. My lungs refuse to work; they've deflated. Wheezing sounds rise from my chest.

The door bursts open, and Reed rushes into the room. He takes in the situation with a single glance, just as he's been trained.

"Stay back," I croak. If I've been drained of Light, I don't want to accidentally draw from him.

Reed ignores me, crouching beside me. He rips the chain from my neck and pours the manna down my throat.

Other TLs rush in behind him. To take care of Javier, I assume. I'm losing focus, the black blending with the white until everything blurs…and disappears altogether.

"—going to heal?"

"Yes, sir. A full recovery. She should wake up any second."

The first speaker I know well—Levi. The second I vaguely recognize. The Healer from the Sanatorium, maybe.

I blink open my eyes and fight a wave of dizziness. My temples throb.

Moaning, I rub my temples. "What happened? Where's Javier?"

A pause. Then, "I'll be going now," the Healer says. "Thank you for entrusting me with our Conduit."

A light patter of footsteps, the soft snick of a closing door. A heavier thump of footsteps. Then Levi is looming over me, concern etched in every line in his face.

I'm in a spacious bedroom with a three-tiered chandelier, two white columns at the foot of the bed and a white rug the same shape as my brands. This isn't a closet at the Sanatorium.

"What do you remember?" Levi asks.

"I—" Memories flood me, and I gnash my teeth. "Everything. Javier and the explosion. What happened?"

He helps me sit up. "You have no control over your Light, and he has no control over his darkness. Light protected you, darkness protected him, and both lashed out at the other. The two forces collided…"

I moan as a new tide of dizziness sweeps through me. "Is he okay?"

"He's recovering. He agreed to stay in our care as long as he's with Dior. The situation isn't ideal, but it's workable. While they're together, I suspect they'll worsen, Penumbra growing stronger. We'll have to be more careful around them."

The reluctance I experienced with Javier suddenly makes sense. The Grid is becoming an intricate part of me, an ever-present help in times of trouble.

"Do I need to attend a debriefing?" I ask.

"Consider this chat your debriefing. Let's start with Lina."

I repeat her song and we discuss possible meanings—to no avail. He's as lost as I am.

A soft knock sounds at the door.

"Enter," Levi calls.

Jeremy's nanny, Millicent, carries my baby brother in her arms. I'm so happy to see him I whimper.

He gurgles and reaches for me. —*Ten!*—

His voice fills my head. "Are all infants able to communicate through the Grid?" I ask Levi.

He frowns. "Jeremy speaks to you through the Grid?"

Chewing my bottom lip, I nod. "He doesn't talk to you?"

"No." Levi rubs two fingers and a thumb against his chin and studies my brother. "To do so at such a young age…"

Means he's strong. I smile.

Deciding not to touch the little boy yet, considering I just came into contact with Penumbra, I wave. "Hey, buddy. I've missed you so much."

Levi collects him—and the ball Millicent is holding—and sits on the floor, placing Jeremy between his outstretched legs.

"Call if you need me." She makes her getaway.

I take a spot on the other side of my brother. He giggles as we roll the ball back and forth.

"Killian wants to defect," I say, watching Levi closely to gauge his reaction. "He won't actually do it, though."

His expression never falters. "Through feed recorded by the Eye, I've seen the way Mr. Flynn looks at you. He'll do it. You are *necessary* to him."

I want to preen, sigh dreamily, ask a million questions and frown all at the same time.

"Whatever you said to him worked," Levi continues. "He released Mr. Prince."

A cool tide of relief washes through me. *Thank you, Killian.* "Is Victor in Troika? Is he okay?"

"He is and he's fine, though he doesn't remember anything that happened."

Wait. "Killian wiped his mind?"

Levi tugs the end of his earlobe. "It's possible, but I don't know how he could have done it."

"I'll ask Killian for details." And get him into more trouble? I chew on my bottom lip. "Will you help me help him?"

He smiles, as if I've just given him the perfect Christmas present. "Yes, Miss Lockwood. I'll help you."

His willingness doesn't surprise me. Levi wants the best for me and even for Killian. He's that kind of guy.

"Why is Myriad in the dark?" If I'm going to win this battle with Killian, I need to know more about his home. "Why are the citizens drawn to shadows rather than Light?"

Levi and I share a chuckle when Jeremy accidently bumps the ball with his foot.

"Did you know a bridge used to connect Troika and Myriad, and Light used to shine upon both realms?" Levi asks. "True Light comes from the Firstking, the sun a little piece of his heart. Then the Prince of Ravens attacked his father's kingdom—the Rest. Myriad was cast into darkness, Ambrosine disowned, and the bridge burned. He attacked his brother's kingdom next."

"Ambrosine is the problem, then. Not the people." A captain decides the direction the ship travels. A leader feeds his people truth or lies, filling everyone with love or hate.

How can I use this information to foster peace? Turn my sights to the death of Ambrosine?

What if the bridge could be rebuilt...?

Levi regards me curiously. "I suppose you're right. The

Everlife Grids flow from their kings. Myriadians are connected to Ambrosine, and Troikans to Eron."

Zero! One step forward, two steps back. "Kill one, kill all?"

"I honestly don't know," he says on a sigh. "As you can guess, a prince has never been killed."

We lapse into silence, lost in our own thoughts. I continue to pass the ball to Jeremy. By the time my brother's eyelids begin to droop, I'm at full strength, certain I'm darkness free. I pick him up, rock him to sleep in my arms, and carry him to the nursery—Levi shows me the way since we're in his house. I place my baby bro in his crib and kiss his temple.

"Where's Victor now?" I whisper.

"He's home, resting. Miss Brooks is with him, ensuring he has everything he needs."

Good.

We exit the nursery, and Levi pats me on the shoulder. "Go home. You could use some rest yourself. You've had a tough day. Forget about Lina's song for the night. My brilliant mind is on the task."

Swept up by a wave of affection, I throw my arms around him. "Thank you. For everything."

He gives me an awkward pat on the back. "Yes, well." He clears his throat. "You had better take off before I decide to make you run laps."

I snort but I also beat feet to the nearest Stairwell. When I exit, I'm a few blocks from the cathedral.

The streets are crowded today, families, friends and coworkers meandering through the different stalls, where linens, hand-carved furnishing and decorations are being sold. I guess everyone decided to visit the outdoor markets at once.

There's a mix of robes and catsuits, a totally different fashion vibe than I'm used to seeing.

"Hi, Ten!" Clementine calls.

Winifred grins and waves. "Glad to see you're back on your feet. Want to shop with us?"

Their warm reception is refreshing. "I'm tempted, but I've been commanded to rest."

"Well, poop. Maybe next time."

They blow me kisses before heading off.

One of the merchants rushes over and places a piece of manna in my hand. "Please enjoy," he says, bowing to me. "My gift to you for all your hard work on our realm's behalf."

"I—"

He returns to his table before I can politely decline. Should I decline, though? A rejection would be rude. I mean, he wanted to do something special for me. The least I can do is appreciate the gesture. "Thank you," I call, and he beams.

As I enter the cathedral, a message from Kayla comes in. You free? I could really use a friend.

Even though I told the newbies no, I can't bring myself to abandon my friend in a time of need. I would love to meet up, but I have to rest. Levi's orders. Come to my apartment!

A pause, then: Let's meet at the Baths of Restoration. Levi would approve, promise. See in you 5!

I switch directions.

When I reach the baths, I take a moment to enjoy the scenery, an elaborate structure consisting of multiple bodies of water—both hot and cold springs—broken up by arched doorways and massive stone sculptures in the shapes of flowers, birds, horses and winged warriors.

Light falls over me, and I soak it up, buzzing with a sudden influx of energy. My body guzzles the rays as if I've been dying of thirst.

The pressure on my lockbox eases. Just like that. I'm stunned.

Kayla exits the Gate, her expression troubled. She gives me a hug and leads me to one of the hot springs. We sit at the edge and dip our toes into the warm, violet-colored water. I gasp as liquid fizzes against my skin.

"What's going on with you?" I ask. "Did something happen with Victor?"

She stiffens, saying, "Another girl showed up at his apartment, and he asked me to leave. Her name is Martha, and she's one of the Leaders under General Bahari. They're in charge of communications. The smart ones. How can I compete with that? He said she's a friend, and she needed a shoulder to cry on. But it looked to me like she wanted a guy to ride." She cringes. "Sorry. That was crude. It's just...this place... the rules. Do you ever feel like it's all too much? Like maybe you would have been better off choosing—" She presses her lips together, shakes her head. "Never mind."

"Better off choosing Myriad?" I ask gently. "Where the party never stops?"

She looks left, right, making sure no one is listening. Then she nods.

"Not really," I answer honestly. "I like structure. But this isn't about the realm or the rules, is it? It's about the boy."

Her chin trembles. She wipes at her eyes with the back of her wrist. "If Victor cares for me, he should want to give me his attention, right? He shouldn't want to spend time with other girls. Hurting me should hurt him."

Well. I can't argue with that. "Have you talked to him about your feelings? Sadly, boys aren't mind readers."

"No, but..."

But? "Are you two dating?" I ask.

"I thought we were. Before his abduction, he told me he liked me. He also told me we had to keep things quiet since our relationship wasn't Grid-approved. But it shouldn't matter, you know? He has free will. Now I'm wondering if his free will is telling him to see other girls."

Ouch. "Maybe ask him about his long-term intentions?" In this area, I have little experience. I've only ever dated James—who lied to me the entire time, and I never suspected—and Killian.

"I've done that, at least," she grumbles. "He says I'm the only one. He says he wants to take the next step with me, to…you know, but every time I push for a legit commitment, he balks."

You know. Sex. I remember a time when I'd been so shy, the S-word had made me blush, too. But I'm not that girl anymore. Prynne changed me.

"I know our rules are in place for a reason, that we're supposed to follow the directions of the Grid because forever is a long, long time, and we don't always see the whole picture like the Grid," she continues, sounding miserable, "but maybe I should just go ahead and sleep with Victor? He'll leave me if I don't. And it's just sex, right?"

"Uh, you do *not* sleep with a guy just to keep him. If your body is more important to him than your mind, he's not worth keeping." My tone is stern. I may not have experience in this area, but I know she's a treasure worth fighting for. "Sex isn't a relationship cure-all."

Killian and I aren't having sex—we can't. And yet he's doing everything in his power to help me. He wants the best for me, no matter what. He *prizes* me.

Just as I prize him. He's strong, smart and witty. He's fun.

He's protective and possessive. He's determined. To those he loves, he's kind. He's giving.

He's willing to die for me. Can I really do less for him?

To me, Killian is worth any hardship. He's worth any pain I'll have to face. Besides, if I won't fight for what I want, I can't cry when I don't get it.

"What should I do?" she asks.

"Listen to your instincts. Follow your heart." Good advice. Advice I need to follow. "Never compromise what's right."

chapter nineteen

"Every mind needs a bouncer at the door."
—Troika

That night, sleep eludes me. My mind returns to Lina, possible ways to convince her to go to court—and win!—and the meaning of her song. By morning, I'm exhausted and still clueless.

Levi surprises me with a visit. "We're doing things differently today," he says in lieu of a greeting. "Rather than training, you're going out on assignment."

My stomach twists with sudden nervousness. "Why?"

"Two birds, one stone."

"Am I supposed to know what that means?" I grumble. "You know, General Nanne, you have a gift. You can make me like and dislike you simultaneously."

Oh, who am I kidding? I love the man. In many ways, he's become a father figure to me. A father figure my own wasn't. Levi supports me. He encourages me.

I might even be used to those annoying life lessons.

Might! I said might!

"You wanted my help with Killian," he says, "and I want your help with a possible recruit."

"I'm listening."

"Remember the woman who begged you to save her daughter Brigitte the day you arrived in Troika? Brigitte is a distant relative on your father's side. She's Unsigned, and Mr. Flynn has been assigned to her."

Myriad clearly believes the more of my family they have, the less I'll fight the realm.

Diabolical fiends!

Their choice—their consequences.

What they don't yet realize? We're *all* connected. If not by blood, then emotion, experience or pain. One person's life will always lead to another's.

"If you accept the mission—" he says.

"I accept," I rush out.

He chuckles. "I'll station TLs in the area. I'll erect a Buckler, keeping other MLs out, minimizing the level of danger you face. Keep in mind Brigitte has a tracker."

Anger gives me a swift kick. I know all about trackers. Dr. Vans surgically implanted one in my side. As my aunt removed it—in one of her rare moments of lucidity—I begged her to leave it inside me. There's a mind-altering drug in it, and it made me think I wanted, no, *needed* the very object of my downfall.

"By the way," I add. "Did your brilliant mind figure out Lina's song?"

One fox in the henhouse. In two days, he'll try to eat his mouse.

Time is running out.

"It...didn't." He drums his fingertips against his chin. "But I'm not worried. We'll figure it out. Go on now. A Shell is waiting for you. By the way, you won't be monitored. The Eye will not record the mission."

"Why?"

"Less questions. More actions."

Suspicious, I ask, "Are you going to get in trouble for this?" To be technical, I've been cleared to work only with humans infected with Penumbra.

He rolls his eyes. "Do you really think I'd send you out without clearance?"

Answering a question with a question. A way to mislead? No, not Levi. He wouldn't. He's too straightforward.

I race off and sure enough, I find my Shell waiting at the Veil of Wings, the pimples brighter than ever. Whells are strapped under a leather coat with slits under the arms for easier weapon removal. On one finger is a Whell for Meredith's ring-gun.

I anchor my spirit inside, fly through the lovely rush of crimson water—such peace—and zoom to...a dark alley, where I'm standing in the only ray of moonlight. In front of me, at the entrance of the alley, humans stroll along a lamplit sidewalk. My sudden appearance has gone unnoticed. Perfect!

I exit, my gaze scanning...scanning...there! My heart leaps with excitement and love. Killian is seated at a table at an outdoor café.

The woman across from him is plump and lovely, with rosy cheeks and a wealth of freckles.

Two birds, one stone.

The streets are cobbled, the buildings around me rich in history and detail. Ancient trees consume the cityscape, adding a delightful country charm.

The hostess asks me if I'd like a table. In French. I understand her, just as I understand the people in Troika, even though I've never learned the language.

I open my mouth to respond in kind, but English slips out. I close my eyes and concentrate on the Grid, where a stream of knowledge flows. Like a thought, but softer. A gossamer thread.

"Mademoiselle?" A hand on my shoulder. *"Est-ce que tout va bien?"*

Is everything all right?

I focus on her. She's human, and she's Troikan. As her hand falls away from me, I see the brand in the center of her palm.

"Oui." In fluent French, I tell her I'm here to meet guests who have already been seated and try not to jump up and down. Too cool!

I don't wait for her reply, but maneuver through the tables. As I sit between Killian and Brigitte, the ground shakes. The people around me huff and puff with confusion and fear, but I know a Buckler has just been set in place.

Killian, who is far from surprised by my sudden appearance, arches a brow, anger darkening his beautiful eyes. He hasn't forgiven me for taking Javier, I see. Tough. I blow him a kiss.

"Sorry I'm late," I say, again in perfect French.

Brigitte frowns, puzzled by the interruption.

Win her. Win him. Try not to alienate.

I hear the ghost of Levi's voice in my head. *Don't try, Miss Lockwood. Do.*

Right. Brigitte doesn't know I'm a Shell. She thinks I'm human. Probably thinks Killian is, too.

"I'm his girlfriend," I say and hike my thumb in Killian's direction.

"Ah. She's the one you were telling me about," she says to him.

He *talked* about me? To a human? What the heck did he tell her?

"She is," he says, his tone brusque.

At least he didn't deny it. I pat his hand and wink. "We're

working through our problems, aren't we, sugar bear? I'll never give up on our love, and I'll never give up on you, no matter how naughtily you behave."

His jaw drops, and he sputters. "*You* continue to endanger yourself, so *I* will be spanking you at my earliest convenience."

I swallow a laugh. "Not that. Anything but that." I bat my lashes at him.

Brigitte looks between us, a little dazed.

All right. Let's get down to business, shall we? I decide on a course of action and say, "Killian is a Myriad loyalist, but we're working on that. He's probably been promising you the world, and hopefully you're skeptical because you've heard the horror stories about the girl who signed with Myriad without reading the fine print. She was a med student, and her contract stated she couldn't help a Troikan supporter without severe punishment." I wave my hand through the air for emphasis, and I know I'm coming across as a whirlwind, but time isn't exactly my friend. "But again, you've probably heard this, so there's no need for me to repeat it."

Her mouth flounders open and closed. "I haven't." She leans away from Killian, saying, "Tell me about the fine print."

"There will be no fine print in *your* contract." Killian crosses his arms over his chest, and though he directs the words to her, his gaze remains hot on me.

"Are you sure about that?" In an effort to maintain my "human" facade, I pick up his mug and drink—and fight to hide a shiver. I taste the bitterness of coffee, the sweetness of sugar and feel the warmth of the liquid as it settles in the Shell's version of a stomach. "With Troika, the contract is the same for everyone."

"I'm sure. And a boilerplate isn't a reason to brag," he says, his gaze now locked on *my* lips. His pupils expand, black swelling over blue-gold.

"How are you sure?" Tingling now, I shift in my seat. "And a boilerplate removes any hint of favoritism."

"Myriadians aren't governed by a strict set of rules meant to control our behavior. If we want something, we take it. We follow our heart wherever it leads us. And favoritism isn't necessarily a bad thing."

"It is when you're not the favored one," I say, and I swear he regards me with pride. "In Troika, anyone who asks receives help. We love. We forgive. We feed you when you're hungry. We help you pay your bills. We are the family you always wished you had."

"A family without fame or accolades," Killian says with no real enthusiasm.

He's not even trying, is he? "Accolades." I wrap my arms around myself and pretend I'm being cuddled. "They keep you *so* warm at night."

He covers his mouth—to stop a laugh?

"You want to know what Troika doesn't do? Surgically insert a tracker inside a human." I meet Brigitte's confused gaze. "You should find yourself a Troikan doctor, get yourself checked."

She begins to shake, the color draining from her cheeks, leaving her waxen. In a burst of movement, she stands, her chair skidding behind her. She backs away from us. "I don't want to hear any more. I've never liked discussing the Unending, and you two are only making it worse. As realm representatives, you are lacking. Besides, you obviously have a lot to work out. Among yourselves! I'm not needed."

I don't try to stop her, because I've said everything I know to say. I've given her things to think about. I've planted seeds, as Levi would say.

To my surprise, Killian doesn't try to stop her, either. As she races off, we stare at each other, trapped by an ever-thickening tension.

"Alone at last." His tone gives nothing away. "Just the way Myriad wanted. You're happy, but you shouldn't be."

"You mean you *hope* I'm happy, sarcastically speaking."

"Not sarcastically. The Greek root for *hope* is *elpís*, which means an unwavering assurance of an expected outcome."

Oh. "Then no. I'm not happy. Not yet. But I hope I will be."

I stand, lean over and cup the back of Killian's neck, yanking him toward me.

chapter twenty

"Every thought has merit."

—Myriad

Killian doesn't accept my kiss—he returns it. His fingers tangle in my hair, fisting the strands at my nape. It's not a power move meant to dominate me, but a possessive one, as if he fears I'll be snatched away at any moment. The same possessiveness roars inside me.

I burn with desire, despite the muted physical sensations caused by my Shell. I'm being branded deep in my soul, and I'm desperate to hold on to him...to hold on and never let go.

He was my last kiss. I want him to be my only kiss.

His lips are soft and silken as his tongue thrusts and rolls against mine, his sweet taste stripping away my defenses one by one, leaving me vulnerable and raw; I love it. I love him.

Different sensations pour through me. Sultry heat. Electricity in my veins, pulsing through muscle and bone. Inside my Shell, my skin grows sensitive. Every move I make, every breath I take, creates an irresistible friction that only makes the heat and electricity worse—or better. Yes, definitely better.

My stomach quivers, delicious pressure throbbing in different parts of me. The first pressure I've ever enjoyed. I'm caught up in a whirlwind of sensation, every cell in my body coming alive. I'm a girl with a purpose—to love the boy who loves me. And this kiss…the kiss is wild, heady. It makes up for every moment we've spent apart, every fight we've ever had, and grounds me in a reality I cannot deny: I'm willing to die for this boy.

Whispers, then giggles and cheers slam into my awareness. We aren't being watched by Troika, but we're certainly being watched by people. Killian and I break apart, and both of us are panting. His gaze remains hot on mine, and my cheeks flush.

"Let's get out of here." He grabs my hand and leads me away from our audience, zigzagging around the tables. On the sidewalk, his pace increases, his stride long and fast.

"The Buckler—"

"Trust me. I'm not ready to die. I'll avoid the borders."

"Are your Flankers nearby?" I search the shadows. "Does your realm have an Eye? Is your boss watching you?"

"I told Myriad you might not show up if too many MLs were in the area. And right now, the Buckler is blocking me from my boss." He throws a wicked grin over his shoulder, and I swear my bones melt. "I think I *hoped* you'd come."

I'm in big-time trouble. That grin…

It's the beginning of my undoing.

If anyone has the power to hurt me, it's Killian. Since we met, he's had a strange hold on me, as if we're somehow linked.

Could *he* be the fox?

The stray thought knocks the air from my lungs. Killian may have changed, may love me, may be willing to die for me, but even at his best he believes winners are adored and failures are abhorred. He craves the attention and affection he never received as a child. Something I understand.

My parents were good to me…at first. The older I became, the more involved they became in their work. Dad was a representative in the House of Myriad, helping to pass realm laws for humans. Mom had her paintings. One day, I woke up, cooked my own breakfast and realized I had been raising myself for years.

They spent time with me only when I required discipline, and the knowledge had hurt. Badly. I'd become an afterthought to the people who were supposed to love me.

At sixteen, I became a bargaining chip.

Because of my supposed Fusing with a Myriadian General, the realm offered my parents more money, more fame—but only if I made covenant.

I wasn't a daughter. I was a key.

The look Killian gives me is fraught with anger and sadness, as if he's reading my mind. "I once asked you to trust me, no matter what. I asked for a good reason. You said you did. You said you would. Have you changed your mind?"

Elizabeth would say he began working on my downfall at the very beginning of my Everlife. After all, what better moment to set me up for failure?

"No," I say. "I haven't changed my mind." So I had a doubting thought. So what? I'm not going to entertain it any longer. I'm not going to allow it to grow into a worry.

It could be foolish to trust him so completely, yes, but I'm going to do it anyway, just as I promised. This boy has more than proved himself.

The alternative? Walking away from him without knowing what could have bloomed between us.

"Good." He stops in the middle of the sidewalk to cup the

side of my face. "Just so you know, hurting you isn't on to-day's agenda, lass."

"Oh, so it might be on tomorrow's menu?" I tease.

"I'm planning to hurt you *never*, yeah?"

I lean into his touch and nod. He gifts me with a soft, swift kiss.

"You do realize *we* are making our relationship happen, right?" *Step out of darkness and into Light, Killian.* "Not Fate. Us."

"No more talking." He leads me to the alley. To the spot I first appeared. Grinning, he pushes me against the wall. "We have better things to do."

I gasp as I meet the cool brick…but the hot male in front of me makes me gasp even harder.

His hands settle on my face again, his grip strong but gentle. "You cause me nothing but trouble, lass. You do realize *that*, right?"

I melt against him. "I thought we had something better to do with our mouths."

"Oh, we do." His eyes sparkle as he presses his mouth against mine.

I welcome him, opening. Our tongues thrust together, and this time, we aren't restrained. We take and give, take and give, the kiss hard and aggressive. The sensations return and redouble, leaving my knees quaking. His breath is my breath, and my breath is his.

Here, in this moment, we exist for each other.

I'm on fire for him. I'm throbbing, aching.

He groans and bites at my bottom lip, staking a claim. "With you, I always want more." He slides his hands under my thighs to heft me up. In an instant, he becomes my anchor.

I wrap my legs around him, clinging to him.

The earth moves—

No, no, it merely shakes, but Killian holds me upright.

"The Buckler is down. We can be seen here," he says, and kisses me again.

I don't know how he does it, but he manages to push a series of buttons on his keyboard without breaking our kiss, whisking us both to—

I lift my head, panting as I take note of my new surroundings. A cave. *Our* cave. The one in the Urals, a few miles from the asylum.

Soon after my escape from Prynne, I had to fight three giant brutes intent on…well, it doesn't matter anymore. I'm scrappy, even wily, but at the time, I was also freezing, not to mention weak from starvation and a recent beating. Killian found me and carried me here, where he patched my wounds.

That was the day I learned about his Shell and his status as a Myriadian Laborer.

A moment of panic. Does he know how close we are to Dior? Then I calm. Maybe he does, maybe he doesn't. He doesn't have to be near her to insist I return her to Myriad, and yet he remains focused on me.

A frigid wind whistles outside the cavern walls. Not that it matters with our Shells. He pulls a switchblade from his pocket. Instinct sends me rearing back. He frowns at me and stabs the blade into his left arm.

I suck in a horrified breath. "Stop! You're hurting yourself!"

"No, I'm disabling my comm." Beautiful Lifeblood trickles from the wound. "But feel free to kiss me better."

"How about I kick you worse?"

With a mock growl, Killian stabs the blade into my left arm. I feel—

A slight prickle. "That was anticlimactic."

He chuckles as he wrestles me to a pallet of soft blankets and pillows. When he pins me, a hank of dark hair falls over his brow.

"No one can see us now," he says. "I can do whatever I want to you…"

I lick my lips. "Oh, yeah? So what are you going to do?"

"This." He tickles me, and I burst into laughter.

"You're a closet romantic," I say, brushing my fingertips over his jawline.

His eyes are hooded, his lids at half-mast. "For you. Only you."

Not just pretty words, but beautiful, exquisite. "Never, under any circumstances, hurt yourself for me."

He gives another mock growl. "I'll do what I want, when I want. You're not the boss of me."

I snort. "How long have you been planning to tell me *that*?"

"Weeks."

Now I smile at him. "Have you been planning this little getaway just as long?"

"Longer."

Ann-nn-nnd I fall even deeper in love with him. Just like that.

"It's one of the reasons I had to enlist Sloan's help," he adds. "I kept disabling my comm and needed a believable excuse."

Butterflies take flight in my stomach. "So she knows everything you're doing for me, and you seriously, without any doubts, trust her?"

"I do."

Still. My earlier nervousness returns. To place our future in the hands of my murderer… "Killian…"

"No. No more talk about Sloan. I want to talk about us… about you. You undo me, Ten." A raw admission, his voice low and husky. "You fight for what you believe in with unmatched passion. You fight for the *people* you believe in. You even fight to help and save your enemy. I've never met anyone like you, with a heart big enough to love a boy who has done such vile things."

Tears well. "We are not our pasts."

"See." He nips at my lips, and pleasure zings through me. "Big heart."

We kiss again, and it isn't long before I'm caught up, swept away, and he is the only life raft. When his hand slips under my shirt to tease me, I writhe against him, already hungry for more. Every caress ignites desire for another. He knows just how to touch me, just how to stroke and knead to drive me to a fever pitch, plying the Shell with maximum sensation.

Even though our realms could get a lock on us at any time—maybe? possibly?—I can't keep my hands off him. I learn him. Every ridge of muscle in his Shell. Every inch of silken skin. Every masculine nuance that makes him different from me.

But I wish I could feel *him*. The real Killian.

He groans when I do something he likes, and he moans when I do something he *really* likes. At the same time, *he* makes *me* groan and moan. He knows my body in ways I never have. He knows where I'm sensitive, and where I ache most.

He's panting as he lifts his head and meets my gaze. Shadows and light flicker over his features; finally the dark captures the corners of his mouth. A mouth pulled taut with strain.

"All right, lass. We need to stop."

Noooo! Gimme! We need to continue.

My fingers comb through his soft, soft hair before settling on his jaw. So strong, with prickly stubble that tickles my skin. I'm trembling. "You're...right." I don't know where I find the strength to halt our interlude. "I don't want our first time to be with Shells."

More than that, I want to give him a reason to live.

His eyes glitter down at me. "And I don't want to go further until our futures are decided."

Do I dare hope? "You mean until you've officially defected?" To survive, he *needs* to defect.

He rolls to his side and tucks me against him. "Until I know for sure I *will* defect."

"You will." I wiggle, settling in, and trace a fingertip down his chest. "I'll encourage you with a kiss every day if I must." I heave a heavy sigh. "Oh, the things I do for love."

"Like you wouldn't enjoy every second of my encouragement." He puts me in a headlock and rubs the crown of my head until I beg for mercy.

Mercy he grants. We resettle on the blankets. As I catch my breath, he scrubs a hand down his face and says, "I'm sorry I shot you."

An unexpected laugh bubbles up. How quickly we can go from kissing to wrestling to apologizing. It's an odd segue, but I can dig it. "You're forgiven. Your heart was in the right place."

"Exactly right." His grip tightens on me, as if he fears I'll float away. Leaning over, he gently runs my earlobe between his teeth. "Ask me anything, and I'll tell ye the truth."

Shivers overtake me. Carte blanche with Killian Flynn? Yes, yes, a thousand times yes. "Has a court date been set for my mom?"

"Not yet. But Levi has agreed—"

"You spoke with *Levi*? How? When?"

"Yes, I've spoken to him. Several times. He sometimes

shows up when I'm out on a mission. Just boom, there he is, in my face. Anyway," he grumbles. "Levi has agreed to find a Barrister for your mother's case."

I'm thrilled. But why hasn't Levi told me?

What else has he been keeping from me?

Deep breath in…out… Okay, I'll deal with Levi later. "Thank you for everything you're doing for her. And my dad? How is he?"

"He's being trained as a Laborer, but not with the new arrivals. He has a private tutor because he's on the fast track."

I'm not surprised. At the end of his Firstlife, my dad's love for me—if he ever really loved me—had darkened into hate. He blamed me for the loss of his fame and fortune, and paid to have me killed.

The memory stings.

I trace the image etched into Killian's wrist. The ten points in Myriad's brand.

"All right. Fair is fair. Ask me anything, and I'll answer honestly," I say, already dreading what he'll want to know.

He doesn't hesitate. "It's time you fessed up. How badly do you want to lick my tattoos?"

I cover my mouth to stop my laugh, but tendrils slip out. "That's what you want to know? Fine. The answer is badly. Terribly. Madly. Are the tattoos on your spirit, too?" I've only seen his spirit from the neck up.

"You'll have to wait and find out. By the way, your Shell's pimples are cute."

I slap his hand away. "You dirty rat! How dare you mention my Shell's flaws."

"Your Shell's *cute* flaws."

I slap his chest now. "I am *so* close to biting off your tongue."

He barks out a laugh, and the genuine display of amusement warms me from head to toe. "You need my tongue more than I do, lass. But go ahead. Do it. I'll just grow a new one."

Yes, I've seen him do that very thing. The day I experienced Firstdeath, in fact.

We both sober, reminded of the harsh reality of our situation. He turns his head to peer into my eyes—to peer at me as if I'm a treasure he can't live without.

"Being without you...it's been harder than I expected," he says.

"I know. I hate being without you."

He rolls on top of me, kisses me again, kisses me hard and deep and thorough, until I'm panting and shaking and aching, desperate for more. For him. Only him.

"Request a court date," I say, close to begging him. "Join me in Troika. You aren't happy in Myriad."

Features ragged, tortured, he shakes his head. "I can't leave yet."

"You can!" I have to reach this boy. "Killian... I know you believe in Fusion. I know you think your mother's spirit is Fused with a human, but Myriad is wrong. Troikan spirits enter into the Rest after Second-death and Myriadian spirits... I think they enter Many Ends. Spirits never die, right?" I rush out before he can protest. "After Second-death they have to go somewhere, and there's a connection between Myriad and Many Ends. Why else would there be a connection?"

He stiffens, but he doesn't argue with me. And I think... I think I'm finally making progress.

One by one...

"I don't know if Myriadians end up in Many Ends after Second-death," he rasps. "You saw no proof of that when you escaped, and I'm not sure how it would work. But I do know Fusion is a lie. When both my General and my Leader refused to tell me my mother's name, pretending they had to jump through hoops to get the information, I took matters into my own hands. I snuck around and got the information on my own."

I tremble as I ask, "What name did you discover?"

"In her Firstlife, her name was Honor Flynn. The human she is supposedly Fused to is Estella Orzo." He tenses as he says, "I visited her. That girl...my mother was *not* a part of that girl."

The anger in his tone gives added weight to his conviction. *Proceed with care.* "You died as an infant and never met your mother. How are you so sure?" What finally convinced him?

"The things that girl was doing... My mother would never act that way. Would never attempt to sleep with me. Honor Flynn has to be somewhere else. Maybe you're right, maybe she's in Many Ends."

I give him a comforting squeeze. "So...what do we do now?"

"I have to find a way in to search for her. If she's there, I can't leave her. I never knew her, but I *need* to know her."

Dread slithers around me, a boa determined to choke all hope out of me. Killian is going to continue endangering himself, and one day he's going to be caught.

"I will find a way back inside Many Ends, Killian. I promise you. I don't know how many spirits are there—whether they're all Unsigned or if Myriadians are part of the mix. I don't know how many are trapped in the mountains, food for the birds and monkeys." The monsters! "But we can rescue everyone...together."

Words Archer once spoke to me. I chose to act without him, and I lost him. I pray Killian doesn't choose to act without me.

"What do you remember about the entrance and exit?" he asks.

"Each time I entered, I died in physical form and simply woke up there. Twice my body was revived and I left as quickly as I arrived. The last time, I had to swim to the bottom of a lake filled with ravenous mermaids." I shudder.

"A lake," he says, and I wonder if there's something similar inside Myriad.

I change the subject—for now—not wanting to give him any ideas. I don't want him traversing Many Ends without me. "Any leads on the spy?"

"Nothing yet."

Who could it be? Kayla, Reed, Deacon, Victor? I trust them. Elizabeth? I would love to blame her. Levi? Even though I'm angry with him, he doesn't strike me as a fox but a shepherd. He *fights* foxes, keeping them away from his flock.

"If I had to guess, I'd say Victor," Killian says. "He defected, but still has ties to Myriad."

"What a shocker. You do remember you admitted you've never liked him, right?"

"Yes, but I like him even less since you met him," he grumbles, and I laugh. "He always had a string of women chasing after him. He promised each of them the world, but never committed."

Well. That certainly fits Kayla's experience. "Is *that* the real reason you abducted him? To keep him away from me? And how did you wipe his memory?"

"I abducted him because I suspected him of being the spy, and I wanted to make sure he couldn't pass information to Myriad. But information was passed even while I had him. And no, I didn't wipe his memory."

I cross Victor off my mental Who's the Spy list. One down.

"Then who *did* wipe his memory? And why did you suggest Victor was the spy if you knew he wasn't?"

"I didn't say I stopped suspecting him. He could have found a way to pass on your secrets while in captivity."

Maybe, but not likely. "Then why did you set him free?"

"I didn't. Sir Zhi Chen found him. My Leader."

My throat constricts. "Did you get in trouble for harming one of your own?"

A corner of his mouth lifts with wry amusement. "I spun the story to best suit my needs. I received a reward."

Phew. "I'm not surprised. Spinning is your specialty."

"Actually, I spun the story with truth, said I had to prove I would do anything—absolutely anything—for you in order to earn your trust. Zhi doesn't know that I'm doing these things because I love you, not because I plan to use your feelings for me against you." He gives me another hard kiss, rocking my world, before standing and drawing me to my feet. "And now I should go. I've been off Grid too long already."

I straighten my clothes, drink my vial of manna and tap my healing comm.

"Wait. I have something for you." Killian won't meet my gaze as he digs into the pocket of his jeans.

I laugh. "If you tell me the gift is your penis—"

"Please. I'll save that *very big* gift for another day." He dangles a necklace directly in front of my face. In the center hangs the symbol for pi.

My hand flutters over my mouth, my eyes widening, my heart swelling. Pi is the ratio of a circle's circumference to its diameter. A circle never ends.

Zero! For the second time today, tears well in my eyes. This is supposed to be a symbol of our relationship, isn't it?

"I made it," he admits, practically growling now. "I make

things. Usually weapons. Which is unimportant right now." Scowling, he presses my thumb in the middle of the symbol, and a soft vibration travels up my arm. A second later, his comm buzzes.

"See?" he says. "If you apply pressure, I'll be summoned through an electrical pulse in my data pad. I'll be able to track you—help you—wherever you are."

I'm not just trembling as I accept; I'm melting all over again. I place the leather cord around my neck and hide the symbol under my shirt. "The fact that you made it makes me love it a thousand times more." As his features soften, I add, "I—I want you to have this."

I step out of my Shell, and motion for him to step out of his. As soon as he complies, I slip off the pistol ring and slide it onto his finger. His finger is much bigger than mine, of course, and the band only fits his pinkie.

We return to our Shells. "It belonged to Meredith, my grandmother," I tell him. "It's a piece of her…a piece of me. Of who and what I am."

He looks at the ring, then at me, then the ring again. His eyes close for a moment, and his expression…he begins to glow, as if he's been lit from the inside out.

"Thank you, lass. I will cherish the ring always." He gently tugs a lock of my hair. "And I hope you'll use the necklace if ever your life is in danger. Promise me you will."

"If ever I'm in the Land of the Harvest and my life is in danger…and summoning you won't endanger you…I promise I'll use it." He can't pass through the Veil of Wings to reach me in Troika, but I suspect he would try if he thought I was in trouble—try until he died.

chapter twenty-one

"There is power in agreement."
—Troika

I'm still reeling over Killian's gift—and his promise—when I step through the Veil of Wings.

Levi is waiting for me, looking dapper in his customary pin-striped suit. No one else is around, and my anger returns full force.

I plant my fists on my hips and glare up at him. "Why didn't you tell me about my mother?"

His lips compress, forming a thin line. "I planned to tell you after I'd found a Barrister for her case."

"Good news. You've found one. *I'll* be her Barrister."

His eyelids narrow to slits. "*That* is the very reason I planned to find a Barrister before speaking with you. I knew you'd volunteer."

"I'll fight harder than anyone else. I'll—"

"No, Miss Lockwood. You won't." He leans down, getting in my face. "This is part of your problem. You think you'll fight harder than anyone else, because you love her. The truth is, we *all* fight our hardest for *all* Troikans and *all* possible Troikans, because we love them *all*. We need you fighting Penumbra, not court cases that could get you killed."

Pop. The air deflates from my anger, and I push out a breath. "You're right. I'm sorry."

A confused pause. Then he nods and straightens, smoothing his hands over his lapels. "I am. But I didn't expect to get through to you so quickly."

"Maybe Killian is a good influence on me?" I ask cheekily.

He tweaks my nose, but says nothing more.

"Is it time for my debriefing?"

"Only with me." With a tilt of his chin, he urges me forward. "Tell me everything."

I relay everything I said to Brigitte and share what Killian revealed: the reason for Victor's abduction, and the results.

"The spy is good," he says on a sigh. "There's been no suspicious behavior among your team."

"Maybe we're looking in the wrong place. What if the spy is higher up? Someone with full clearance, who can access our feed and study our cases with zero redactions."

He frowns. "One of our Generals?"

I despise the thought, but why not?

We enter and exit a Gate. In the Capital of New, the streets are congested with citizens headed to training or work or home after a night shift. Everyone who spots us stops to bow. Even Elizabeth and Raanan.

Nico is with the redheaded twins who were friends with Archer, and Hoshi and Rebel are leaving a manna restaurant. Levi nods at everyone, and I mimic him, doing my best to appear oh so chill, even though I want to shout, *We're equals! Stop bowing.*

I also want to shout, *Vote for Archer! No, no, vote for Meredith!*

No, wait. Vote for Archer! The Resurrection approaches, and Troika could *really* use a third Conduit.

"The Conduit who died this year," I say. "What was her—his?—name?"

"His. Orion Giovante. A good man. Strong. Brutally honest. A little hotheaded. A warrior who preferred to lead his army on the ground rather than from behind the scenes. He refused to leave wounded soldiers in battle and died trying to save them."

He sounds amazing. "We really need him, don't we?" I ask softly.

"We really need *five* more Conduits."

Not an option right now. Unless… "If Myriad can make Abrogates, why can't we make Conduits?"

"If I knew the answer, Miss Lockwood, we'd already have more Conduits."

We take a Stairwell to Levi's neighborhood. At his house, I leave my Shell by the front door, knowing he will beam it to my apartment later. *Note to self: learn to beam.* We go straight to the playroom. Jeremy and Millicent are stacking blocks. Or, more accurately, Millicent is stacking and Jeremy is knocking down.

Jeremy spots me, squeals and crawls toward me. *Crawls!*

"Dude. You've grown leaps and bounds overnight!" I'm so proud I could burst.

"He's strong and wise," Millicent says with a grin.

I pick him up, carry him to the toy box and sit down with him in my lap. Golden sunlight streams through the oval window, stroking us both as he selects a squeaky ball for us— nope, he rolls the ball away from me and giggles.

Millicent excuses herself, granting us privacy, and Levi shuts the door. He leans against the wall, his arms crossed.

"I'm sorry to report I'm stumped by Lina's warning. My one certainty is that you are the mouse."

The subject change throws me, but I rebound quickly. "Yeah. I figured. Maybe the henhouse is Troika? I'd guess my apartment, but henhouse suggests more than one hen, and I live alone." I scrub a hand down my face. "Maybe I should visit Lina again."

He winces. "I received word she asked to be released. We had to let her go. We couldn't violate her free will."

My first instinct is blast him for failing to inform me the second he found out. But honestly? I should be grateful he told me anything at all. He doesn't owe me information. As a General, he must deal with thousands of subordinates and all their loved ones and friends.

More than that, he suggested I go see Lina days before I agreed to do so. Had I gotten my butt in gear sooner, I could have spent more time with her. I could have had a second chance to talk to her about going to court.

"Where is she?" I ask.

"Good question. Not with Myriad, I don't think. They would have tried to use her against you."

True.

He gives me a half smile. "I think you'll be safest in your apartment. Your team can stay with you. I'll station men and women I trust in and around the rest of the building."

I don't want anyone endangered on my behalf, but I also know preparation can mean the difference between victory and defeat. "All right. Yes. Thank you."

He blinks at me. "What's with you today? What happened to your stubborn refusal to obey orders?"

"I'm not stupid. Not all the time," I add with a grumble. I kick out my legs and tap my shoes together. *Tap, tap, tap.* The rhythm sooths me. "Aren't you tired of this war, Levi?" I am, and I've only been part of it for a few months. "I crave peace."

"Victory matters more than fatigue," he says, offering no more.

"Have the realms ever attempted peace talks?"

"No. Why would we? We can't exist in harmony. We want the same prize—humans—and only one of us can win."

"Sharing is caring."

"To share with Myriad, we must compromise. When we compromise we lose the essence of who we are."

Tap, tap, tap. "I'm going to prove you wrong, Levi. I'm going to fight for peace. One person at a time."

His brand glows. "Do what you feel you must." He checks the message, and his good mood fades. "I've had a group of TLs following Brigitte since she left the café. They were ambushed by MLs, and our injured are returning." He waves toward the door. "Go to the Sanatorium. Today's training will come from the Healers. You need to better understand their job."

Eager to help, I blow Jeremy a kiss and head out. Light strokes me, warms and fills me. I inhale deeply, exhale slowly and try to push the rays through my pores. To warm and fill others.

The rays fizzle, and my disappointment is keen.

I spend the next few hours at the Sanatorium, doing whatever my Healer—Dawn—tells me. And for the most part, my patients are kind and grateful.

Then I enter the last room on the second floor.

Elizabeth is perched on the edge of a gurney. She's wearing a bra and a pair of panties, and there are gashes all over her.

She's hemorrhaging, being drained of Light.

This is going to be fun.

She scowls at me. "Why are *you* here?"

"Levi's orders." I set my tray of supplies on the table next to her bed. "Let's get you patched up before you bleed to Second-death." I lift a fat syringe filled with concentrated manna.

"I'm not going to let you stick me. You'll enjoy it," she mutters, and bats at my arm. "Healer! Someone! Anyone!"

"Come on. Don't be a baby." I sidestep her and insert the needle into one of her many injuries.

She hisses and snaps, "Your *mom* is a baby."

"A mom joke? So mature." I empty the syringe and drag a chair next to her bed. "I don't care how rude you are. I'm staying here until I know you're healing properly."

"Whatever." She grabs another syringe from the tray and injects another wound. After a few seconds, the medication eases some of her pain, allowing her to spread ointment and apply a bandage.

"Done," she says, waxen. There are dark circles under her eyes. "You can go now."

"What's your problem with me? Besides the obvious, I mean. Yes, I made mistakes and people got killed. But you punished me, right?"

A flush of shame spills over her cheeks.

"The spiked board," I add, just to be clear. "That was you."

A pause. Then a single, curt nod.

"Who helped you?" Most likely Raanan. But who else? I remember three.

Her scowl returns in a hurry. "I convinced the others to act against you. The crime is mine and mine alone."

I admire her loyalty. "I'm sorry, Elizabeth." Because of Meredith, I know how deeply I hurt this girl. She misses her boyfriend, and I am to blame. "The day of my Firstdeath, I protected Killian because he's important to me, as your boyfriend was—is—to you. No matter his realm affiliation. Protecting him was instinctive. I just wish... I wish we weren't at war. No battles, no deaths."

I'm as bad as Archer and Killian, aren't I? Using every opportunity to work my agenda.

The fight drains out of her, and she reclines. "I feel so guilty. The Resurrection... I'm not going to vote for Claus. We need the Conduit too badly."

Her willingness to let go of her boyfriend for the needs of the realm tears me up. "I know," I say softly. "I want to vote for Archer or Meredith, but..."

My brands begin to glow, a short message from Clay hovering over my palm.

We've got problems.

Can't catch a break. "I have to go." I jump to my feet, saying, "Dior might be in trouble."

"Go," she says, and waves me away. "And, Ten?"

I pause. I think this is the first time she's used my name.

Raanan enters the room, his features tight with concern. "You okay? I just heard."

Elizabeth's focus remains on me. "I forgive you."

"I forgive you, too." I return to her side to hug her before patting Raanan on the shoulder. "Both of you."

"Me?" He snorts. "What'd I do besides look too good for your peace of mind?"

I roll my eyes and race out. I take a Stairwell, messaging Levi along the way. At my apartment, I collect my Shell and cover the hands with leather gloves. Consumed by urgency, I race to the Veil.

Kayla, who is at the Eye, speaks to me through the Grid. —*All clear.*—

Through the water...*whoosh*...I land inside Prynne, greeted by chaos.

Javier is whaling on Clay, who is doing his best to stop the human without inflicting injury. Dior is screaming, begging the boys to stop.

Heart a thunderstorm in my chest, I shove the combatants apart. The gloves prevent skin-to-skin contact.

Worked into a rage, Javier shouts, "You don't touch her. You don't *ever* touch her." He tries to bypass me to get to Clay. I shove him with more force, and he stumbles back.

"Enough," I command. "Calm down or head for the mountains."

He huffs and puffs like the big bad wolf, but he stays put.

Clay rubs his jaw, his Shell's skin shredded. He's always been a lover, not a fighter, but I'm proud of him. He held his own.

"She had a seizure." He drains the vial of manna hanging around his neck. "I rolled her to her side and, well, you saw the results."

Dior rushes to Javier. She rips a piece of material from her T-shirt and covers the cuts on his knuckles. "Thank you for protecting me, baby. I love you so much."

Protecting her? From Clay? This doesn't strike me as very Dior-like behavior. Has Penumbra strengthened her feelings for Javier, a meathead willing to sleep with anyone breathing? Black veins now wind across every inch of visible flesh.

I bite the inside of my cheek. "Why don't you take a break, Clay, and—"

"No," he says with a shake of his head. "I'm staying. I'm useful here."

"Fine." I hold up my hands, palms out. Stupid free will. I glare at Javier. "If you attack Clay or any other Troikan, you'll have to deal with me. You remember what happened the last time we touched, don't you?"

Free will works both ways. I can choose to kick his butt.

He glares right back.

To err on the side of caution, I message Levi to request a handful of TLs and TMs to help Clay. We've kept the location secret to protect Dior and Javier from Myriad but—if Killian is right—the realm doesn't really want to steal either one of them.

I try to speak with Dior, but she steps back every time I step forward.

"Will you just go?" She rubs her arms, as if she's cold.

"You heard her." Javier points to the door. "Go."

I'd take it personally, but I think I know what they're feeling toward me. Repulsion. Their darkness is a revolting pulse against my skin, one I can't wait to escape.

Clay hugs me and whispers, "Believe it or not, I'm making strides with Dior. I can't give up."

I understand, and I admire his tenacity, his tender heart. "Message me if you need me."

"Will do."

Good luck, I mouth and return home.

Midnight. 2:01. 4:39. I pace through my bedroom, the Blessing and Cursing clutched in my hands. I continue to watch the clock.

As promised, my team is inside my apartment while guards patrol the rest of the building. Lina's song plays through my mind again and again, and I exhaust myself digging for answers.

One fox in the henhouse. In two days, he'll try to eat his mouse.

Two days have passed. Today is the day. Anytime now.

Three, yes, three warnings will come. By four five six, you'll be glum. Look, look, look, for the seven. Eight, nine, Ten is in heaven…

Does "Ten is in heaven" mean I'm going to experience Second-death and enter into the Rest?

My nerves are razed, my calm facade nothing but rubble. I'm not ready to die. I have too much to do.

The lights suddenly switch off, a total eclipse of darkness, startling me.

My brands glow as the lights flick back on, and I moan, expecting the worst. Levi says: Every TL in your building just fell into a state of unconsciousness. The fox is in the henhouse. I'm on my way. Tell me you're safe.

Three warnings. This must be the second, the lights the first. Zero! My apartment *is* the henhouse. Because I'm not alone anymore. My team is here with me. Victor, Deacon, Elizabeth, Reed and Kayla.

A kernel of panic unfurls. Is everyone okay?

"Guys," I call, even as I respond to Levi, letting him know I'm on my feet.

Silence.

A thump echoes from the walls, and icy dread slides down the ridges of my spine. The third warning?

My nerve endings throb as I glance at the clock. It's 4:56. 4. 5. 6.

By four five six, you'll be glum.

The numbers in the song—four five six. The time of the attack?

Suddenly the hinges on my bedroom door splinter, the entrance swinging open to reveal a scowling Victor, a gun raised, aimed and ready.

chapter twenty-two

"Never rely on anyone else."
—Myriad

My first thought is, *He's here to whisk me away from danger.*

My second, *He's the fox.*

A sense of betrayal sends me stumbling back. Lifeblood is splattered over his face and clothes, and it's not his. He's uninjured.

He hurt my team.

He fires a Dazer at me. I dodge and swing my swords, blazing shards flinging his way, knocking the gun out of his palm. He's fast and palms a semiautomatic, quickly emptying the clip. I block the way Levi taught me. The bullets ping off the metal and fall to the floor.

"Someone's improved," Victor says with a cold smile.

Levi is on his way. I need to stall. "How did you keep Myriad informed of my activities while you were Killian's captive?" I demand.

"How else? I planned ahead and left a mic in your kitchen. Other places, too." He changes the clip in the gun, but he doesn't fire a second round. Not yet. "I don't want to hurt you, Ten."

"Then why shoot at me?" I screech.

"Weakened, you won't put up a fight when I drag you to the Land of the Harvest to meet with my boss."

"I've already met your boss. His name is Levi."

"I have *never* worked for Levi." He takes aim. "I work for Myriad. Always have, always will. I have family there, and I want the best for them. An eternity without Troika."

His family. Meaning his father? The one responsible for the rift between realms, the destruction of the bridge. The one who fans the flames of hate.

I lift my chin. "I love Archer, and I don't want to hurt his brother. Or worse! I'm begging you not to do this. If you have any love for Archer, you'll—"

"I have *no* love for him. He was a traitor to our realm. And you…you were only as good as the intel you provided. I'm not sure if the handler at the end of your leash is leading you or his boss, but I'll find out."

Handler… Killian?

I fight a new wave of panic, the pi necklace nearly burning a hole between my breasts.

"So? Are we doing this the easy or hard way?" Victor asks.

"Hard." I'm wearing my armor, and I have weapons strapped all over my body. I won't go down easily.

"Very well."

I step backward. He steps closer—and triggers the traps I set. An arrow shoots from the crossbow anchored on my wall. He manages to duck and even picks up speed. He dodges when he accidentally activates my second trap, a Dazer, his finger hammering at his gun's trigger.

The bullets meet my swords.

Time seems to slow to a crawl as he dives at me. I lunge, thrusting my swords up and out. But he twists before he lands and rolls to his feet, missing my weapons while remaining trained on me. I am a whirlwind of motion as I walk backward…over the bed…

He pins me against the wall and hammers at the trigger. The swords act as my shield. I kick out my leg, and Victor stumbles backward. I dive over the bed and skid to the door, then rush out of the room, my ponytail slapping my cheeks.

I need to find the number seven. Where is the seven? *What* is the seven?

Footsteps behind me.

Turn! Now!

The command whispers from the Grid. Not another person, but the Grid itself. I spin, and manage to block another blast.

My boot catches on something solid. Zero! I trip and crash-land on an unconscious, hemorrhaging Elizabeth, who shouldn't have been assigned to me in the first place, considering her previous injuries.

Victor reloads and fires. At me. At Elizabeth. I guard her as best I can. A bullet grazes my arm. I hiss as my flesh splits open and Lifeblood pours out like a molten, glittering river.

My strength wanes, and I tremble. My head fogs. I'm panting, struggling for every labored breath.

No time to apply pressure to the wound. He fires off another round. I'm sluggish, every action igniting searing, burning agony, but I block.

When he's forced to pause to reload, I swing my swords at him, and shards of pure Light once again fly from the tips. He dances out of the way—but not fast enough. One of the shards nails him in the chest and pitches him across the room.

He smacks into the wall. I seize the opportunity to both attack and cauterize my wound, slamming the swords together.

The staff flames. With a roar, I swipe one end at Victor while pressing the other against my injured shoulder.

The pain! My vision darkens, and I scream; a black crust forms over the top of my wound, ending the flow of Lifeblood.

Victor bellows and wrenches away.

I knock the staff into one of his wrists, then the other, and he drops the guns.

We circle each other, two predators unwilling to bend. Around us, Deacon, Kayla and Reed remain unmoving, each surrounded by a pool of Lifeblood.

Can't react, can't react. "How did you take them out?"

"Easily. You're all so gullible."

Son of a Myriad troll! "Why wasn't I affected?"

"Why else? You're a Conduit."

The flicker of Light. Had he somehow hit everyone with a bomb of darkness?

Enough stalling. I swing. He spins to the right, and I yank the staff apart. I toss a sword, end hurling over end. The blade slices through his chest and comes out the other side. He wobbles on his feet and stares at me with confusion.

I close in on him, intending to stab him with the other sword.

Suddenly, I'm in my bedroom, and Victor is standing in my doorway. I'm holding my swords, and he's holding his guns. We're both uninjured.

Shock puts me in a choke hold, my brain whirling with—

The answer slams into me. This is a blessing. A second chance. A chance to start fresh with full knowledge of what will happen if we fight.

"How did you do that?" he demands.

"I didn't do anything. The sword did. It's giving you a chance to walk away. I suggest you take it. Otherwise I *will* kill you."

His eyes narrow, his fingers twitching on the triggers, but he doesn't fire. "Or *I* will kill *you*. I've had multiple opportunities. I convinced Elizabeth to attack you. As she ran away, I could have beheaded you and no one would have known. The time I came over, I could have poisoned you. I let you live—I knew you could aid Myriad."

Killian, yes. Myriad, never. "You can't return to your precious realm without going to court. Will anyone sign on to be your Barrister?"

"I never planned to go back. I'll be put to death here." He lifts his chin. "A punishment to fit the crime, because I will never be remorseful. An end I'll gladly endure for Myriad."

Banging at my front door. "Ten!" Levi calls. "Ten!"

Time hasn't started over, I realize; only we have. "Last chance," I tell Victor.

"Ten!" *Bang, bang, bang.*

Victor's teeth flash, a menacing growl leaving him. He hammers at the triggers. *Boom! Boom! Boom!* I rotate my swords to block the bullets. I force Victor to back out of the bedroom while avoiding my own traps. Too cramped in here, need more space.

This time, *he* trips over Elizabeth. As he falls, I strike, using the swords as scissors, slicing through his wrist. Thud. His severed hand lands on the floor, the gun within his useless grip.

He bellows, Lifeblood gushing from the wound. I slash, and he rolls. Rinse and repeat, until the tip of my sword wedges in a floorboard. I jerk to no avail. He aims the second gun and fires.

I swivel, but it's too little, too late and a bullet burns through my hip. Agonized, I lose Lifeblood at a rapid pace. Adrenaline and determination become my only means of strength.

Victor fires another shot. I dive over the couch, pain wrecking me.

Midair, the *Book of the Law* appears. I pass through it, my arms stretched to catch me when I land; one of my number brands glows over the open page, and in that split second, a lightbulb goes off in my head, the cypher suddenly clear.

The first number of every sequence is a page number, and the others will correspond with either a letter or a word.

Excitement unfurls, every fiber of my being ready to decode. *Later!*

The seven, Lina said. I need the seven if I'm going to survive this.

I land and roll, ending up under the coffee table. I'm about to crawl to the other side, intending to upend the table to use as a shield, when its legs catch my attention. They are wooden and, because of the way they are anchored underneath the tabletop, they are angled...creating the number seven.

Yes! I kick, kick, kick at a leg and...zero! It refuses to budge.

Victor grabs my ankle and drags me out from under the table. A mistake. I kick *him*. He's weak and already winded, and as he doubles over, I deliver another swift kick to the table. Sweat trickles from my temples, and my muscles tremble. Finally the hinges bend, the metal loosening from the top, sticking out.

Not the miracle I needed. Victor drags me out a second time. I claw at the wooden leg, desperate to hold on, but he uses my momentum to flip me over and jam both knees into my shoulders, pinning me down.

The cold end of a gun presses into the back of my head.

No, no, no! I can't lose. Not like this. Not to him.

Panting, he says, "Round one, Ten. Round two, Victor."

Boom!

Victor falls off me. I jump up, confused. Elizabeth is leaning against the kitchen counter, a gun extended, smoke curling from the barrel.

No time to rejoice—she's alive!—and no time to thank her. Victor lumbers to his feet and aims his gun at her.

"No!" I smack into him. We slam into the wall but remain on our feet.

With his good arm, he punches me once, twice, thrice, and I topple. He follows me down, lifting the gun he dropped earlier. I work my leg up and kick his arm, and the shot flies past me.

He puts all his weight into his heel, preparing a kick of his own, but I push to my knees and shove him with all my might. He stumbles, trips over a body and—stops. Just stops. The wooden table leg I dislodged has cut through his middle and now sticks out of his back.

He struggles for several seconds, Lifeblood gurgling from the corners of his mouth.

The seven. It's done. *He's* done.

More defeated than relieved, I fall to my face. My mind hazes, a sharp sting razing my cheek. Whatever. Too many other pains to worry about.

This can't be heaven.

"Ten! Ten!" Levi's voice. Fists pounding at my door. "You have to disable the shield."

"How?" My lips form the word, but no sound leaves me. Black stars swell in my vision, and I'm tempted to use my necklace. To summon Killian. I want Killian. I want his arms around me, holding me. Want his breath fanning my skin, his scent in my nose. Want his words of comfort in my ears. He'll tell me everything is going to be okay, and I'll believe him.

But I can't risk him. I won't. Even if he made it through the Veil of Wings without burning to ash, he'd have to fight legions of Troikans to reach me.

"The fox will have some kind of device. Find the device, Ten!" More pounding, harder and faster.

I try to move, but fail. I think I see Elizabeth crawl to Victor and dig through his pockets.

She must have found the device, because the door bursts open and Levi leads an army into my apartment.

Knowing we're safe—the fox conquered—I allow myself to drift into the darkness…

Hey. Maybe the darkness isn't so bad, after all…

…I'm not sure how much time passes before an array of voices enters my awareness. I blink. I'm lying on a gurney. I'm sore and light-headed, and Levi is seated beside me.

The voices continue, but none are directed at me. They drift from other rooms, I realize. I'm in the Sanatorium.

Memories flood me. "Elizabeth," I croak. "Deacon, Reed, Kayla."

"Deacon, Reed and Kayla are recovering. Elizabeth…" He looks away for a moment, the only sign of his inner turmoil, before facing me head-on. "Coupled with the injuries she received this morning, she couldn't be saved."

"No." Only a short while ago, she crawled to Victor, dug through his pocket…and that's probably when she breathed her last. The realization hits me and a whimper escapes. She bled out saving us. "No" I whisper this time.

His expression firms. "Refusing to believe a truth doesn't make it a lie, Miss Lockwood."

I long to rant and rail at him. To shake him. I long to curl against him and sob. Because he's right. I know he's right. I know in my heart Elizabeth is gone. She's gone, no longer a Light inside the Grid.

Troika lost a valuable soldier today. A girl loyal to the end. I lost a potential friend.

I won't cry. I will be strong. I will honor *her* strength. "Why did you insist she guard me?"

"I didn't." He gives me a small smile. "She did."

My grief sharpens to a razor point. I fight the tears desperate to spring free. "She will be missed," I whisper.

If I'd just figured out Lina's riddle sooner…if I'd suspected Victor's treachery…

Levi takes my hand, squeezes. "The blame doesn't rest at your door, Miss Lockwood. It rests at Mr. Prince's."

I know that, but knowing doesn't negate *feeling*. "Did he survive?" My chin trembles. A funny thought takes center stage: during the frenzied attempt to enter my apartment, Levi had called me Ten.

"Yes, but he had help. Someone put our prison guards to sleep the same way Mr. Prince put my team to sleep. A flash of all-encompassing darkness. Then someone opened his cell."

I hate that Victor is out there—with a partner! "What about his contract? Hasn't it been voided? Shouldn't he lose his connection to Troika?"

"Even people like Mr. Prince are given a grace period. We do not favor one over the other." Levi gives my hand another squeeze. "Don't worry about him. We'll be talking with his friends and every girl he's dated. We'll find him and who-ever's working with him. Rest up, Miss Lockwood. You have begun to unlock the Grid. I can feel it. You have work to do."

"Don't I always?"

He ignores me. "The moment you succeed—and you will—the war will heat up. Everything will change."

MYRIAD

From: Z_C_4/23.43.2
To: K_F_5/23.53.6
Subject: What am I to do with you?

You failed to sign the French girl, and this morning one of your former protégés was caught hiding Miss Lockwood's mother.

I hope you're pleased to learn both citizens have been placed in the Kennels.

As for Miss Lockwood, she's learned of Victor's allegiance to Myriad, and she's close to using her Key. The Generals have decided she's more trouble than she's worth, a true threat to our freedom. You are to draw her out and kill her.

Another failure will not be tolerated, Killian.

Might Equals Right!

Sir Zhi Chen

chapter twenty-three

"With kindness, you brighten the world. With cruelty,
you darken yourself."
—Troika

The next day, I'm released from the Sanatorium. I return to
my apartment, which has been cleaned, the broken furniture
replaced, Victor's recording devices found and removed. I
consider asking for new digs; the furniture may be different,
but my memories are vivid.

Death came to visit and left his mark. Shadows have moved
in, and they are named Sorrow and Sadness.

During Firstlife, death is expected. We are human, and
no matter our station, our bodies age. A fact as certain as the
passage of time. Here in the Everlife, we are spirits with the
potential to live forever.

Tired, I place the Blessing and Cursing on my brand-new
coffee table.

When Levi whisked me to the Sanatorium, he brought the
swords with us. He'd known what I hadn't. I would never
want to be parted from them again. I must always remain
alert. I must be ready for battle, even during times of seeming peace.

Looking back, the signs of Victor's treachery are vivid. His deceitful method of campaigning for Archer. An attempt to prevent the Resurrection of a Conduit, I'm sure. The pressure he placed on Kayla. Killian's innate distrust of him.

I flop onto the couch, determined. The *Book of the Law* opens in front of me. Enough wallowing. What's done is done and cannot be changed. It's time to move forward, to work and find answers.

I brace as I follow the cypher and flip to page 10.

The second number can only be a letter within a word or the word itself, and it doesn't take long to figure out it's the word. Excitement blooms.

The meaning clicks, and I laugh. Loyalty. Passion. Liberty. Three things I need more than any weapon. They will get me through any hardship.

Doors in the Grid begin to open for me, Light pouring through me. Light is knowledge. Darkness is confusion. Light is strength, like being connected to a battery. Light is love, the reason we live. It is hope. No matter how magnificent or how bleak our situation, we can have better. Light is truth. There are no shadows where secrets can hide.

I must fight for what I believe. I must be loyal to my heart. I must fight with passion. In the end, I can free the people trapped in Many Ends. I must shine my Light in a very dark world. I must do what's right even when others do me wrong.

My number brands *move* on my skin, elongating, bleeding together to form a Troikan symbol. I laugh.

The Light streaming in from the window is drawn to me, ray after ray wrapping around me, sinking inside me, warming me. Filling and consuming me. Goose bumps cover me.

More doors open. A torrent of images crystallizes in my

mind, and I gasp. I close my eyes and concentrate on my favorite. A sea of unimaginable colors.

In the distance, lightning strikes. Clouds dipped in diamond dust twirl together, dancing in Light and luminance, yet still stars shine bright enough to be discerned.

Someone is floating toward me...someone with hair the color of spun gold and an impossibly handsome face.

My heart leaps as he smiles at me.

"Archer!" I feel myself rushing toward him. *This*. This is joy, pure and unadulterated.

He catches me and, with a laugh, spins me around.

"I've missed you so much." When he sets me on my feet, I can't bring myself to let him go. I cup his face. "How am I seeing you?"

He kisses both of my eyes. "You're a Conduit. You're able to open doors others can't."

Whoa. "I can open a door into the Rest? I can visit anytime I want?" I'll be able to see Meredith and Elizabeth and even meet with the other Conduit? I squeal.

His smile brightens. "You surely can."

I bear-hug him. "Where are the others? What do you do up here? Are you happy?"

"One question at a time," he says, tweaking my nose. "The others are in the Viewing Room. After entering the Rest, we're shown a playback of our lives. For the first time, we see the whole story, know the mind-set of those we interacted with and find out what would have happened if we'd made different choices. The longer the life, the more memories there are to watch."

"So why aren't *you* in the Viewing Room? Shouldn't a playback take nineteen years?"

"Time passes differently here, a day like a thousand years

and a thousand years like a day. And yes. I'm happy. But if anyone can ruin a good Rest, it's Ten Lockwood."

"Hey!" I poke his chest.

He snickers at me.

Treading carefully, I say, "Are you aware of the happenings in Troika?" Do I need to tell him about his brother? Or Dior?

He sobers in a snap. "Yes, I know." He winds an arm around my shoulders, and I rest my head against him. "Before entering the Viewing Room, Elizabeth told me."

"I'm so, so sorry, Archer."

"My brother…" He releases me to walk to the edge of the cliff. "He signed with Troika, but his heart has always belonged to Myriad."

I join him. "Do you know where he is?" I'm willing to bet Victor stayed inside the realm, fearing he would lose the bond, no longer able to pass through the Veil of Wings. "Where he might go?"

"He had a plan B, I'm sure. A safe house." He closes his eyes and takes a deep breath. "Thank you for helping Dior."

"Hey, don't thank me. So far I've botched everything." I stand up a little straighter, adding, "At least I'll be able to use my Light to fight Penumbra."

"Promise me you'll be careful."

At the moment I'd promise him so much more. "I will. You have my word."

"Great. Now stop dating Killian."

I roll my eyes. I won't promise him *that*. "Nice try. I think he might be my soul mate. I love him, and he loves me."

"I'm sure he does. You're pretty amazing, and he isn't stupid." He glares at me to prove he means business. "But love isn't always enough, Ten."

"Actually, according to the *Book of the Law*, love never fails. Love is *always* the right answer. Love is life."

He makes a disbelieving sound. "Using my own beliefs against me...shameful! I'm as impressed with you as I am furious."

I fluff my hair. "I try."

We share an adoring smile.

A soft vibration glides along the Grid, accompanied by a sense of urgency. Frowning, I back away from Archer, as if I'm being pulled by a cord. "I think I'm needed in Troika."

His eyes glimmer with disappointment. "I understand. Go."

I can't leave him like this. Knowing he loves poems—but only poems that rhyme—I tell him, "You're tough and strong, that hasn't changed. From now on, let's not be estranged. I have to bail, there's work to be done. You lucky duck, you get to stay and have fun. But don't despair, sweet Prince, for I *will* come back. If only to knee you...in the sac."

He barks out a laugh. "You've gotten rusty. Work on this one, and get back to me." He waves me away. "Now, go on. Kick butt and take names the way I taught you."

I blow him a kiss with just a little bite and open my eyes. I'm sitting on the couch in my living room.

A high-pitched ring sounds in the back of my mind. An alarm... I'm being summoned into battle. Unlike last time, details register.

A massive number of MLs have attacked Prynne. Thanks to Victor's intel?

I suspect Killian's boss has changed his mind about Dior and Javier. He no longer wants me to have access to the infected pair.

I grab my swords and jump to my feet. As I run out of the

cathedral and into the streets, I'm surrounded by TLs and TMs who are heading for the Gate.

I notice the people have different levels of brightness. Some sparkle, as glittery as Lifeblood. Some possess a barely detectable glow.

The guy beside me looks at me and does a double take. "You're brighter than the sun!"

I am?

Reed pushes his way to my side. "Good job. You decoded your Key. The Grid exploded with Light the moment it happened."

Yay me?

We reach the Veil of Wings, dart through and land just outside the asylum.

Wind blows, and ice crystals whirl like little missiles. Night has fallen. The moon is high and golden, the beams peeking through clouds to find and stroke me, as if summoned. They strengthen me, and I think I strengthen them; they thicken, pushing back the clouds.

Thump. An ML drops from the roof and lands in front of me. He's ready for war, a bodysuit covering him from head to toe to ensure his skin never encounters a single flicker of light.

He swings a Glacier at me. I block with one sword and strike with the other, cutting through his stomach. Not a killing blow, not for a spirit, just a disabling one. But the handle of the Cursing vibrates, and the boy turns to ash.

That kills him. The condition of his heart.

Other MLs leap at me, but they never reach me. In a blaze of Light, over a hundred TLs land around me, shielding me.

A war cry cuts through the air. Troikans clash with Myriadians. Enemy against enemy. Grunts and groans of pain sound. Metal clinks together. Flames crackle.

The fight is on.

Save the humans. "Anyone see Dior and Javier?" I shout.

"Inside!" Reed's voice rises above the others.

I fight my way into the lobby. I'm lightning fast, no one able to catch me. The Grid guides me, instructions clearer than glass—because I'm finally listening. I know when to duck, thrust and spin.

But every time I fell one soldier, two more take his place, more and more MLs concentrating on me. Can I pull off a victory? By the time I make it to the staff's quarters, I'm surrounded, one of my swords knocked out of my grip.

Zero! There's no sign of Dior or Javier. Where are they?

The ground shakes, and I stumble. Myriad has erected a Buckler. I can hear the hiss of shadows. I'm trapped, but I'm glad for it. *Let's finish this!*

I twirl the sword, the tip spitting out pure Light. MLs drop like flies, but of course, a new crop quickly swoops in. How much longer can I hold them off?

A whip cracks me from behind, coils around one of my blades and yanks. Before the loss has registered, I've lost my other blade, too. Fear sparks, but I tamp it down. Fear is darkness. Fear has no place in this battle.

Remember, the Grid whispers to me.

I...do. I remember the words Killian once spoke to me. His opinion of me the first time we met.

The warhorse paws fiercely, rejoicing in its strength, and charges into the fray. It laughs at fear, afraid of nothing; it does not shy away from the sword. The quiver rattles against its side, along with the flashing spear and lance. In frenzied excitement it eats up the ground; it cannot stand still when the trumpet sounds. At the blast of the trumpet it snorts, "Aha!" It catches the scent of battle from afar, the shout of commanders and the battle cry.

I am the warhorse, and I will do what needs doing. I will rush headlong into battle, unwilling to concede defeat—even if it means the end of my Everlife.

MLs converge. Determined, I go low, kicking out my leg and spinning. Multiple soldiers hit the ground as their ankles bounce together. As I straighten, I punch, and as I punch, my Troikan symbol flares with Light. The next blow burns *through* the MLs chest, my fist coming out the other side—a sword of fire in my grasp.

I reel, but he reels harder. His body seizes, Light spreading through his veins, racing under the surface of his skin. He screams in agony as he topples.

"I'm sorry," I tell him. "I didn't want it to be this way."

Other MLs back away from me. Afraid of me?

A mass of TLs come in behind them and, without hesitation, renders the necessary deathblows. Had to be this way, and it's Myriad's fault. They threatened the humans; they pay.

"I'm sorry," I repeat. I open my palm, and the Pyre disappears. I swipe up my swords. The one who'd wielded the whip, stealing them, is now dead.

My gaze locks with Reed. He nods at me. Shadows move behind him. Behind all the Troikans. I shout a warning, but I'm too late. Spears pierce the TLs from behind, coming out of their chests.

Reed's knees give out, and he collapses.

"No!" I rush to him, but just before I reach him I'm propelled up, up by a force greater than myself—

Carried by a beam of Light, I blaze through the Myriadian Buckler as if it's butter. I reach a plateau, where I hover, looking down at the raging battle. Violent. Brutal. Bloody. My stomach twists. Reed is nothing but a speck on the ground.

He is spirit. He can survive. He must.

Can't lose another friend.

A dark dome surrounds a mile-long stretch in every direction. The hole I created is growing together, closing. I don't know how or why this happened.

I need to go back. I can't abandon my troops.

—Orion died with those same words on his lips.—

The feminine voice flows from a room in the Grid. Princess Mariée. She's helping me. One day, I'll be strong enough to do this.

"I'd rather die fighting than live safe," I tell her.

—Without you, we'll crumble.—

Loyalty. Passion. Liberty. "No. I don't believe that. The heart of Troika will never stop beating."

Suddenly I drop. Whoosh! My heart and stomach switch places as I blaze through the shield once again. Impact throws me but I roll and come up swinging, taking down three opponents in quick succession.

Necessary. Must save Reed, must save the humans.

Another ML rushes into my path. Ready, I raise my swords—Sloan trips him, clearing the way for Killian.

I shout with relief, battling a painful urge to throw my arms around him. He's here, and he's alive!

His dark hair is matted to his scalp, wet with Lifeblood. He has several gashes on his face, and the collar of his shirt is ripped and hanging low, revealing thick scars around his neck. His only remaining weapon? Meredith's ring.

His gaze slides over my still-glowing arm, and he nods, as if satisfied I'm healthy and whole.

A TL sprints up behind him, sword raised, but I grab the tattered remains of Killian's shirt and push him out of the way, shouting, "No!" No more.

Loyalty.

What if Killian had been killed today? What if Reed is already in the Rest? What if the humans got caught in the crosshairs?

My determination changes course. "Stop! Everyone—just—stop." Passion.

A round, disc-like beam of Light explodes from me, shocking me as it swoops over the masses.

MLs drop to their knees, even Killian and Sloan, and TLs freeze, the battle suddenly on pause. Every eye finds me and widens.

Tensions remain high, peace a fragile thing, as delicate as a gossamer thread. Uncertainty floods me. What do I do now?

Killian lumbers to his feet, his arm extended toward his brethren, the ring-gun aimed and ready. "Hear her," he tells them. "Dare you."

Liberty. I can lead these people. I can see myself. *See it, do it.* My life is a book filled with blank pages, and my actions and words are the pen.

"We have fought and warred against each other, but we've only birthed misery and pain," I call. My gaze finds two Troi-kan Generals. Mykhail and Luciana. Both are drenched in Lifeblood, their tense posture proclaiming a fierce desire to return to battle. Next my gaze catches on Reed. He's clutching his side, but he's breathing.

Relief is a cool tide. "Myriadians, you hate us for our Light, and we despise you for your darkness. The two cannot coexist. We know this. We *all* know this. But why must we war because of it?"

Hear me. Please.

Silence reigns, but I'm certain not everyone likes the story I'm writing. Soldiers on edge, gearing to fight.

"I'm willing to call a truce," Sloan shouts, and I'm grateful to her.

"Die," someone calls.

The starting bell. Cries ring out, warriors blazing back into motion.

The same TL sneaks up behind Killian, intent on harm. I have a split second to make a decision. Stop the TL and save Killian, betraying my people yet again, or let Killian take the blow and pray he recovers.

No contest. I spin in front of Killian, my swords lifted and ready. Come what may. I love him. Enemy or not, I will protect him. I will fight for him until my dying breath.

I will do what's right even when others do me wrong. Saving him is right. Helping him—helping others like him—is right. If my people die, they will end up in the Rest. Happier. If Killian dies, we don't know where he'll go. I won't risk a trip to Many Ends, where he'll be trapped.

The TL pauses, unwilling to harm me.

"It's okay, lass." Killian pulls me to his side. "It's okay."

He is willing to take a killing blow simply to stop me from hurting one of my own people? An act he knows I'll abhor.

My heart constricts. This boy…he is so precious to me. He is precious, period.

I haven't forgotten my goal. Stop the war—save my enemies—one at a time.

In a show of unity, Sloan takes a post at my other side. I marvel. The girl who killed me is willing to die to save me.

The TL backs up, but others have spotted Killian the mighty Troikan-slayer, seducer of humans, a prize among prizes.

There's no way we can block them all.

Two TLs leap at Killian. Guided by the Grid, I summon

a beam of Light. It rockets in my direction and catches me around the torso and ankles, yanking me flat. I hover, horizontal, a block to both Killian and Sloan.

A sword cuts through my rib cage, another through my thigh. A deluge of pain. I gnash my teeth. At least Killian and Sloan are safe.

Realizing they've hurt their Conduit, both soldiers drop to their knees.

Killian bellows with horror and rage—rage he then focuses on those responsible for my injuries.

"I will *murder* you for this," he hisses, taking aim.

"No," I grate. "Don't hurt them. Please." The beam gently lowers me to the ground. "Don't...hurt...stop...war..." Breathing is becoming more difficult, my lungs constricting, my throat burning. "Please."

Concern for me must outweigh the need to avenge me, because Killian doesn't shoot. He bends down to pick me up and clutches me close to his chest.

TLs reach for me, determined to wrench me from the arms of their enemy. Sloan beats them back, as fierce as a shark that has scented blood.

"She is *mine*." Killian's heart pounds against my temple, and it comforts me, lulls me. But we aren't in Shells, and contact is painful.

I swallow a whimper. He hangs on to me, carrying me through the battle.

"Dior..." I say. "Javier."

"Your team is winning the battle, lass, and mine are re-treating. The humans will be left in the care of their TLs, perhaps even moved to a new location before I finish this sentence. But you..." Killian growls low in his throat.

"Love you, too...almost died before..." I mean to tell him

I recovered then, and I'll recover now. This? This is nothing. But my body shuts down, the frigid cold too much, icicles filling my throat.

Darkness blankets my mind.

chapter twenty-four

"With violence, you ensure victory. With kindness,
you welcome betrayal."
—Myriad

Warm rays of Light drift through me. Remembering how
Meredith stored precious beams throughout the Grid to be
used whenever needed, I do the same, filling up room after
room. When I finish, no more doors before me, I open my
eyes...and find I'm centered in a beam of bright sunlight.

I stretch with languid satisfaction. Memories flood me,
and I go still. The battle...taking blows meant for Killian and
Sloan...no one else willing to embrace peace...being carried
out of the danger zone.

With a gasp, I jolt upright.

My swords are beside me, and I snatch them up, ready to...
swim? I'm surrounded by water, sand and banana trees rather
than armies at war.

In the trees, limbs and leaves shake as monkeys climb.
Overhead, birds soar. Normal monkeys and birds. This is
not Many Ends.

Salt scents the warm breeze and strokes me. *All* of me. I've
been stripped to my bra, panties and two necklaces. My vial

of manna is empty. Killian must have poured the contents down my throat and cut away my clothes.

I can't really complain about my seminakedness. I think I needed sunlight as much as manna. There isn't a scratch or bruise on me. I'm healed.

A few feet away from me, sitting pretty in his Shell, crystal waves lapping at his feet, is my rescuer. He's lost in thought, staring into the distance.

Love for him is undeniable and inescapable.

I've been fascinated with him since our first meeting. Over the ensuing weeks, as I got to know him better, that fascination only intensified.

In the beginning, I was a broken thing. A girl who'd been shattered into a million pieces of pain and heartache, betrayed by nearly every person in her life. A girl with no anchor or purpose, who'd fallen deeper and deeper into an abyss of misery. I thought I could fight my way out on my own, but indecision made me weak. I see that now.

Piece by piece, Killian and Archer carried me out of the abyss. They welded me back together and protected me no matter the cost, ensuring the girl I became would be stronger than the girl I was.

At any point, Killian could have betrayed me. He could have chosen his realm over my fragile trust, but he never did. Not once. He picked me. He put me first. I see that, too.

I matter to him.

He is the answer to my every equation... I am Juliet to his Romeo, and oh, zero! I don't want to end up like the fictitious, doomed lovers. Forced apart because a war between our families is stronger than our love.

Nervousness pricks at me as I set the swords on the ground and fist handfuls of sand, the grains falling through my fingers.

He notices the movement and turns his head to scowl at me. Not quite the reception I anticipated.

"Where are we?" I ask.

"Fiji."

Nice. "What happened to—"

"The humans were transported to a new Troikan safe house, just as I told you. So let's focus on what *you* told *me*. You almost died *before* this? Tell me what happened. I'm close to blowing a fuse."

He's been sitting there stewing, hasn't he?

I scrub a gritty hand over my face. "I'm sorry. I didn't mean—"

"Less apology, more detail. I've been waiting twenty-eight hours, lass."

What? "I've been out for more than a day?"

Even as I speak, the number twenty-eight rings inside my head. In the *Book of the Law*, page twenty-eight states: *There is a time for planting seeds and a time for harvesting what has been planted, a time to fight and to a time to heal, to destroy and to build, to cry and to laugh, to mourn and to dance, to embrace and to turn away, to search and to wait, to keep and to discard, to tear and to sew, a time for keeping silent and a time to speak, to love and to leave... a time for war and a time for peace.*

Peace...the word teases me. Still a pipe dream?

"Yes," Killian says. "More than a day. Every second has been agony. *For me.* I've wondered if you would wake up. I've weighed the pros and cons of taking you to Troika's Veil of Wings. I've cried, Ten. Cried like a baby—for you."

I *melt* for him.

As I tell him about Victor's sneak attack, he radiates aggression and menace. It's easy to imagine him as the cold-blooded killer so many Troikans believe him to be.

"I wish I'd been there, wish I'd protected you, but I can't even protect your mother," he says with a scowl. "She and a Laborer I trained are now in the Kennels. I've failed one too many times lately, and today might have sealed the deal. Myriad wants you dead, and I shielded you. I'll spin my actions to the best of my ability, but I fear my treachery has been exposed. I could be sentenced to life in the Kennels the moment I return to Myriad. I could be used against you."

My heart sinks. For Killian, my mother and even his friend. "Don't go back," I say. "Stay in the Land of the Harvest until we can set a court date."

"I have to free them. Which means I have to continue my charade as long as possible. If I'm locked up, I'm locked up. I'll still have a chance to rescue our people. The moment I defect, I lose that chance."

"Killian, please. There has to be a way we can keep you safe *and* save the others...together."

Silent, he stands. He's so tall, I have to look up, up, up. The sun hits his back, shadows and radiance dancing over his chiseled features. Because he's in his Shell, the sunlight doesn't bother him.

He walks over, sits beside me, the scent of peat smoke and heather enveloping me.

Yearning consumes me. *Hold on to him and never let go. Be his buffer in this time of trouble.*

I reach for his hand, desperate for contact, but my fingers ghost through his Shell and reach his spirit. We hiss and jerk away from each other.

Disappointment consumes me.

"When you fought the Myriadian army," he says, "you were glowing. There's still a halo around you." He stretches out to peer up at the sky. He is shirtless, wearing only a pair of ripped jeans and leather bracelets he gave me before I died, his tattoos on magnificent display. "It's beautiful. *You* are beautiful."

Touch him...every glorious inch...

My gaze follows a line etched through a skull that is crying tears of blood...through a cracked and crumbling moon, with pieces falling onto a blanket of dying stars...through a rosebush. The roses are black, the leaves withered, the thorns sharp.

"Since your Firstdeath," he says, his tone gentle, "I've turned my entire life upside down. I've sabotaged the only home I've ever known. I'm doing what you said, putting word into action. For you. I regret nothing. But I can't turn away from those in need. Not anymore. You taught me that."

"Killian..."

"You were right. I think we can do more together. I think we should make covenant...with each other," he says, and looks away.

I feel as though my head is spinning. "Make covenant... the way humans make covenant with realms? Like, pledge our lives to each other?"

"I've heard stories," he says. "Of Troikans and Myriadians who have fallen in love. Through covenant, a bond forms between them, like our bonds to our kings. If we do it, what's mine becomes yours and what's yours becomes mine."

Head spinning faster... "Why do you want to do this? What happened to the others?"

He rolls toward me, facing me at last, but his gaze is hooded. "I want...so many things. I want to touch you, spirit to spirit. I want you to touch me. I want us to be a family. I want peace between us. I want to find a way to save your mother and Sloan together, just like you said."

My heart kicks into a too-fast rhythm. There are probably a thousand rules against what he's suggesting, and a thousand punishments. Maybe even banishment. "Will you be able to pass through the Veil of Wings and enter Troika? Will I be able to enter Myriad? The Kennels?" Will I be able to return to Many Ends?

"Some stories say yes, some say no."

If the answer is no, we could try and die? "Let's say it works, and we can. Where will we live after we've checked off each of our goals? When will we be together? Will we still fight for our realms, knowing we could be hurting each other?"

He heaves a sigh. "I never said I'd worked out all the details, lass. I only know I'm willing to risk everything to be with you."

I flounder…reel…entertain a million different thoughts… but only one thought matters. What will I risk for him? Everything.

"Would you set a court date?" I ask.

"After we've found a way inside Many Ends…yes."

Spinning faster and faster. "Killian… I…"

"Just think about it. All right?" He sits up and types into his brand. "As for today, dress and return home. Your people are missing you something fierce."

A pile of folded clothes appears. He offers me a black T-shirt, which I pull over my head, hiding my necklaces, and a pair of leather pants. I shimmy into the too-tight material, sheathe my swords and stand.

Killian joins me, and we face off. He is everything I ever wanted, and I yearn to accept his offer. Can we overcome the obstacles between us?

I'm about to set a course for home when a message from Levi comes in.

I see your Light on the Grid. I've hidden Killian's darkness, and I've asked Kayla to beam you to Dior's new safe house in five...four...three...

"I love you," I tell Killian, already missing him.

The look he gives me is one of abject starvation. "I love you, too."

I reach for him—

Whoosh! I travel in a blaze of Light, landing on the porch of a small log cabin hidden in a forest in Montana.

I listen as I scan the surrounding area, searching for anything out of place. The snap of a tree limb. The crunch of fallen leaves being stomped on. A light pitter-patter of footsteps. A shadow. A print. There is nothing.

A Shell awaits me at the front door. I anchor, and my swords bond with the special Whells strapped to my back. Remaining on guard, I step inside.

The furnishings instantly charm me. A floral-print love seat has a colorful quilt draped over the top. The coffee table has legs made from deer horns. A lace doily covers the surface. Antique dolls perch inside a glass case. On the walls hang pictures of Troikan gardens.

Levi is seated at a hand-carved table with Dior and Javier. He motions me over. "Join us." His voice is tight, tension thick in the air.

"Where's Clay?" I ask. Injured in the battle?

"He's fine. I sent him home to rest."

Finally! *A mark for the Going Well column of my life.*

I slide into the empty seat next to Levi, peering at the humans across the table, unable to hide my horror. Both Dior and Javier are riddled with Penumbra. A black cloud surrounds them. Her eyes are no longer gold, and his are no longer brown. Instead their irises are black, utterly indistinguishable from their pupils.

Sizzling sounds echo in my head, my Light repulsed by the pair.

An-nn-nd one mark for the Going Poorly column.

At least I have the tools to help them now.

"Dior has consented to being cleansed," Levi says.

"All right. Yes." Can I do this? "How would you like me to—"

Bang, bang. The sound comes from the Grid, and I frown.

"You'll want to answer that," Levi says.

How does he know—

Bang, bang.

I rub my temples as the image of a beautiful blonde flashes through my mind. I know her. The princess. A long white braid drapes her shoulder, her beautiful features so delicate and pure I almost can't bear to look at her.

Instinctively I close my eyes to concentrate, and a door opens in the Grid. The princess glides through and smiles at me.

"I'm so pleased to meet you outside a battlefield, Tenley. I've been watching your progress on the Grid, and your Light has only grown brighter."

I bow to her.

"No, no. Rise. Together, we will save Dior. Shall we begin?" She twines our fingers. Her grip is weaker than I would have expected, and cold. So cold.

But a stream of warmth flows through our connection, filling me. Warmth and strength, as solid as gold. But the warmth begins to fade, and a chill wind beats against me. Tremors rock her.

"That's the way," Levi says.

My eyelids flutter open, the sight before me startling. I'm leaning across the table, Dior's hands in mine. I must have reached for her when I reached for the princess. Dior's mouth is open to release an endless silent scream. Her features are contorted in sheer agony.

My fingers jerk, but Levi moves beside me, and he clasps our hands to ensure we remain linked.

—*Give her our Light.*—

With my eyes open, the princess has become a whisper in the back of my mind. And yet she issues the command with so much force I instinctively shove a ray of Light from the Grid into my hands. Dior quakes and shakes with more fervor, the darkness *thrashing* underneath her skin. But the ray hits a wall—and it can't go up, down or around and returns to me.

Another chill wind beats at me, pricking me with thousands of needle-points. Ice crystallizes in my veins, and my heart slows to a sluggish crawl.

—*More.*—

Another ray leaves my fingertips. Then another and another. The cold worsens, and a terrible pressure builds inside me. Too much Light for me to contain!

Dior shakes with more vigor, her chair rattling.

Javier grabs hold of her arm in an attempt to pull us apart. His mouth is moving. I know he's speaking, but I can't hear him.

"Let Miss Nichols go. Now." Levi. I hear Levi. I hear the General in his hard tone.

Javier obeys. A miracle.

—*More.*—

Doors in the Grid are ripped open. Doors to rooms I've filled. Light rushes out...only to hit the wall and return to me, just like the others. The pressure continues to build, becoming a searing agony on top of the still-worsening chill.

Dior stands—no, she *levitates*. Our arms stretch across the table as she lifts higher and higher. This is a scene out of a nightmare.

—*More.*— The princess's voice is strained, beginning to weaken.

No, I try to tell her. Any more, and we'll all explode. We can't risk losing Troika's strongest Conduit. I'll continue, but she must disengage.

—*More!*—

Light obeys, banging at the wall. Then we *do* explode. Or I feel like we do. Our screams blend with Dior's as the wall crumbles and the rays shoot through Dior, filling her up. Golden Light shines from her pores, pushing what looks to be *another person* out of her—a screaming teenage girl with black hair and freckles.

The girl shatters into a million pieces of broken glass and evaporates.

—*General Rosalind Oriana…must have possessed Dior as if she was a Shell… General is now dead…her Second-death…our Light… Tenley! Pull the Light back inside the Grid before Dior experiences Torchlight!*—

I pull and pull and pull, my mind whirling. If General Rosalind Oriana possessed Dior…that meant the other presumed dead Myriadian General possessed Javier. That's one of the ways Myriad stayed a step ahead of us. Not just Victor. That's how the other realm always knew where we'd stashed the humans. The Generals had sent word.

Dior crashes to the floor, unconscious, our hands finally unlocking. I slump over, laboring for every breath.

"The princess," I manage to wheeze. Is she— Yes! She's alive. I see the glimmer of her Light on the Grid.

Levi checks my vitals while a pallid Javier checks Dior's.

"You'll recover." Levi grins and pats my shoulder. "I'm so proud of you, Ten."

"Javier...shouldn't touch..." If she contracts Penumbra again...

"He's not." Levi waves in the couple's direction. "He can't. Not without pain. She's still filled with Light. But not too much Light," he adds as I struggle to rise.

Too weak. *So* weak. All I can move is my gaze. Levi is right. Javier is crouched beside Dior, who is rousing, but no part of him touches her. He's maintaining distance.

Realization dawns. The other General knows Light will force him out of the human, ending his Everlife.

We have to...to...my one-hundred-pound eyelids close, too heavy to hold up...

Lights-out, Ten.

The Lights flicker, until they are shining brightly. I straighten gingerly, careful of new aches and pains, memories and questions rolling through my mind.

The Grid answers each question as soon as it forms.

Can any spirit possess any human?

Only higher-ups have the necessary skill. More than that, the human must grant permission—even if they do not know they are granting permission.

I remember how I used a human as a shield and flinch. Can Troikans possess humans?

Possession is forbidden to Troikans. It removes free will.

Why don't all Troikans know about this?

Too many TLs would kill the possessed humans rather than risk the lives of their Conduits.

My temples begin to throb. Javier needs to be cleansed, too, but I'm in no shape to help him. If I rush headlong into battle right now—and cleansing is a battle—I'll lose. I'm ready to win! Time isn't our friend. As the days pass, Penumbra—the Myriadian General—will only strengthen his hold on Javier.

I catalog my surroundings. I'm still in the cabin, but I've been moved to the couch.

Levi sits on the arm. He winks at me. "Have a nice nap, Miss Lockwood?"

"How long was I out?"

"Only an hour."

A radiant Dior dances through the house, her smile wide and infectious. Javier watches her with a scowl.

She bounds over to hug me. When her skin brushes against mine, warmth arcs between us, and she laughs. "Thank you. Thank you so much. I hadn't realized…the difference is astounding. I've never felt better and…thank you!" She releases me to hug Levi.

Though his eyes glow with affection, he clears his throat and says in a stern tone, "All right. Let's continue this meeting."

She sits at the table, but practically bounces in her chair. "Is Javier next?"

"No," Javier says.

At the same time, Levi says, "Not today. Miss Lockwood must recover." He frowns at Javier. "I know you objected to Miss Nichols's cleansing, but as you can see, she survived. So will you. Trust me, kid. You want to be cleansed. I know you couldn't see what came out of Miss Nichols, but it wasn't pretty, and the same type of thing lives inside you."

"Don't care."

Levi is a bundle of irritation as his gaze lands on me. "Because of the brutal battles being fought over Miss Nichols, the judge has decided to move up her trial. It begins tomorrow."

No way! "She doesn't even have a Barrister yet."

"She does." He reaches out to pat Dior's hand. "Me."

"You can't. You're a General. You're needed in the realm. We can't risk—" The rest of my words die on my tongue, killed by the Grid.

Humans aren't to know the price we pay. Our sacrifice isn't to drive theirs.

My hands fist. —*We need you, Levi.*— I throw the statement through the Grid as if it's an accusation.

—*She needs me, too. She needs someone strong to lean on. She needs to know someone will stand beside her, no matter what.*—

—*Levi!*— He's willing to risk his life for someone who is currently his enemy.

And I'm not?

—*If she fails, you die.*— I plow on. —*No if, ands or buts about it.*—

He offers me a soft smile. —*One at a time. That's how we end a war, yes?*—

Jerk! He's fighting fire with water.

"What's wrong?" Dior asks, looking between us. "What's going on?"

Helpless to do otherwise, I say, "Let's prepare." We have to convince her to believe in herself and what she wants, no matter what, and all of Troika has her back, no matter what.

Levi's brand glows in time with mine. A message from Kayla has comes in. I read it and go cold.

Clay returned to the LotH. I don't know why. A short while later, he sent me an SOS. Said someone from Myriad was tailing him. I sent TLs out to aid him, but they can't find him. Neither can I. His Light has vanished from the Eye. I think Myriad has him.

chapter twenty-five

"Do not be deceived. In everything, there is right,
and there is wrong. They are no shades of gray."
—Troika

Levi leaps into action, sending out messages. TLs appear to whisk Dior and Javier away. I'm glad. I don't want Javier—and the General possessing him—to hear what I have to say.

"I'm hunting for Clay," I tell Levi. Why did Clay return to the Land of the Harvest? A General had commanded him to rest.

"We can't risk you," he replies with a shake of his head. "I know you're probably tired of hearing those words, but they are true nonetheless. Deacon will—"

"I *have* to help him." Somehow. I've let Clay down too many times. "I've never declined a mission, Levi. Let me do this. I can do what Deacon can't. I can talk to Killian and gain inside info." I don't like pitting the boy I love against his realm, but today I'm going to do it. I love Clay, too, and I will do anything to help him.

Levi offers a stiff nod and types another message into his keyboard. "No fighting for you," he insists. "You can stay here, speak with Killian. I'll give you five minutes. Relay all intel to Deacon when he arrives and return to Troika. Meanwhile, I'll have other troops out searching."

At least Levi trusts Killian to help us and not betray us. A huge step forward. And whether Levi realizes it or not, this trust heralds peace. Not with Myriad, but with Killian himself.

One person. One change.

Levi's gaze locks with mine. "I'd stay with you, but I've set a meeting with the other Generals. May your quest be enlightened." Then he's gone, vanishing in a blaze of Light.

Alone, I press my thumb against the symbol for pi that hangs from my neck. As I wait, I pace, too rattled to stay still.

A burst of shadows suddenly shoots through the ceiling and hits the floor. In the center, Killian appears. He's in a Shell, like me, concern pulling his features taut.

"Clay is missing." I rush to him, throwing my arms around him. "We think Myriad has him."

He holds me, and I imagine his peat smoke and heather scent surrounds me. "They do. I managed to convince my Leader I've got you at the end of my hook, so I'm still somewhat in the loop. Victor recovered enough to trick Clay into thinking you'd been captured. Clay went to save you, walking right into a trap."

This is the worst possible news.

No! He lives. There's hope.

"Do you know where Clay's being held?" I ask.

"I don't. I'm sorry, lass. I'm only being fed select information while I *prove my loyalty*." With a sigh, he sits on the couch and tugs me onto his lap. "I know you, and I know you're planning to go after him. Don't. His abduction is meant to draw you out." He reaches in his pocket, pulls out a flashscribe—what looks to be nothing more than a small black button. "After what you did during the last battle, our Generals fear you."

"They should! I'm bad to the bone. Or *good* to the bone."

He smiles and kisses the corner of my mouth, admiration glinting in those blue-gold eyes. "Yes, you are."

I snuggle closer. He pets my hair.

We touch as if we'll never get another chance.

My internal clock buzzes, and I stiffen. "I don't want you to go," I tell him, "but Deacon is headed this way and—"

A blaze of Light erupts in front of the door.

Too late. Deacon appears. He's dressed in black and armed for war. Fastened to him are a sword, spear and shield. He nods to Killian, then to me. Killian nods back.

I look from one to the other. "You guys are cool with each other?"

"We've...chatted." Deacon sits in the chair across from us. "Someone update me."

"Clay is alive." Killian relays the details he shared with me. "He's bait, and he won't be killed as long as Ten is alive." He motions to the flash-scribe. "You need to listen."

Trembling, I press the center of the device. At first, there's static and huffing, as if someone is running.

"We have the boy?"

"The speaker is the Prince of Ravens," Killian informs us. "One of his assistants gave me the flash-scribe, said he heard I had a thing for a Troikan girl. I think he was told to give me the flash-scribe. I think this is a test to find out what I'll do, maybe even an attempt to manipulate you through what you hear. But if what comes next is true, you need to know. You need to prepare."

The recording continues.

"Yes, sir."

"Excellent. Spread the word. Make sure the Conduit learns of his capture."

Footsteps. The click of a door being opened and closed.

The male who'd issued the orders speaks again. "Ready the troops. Every Messenger, Laborer and Leader. Keep the Conduit outside Troika. I want our people surrounding the realm by the end of the day. Block all Light. The weaker their people, the easier our victory."

The hate in his tone is just as clear as his words. This man…he taught Killian that victors are adored and failures abhorred, encouraged Killian to do anything—lie, steal and kill—to win a battle.

No wonder he named one of his sons Victor.

There's a rush of pounding footsteps. The door being opened and closed again.

"How many agents do we have inside Troika?"

"Nine."

"Excellent. Have them—"

The device goes quiet, revealing the hard rasp of my breathing.

Killian rubs my arm up and down. "If this is true… I'm sorry."

Zero! There could be more monsters walking among us. Evil cloaked in righteousness.

Overcome by urgency and uncertainty—a toxic mix—I fight the urge to curl into Killian's arms and check out. We need to act, but action without clear direction will get us nowhere fast.

"How do we know *you* aren't part of this?" Deacon grates, his jaw clenched. "How do we know you aren't setting us up for failure?"

Killian gazes at me, his expression grave. "You don't."

"*I* know," I insist. "I trust you. Always. You and I will rescue Clay. Deacon, you go home and warn our king of a possible attack. I'll return as soon as I can."

Killian shakes his head before I finish. "I told you, lass. There will be traps set specifically for you. *I'll* look for Clay. I can sneak attack. You can't. You are Light, and you can't hide anywhere. Your presence is a beacon."

"I hate to say this but he's right." Deacon stands. "I'll accompany Killian. You return to Troika. If we can't stop the attack, the people will need your Light."

Logic I cannot refute, no matter how badly I want to.

"I won't let anything happen to Clay," Killian vows, his arms tightening around me. "I will find him, and I will keep him safe."

During my Firstlife, Killian's actions led to Clay's First-death. He attacked Archer while we were racing down a snow-covered mountain, and it caused the avalanche that tossed Clay over a ledge.

Whether Killian admits it or not, he's not doing this for me. Not entirely. He is atoning for a crime his king once praised him for committing.

"I know you will." My chest constricts. We're both heading into dangerous situations. "If something happens to me—"

"*Nothing* will happen to you." He grips my shoulders to shake me. "You will fight, and you will survive. No other outcome is acceptable."

I kiss him hard, and I kiss him fast, Deacon momentarily forgotten. Killian kisses me back, his strength seeping into me, as if I'm drawing Light from him—because I am?

Yes! I am, and the realization stuns me. Despite his tie to Myriad, there *is* Light in him.

Light springing from his love for me?

Love is always the answer. Love never fails. Love is life.

I stop taking and start giving, fanning the flames. Just a little. Not too much. I don't want to overwhelm him or cause Torchlight.

When he hisses, I know I've pushed the boundaries as far as I can. I jump to my feet, ending the kiss, and punch in the code for Troika. I'm trembling.

He stands, a tower of menace and aggression, ready to raze his own world to save my friend, just because I asked.

Any wonder I love him? "You are amazing, Killian Flynn." I hold his gaze until the cabin vanishes around me.

I appear outside the Veil of Wings—and frown. The Light...where is the Light? Despite my urgency, I pause to gaze at the sky...and groan. There *will* be a battle. I'm too late to stop it. Dark shadows have fallen over the water. So many shadows, cast by Myriadian soldiers.

Life can change in a blink, going from bad to good, or good to bad, or anything in between. With combat on the horizon, everything in Troika is about to change. Lifeblood will be spilled, and people will die. *Innocents* will die.

Disregarding the burn of panic, I soar through the Veil. My necklaces bounce against my chest. I refuse to hide the one Killian gave me under my shirt any longer. We hide because we fear the opinions of others, the outcome or whatever big bad we think will happen. I'm done with that.

Today I fight. For one—for all.

chapter twenty-six

"Do not be pressured. There is no right or wrong, only what is within a thousand shades of gray."
—Myriad

I race through the first Gate, a Stairwell, then another Gate, exiting in the Capital of New—and finding utter chaos. Smoke billows around the buildings, thickening the air. The streets are congested with citizens running in a mad haze. I can't see through the masses. Nearly everyone is covered in soot, their clothes ripped and stained, Lifeblood trickling from different wounds.

"What happened?" I demand of the man slowly spinning in circles.

He ignores me, his gaze unfocused.

"Bombed," a sobbing woman tells me. "We've been bombed."

"Thomas! Thomas! Have you seen my son? Where's my son?"

"Matilda!"

Other cries ring out as I push my way through the crowd. *Jeremy.* I have to get to Jeremy. Myriadian spies have begun their attack, and even babies are fair game.

Up ahead, an injured little girl trips and falls. No one else notices her. She is going to be trampled.

I fight my way to her and, reaching her, sweep her into my arms. At the second of contact, my Troikan brand glows, the Grid ensuring my Light rushes into her. She gasps, the cuts on her face and chest beginning to knit together. All the while I continue moving forward.

I'm as grateful as I am amazed. I understand now. A Conduit is a vessel used to protect and route a substance into another vessel.

I carry her through the throng…but soon the masses part of their own volition, the people switching their focus to my Light. A chorus of frantic bellows suddenly quiets.

"Matilda!" A woman with tears wetting her cheeks rushes over to pull the little girl into her arms. "You're okay, you're okay."

The two embrace, the girl sobbing, "Momma, Momma. I'm so scared."

I face the crowd, suspecting I have but a moment to fan the flames of calm before fear once again takes hold. My gaze finds Winifred, Rebel, Clementine and Nico. And there is Sawyer with Fatima in his arms. Relief helps ground me. I'm so glad they're okay.

"Myriadian armies are here," I call. "They want us confused and panicked, so we'll be easier to pick off. Not all of you consider yourselves warriors, I know. Some of you work in the gardens and manna fields. Some of you make our clothes and clean our cities. But the heart of Troika beats within us all. Together, we are strong. Stay calm, stay smart. Guard our children. Do not give Myriadians what they want: our fear. We will find the ones who did this. We will prevail!"

I don't know if I've reached them. I leap back into motion and rush through a Stairwell. When I exit, I choke on smoke, my throat on fire. My eyes water. Still I sprint down the streets…

A dark haze opens, and I come upon General Tasanee and

General John working alongside Hazel and Steven to dig through what's left of the cathedral—rubble, only rubble. I cover my mouth with a trembling hand. Hazel spots me and cries out with joy. She nudges Steven, and the two rush over to hug me.

A knot grows in the pit of my stomach. The spies must have struck the Laborers first to take out our best fighters.

I try to concentrate on numbers to calm myself. The possible number of people inside versus the possible number of survivors.

The odds are poor.

No grief. Not here, not now. I'm needed.

"Help us," General Tasanee rasps. Her jet-black hair hangs in tangles around a soot-streaked face. Her leather catsuit is torn in multiple places.

"I've got to find my brother, Jeremy."

She nods her consent. I'm about to race off when Hazel grabs my wrist.

With tears in her eyes, she says, "We found Reed. He was... he... Kayla escorted him to the Sanatorium."

I tell myself Reed will heal. I tell myself we'll all heal. But I'm trembling as I run, run, my surroundings whizzing at my sides. I enter another Stairwell, braced for the worst. Thank the Firstking! The houses are still intact.

Boom!

The ground shudders, a gust of wind knocking me back, every molecule of air abandoning my lungs. I lumber onto unsteady legs, dark smoke rising in the distance...where Levi's house used to stand.

No. No, no, no.

I leap over an obstacle course of debris, my eyes burning, my chest boiling. When I reach the remains of Levi's home, I search the wreckage...there! Millicent, Jeremy's nanny. She's cut and bleeding, barely conscious, but she's alive.

"Jeremy," I rush out. "Where's Jeremy?"

"He w-wasn't here," she manages.

"Where is he? Please! Tell me where he is!"

"D-don't know. Sorry. So sorry." Her head lolls to the side, her eyes closing.

Guided by the Grid, I flatten my hand over her heart, and a ray of Light rushes into her.

Her eyelids flutter open, color quickly returning to her flesh. The Light...she's charging like a battery.

"Look out!" The warning comes from behind me.

There's no time to react. A hard weight slams into me, knocking me to the ground. I buck, and General Bahari rolls off me, an arrow lodged in her chest.

She...saved me?

She reaches for me, a silent plea for help...and then she begins to seize, her entire body shaking. Foam drips from the corner of her mouth. Poison?

Around us, Troikans are climbing free of the rubble and gathering their wits. We are unnoticed. I tremble as I yank out the arrow. She goes still, and I press my fist into the wound to staunch the flow of Lifeblood, at the same time unleashing a ray of Light.

Her eyes open and widen. I turn to see what she sees. A guy I've never met is racing toward us, notching a second arrow in his bow. He has no Light.

The arrow flies. Another guy jumps in front of me, shielding me—he is lit up like a Christmas tree. We weren't unnoticed, after all. With a grunt, Christmas drops. Just like the General, he seizes, his mouth foaming.

I remove the arrow, feed him a ray of Light and lumber to my feet, determined. No one else is taking a hit meant for me.

As I race forward...faster and faster...another arrow flies

my way. Got this. I unsheathe and twirl my swords, the arrow pinging and falling uselessly to the ground.

To my right, another guy races from the shroud of smoke, a spear in hand. He takes aim. His Light is faded—he's another of Myriad's spies. I dodge the spear and swing my arms, sparks of pure Light flinging from the ends of my swords, cutting through his chest.

I should feel triumphant. I just feel sad.

The other spy notches an arrow, but I duck, still running. Finally he's within reach. I slam my swords together, creating a staff—and slam the fiery end into his temple. He stumbles, and I hit him again, disorienting him before swiping his feet out from under him.

As he topples, I yank the staff apart. One of the hilts vibrates, ready, and when he lands, the tip is there to greet him, sliding deep into his chest. He shakes, like the General he nearly killed, before rivers of black swim through his veins, his flesh beginning to harden.

Only when his entire body is stone do I straighten. Again I entertain no triumph. I take no satisfaction in my actions, but I will accept no regret, either. Those who come into my house better mind their manners. These people are my family. I will protect them until my dying breath. If that means peace can never be reached, so be it. Not that I will ever stop trying.

Troikans do not try. They do.

I wipe my bloody mouth with the back of my hand, my gaze landing on Raanan, who snatches up the spy's weapon.

"What do you want me to do?" he asks me.

The entire realm shudders, the rubble at my feet banging together. A new chorus of screams erupts, a thicker wall of smoke billowing in the distance, rising to cover the sky and darken more of our precious Light.

Horror descends. Myriad wanted me to cleanse Dior and weaken. They wanted me helpless as they attacked my people. *One step ahead of me all along.*

"Ten! Ten!"

I spin and catch sight of Kayla, who is headed my way, pale hair flying behind her, a multitude of weapons strapped to her small body, metal swords banging against her legs with every step.

She's alive!

"Levi sent me to gather any Laborers who survived the blast. He's sending soldiers through the Veil of Wings to clear the armies outside our walls so Light can reach us." As she speaks, she tosses a weapon at anyone within reach.

I share what little Light I have left, guaranteeing everyone is steady.

"Go. Help the others," I say. "I'm searching for my brother."

Raanan pats my shoulder, and a spark of Light ignites between us. Not one created by me. He gasps. Is he... Could he be...?

The group rushes off, led by a fully recovered General Bahari.

"I know where Jeremy is," Kayla tells me.

Thank the Firstking! I'll consider Raanan's status later. "Take me to him." Maybe I shared too much Light. I'm weak, trembling, swaying on my feet. "Please."

"Come on." She heads in the opposite direction. "He's in the Tower of Might."

I follow, my relief potent and powerful. The deeper we go, the more shadows that descend over the watery sky, and my brands dull. Vibrations erupt in the back of my mind, telling me something's wrong.

"Kayla," I rasp as we approach the Gate.

She enters without pause. I trail behind, intending to grab her and retreat. Jeremy must have been moved, because—

Whack!

A spiked board smacks me in the face, and I career, nearly losing my grip on my swords. Dizziness and pain are instant and excruciating, Lifeblood washing over my eyes and coating my tongue.

Male laughter rings out. "That never gets old."

"Stop! Victor," Kayla cries. "You said she wouldn't be hurt."

Victor. *Of course.* But I have a hard time wrapping my head around the fact that Kayla set me up. That she helped him plan a mass destruction of innocents.

I blink in an effort to clear my vision. "Where's Jeremy?"

"He's fine," she assures me. "I put him in a bunker before...before..."

The first bomb went off, I finish for her. She did. She set me up and helped plan this. Betrayal nearly rips me in two.

Victor drops the board and palms a .44. "Surprise! Your good pal is out of hiding and better than ever." He waves, his hand almost fully regrown.

The realm shakes with great force, rattling my brain against my skull. Another bomb? I remain on the ground, feeling utterly defeated. First I loved and trusted Sloan, and she killed me. Then I loved and trusted Kayla, and she does this.

"How?" I croak.

She bows her head, radiating shame. "I'm sorry, Ten. I am. But I love him."

This isn't love, I want to scream. "He tried to kill me. Numerous times! In my apartment, he even tried to kill you."

"No," she says. "He only tried to weaken you. And he only wounded me, so no one would know I'd helped him. He did me a favor."

She can't be so foolish. She can't.

"Poor Ten." Victor smiles, smug. "Outsmarted and out-played."

"You want peace, Ten," Kayla continues, desperate to make me understand. "This is how we get it."

"This? *This?*" I shout. "You mean slaughtering innocents?"

"A few will die to save many," she rushes out. "Victor promised me. Your Light is going to be dimmed with Penumbra, and the realms will be on equal footing." Her gaze pleads with me to consent to my own downfall. "The fighting will stop."

Fool! "Light and dark cannot coexist." Archer and Killian have said the same to me on multiple occasions. "I can't be infected with Penumbra, only killed."

"No." She shakes her head, vehement. "Victor promised."

"Ten is right. At some point, we *are* going to kill her. But don't worry, baby. You won't be around to see it." He aims and fires, a bullet nailing her between the eyes.

"No!" I jump up. In that moment, I don't care what she's done or how terribly she's hurt me. I only want her to be okay.

I hurry to her side—or try to.

Victor fires at my feet, stopping me in my tracks. "Stay where you are."

"How could you hurt her?" I grate.

"Easily. She served her purpose. Now toss the swords in my direction."

I hesitate. There are no other Troikans nearby. None that I can see, anyway. They were called away to fight the threat outside.

Victor is smart. He knew exactly where to draw me.

Did the armies put more soldiers above this area, knowing he would lead me to it? Knowing I would need only a single ray of Light to start a conflagration?

I lick my lips and toss the swords…but only a few feet away from me.

Scowling, he stomps over to kick the blades behind him. While he's distracted, I reach up to rub my thumb against Killian's necklace. I know he can't get inside the realm, but maybe, just maybe, he can pinpoint my location and help clear the area above the Tower of Might.

I just have to keep Victor talking long enough for Killian to arrive.

"Why haven't you killed me already?" I ask. "Didn't you learn your lesson about letting me live?"

He smiles without humor. "I've decided to make covenant with you."

I snort-laugh. "Are you kidding? Why would I ever agree? Why would you *want* me to?"

"Why else? Power. With you on my side, the Prince of Doves will have no choice but to surrender to Myriad. The war will end, as you claim to desire, and I will take my rightful place in Troika. The new Secondking."

I would rather die. "You'll never have enough power to become king."

His comm glows, but he pays it no heed. "Choose, Ten. This is your only means of survival. And you want to survive, don't you? You want to continue fighting me, at the very least. To ensure you save your friends from my wrath."

Every decision matters. Every action has a consequence. What you sow, you will reap. As he deceived Kayla, he has deceived himself. "Love gives rather than takes. By saving myself, I would be condemning others. That, I won't do."

A minute beam of Light slips through the shadows above, shining a few feet in front of me. Killian is here!

Victor frowns and glances up at the sky.

Now! Heart hammering, I dive for the Light.

chapter twenty-seven

"A problem should never be the sole focus of your life."
—Troika

I land in the center of the beam, going from cold to hot in an instant, suddenly jacked up as if I've just been plugged in to a generator. The brand on my arm flickers once, twice... glows...and the Grid begins to buzz in the back of my mind.

First up: disarming Victor.

He plans to destroy Troika from the inside. He must be stopped.

As I straighten, he realizes his mistake—never lose track of your enemy. He adjusts his aim and squeezes the trigger, but I'm on a roll, literally, and the shot soars over my shoulder.

I swipe up my swords and come up swinging.

Boom, boom. The bullets whizz past me. I strike at him. We move in tandem, one of us attacking, the other dodging. I manage to drive him backward.

"You're not going to beat me." I *see* my victory playing along the Grid, leading my every action.

"Wrong. You're *already* beaten."

A lie. Just another in a long line.

In a single, fluid motion, he reloads his gun. Another bullet heads my way. I duck, beginning to detect a pattern to his movements, as if he's dancing to music I cannot hear. Step, step, duck left, duck right, fire. Step, step, duck.

Using my Light as fuel, I pick up the pace, changing the beat. I block and press my swords together. With a swipe of the staff, he falls to the side, but also fires another shot. He lands and leaps at me. I dart in the opposite direction, going low, as if I mean to knock his feet out from under him.

When he jumps, I jerk the staff up instead of down, hitting his calves to disrupt his balance. He falls again. I yank the staff apart and twirl a sword, cutting off his foot before he lands. Thud. He's on the ground, reaching for his spurting stump. I cut off his hand, the gun still in his grip.

He screams. I pivot around him...and remove his other hand.

His next scream makes a mockery of his first, Lifeblood pouring from all three wounds.

Determined to end this, I relock the swords and press the tip of the staff against the pulse at the base of his neck. A flame burns him.

"Mercy, mercy," he cries.

I'm panting, my heart pounding. This boy has caused me all kinds of problems. He has deceived me, hurt me, and killed my friends. If given the chance, he'll do it all again.

My heart weeps. *Allow him to live. Save the enemy, one at a time... As long as there's breath, there's hope.*

...but I'm tempted, so tempted to finish him. Death is what he deserves.

A thick beam of Light spreads over us, bright and warm. I glance up and exhale a breath I hadn't known I'd been holding. MLs are fleeing. Has Troika won?

"Mercy." Victor's voice weaker, his strength draining as quickly as his Lifeblood. "Mercy. Please, Ten."

"If the situation was reversed and I asked you for mercy, you would strike me down with a smile on your smug face."

But I am not him. My choice today defines who and what I am tomorrow.

He flinches, the truth of my words irrefutable.

I straighten, removing the tip of the staff from his pulse, adding, "I'm not going to kill you. I'm not your judge, and I'm not going to decide your punishment."

Footsteps sound in the distance. I spin, ignoring an influx of dread as I lift my weapon, prepared to battle.

A Troikan army rushes through the Gate, Levi at the helm.

Relief opens a floodgate, and tears fill my eyes. I pull the staff apart and sheathe the swords as I rush over to Kayla. She's unconscious, unmoving, but she has a pulse.

I push every bit of Light I can spare into her and shout, "Help her!" Victor is proof spirits are harder to kill than humans. I think...pray...she can recover from this.

Levi issues a series of orders. Three soldiers see to Kayla's care while another two deal with Victor. As both individuals are carted to the Sanatorium, I begin to tremble.

"Kayla told me Jeremy is safe," I say. If she lied...

"He is safe. I've seen him."

My knees give out, and I topple. My tears spill over and rain down my cheeks. "According to intel, there are—were—nine Myriadian spies in our realm," I tell Levi. "I killed two. Victor is the third."

"The Secondking can do what we can't, unearthing those who disabled their comms and locking them away until they can be questioned." He closes the distance and, with a quiet hiss, eases beside me. There's a wet spot on his rib cage, and it's growing, his Lifeblood hemorrhaging.

"You need Light, but I have none left," I say. "Why don't you go to the Sanatorium with the others."

"I'll go. Eventually. You'll be happy to hear we were also able to drive the enemy away...with Killian's help."

My heart skips a beat. He came through. After everything, he came through for me. He chose me, fighting his peers to save me.

I cry so hard I dry heave.

I want my arms wrapped around him. I want his heart beating against mine and his scent in my nose. I want his breath fanning my skin, branding me as effectively as the Troikan symbol. I want his lips pressed against mine.

I want to thank him.

"What about Clay?" I rip the hem of my shirt and press the material into Levi's side.

With another hiss, he takes possession of the cloth to maintain pressure on his wound. "Killian and Deacon found and freed him before joining the battle. Apparently there are Troikan sympathizers inside Myriad. Clay helped them fight outside the walls."

Killian kept his promise to me, finding my friend and bringing him home.

A promise kept is a star in the darkest of nights. A bridge between us. A bridge no one will ever be able to destroy.

I tell Levi everything that happened. Kayla's betrayal. Victor's plots and plans. Sadness fills his eyes.

"What will happen to Kayla? If she survives?" I ask. Punishment? Banishment?

"The Secondking will decide."

"And Victor? What will happen to him?"

"His covenant has been broken, his grace period over. He'll be banished. He wanted Myriad, he can have Myriad."

My hope is that he is haunted by the kindnesses shown to him today—and every day he lived here—that he realizes he lost a prize.

"Our realm…" I say.

Levi heaves a sigh. "We have much to rebuild."

Much is an understatement. "And the casualties?"

"I would say they are too numerous to count, but I'm sure you'll find a way."

I have no humor to spare. I dig my fingers into the ground, dirt sinking under my nails. "How was Myriad able to do this?"

"They distracted us with smaller battles in the Land of the Harvest, dividing our focus while launching a bigger battle on our own soil." He pauses, sighs again. "You did well today, Miss Lockwood. You saw past your emotions, putting the needs of others above your own wants. I'm proud of you."

A hard lump clogs my throat.

Through the Grid, a Light brighter than any other shines. My cells sizzle and snap with new life. Strength blooms inside me, a rose opening for the sun. I'm no longer slumped over but sitting up straight.

The princess! She is energizing me. No, not just me but all of us. Levi is sitting straighter, as well.

"One day," he says, "you will be able to do that. As for this…we will overcome. We have been knocked down, but we won't stay down." He stands and offers me a hand, helping me to my feet. "Today we salvage."

We take different Gates and Stairwells through the realm. The Capital of New, the Baths of Restoration and the House of Secrets sustained the most damage.

For the next several hours, we dig through the rubble, searching for survivors. The other Generals work alongside us, and so do the newbies. Old and young have come together as one.

The jagged rocks cut my hands, and I lose a couple of nails, but as we find survivors, my determination is renewed and I continue on. At some point, Deacon joins us. He's covered in soot and grime and there's a bruise on his jawline, but he's steady.

A little while later, someone taps my shoulder, startling me. I turn to find Clay and launch into his open arms. He hugs me tight, as if I'm the only life raft in the middle of a typhoon.

When we part, he chucks me under the chin. "Why didn't the two fours feel like eating dinner?"

How much do I love this boy! "Because they already ate. Sorry, I mean *eight*." I press my forehead against the center of his chest. "I'm happy you're alive and well."

He gives me another hug. "I wish you could have seen Killian. He swooped in, armed and dangerous. Slayed and took names. No one could stop him."

That's my guy.

A door opens in the Grid, and I see Archer's beautiful face. My tears return.

I whisper, "Today we will mourn, but new strength will be born. For those who have fallen, we will not be downtrodden. We will rise and we will shine, and in the sand we will draw a line. We will fight for what we believe, and to our hope we will cleave. Victory will be ours, and in the darkness, we will glitter like stars."

Archer offers me a sad smile.

Clay frames my face with his hands, lifting my head to kiss my temple. "The past is in the past, where it belongs, and the future awaits us…but there's something else we need to discuss."

Archer snorts. "Tell him he sucks."

I laugh and say, "Not bad."

"Thank you." Clay wipes a tear from my cheek. "I hunted you down to deliver a bit of good news. Kayla's awake, and she wants to see us."

While half of the Sanatorium is in perfect condition, the other half is destroyed. Triage tents have been set up around the rubble, Healers doing everything they can to save the injured.

Kayla has a gurney in back of the tent farthest from the others. She's propped up on a mound of pillows. The enclosure holds fourteen other patients, some missing limbs, some thrashing in pain.

War is never pretty.

Levi beat us here. He's sitting in a chair next to her bed, holding her hand. The two haven't noticed us; they're too focused on each other.

"Did I…did I lose my citizenship?" Her voice trembles. There's a bandage between her eyes, hiding her wound.

"No, Miss Brooks. You didn't lose your citizenship. You simply lost your way."

The words surprise me, even though part of me expected to hear them. Levi is the epitome of the Troikan way of life. He doesn't tell us the path to walk; he *shows* us. And this… this is what changes people for the better. Unconditional love.

A sob bubbles from her. "I'm so stupid. I never should have believed—" Her gaze lands on me, and she sobs again, sobs so hard she can no longer speak coherently.

Levi stands. Though his dark hair is in complete disarray,

he's wearing a clean shirt. He pats my shoulder as he passes me, and says, "Give compassion, receive compassion."

Then he's gone. I take his place at Kayla's bedside, and to my amazement, it's not resentment or anger I feel but pity and compassion. I could just as easily have been the one to turn on my friends. The only difference is, I placed my trust in someone deserving; she didn't.

"I'm so, so sorry," she chokes out.

"I forgive you," I say, and not because she's apologized. I forgive her because I refuse to give hate a place in my life. Hate carried Victor to his disastrous end. Hate drove Myriad to attack a realm where innocent children played.

She only sobs harder.

On the other side of her bed, Clay pulls up a chair. "Enough blubbering like a baby." His tone is stern and unbending. Un-Clay-like. "You made a mistake. Who hasn't? Use the mistake as a tutor, learn from it, and move on."

"P-people died." She wipes at her tears with trembling hands. "I helped kill... I'm a *murderer.*"

"Yes," I say. "You are." It's true. There's no denying it, no coating it with sugar. "But don't stay in here and wallow. Get out there and help the people you hurt."

Reed joins us, squeezes my hand. "Victor and the other Myriad supporters would have found a way to attack us even without you." A bandage covers his left eye and there's a gash on his neck. "I just wish you'd come to me, told me what you were planning. I could have talked some sense into you."

She sobs again. I let her cry it out, and as the minutes turn into hours, I doze on and off in my seat. I'm aware of people coming and going, but don't snap to full attention until Deacon peeks his head through a slit in the tent. Our gazes meet, his expression grim; he motions me outside. I stand a little too quickly, bid the others a hasty goodbye and rush out.

As soon as I'm standing in front of him, he says, "Despite the attack, Dior's day in court has kicked off."

You've got to be kidding me. "We should reschedule. Just for another day. Levi needs rest, not stress." We all do!

"In the chaos, we missed the deadline to reschedule. To postpone now is to lose."

I rub the back of my aching neck. "So what do we do?"

"The warehouse where Shells are made still stands. Now we collect a Shell, go to the Courthouse and offer what support we can."

chapter twenty-eight

"Focus all your energy on your problem until it's solved."
—Myriad

I'm a jumble of apprehension as I enter the courtroom, Deacon at my side. The room has to be at maximum occupancy, Myriadians on one side and Troikans on the other. As the doors close behind us, emitting a high-pitched squeak, every eye darts to us.

The proceedings—which are already in session—pause. Quiet reigns.

Game face on.

I lift my chin as I move deeper into the chamber. Javier is seated on the front bench of Troika's side. He's got his own game face on, hiding the thoughts rattling inside his head.

Because Deacon and I are encased in Shells, Javier can see and feel us. Deacon sits next to him and gives him a little push to make room for me at the edge, Deacon remaining a buffer between us.

Javier's hands are wrapped over his knees, his knuckles white. Well. There's a hint of his thoughts, after all. He's petrified.

His infection reacts to my presence, the veins of black writhing. The Grid buzzes, irritated by our close proximity. Light spills through me, lining every inch of me to create a barrier.

I skim the faces of other spectators—

My gaze collides with Killian's, my heart nearly kicking down my ribs in an effort to escape my chest and get to him. He's sitting with Sloan on Myriad's side. He gives me an almost imperceptible nod.

Why did he come? To see me? Or Dior? He has to know she'll take one look at him and be more determined to side with Troika.

My spine suddenly snaps straighter, as if it's been strapped to a board. He's here for us both, isn't he?

Brilliant boy. *My boy.*

I'm not sure I'll ever have the words to thank him for everything he's done for me. I just hope he sees the gratitude and love in my eyes.

Concern and longing stare back at me. I force myself to look away and nod at Sloan. She offers me a wobbly smile.

The proceedings resume, and much like the other case, the judge's chair is centered on the dais at the back of the room. Dior sits next to him, and Levi sits next to her. He's in a Shell and draped in a pale blue robe.

The same Myriadian Barrister who presided over the last case presides over this one—and he's doing a great job. Dior is already crying, scenes from her life playing over the walls. He makes sure to emphasize the many times she allowed a Troikan loyalist to be hurt or killed, simply to avoid being punished.

"You're selfish," he says, his tone harsh. "Yes, you made covenant to help your father, but in doing so, you hurt so many others. I know, I know. You've stated your defection will allow you to help others—to help Troikans. Do you truly believe those Troikans want your help? How many times did you allow their brethren to *die* simply to save yourself from castigation?"

She keeps her gaze downcast, as if she can't bear to face the crowd. "I don't... I don't know."

I stifle a moan. *Come on. Get your head up! Resist self-loathing and forgive yourself.*

As the footage continues to play, hour after hour, and the Barrister continues to berate her, her shoulders sink in and her head dips lower.

When the recordings finally end, he slams his hand on the wooden bar between them, leans in and shouts, "This man, Levi Nanne, claims he knows everything you've done and wants you to be part of his realm, anyway. Do you think it's possible he wants you there simply to get revenge? And what of the others? Your actual victims. They live there. Do you think they want to see your face every day? They must hate you."

The unexpected suddenly happens. Around me, one after the other, Troikans stand and speak.

"I forgive you."

"I forgive you."

On and on, until they've all spoken. And I think... I think they are the very people the Barrister mentioned. The ones she allowed to suffer and die.

Her head begins to lift at last.

The Barrister sneers. "Pretty words. And maybe they're true—but maybe they aren't."

"They are true," Levi announces, jolting me. "I won't speak for you, Barrister, as you've attempted to speak for me, and

I won't claim to know what *you* see when you look at Miss Nichols. I will only state what I know to be true. Everyone in this courtroom has made mistakes, in Firstlife and in Everlife. None of us can cast stones. When I look at Miss Nichols, I see a woman with great potential. A woman with a heart that beats with kindness. A woman I will be proud to call family."

I want to stand and cheer.

The Barrister blusters, but it isn't long before he regains his equilibrium. "I'd like to present to the court a statement made by Miss Nichols's boyfriend, Javier Diez, this very morning."

The crowd quiets, tension thickening. And yet, Javier relaxes in his seat, *his* tension gone. He expected this, whatever it is—he wants it to happen.

My gaze meets Levi's. He gives an almost undetectable shake of his head. He has no idea what's coming, either.

The Barrister points to a spot on the wall, where new footage plays. In it, Javier is speaking to Dior. "We can be happy in Myriad. We can have the life you once claimed to want. My covenant will make provision for you, ensuring you're able to practice medicine for the rest of your Firstlife—on anyone— without consequence. If you defect to Troika, they'll insist you practice only on Troikans. You know they will. You'll be in the same situation, only you'll be stuck, with no way out."

In the video, he caresses her temple, and I stiffen. Does no one else see the shadow he left on her skin? An oily residue now absorbing onto her pores.

Did he…infect her? Without the possession of a Myriadian General?

I can't allow this. "He's wrong. He's *so* wrong," I call. "Don't listen to his lies."

"Order," the judge demands.

In the present, Javier stands and says, "I accept the covenant offered by Myriad. I pledge my allegiance to Myriad."

Gasps abound through the crowd, some of shock, some of glee.

Dior ducks her head, and my nails cut into my palms. I meet Levi's gaze, and this time he offers me a small smile. A sad smile. He's expecting the worst from this point.

"I said order!" *Bang, bang.*

I want to fall apart, to scream and to rage. To hug Levi and shake Dior. "Remember the Light."

Bang, bang, bang.

—*Prepare yourself, Miss Lockwood.*— Levi's voice whispers through the Grid.

"Javier," Dior whispers. "I can't. They helped me. I don't want to get sick again. I want—"

"If you defect today," he tells her, his tone cajoling, "we'll be enemies. I won't be able to help you. You have to trust me, baby. I'm doing what's best for us. I'm doing what's best for *you*. I know you hope you can one day see your first love again. But your father is in Myriad, and he needs you. My contract provides for him, as well. On the condition you drop this trial."

She closes her eyes, tears catching in her lashes. In that moment, I see the shadows whirling underneath her skin. My stomach churns. She *is* infected. The disease has spread. The beginning of a pandemic?

"I'm sorry, Levi. I'm so sorry, Ten," she says. "But I'm... I'm withdrawing my request to defect. I choose to remain with Myriad."

Those on Myriad's side cheer. Horror rips through me because I know what she doesn't. A ransom must be paid—in Lifeblood.

"No!" I leap to my feet.

Deacon grabs my wrist, holding me in place. By the time I wrench free, Killian is at my side. He wraps his strong arms around me, his grip a shackle.

"There's nothing you can do, lass. I'm sorry."

I struggle against him, determined to reach Levi, to protect and shield the General who has so often protected and shielded me. I remained chained to him.

"Let me go!" Levi doesn't deserve to die. He's done nothing wrong and everything right. He's a good man, and as I'm learning, there are too few of those. "Now, Killian."

"I'm sorry," he rasps.

Levi stands, his head as high as I'd wanted Dior's to be. He approaches the Barrister, who is given a blade.

"Kneel," the Barrister says with a cold smile.

Levi only raises his head higher. "You are not my king. You have no power over me but that which I willingly grant you. I gladly die for the chance to help Dior Nichols."

"No," I scream, bucking and kicking to gain my freedom. "Please! Don't do this!"

Killian only tightens his hold, nearly crushing my bones. A warm tear splashes onto my cheek, but it's not my own.

—*Levi! You have to run. Okay? All right?*— I throw the words across the Grid.

He offers me another small smile. —*I have no regrets, Miss Lockwood. I will enter into the Rest knowing I did everything I was meant to do. I helped my realm to the best of my ability. I died to give a human Light, whether she accepted it or not. So let my Lifeblood spill. Let it speak throughout the ages to come. Let it say darkness may win a battle but goodwill always wins the war. And you…forgive her and fight for what's right. Let nothing stop you.*—

"Wait. Wait!" Dior shouts as Javier leaps over the bar to reach her. "What's happening? Why do you have a knife?"

The Barrister's smile widens—he strikes.

The blades slashes through Levi's throat. Slashes through Shell and spirit alike.

"Noooo!" I break free of Killian at last and bound over the bar to throw myself into the Barrister, knocking him to the floor. Fury and grief have gained control of me, and they use my fists to punch his horrible face.

He's not smiling now. No, he isn't smiling now.

Strong arms fetter my waist and wrench me backward. Again I punch and kick to regain my freedom.

—*Stop...stop, Miss Lockwood... Ten...*—

Levi's voice penetrates my awareness. The guard who grabbed me releases me when Killian punches him. I dive down, skidding across the floor to reach Levi's side and take his hand.

I fight sobs. —*We can get you to a Healer.*—

—*A life for a life. The price must always be paid. You know this.*—

"No. No!" I shake my head as I gather him close, intending to lift him. I'll carry him if I must. But I'm not strong enough, not right now, and all I can do is hold him and cry. "Not yours. Never yours."

His Lifeblood soaks me. It's so beautiful, glittering like diamond dust.

—*I will live on.*—

"In the Rest." I choke on another sob. "I know. I know I'll see you through the Grid, but that's not good enough. I need you in Troika. I need you with me. You're not done with my training. There's so much more you need to teach me. And what about Jeremy? Levi, you can't leave him. He needs you, too."

—*I will be with you both, always. In your hearts, I'll be with you.*—

Not just ours, but every heart he's ever touched. To so many, he's been like a rainbow after a storm.

He gifts me with another smile, this one slow, the sadness gone. —*Until we meet again.*—

"No!" My voice cracks at the edges. "You can't do this."

The Light fades from his eyes, and his head lolls to the side. I dry heave.

He's dead. He's dead and gone, his spirit transported into the Rest. I thought the worst was over. I had no idea the worst was actually on the horizon.

"I didn't know. You have to believe me, Ten, I didn't know this would happen..." Dior drops to her knees and frantically pats Levi's face. "I'm sorry, I'm so sorry. Levi! You didn't tell me. Why didn't you tell me?"

Javier jerks her to her feet.

My gaze locks on him and narrows. I've lost too many people lately; I've forgiven too many crimes. Here, now, I'm broken. I'm nothing but shattered pieces.

"You." I point at him. One decision can change everything. In a single second, your entire world can shift. The things we say, the things we do...we affect everyone around us. "*You* are responsible for this."

A flush of shame darkens his cheeks, and yet he never stops tugging at Dior toward the door, eager to escape the poisonous fruit of his labors. "I did what was right for her."

"*Liar.* You did what *you* wanted, not what she needed."

In the stands, hostilities bubble over, even as Sloan attempts to be a voice of calm.

"Walk away. This isn't the place—"

Troikans and Myriadians charge each other. They might be weaponless, but they have fists and they aren't afraid to use them.

"Order! Order!" the judge shouts from his podium.

No one listens. Once again, strong arms wrap around me. Killian drags me through the crowd. Deacon remains at his side, ensuring no one is able to harm me. Once we clear the room, the boys pick up speed and hurry out of the building, down the steps and to the Gate that leads to Troika.

I stop struggling, knowing I'm not doing anyone any favors. Least of all Levi.

"I wish I could go with you." Killian reluctantly hands me over to Deacon. He traces his knuckles along my jawline. "After today, I'll have to go into hiding. I'll have to find a way into Many Ends from the fringes. But when you're ready, summon me. I'll come. I'll always come. I love you. Never forget."

My heart squeezes, trapped in a vise-grip, but I'm too broken to respond.

As Deacon ushers me through the Gate, my fingers trail from Killian's, my gaze staying hooked with his until the last possible second. Then he's gone, and I'm stepping through the Veil of Wings to enter Troika, where I'm greeted by the same devastation I left.

When will the heartache end?

News of Levi's death has already spread, everyone Deacon and I pass bawling. Most people knew him as a General, a warrior who helped save spirits and humans alike. An icon. A symbol of Light.

I knew him as a friend.

Hopeful glances find me, and part of me withers. I'm not

the answer to their problems. I'm not as strong as I thought I was. I'm just a girl torn and shattered by the ravages of war. I'm the defeated one. The loser. The failure. Abhorred...by myself.

Even as Light shines over me, I am surrounded by darkness.

Love is not the answer
How could anyone believe that
Love empowers!
Hate
Is the true treasure and far better than
Love
Hate allows you to do what's necessary for victory,
    and victory is the source of your happiness.
Never allow yourself to be convinced that
Love is not a weakness
The truth is
Love is an anchor that holds you down
Be wise, and refuse to believe the biggest lie of all:
Love gives you wings and makes you soar.

A woman steps into my path, stopping me. I know her. Brigitte's mother. Smiling, she grabs my hands; she's the only bit of happiness amid the gloom. "Thank you. Thank you!"

I simply blink at her.

"Brigitte signed with Troika this morning!"

My brow furrows with confusion. "Why?" I don't understand. I spoke to her once, only once.

"Whatever you said kept her thinking. She couldn't escape your words and finally visited a TL stationed in Paris. They spoke at length. She left crying but returned a few hours later to make her pledge."

"That's wonderful," I say, only sounding more depressed.

I pull from her hold, pull from Deacon's hold and run... I run, and I don't look back.

I end up in the scorched manna fields, my heart pounding. No matter how far I go, I can't escape my problems.

I stop and press my fists into my temples as I look up at the water-sky and scream. I scream until my lungs empty, and my voice breaks. I scream with all the rage trapped inside me. I scream with agony I'm not sure I'll survive, and helplessness I despise with every fiber of my being.

We have been knocked down, but we won't stay down.

Levi's words are beautiful and uplifting. And yet I still cannot see the Light.

"I fought for what was right, and I failed. Where is my justice?" I shout to no one. To everyone.

"Justice comes, its wings steady and sure." The soft voice drifts from a room in the Grid. "Though it doesn't always come on our timetable."

I close my eyes and see a woman clad in a white robe. She—Princess Mariée—stands in a doorway, regarding me with eyes free of tears but filled with...joy?

"Levi lived a good life," she says. "He achieved great victories and will enjoy great peace."

"Agreed, but I can't see past the sorrow of his loss."

"Why? He isn't lost. We know exactly where he is. And one day, we will join him."

But *one day* isn't *now.* "Why can't we enjoy peace *here*? Or, if we must fight, why can't we fight to free the spirits trapped in

Many Ends?" Killian's proposal—making covenant with each other—burns through my mind. Perhaps it's our only way in.

"You can't make peace with a monster. When you try, you only deceive yourself. You leave yourself vulnerable to attack. And there will be attacks. They will be subtle rather than overt, and that is where true danger lies. Victor is the perfect example of this."

"The monster. You speak of Ambrosine."

"And those like Victor and Javier, who want nothing to do with the truth."

"But shouldn't we try to reach those people? We say we love. So let's put action to word. Let's love our enemy and help even those who have hurt us."

"You've seen what happens when we fail." She spreads her arms wide, whether to indicate the barren field, or the pain arching through the Grid, I'm not sure. "You see here and now. I see the future."

Does she mean that literally? "Let's forge a new path," I say, and my grief begins to lessen, leaving room for determination.

For a long while we simply stare at each other. Then she lifts her hand, a light glowing at the end of her index finger. She traces that finger around each of my eyes, imprinting warmth into my skin, almost as if she's created an invisible pair of glasses.

"We Troikans are of one body...one heart," she says. "The Secondking has decided you will be our mouth and speak for us. You will choose who will be released from the Rest."

"No." I shake my head. "The decision should not be mine." The pressure!

"And yet, the decree has been issued. In two days, you will choose."

"But the people...the Generals. They must be upset about this."

"Their reaction is not your concern. Go now," she says. "You have many choices to make. Do what you see is good and right."

I gulp. "And if I'm wrong?"

"We will all pay the price."

Do what you see is good and right.
What you see.

The words reverberate through my mind as I set a course for the Urals—for my special cave—and summon Killian.

The moment he arrives, he pulls me into his arms. Though we've been parted for only a short time, I feel as if forever has passed. I return his embrace with equal fervor.

He lifts my face, his gaze searching. With his thumbs, he caresses the rise of my cheekbones. "There's still darkness in yer eyes, lass. I much prefer the Light."

"So much has gone wrong." I clutch the collar of his shirt. "So many people have died."

"That is the way of the world."

"But it shouldn't have to be." I rest my head in the hollow of his neck. "I'm supposed to choose who's released from the Rest. Me alone. But who do I bring back? Archer? My grandmother? Levi? Elizabeth? Another Conduit? I had begun to think the Conduit was the answer, but I think Conduits can be made, like Abrogates." I haven't forgotten the spark I shared with Raanan.

"Peace is your goal, lass. Bring back the one who will help you achieve it."

He makes it sound so easy.

He kisses me then, and I welcome him eagerly, losing my-

self in the moment…losing myself in him, in all that he is—
the boy I love, the boy who loves me back. His hands slide
down the ridges of my spine while I cling to him. All the
while his scent and taste remake me into something—someone—new. I'm no longer Ten, the Conduit who stands alone.
I'm Ten, one girl forged by two, with the heart of her entire
realm beating in her chest.

When Killian lifts his head, we are both trembling.

His gaze remains hot on mine as he whispers, *"An té a
luíonn le madaí, eiroidh sé le dearnaid."*

The Grid translates. *He who lies down with dogs, gets up with
fleas.* A little laugh escapes me. "Not exactly the romantic
words I dreamed of hearing."

"They should be. I'm no longer going to lie down with
dogs," he says. "I'll lie down with the treasure of my heart."

I melt. And then I gape at him. "You're going to defect,
now rather than later." I lick my lips, nervous energy over-
taking me. Court won't be pretty for either of us.

"I am."

"Ar scáth a chéile a mhaireann na daoine," I tell him.

Under the shelter of each other, people survive.

He smiles at me, and I give him a swift kiss.

"Killian," I say on a wispy catch of breath. "My answer
is yes."

His hold on me tightens. "You mean…"

"I mean, yes." I nod. "Yes, I will make covenant with you."

Shock registers, then pleasure. Then his own bout of nervousness. He cups my face with his big, calloused hands, his
thumbs once again brushing over the rise of my cheeks.

"You're sure, lass? I'm now being hunted by my own people. I can get inside Myriad, but the moment I pass through
our Veil, I'll be met with resistance."

"We can sneak me inside and we can overcome any resistance together."

Together, we can find a way into the Kennels and Many Ends. We can save the people being tortured. Maybe, just maybe, we can dethrone Ambrosine and finally usher in peace between the realms.

"You're sure?" he asks again.

"I'm sure," I say with a nod.

A radiant smile lifts the corners of his lips. "Then let us begin."

"Victory comes one day at a time."
—Ten Lockwood

MYRIAD

From: S_A_5/46.15.33
To: K_F_5/23.53.6
Subject: Penumbra

I know you're in hiding, Killian. I know you're in trouble. But you have to come back to Myriad. After Dior's court appearance, I overheard something I shouldn't have. We knew the Penumbra had begun to spread but we didn't know our realm had found a way to mass-produce the infection. Thousands of humans are going to be affected—and soon.

Killian, please! You have to come back. I can't fight this alone.

ML-in-training,
Sloan Aubuchon

MYRIAD

From: Mailer-Erratum
To: S_A_5/46.15.33/K_F_5/23.53.6
Subject: THIS MESSAGE HAS BEEN DEEMED UNDELIVERABLE

Report to Zhi Chen for debriefing.

★ ★ ★ ★ ★

Thank you for reading LIFEBLOOD!
Change can begin with just one person...and one spark
can ignite a conflagration.
Killian and Ten's new bond will be tested. Myriad will strike
as Troika rebuilds.
Who will emerge victorious, and who will be left in the rubble?

Turn the page to read an excerpt from EVERLIFE,
book three of the EVERLIFE novels.
Only from Gena Showalter and Harlequin TEEN!

TROIKA

From: A_T_3/23.40.29
To: L_R_3/51.3.15, J_A_3/19.37.30, S_C_3/50.4.13, C_M_3/5.20.1,
Y_L_3/59.1.2, A_S_3/42.6.31, T_B_3/19.30.2, B_S_3/51.3.13,
M_V_3/54.5.8, J_B_3/19.23.4, S_J_3/62.5.5, M_P_3/45.10.9
Subject: Tenley Lockwood

Fellow Generals,
We have two orders of business to discuss. The first: animals. Because of the recent bombings inside our realm, our Secondking has issued a decree. Every citizen will be appointed a guardian, whether four-legged or winged. However, we all have the right to decline. I suggest you do so, and encourage your people to do the same. We haven't trained with these animals. There's a good chance they'll be more of a hindrance than a help.

The second order of business is the most important. For the first time in our realm's history, the Prince of Doves has decided NOT to hold a vote for the Resurrection. I don't know why, only know protests will not change his mind. Instead, Tenley Lockwood is tasked with selecting which of our fallen soldiers will leave the Rest.

No doubt she plans to choose one of the following (in order of rank):

General Levi Nanne, her trainer

Leader Meredith Cordell, her grandmother

Laborer Archer Prince, her friend

Laborer Elizabeth Winchester, her teammate

We have twenty-four hours to plead the case of our revered brother, General Orion Giovante. While I love and respect the others, Orion is the one we need. The war with Myriad is heating. We are outnumbered and outgunned, and Orion is a warrior among warriors, our greatest hope for victory. He has what Levi doesn't: a killer instinct. Toward the end, Levi softened. He worked with Killian Flynn, known by our Laborers as the Butcher. Mr. Flynn is also Miss Lockwood's biggest weakness. Their romantic relationship puts us all at terrible risk.

Orion will deliver Mr. Flynn's Second-death without pause or concern for Miss Lockwood's feelings. He will help us focus on the only thing that matters: Myriad's annihilation.

First, we must find Miss Lockwood. Second, we must convince her to do what will help us but hurt her. For some reason, I'm unable to find her in the Grid.

Jane, do you see her in the Eye?

Light Brings Sight!
General Alejandro Torres

TROIKA

From: J_A_3/19.37.30
To: A_T_3/23.40.29, L_R_3/51.3.15, S_C_3/50.4.13, C_M_3/5.20.1,
Y_L_3/59.1.2, A_S_3/42.6.31, T_B_3/19.30.2, B_S_3/51.3.13,
M_V_3/54.5.8, J_B_3/19.23.4, S_J_3/62.5.5, M_P_3/45.10.9
Subject: Foolish girl!

Miss Lockwood has disabled her comm. Does she *want* Myriad to kill her?

Worry not. I'll find her. I just need time.

General Shamus, gather your army and await further word at the Veil of Wings. The moment I've located Miss Lockwood, I'll transport you to her side.

Light Brings Sight!
General Jane Adamson
PS: I have rejected my guardian

TROIKA

From: S_C_3/50.4.13
To: J_A_3/19.37.30, A_T_3/23.40.29, L_R_3/51.3.15, C_M_3/5.20.1,
Y_L_3/59.1.2, A_S_3/42.6.31, T_B_3/19.30.2, B_S_3/51.3.13,
M_V_3/54.5.8, J_B_3/19.23.4, S_J_3/62.5.5, M_P_3/45.10.9
Subject: I'll be ready

However, I doubt I'll be gentle. But then, I have a feeling "gentle" isn't necessary or even desired. Why else would you assign the Brute to retrieve her? You'd like someone to teach her the error of her ways, perhaps even scare her into doing what we desire.

Consider it done.

Light Brings Sight!
General Shamus Campbell
PS: I was appointed a guardian poodle. You did not misread. I said POODLE. If you want to be insulted on my behalf, feel free. I turned her down—of course.

TROIKA

From: L_R_3/51.3.15
To: S_C_3/50.4.13, J_A_3/19.37.30, A_T_3/23.40.29, C_M_3/5.20.1,
Y_L_3/59.1.2, A_S_3/42.6.31, T_B_3/19.30.2, B_S_3/51.3.13,
M_V_3/54.5.8, J_B_3/19.23.4, S_J_3/62.5.5, M_P_3/45.10.9
Subject: I'll go with you, Shame-us

And I'll hear no protests on the matter. Anger has clouded your judgment; it is Myriad, not Troika, that deals in fear. Also, if we punish the girl, we risk alienating her. We cannot make her feel as though she has no allies, otherwise she'll vote for someone other than the General she's never had the privilege of meeting.

Do us all a favor and think before you speak, General Campbell.

Light Brings Sight!
General Luciana Rossi
PS: I was assigned a grizzly bear. Suck it.

TROIKA

From: S_C_3/50.4.13
To: L_R_3/51.3.15
Subject: Admit it

Your concern isn't for the girl or even our great realm. You've always lusted for Orion, and you'll do anything to bring him back—even pander to a Conduit too ignorant to pick a good decision in a lineup.

I'm sure Orion's wife will thank you for your efforts, eh. Or not. Yeah, probably not.

If ever YOU stop acting like a Myriadian and want to tup an *un*attached male, all you have to do is beg me. I'll do the dishonors, you have my word.

Light Brings Sight!
General Shame-on-you
PS: I guess Eron thinks you need a stronger guardian… because you are weaker.

MYRIAD

From: S_A_5/46.15.33
To: K_F_5/23.53.6
Subject: Penumbra

I know you're in hiding, Killian. I know you're in trouble. But you have to come back to Myriad. After Dior's court appearance, I overhead something I shouldn't have. We knew the Penumbra had begun to spread but we didn't know our realm had found a way to mass-produce the infection. Thousands of humans are going to be affected—and soon.

Killian, please! You have to come back. I can't fight this alone.

Might Equals Right!
ML-in-training,
Sloan Aubuchon

MYRIAD

From: Mailer-Erratum
To: S_A_5/46.15.33, K_F_5/23.53.6
Subject: THIS MESSAGE HAS BEEN DEEMED UNDELIVERABLE

Report to Zhi Chen for debriefing.

MYRIAD

From: Z_C_4/23.43.2

To: S_A_5/46.15.33

Subject: Your loyalty is rivaled only by your stupidity

Your devotion to Killian Flynn would be admirable, if he hadn't made the grave mistake of siding with a Troikan and disgracing his realm. The moment he's found, he'll be placed in the Kennels or killed. There are no other options.

Get your priorities straight, Miss Aubuchon, or you'll join him, whatever his fate.

Now, on to more pleasant news. I'm assigning you a mentor to help steer you in the right direction. His name is Victor Prince, and he's an exalted son of our Secondking.

Years ago, Victor made covenant with Troika in order to spy for us. Just last night, he managed the impossible. He defected and returned to our midst without having to go to court. Unfortunately, he lost both hands in the process.

Side note: As new as you are, you might not know spirits regenerate limbs. In time.

Until Mr. Prince is whole again, he'll remain inside a Shell. You'll remain inside one, as well, since he is now responsible for your training. Yours, and your new partner's, who is rising through our ranks. His name is Leonard Lockwood, and he is Tenley Lockwood's father.

I know you'll treat him with respect, because you know what will happen if you don't.

Might Equals Right!
Sir Zhi Chen

MYRIAD

From: H_S_3/51.3.6
To: Z_C_4/23.43.2
Subject: Javier Diez and Dior Nichols, among other things

Yo! I heard from one of our queens, who heard directly from our Secondking. Ambrosine wants the spirits of Jaiver Diez and Dior Nichols in Myriad, el pronto. No more waiting. Find someone to do the honors. I'm busy managing a warehouse full of ticking time bombs.

Speaking of, I flagged all messages about this particular topic, and came across one sent by a Laborer under your command. Sloan…something. Abadabado? Whoever she is, send her my way. I'm ensuring Troikans find the warehouse later today. Considering she's a sympathizer, she'll make excellent bait.

You might be willing to pardon her for her loyalty to Killian, but I am not. She can no longer be trusted, but she can be used.

Get ready. The war is about to take a drastic turn—for our better!

Might Equals Right!
General Hans Schmidt

chapter one

"Life isn't about what you gain; it's about what you give."
—Troika

Ten
Present day

I peer up at the indomitable Killian Flynn, my heart thudding against my ribs. Every breath I take fills me with hope, wonder...and dismay.

Our relationship is about to change. *Everything* is about to change.

Earlier we snuck out of our realms to meet in the Land of the Harvest. A secret cave in Russia's Ural Mountains, to be exact. Now we stand face-to-face, hand in hand. Jagged rocks create the perfect frame for Killian's wild, ravaging beauty and the unwavering strength he wields. Strength forged on the bloodiest of battlefields.

There's no other warrior I'd rather have at my side.

Our people might be at war, but we are going to usher in peace. One step at a time.

I drink him in, this boy I'm trusting with my present—and my future. His skin is a magnificent shade between bronze and gold while his hair is jet black. His eyebrows are thick, masculine, and his nose sharp as a blade. His mouth is soft and lush. Pure temptation…

A shadow of a beard dusts his triangular jaw. Under his T-shirt and jeans, his deliciously muscled body is covered in tattoos. Skulls, stars, roses and other images, all connected by lines, creating some sort of map. That map appears on both his spirit and his Shell—an outer casing made to resemble a spirit—but he's never told me where it leads.

One day, he'll share all. We both will.

But it is his eyes that draw me in and hold me captive. His eyes are soulful gold with flecks of electric blue. Always those flecks strike a chord inside me, different songs piercing my soul. Some are fast and erratic, eliciting passion, while others are slow and dreamy; always they are haunting.

Today I hear a seductive melody that sets my blood aflame *and* chills me to the bone. Makes sense. I am fire, he is ice, yet we fit. After all, the warmth of a fire is best enjoyed on a frigid winter's day.

So many differences. Too many, most would say.

Just enough to rock the entire world.

I am day. He is night.

I strengthen in Light. He is unrivaled in darkness.

I like rules, structure. He thrives in chaos.

I believe our worst emotions should never dictate our actions; we should help, forgive and care for others. Emotions are fleeting, after all, and subject to change. Why let one ruin your life? He believes emotion should drive us every moment of every day, and caring for others is foolish. Those you help now will stab you in the back later.

To me, today's choices dictate tomorrow's reality. To him, Fate decides for us.

I'm a Troikan Conduit. He's a Myriadian Laborer. We are Lifeblood-born enemies, and yet he is the love of my Everlife.

As different as we are, we are also the same. Painful pasts shaped us, made us stronger. We hold on tight whenever something—or someone—threatens the people and things we love. We fight for what we believe is right, no matter the obstacles in our way.

I'm one of only two Conduits responsible for lighting Troika, and I'm supposed to kill Killian, our enemy. I'm going to marry him, instead.

Chemistry doesn't care about expectations. I love and adore this boy, and I hold on tight, remember?

Even if I despised him, I would say "I do." There's more at stake than our hearts.

Once we unite our spirits, we will have the opportunity to unite our realms and facilitate the peace we so desperately crave. Together, we will enter Myriad and slay Ambrosine, Prince of Ravens. The realm's corrupt Secondking.

A corrupt leader corrupts his people absolutely.

Then Killian will take the crown, and command, and order his armies to stand down. He will accept the truce Troika once offered. A truce Eron, Prince of Doves and the Second-king of Troika, has wanted for centuries.

Finally the war will end.

Once that is accomplished—or maybe before, we haven't decided on an order yet—we will save the poor souls trapped inside Many Ends, the hellish sub-realm connected to Myriad.

Many Ends is home to the Unsigned who experience First-death, as well as monstrous beings with a single goal: *kill every-one*. Spirits are hunted and killed in the most horrific ways. Again…and again. Because, once a spirit "dies" in Many Ends, it comes back to life, ready for round two…three…four…

Four, the number for stability, order and justice. A strong foundation, considering there are four sides in a square. Four cardinal directions—north, south, east, west. Four seasons to complete a year—winter, spring, summer, fall. Four winds, and four phases of the moon.

Four is the only numeral spelled with the same amount of letters as its numerical value.

Focus. I *believe* the spirits trapped inside Many Ends come back to life, but my theory hasn't yet been proven.

Another uncertainty? Killian's mother, Caroline, and my friend Marlowe could be there. But here's the thing. Neither Caroline nor Marlowe were Unsigned. Caroline made covenant with Myriad years before, only to experience Second-death within days of reaching the realm. Marlowe made covenant with Troika, only to void it when she committed suicide. Different people, different policies.

Myriad claimed Caroline's spirit Fused with the spirit of a newborn infant the day of her death, but I think they lied. I think all Myriadians wind up in Many Ends, like all Troikans wind up in the Rest.

If people knew, they might not sign with Myriad. Falsehoods and propagandas keep business booming.

I *need* to save the damned, and I can. I know I can. Not because I'm special. Please. I'm just a girl who can navigate Many Ends' treacherous labyrinth better than most, because I've been there.

A shudder of dismay rocks me.

"I hope ye weren't thinking of me just then, lass." Killian lifts my hands to his lips and kisses my knuckles, sending tingles down my spine.

"Are you kidding? The great Killian Flynn only ever makes girls shiver with desire."

"Or vibrate with anger."

Smiling, I nod. "That's fair."

The ring on his thumb glints in the firelight, warming my heart. After my grandmother Meredith experienced Second-death, I was presented with a token of remembrance. A gun-ring with six-round cylinders, 2mm pinfire. A gorgeous piece of weaponry *and* a fashion statement. My most prized possession.

I could think of no better gift when Killian gave me a hand-carved pendant in the shape of pi. Infinite possibilities rest within the ratio of a circle's circumference to its diameter; every possibility for every life. A number without end. Convert letters to numbers, and they, too, can be found within pi. Meaning, every number with any meaning—from our birthdays to the date we die—and every word ever spoken, every word that *will* be spoken, exist within pi.

"I love you" becomes $9 + 12 + 15 + 22 + 5 + 25 + 15 + 21 = 619$.

Or as Killian says:

I = one letter.

Love = four letters.

You = three letters.

143, 10.

Even now, the pendant hangs from a string of leather around my neck, both beautiful and useful. Whenever I'm in trouble, I can press the center, and my location will be sent to Killian's comm. He can find me in an instant and help.

Now, we're going to help each other and intertwine our futures with an unbreakable covenant.

What if, despite this, I'm unable to enter Myriad?

Zero! The doubt devil surfaces, and swarms of others follow. Will my Light hurt him? Will his darkness harm me?

Will we weaken or strengthen each other? Will our covenant to the realms be voided? What if, after this, neither of us can return home?

Firstlife was a dress rehearsal. Now the curtain is up, and we're performing in front of a live studio audience. Every word, action and decision comes with a consequence. There are no second chances to right our wrongs. No do-overs.

I've been told I'll turn the tide of the war, somehow, some way. What if my bond to Killian turns the tide in *Myriad's* favor?

Maybe I should back out. Except...every fiber of my being suddenly screams in denial. Both realms have reached a boiling point. Every day innocents are slaughtered. Something has to change, and fast. This is our best shot at peace. Our *only* shot. And really, I want to save Myriad just as much as I want to save Troika. I shouldn't put one realm above the other.

Face it. If I back out now, fear wins and *everyone* loses.

I will not make decisions based on "what if." I will do what's right, always. Because, in the end, I'm the only one who has to live with my regrets.

Doubt devils can suck it.

Killian squeezes my hands. "Yer paler by the second, lass. There's still time tae back out." His accent is thicker than usual, his voice low and husky, and irresistibly sexy. "I doona want you feelin' pressured."

"I just... I wish we could speak with other inter-realm couples. We aren't the first Troikan and Myriadian to fall in love. We can't be." Though we've searched high and low, we've found no one else. Either the others are in hiding...or dead.

He stiffens, as if he's expecting a devastating blow. "We can put this ceremony on hold and continue searching."

And end up right where we are, perhaps far too late. "We're

doing this. I'll share my Light with you, and you'll share your darkness with me. I'll pass through the Veil of Midnight." The doorway that leads into Myriad freezes Troikans to Second-death. But I'm about to become half-Myriadian. Maybe. Probably. Fingers crossed.

"If yer doing this for your mother…"

Mom is locked in the Kennels, a prison in Myriad. I'm going to find and free her, so she can defect to Troika to raise my little brother, Jeremy. "She's one of many reasons," I say.

He relaxes, but only slightly. "Yer only seventeen years old. We can revisit the bond in a few decades, yeah."

Decades? I inhale deeply, drawing in the familiar and beloved scent of peat smoke and heather. His scent. A new wave of calm flows over me, as warm and sweet as honey. "I'm almost eighteen, and you're only nineteen. So what? We've lived, died and lived again. I'm not going to wait to fight for what's right, and I'm certainly not going to wait to claim you."

"I doona want you doin' something you'll regret."

His accent has reached maximum thickness. Aka sweet, mouthwatering molasses. Meaning his emotions are engaged and running rampant. "How could I regret a miracle?" I ask.

One dark brow arches as his incredible eyes glitter. "Explain."

"There are over one hundred billion galaxies. And counting! There are incalculable universes, two realms in the Unending, two sub-realms, nine planets in our solar system, one hundred and ninety-six countries, seven seas, and over seven hundred islands. The fact that we found each other—miracle."

He laughs. "Ye trying to seduce me, lass? 'Cause it's working."

This boy. Oh, this boy. He's the one seducing me. Heart, mind, body. I love him.

But go ahead. Remove love from the equation. It doesn't matter. Still I trust him. Time and time again, he's defied the orders of his Secondking in an effort to protect my family. He's helped me when he should have harmed me.

"It's working, but it hasn't carried you to the finish line yet?" I mock-growl. "I can't believe you're making me talk you into this. It was your idea. Maybe I should wait until you get down on one knee to beg for the honor of becoming my husband."

His good humor fades in an instant, his features tight with tension. "I willna beg. I had tae beg for scraps as a child, simply to survive. Now I'd rather die than beg for *anything*."

"Hey, hey." Amusement gone, I gently cup his face. Tenderness wells inside me. There's so much I don't know about him. So much I'm eager to learn. "I was only teasing, I promise."

He releases a shuddering breath. A second later, his lips curve in a slow smile full of promise, and tendrils of heat unfurl inside me. He is beautiful beyond imagining, though every chiseled line is cut by cruelty, as if pain lives and breathes inside him. I look at him, and I want to kiss him, hug him and shake him all at once.

"I'm sorry," he says. "You get I'll be cherishin' ye every day of my Everlife, yeah?"

Just like that. I'm undone. One smile—and I fall deeper in love with him. One moment of time—and I can't imagine a single day without him. One sentence—and I'm happier than I've ever been.

I rise on my tiptoes and press a soft kiss to his lips.

"Will *ye* be cherishin' *me*? I mean, yer wearing Troikan armor. Think your marriage is going to be a battlefield, eh?"

I give the collar of my black catsuit a self-conscious tug.

"I kid, I kid." Killian brushes his knuckles across my jawline. "Ye look good in anything." His voice takes on a husky timbre. "Later, ye'll look even better in nothing."

Heat blooms over my cheeks.

His smile returns, and it's full of mischief, wonder and adoration. He brushes his thumbs over the rise of my cheekbones. "Yer eyes are like mini-TV screens. They broadcast yer emotions."

Others have told me I'm *impossible* to read. But then, Killian knows me better than most, and he wants me anyway. Not because I'm a rare Conduit, but because I'm me. Tenley Lockwood. A girl who's messed up, time and time again, but continues to get up and keep fighting the good fight.

"Today, a new future will be forged," I say. "Enemies become family."

"The first step toward concord between our realms."

Wind whistles outside our cave, snow billowing, while a fire crackles inside. My gaze snags on the far wall, where the numerical equivalent of our names is carved. 68 + 39.

Killian: $11 + 9 + 12 + 12 + 9 + 1 + 14 = 68$

Ten: $20 + 5 + 14 = 39$

$68 + 39 = 107$

Sonnet 107 by William Shakespeare.

Not mine own fears, nor the prophetic soul
Of the wide world dreaming on things to come,
Can yet the lease of my true love control,
Suppos'd as forfeit to a confin'd doom.
The mortal moon hath her eclipse endur'd
And the sad augurs mock their own presage;
Incertainties now crown themselves assur'd
And peace proclaims olives of endless age.
Now with the drops of this most balmy time

My love looks fresh, and Death to me subscribes,
Since, spite of him, I'll live in this poor rhyme,
While he insults o'er dull and speechless tribes;
And thou in this shalt find thy monument,
When tyrants' crests and tombs of brass are spent.

In other words, love is not subject to time, or even death.

In the back of my mind, the Grid ripples with approval and delivers a new surge of confidence. I *am* doing the right thing. We *will* succeed in our endeavors.

Once, I lamented my invisible link to other Troikans. Now I rejoice. Support can mean the difference between victory and defeat. But who would approve of this union? No one but me knows about it.

"Whatever happens next," Killian says, "doona forget I love ye." The brawler capable of any dark deed leans down to rub his nose against mine. "All right?"

"All right." I'll never forget, and I'll never tire of hearing those words. "I love you, too."

His smile reignites, and oh, wow, it's like Cupid's arrow through my heart. Killian is more than beautiful. He is life. The crystalline flecks in his eyes…there are eight. Eight is the atomic number for oxygen. Killian is my oxygen, the reason I breathe.

"Ready?" He lifts my hands to his mouth once more and traces his tongue between my knuckles.

My stomach flips over. If not for Shells, Myriadians and Troikans would be unable to touch without agonizing pain. Usually Shells mute sensation. Today I feel *everything*.

"Tell me what to do," I rasp.

"Our word is our bond. Speak, and it's done. We'll pledge our lives tae each other. Simple, easy."

As simple and easy as pledging our Everlife to one of the realms. Okay, I can do that. The simplicity doesn't negate the difficulty, however. I'm giving my life—my future—to another person.

He raises his chin. "I'll go first, aye."

"Aye. I mean yes." My heart thuds against my ribs, and I lick my lips.

When he releases my hands, panic invades. I've lost my anchor. Then he cups my face, holding me as if I'm more delicate than glass. "Tenley Nicole Lockwood, you've given me life beyond the grave. Until ye, I never knew the power of being connected tae another person. Ye saw the best in me even when I showed ye my worst. Ye trusted me when all evidence pointed tae my guilt. For that, I give ye my Everlife. Everything I am, everything I have, is yers."

Hot tears well in my eyes, catching in my lashes. How am I supposed to match such a glorious pledge? Well, I have to try.

Nope. Troikans do not try. Troikans do. "Killian—" *Zero!* "I don't know your middle name."

"Niall."

Killian Niall Flynn. Five Ls. Four Ns.

$5 + 4 = 9$

Killian Niall Flynn + Ten = 5 Ls and 5 Ns.

$5 + 5 = 10$

10 = existence. $1 + 2 + 3 + 4 = 10$. (1) the FirstKing (2) the Secondkings (3) human life (4) the four elements: earth, air, fire and water.

Ten is completion: the end of one cycle, the beginning of another.

Concentrate!

Oops. My bad. I tend to lose myself in number trivia when I'm nervous. But there's nothing to be nervous about, right?

This is Killian. *My* Killian. Together, we can handle what-ever comes next.

"Killian Niall Flynn." I wrap my fingers around his wrists as I peer into his eyes. "You found me before the grave and taught me how to live. Until you, I'd known only disappoint-ment and betrayal, but you picked me up every time I fell. You carried me when I was too weak to walk, and you put me first, even when it meant torture and possibly Second-death. For that, I give you my Everlife. Everything I am, everything I have, is yours."

His expression softens, and I wish, so badly I wish, that my family and friends could witness our union. While my mother is in the Kennel, my father is training to be an ML. He hates me, anyway. My aunt Lina, his twin sister, is miss-ing. No one knows where she is.

Lina can see into the future. As a child, she taught me a rhyme that aided my escape from Many Ends. Only a few weeks ago, she taught me a second rhyme, saving my life when a supposed friend—Victor Prince—attempted to kill me.

I frown. "I don't feel any different."

"We aren't done." Killian steps back, his arms falling to his sides. "Out of yer Shell, lass."

I'm confused by the command, but still I obey. He steps from his Shell, as well, gifting me with the sight of two po-tential husbands. The inanimate Shell, and the spirit man—the *real* Killian. Usually darkness surrounds him, his own per-sonal veil of smoke. Now the darkness is muted, but there's no Light emanating from him, either.

He's so much taller than me, I'm forced to look up, up, up. Scars circle his neck, proof of the pain he's suffered through-out his Secondlife.

I reach out, intending to trace a fingertip along the raised flesh, but stop myself just before contact. "You've been a spirit all your life. Why didn't you regenerate after you were injured?"

"Spirits are unable to regenerate fully until they reach the Age of Perfection. What you receive as a child, you keep." He crooks his finger at me. "Come here. I'm goin' tae kiss ye now."

A kiss. Of course! A wedding always ends with a kiss.

I move toward him, eager, and he enfolds me in his muscular arms. His lips descend, claiming mine in our first spirit-kiss, no barriers between us, and he isn't gentle about it. He's demanding and possessive, pure masculine aggression, and I love every second.

Everything about him makes me think of forbidden nights and carnal indulgence.

I'm burning up rather than freezing as usual, pleasure consuming me, the pain I'm used to feeling nothing but a distant memory.

Realization: We can touch without consequence!

I melt into him, the rest of the world is forgotten as I luxuriate in the sweetness of his flavor.

Now the deal is sealed. This boy is now my husband. And this, our first kiss as a bonded pair, is everything I've ever dreamed and more. It's—

A bolt of ice slams into me, tossing me across the cavern. I collide with the wall and slide to the ground, fighting for breath. Agony sears my right arm. Panting, I look down. Doubletake. An image appears in my flesh, as dark as ink and in the shape of...a horse?

The animal rests under the words *Loyalty, Passion, Liberty.*

Loyalty to my realm. Passion for the truth. Liberty for all.

The words appeared immediately after my Firstdeath. Actually, numbers appeared. The moment I figured out what those numbers represented, the words took their place.

Why a horse? There has to be a reason. There's *always* a reason.

I rack my brain, but all I can come up with—Killian once likened me to a warhorse.

The warhorse paws fiercely, rejoicing in its strength, and charges into the fray. It laughs at fear, afraid of nothing; it does not shy away from the sword. The quiver rattles against its side, along with the flashing spear and lance. In frenzied excitement it eats up the ground; it cannot stand still when the trumpet sounds. At the blast of the trumpet it snorts, "Aha!" It catches the scent of battle from afar, the shout of commanders and the battle cry.

But I'm not here to fight him. I'm here to make peace. Unless...

The moisture in my mouth dries. Ready or not, a new battle is headed our way.

My vision goes hazy, and I moan. I am Light, and I've never needed to see more! Blinking rapidly helps, allowing me to search for Killian. The same terrible phenomena must have bombarded him, because he's slouched against the opposite wall. When our gazes meet, he reaches in my direction, the numbers tattooed on his wrist visible.

143, 10. *I love you, Ten.*

Beneath the numbers I spy a new image. A horse. A match to mine, though his is white and mine is black.

His eyes are alight with...no, impossible! The flecks I so adore cannot be doused in literal flames, flickering with both light and shadow.

I need to get to him, *now*, but my muscles are like frozen blocks of ice. And the Grid—

The Grid! My connection to Troika, and a reminder that

there is so much more to the world—to my world—than what I can see and feel at any given time.

Shadows dance along the Grid, where multiple doorways loom. Those doorways lead to rooms. In some, I've stored extra Light. Others provide a link to the conscious minds of different citizens. One in particular opens up to the Rest, where our dead spend eternity at peace.

A pang of homesickness strikes me. Meredith, Archer and Levi are there. I miss them desperately.

Radiating hatred, the shadows try to sneak into one room after another. I fight to keep the doorways closed as information bombards me. Darkness is measured by the absence of Light. These shadows, whatever they are, must have come from Killian, and our bond, and yet they are so familiar to me...as if they are old friends. How is that possible?

Doesn't matter. Must...do...something. Now!

Left with no other choice, I change tactics and open a door to one of my storage rooms. In a vivid, dazzling rush, bright Light escapes. Shadows hiss, some dying the second they come into contact with a beam, others slithering away, and, oh, zero, sharp pains explode through my head, and I scream.

Can't give up. Strengthen in the Light, die in the darkness.

Between one breath and the next, the pain leaves me, and a scene opens in my mind. A memory that is not my own.

I'm standing in a doorway, watching a young couple walk down the center of a hallway. There are thirteen children lined up beside me, all under the age of ten. The couple stops to question a little girl before dismissing her and moving on to a little boy. He, too, is dismissed. The next three children are ignored, but the couple pauses to inspect the teeth of the fourth.

Closer to me by the second...

I'm nervous. I would kill to have a family of my own—literally—but no one will look at me twice. What's wrong with me? What do I lack?

Easy: absolutely everything.

Once, my superiors thought I was destined to become a General. Everyone wanted me, then. When I failed to develop the necessary skills, the want turned to disdain.

I try so hard, and I train harder than everyone else combined. I learned how to use a sword and every type of gun. Even the Stag and the Oxi, the most dangerous weapons in a Laborer's arsenal. One day I'll kill more Troikans than any General in our history. I vow it.

Just give me a chance. Please!

The couple is on the move again...so, so close to me... the woman looks me over and gives an almost imperceptible shake of her head before passing me, silent. My heart sinks, tears threatening to spill down my cheeks.

Me? Cry? Never! I keep my head high. If this family doesn't want me, fine, I don't want them, either. They aren't good enough. I'm better off at the Learning Center, anyway.

The scene goes blank, and I—Ten—blink open my eyes. I'm back in the present, back in the cave, panting and drenched in sweat yet shivering with bone-deep chill. I was wrong. The pain didn't subside; it ramped up.

The memory...it came from Killian. I know in my heart. Having died soon after his mother gave birth to him, he spent his childhood inside the Learning Center, a Myriadian orphanage.

Humans—both in flesh and spirit form—could be ugly in so many ways. Rotten inside. Vile and cruel. But they were also layered. Pull back the ugliness, and you might see a hurt.

Pull back another layer, and you might see a child who used to crave approval, affection and acceptance.

A child like Killian had been. My husband has seen the worst the world(s) have to offer. I want so badly to hold him in my arms and comfort the boy he'd been, and praise the man he'd become.

My gaze seeks him. He's on his back, pulling at his hair. Like me, he's panting and drenched in sweat. But he's muttering, "Kill, kill, kill."

Kill...who? Is he seeing into *my* memories?

"I'm here," I tell him. "I'm—"

My heart stops, stealing my words as a man and woman storm into the cave.

Don't miss book one in The Androma Saga from #1 *New York Times* bestselling authors

SASHA ALSBERG & LINDSAY CUMMINGS

Intergalactic adventures. Dangerous bounty hunters. A galaxy-wide war to devour worlds.

Androma Racella is the Bloody Baroness, a powerful mercenary whose reign of terror stretches across the Mirabel Galaxy. On her glass starship, *Marauder*, however, she's just Andi, captain and fearless leader.

When a routine job goes awry, the *Marauder*'s all-girl crew find themselves placed at the mercy of a sadistic bounty hunter from Andi's past. Coerced into a dangerous, soul-testing mission, they'll either restore order to the ship—or start a war that will devour worlds.

"A whirlwind, out-of-this-galaxy adventure!"
—#1 *New York Times* bestselling author **Sarah J. Maas**

ZENITH
THE ANDROMA SAGA

#1 NEW YORK TIMES BESTSELLING AUTHORS
SASHA ALSBERG &
LINDSAY CUMMINGS

READ IT NOW!